"I was amazed at the high level of quality that permeates all aspects of the series. . . . It's such a pleasure to see Dell doing something original with dark fantasy/horror."
—Richard L. Cooke, Literary Editor,
Tekeli-li! Journal of Terror

"The most exciting line of horror novels to hit the field in a very long time. . . . The Abyss line will not only leave its mark on the field but may very well revitalize it."
—From the *Time Tunnel* newsletter

"The new Abyss line of horror fiction has provided some great moments in their first year."
—*Mystery Scene*

"Inaugurating Dell's new Abyss Books series, this powerful first novel [THE CIPHER] is as thought-provoking as it is horrifying."
—*Publishers Weekly*

"Claustrophobic, paranoid . . . compelling, Dell's new horror line is definitely worth keeping an eye on."
—*Science Fiction Eye*

Also by Dale Hoover
SHADOW TWIN

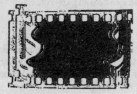

DALE
HOOVER

A DELL BOOK

Published by
Dell Publishing
a division of
Bantam Doubleday Dell Publishing Group, Inc.
1540 Broadway
New York, New York 10036

ISBN: 0-440-21338-X

Printed in the United States of America

Published simultaneously in Canada

April 1994

10 9 8 7 6 5 4 3 2 1

RAD

For my good friend, Crazy Jo Trekas
Because she is always there,
even when she isn't

And for Lori Perkins
Because Old Business is as eminent to her
as it is to me

Humble thanks to Jeanne Cavelos, The Storyteller,
for her enduring kindness and
immeasurable patience.

Quiet thanks to Alan and John,
because they wouldn't have it
any other way.

And, as always, eternal thanks to
my brother, The Lump.

Prologue: Sour Rain

"Feel the wind? Can ya feel it?" She had the door to Rozina's bar open only a crack, just enough to stick her head out and let the new wind brush her cheeks, turning her dried old wrinkled skin cold. Jeff had known the old woman for only a few short months, but he'd come to think of her as a sister in some way. They were not blood, but he and Janice D'Lacy had a bond. When she cracked open the large carved oak door that seemed more appropriate in a cathedral main entrance and stuck her head outside, Jeff had felt the chill of the wind and had thrown an anxious glance toward Rozina. But there was no hope there. Rozina didn't even acknowledge him. Her eyes were trained on Janice, who now had her shoulders pushed through the crack as well.

"It's from the south," Janice was saying. "Always comes from the south, can ya feel it?" When her body went from a fine soft tremor to the stiffness of a corpse, Jeff Baines could no longer restrain himself.

He moved off the stool swiftly and crossed to Janice. Rozina watched him with regally quiet repose, but her eyes were dark and glittering, seeing things. Seeing things and knowing what they were. She'd felt the wind, and she knew the depth of its cold.

Jeff laid his hand softly on the old woman's back. "Come away now, Janice. Come back to the bar and finish your ginger ale."

Janice ignored him. She leaned farther out the door, as if to catch the brass ring as it fled swiftly by her grasping fingers. "Storm's comin'. I can feel it. Felt it before, so I know. I know when the wind changes like this. Changes. Felt the rain.

Felt it sour. Now it's come again." She shuddered. "Storm's comin', with the wind."

Jeff grabbed Janice by the arm and began to tug. "Janice, please. Come away from the door. The cold is getting inside."

It was only then that the old woman relented, her body slackening into a bend of defeat and despair. She let herself fall back into Jeff's arms. It was a maneuver for which he was not prepared, and the two of them slumped nearly to the floor.

As he carried her to the bar her breathing grew more labored, like the puffing sound of an engine too long working at maximum capacity on a job it was not made to handle. Jeff watched her with deepening concern, casting his anxious glances at the stolid Rozina as he sat her stiffly on a barstool and motioned for a drink.

Without saying a word Rozina turned, reached for a shot glass, and quietly set it upon the bar. She bent low, brought up a bottle of Irish whiskey, and poured a shot. Janice watched blandly as the clear brown liquid filled the shot glass, but once her fingers were wrapped around it her eyes came alive. She brought it shakily to her lips, then threw her head back and sent the fire into her stomach with one swallow.

Jeff sat quietly, studying her. How frail she was, and yet her eyes held the flair of youth, the spark of memory now suddenly ignited with new fear. It was not a pleasant thing to see. It made him feel twisted inside, like an already too-tight knot being torqued to greater tautness. When he finally looked away he saw that Rozina was carefully watching him.

He returned her gaze, but said nothing. What could he say? He did not know the cold personally, except where it had touched his heart in its own way. But as for the past, he was ignorant. And Rozina had heretofore kept it secret from him.

He believed that was about to change.

Outside, the wind began to gust. It sent thrusts of cold beneath the threshold as it buffeted the door. Tendrils of cold, like the icy fingers of something ancient and forbidden, writhed across the floor and around his ankles. The cold was like a living thing.

Janice slammed the shot glass down, tucking her head so that her chin was buried against her upper chest. "Another."

Silently, Rozina poured another shot. Janice took it as quickly as the first.

Slammed it down. Was silent. Eyes closed, her mouth worked with the fire in her stomach. She got up from the stool and swayed to the nearest table, where she slumped into a chair.

Jeff turned to Rozina. "Will you talk to me?"

Rozina replaced the bottle beneath the bar, then straightened and looked Jeff straight in the eye. She took him into her gaze, and as she did he saw her for what she was. Not a tall woman; not sinewy and graceful as one would think a woman of Nubian ancestry would be. Rozina was short and almost pudgy, with thick lips and a broad nose. Her jaw was straight and strong, and in her countenance was the impervious mystique of her race. Unencumbered by the constrictions of contemporary political correctness, Rozina was Africa. Dark and mysterious, the ancient plight of Africa weighing on her face like a mourner's veil. He couldn't say her skin was black. It had more the color of manzanita, which caused him to often think there might be some American Indian blood flowing through her veins. But her eyes . . . yes, her eyes were Africa, black silver, liquid and visceral. It was as though she could look into his heart and see the blackness there. Sickly blackness like a disease gone unchecked for far too long. He didn't like her looking that far into him. He didn't like it at all. But he had very little to say about it. Rozina had the gift, he knew, and when she looked at him she touched his heart for a second, just a second, and during that time she rescued him from the cold. So he let her look, and he let her feel him and sometimes, in spite of himself, she comforted him.

"It's the storm, isn't it?" he asked.

Rozina nodded.

Jeff sighed deeply, feeling a shudder go straight through his gut. He looked over at Janice slumped in the chair, her

labored breathing rocking her body rhythmically. Back and
forth, back and forth, like rocking a child to sleep.

"Do you know his name?" he asked Rozina without looking at her.

"I do."

Jeff turned to her then and looked at her with the look of a
frightened child. "What will we do?"

"What will *you* do, Jeff?" Rozina said.

Jeff stared at her, frightened.

"Time for you to decide where your heart lies, boy. Time
to decide what you will do."

"I'm scared," he whispered in a small voice.

"Course you're scared. We all scared, boy. But you ain't
got much time left. You gonna deal with it or are you gonna
run away and hide? Make your decision, don't wait until it's
too late. I got my own skin to think about."

"I'll stay," Jeff said hollowly. "I'll stay, Rozina. I don't
really have a choice."

Rozina's eyes flitted a little. She pulled a white cloth from
beneath the counter and began to wipe up the bar sweat.
"We all got choices, boy."

Choices.

There had been a time when Jeff believed that everybody
had choices. Everybody had the time and opportunity to
weigh the consequences of any given circumstance. But in
this past year the rules had changed. His past was no longer
fodder for the philosophical meanderings of a man too drunk
to do anything more than sit on a barstool and ponder his
mistakes. In this past year things had gotten very real. When
the time had come for him to make his choice, Jeff Baines
wondered just how much control he'd had over the choice
he'd made.

"I did what I had to do," he said, almost flimsily.

"And now you be payin' for it with your heart," Rozina
said. "And you gotta decide."

Jeff frowned. "Decide what?"

"Where is your soul, boy?" Rozina barked. "In your heart?
Or in your mind?"

"I don't understand."

Rozina sneered at him. "More choices, fool. They're comin' fast and furious now." She leaned forward and lifted his chin with two fingers. "You're very good at savin' your own skin, boy. You're very good at that. What will you do when your own skin's got nothin' to do with it?"

For the life of him Jeff couldn't think of an answer.

The first thing Joe Moreson thought about whenever Richards came into his cubicle was how his boss's presence always made his stomach tighten. The second thing he thought about was why, and that was when he stopped trying to think at all.

It was almost an animalistic thing; the surge of adrenaline through his veins when that man with the fat red sweaty face lumbered in and set his puny squinting eyes on Joe. It was always the same: a hunt. A search for Joe's guts. And the predator always won.

Even Kelsie couldn't save him when Richards was on the hunt, and he was on the hunt now, setting his blubbery mass over Joe's right shoulder to peer myopically at the computer screen. His caustic wheezing filled Joe's ear with its unpleasant sound.

Joe snatched a look at Kelsie, who leaned casually against the corner of Joe's desk and watched calmly, keenly.

Finally Richards spoke. His voice was as gritty as his wheeze. "That's as far as you've gotten with this?"

Joe nodded silently.

"Hell, man!" Richards rasped. "We only got two months before this goes out to the field! What've you been doing all this time?"

Joe closed his eyes. "I've been on the phone all day, Mr. Richards. The guys in Pasadena are having trouble with the test program we sent out the beginning of this week." He tried to type, but his trembling fingers only spasmed.

Richards straightened. "You sent that program out with bugs in it?"

Joe felt his lips tighten. "It was a test, sir."

"You're going to have to be more careful, Moreson."

Joe clenched his fists. "We expected it to have bugs, Mr. Richards. That's why we sent it out, to find the bugs."

But Richards knew this. Joe knew he knew it, and Joe knew it didn't matter. Not now. Not in this game of catch-the-mouse-and-watch-it-squirm. Richards stared down at him, those pig eyes all weepy and red rimmed with tension. He stared at Joe, silent except for that horrible morbid wheeze, and played the game to its maximum.

"You're just going to have to be more careful," he said finally. "Understand?"

Then he stood there. He actually stood there and demanded with his hulking presence that Joe reply.

I won't do it. Not this time. Not this time.

"Yes, sir," Joe said. "I'm sorry."

Richards's face formed a grin. He touched the side of his nose with his finger, then turned and lumbered out.

Joe breathed a heady sigh. His heart was pounding now; he could see it at his wrists. He raised them and peered at them, as if studying the results of some laboratory test. Then he looked at his computer screen. What had been the comfort of a familiar face now seemed alien to him. He hit the break key and looked away, swiveling in his chair to lean back and take a shot at ignoring Kelsie's keen gaze.

"He talks like that to you because he knows he can get away with it," Kelsie said calmly. "Why do you let him get away with it?"

Why. Why. Why.

He turned back to the screen, stared at it with a hatred ready for the harvesting.

"I had a dream last night," he said, surprised at how wistful he sounded. "Funny dream, about being in this old house where there were a lot of bodies all piled over in dirt and dust, and I was digging through the dirt and uncovering the bodies. And you know what I did with them?"

Kelsie shrugged.

Joe turned on the computer, called up the program, and stared at it. "I stole their rings. All the rings. I stole them." He closed the program, hit *X,* and entered the system. "Then I put them on my fingers, admired them."

"What are you doing?" Kelsie asked.

Joe glanced at Kelsie, noted the knit in his friend's brow, then turned back to the computer.

The *C* prompt blinked at him.

Joe typed in his command. "I stole them, from dead fingers, and put them on my own."

On the CRT the words *erase comex.exe* shone dully. Joe sharpened the brilliance a little, then hit "Return."

"What are you doing?" Kelsie asked again. He didn't sound confused, and he didn't sound frightened. He sounded like a man who'd played this game before and was tired of it. Had Joe been a little less fed up, the tone would have made him acquiesce,

or come to your senses? Come to your senses, Joe.

No. I don't want to. Not this time. Not anymore.

The screen printed out the words, *are you sure?*

Joe stared at it for a moment. "I admired them." Then he hit the letter *Y.*

Kelsie gasped.

The computer hummed for only a second, then printed the words *file erased.*

Joe turned the computer off.

Kelsie closed his eyes, sighing with tired annoyance.

"I'm leaving," Joe announced, rising. Kelsie turned on him as he walked past, into the hallway.

"You always do this, Joe," Kelsie said. "You walk out with righteous indignation, then slink back here the next day with your tail between your legs. It's getting old."

Joe barked a hoarse laugh. "That's what I like about you, Kels. I can always depend on you to be on my side."

"I am on your side," Kelsie said. "You know that."

"Sometimes . . ."

Joe looked at the man he'd called a friend for more than two decades and saw for the first time that Kelsie was taller than himself. He had always thought of the two of them as being brothers, both big men but slender and agile. Except for Kelsie's crown of prematurely gray hair, they were nearly identical, with blue-gray eyes shaded by healthy dark eyebrows. Kelsie's hair had been dark like Joe's until sometime in college. It had seemed to happen suddenly, and now that he thought about it, standing here gazing at the man with the shimmering gray hair, Joe realized that it was then that Kelsie had seemed taller. Joe had put it out of his mind, denied it, until now.

Why would he think of it now?

He gathered himself up, straightening his shoulders to dispel the feeling of smallness as he stood gazing at Kelsie. "Sometimes I'm not sure, Kels. Sometimes I'm not sure where you stand." He cocked his head a little. "Are you on my side? Or are you just waiting around? Like a vulture, circling?"

Kelsie narrowed his gaze until his eyes were angry slits. "I deserve better than that from you."

Without answering, Joe turned and began to walk down the hallway.

"How long this time, Joe?" Kelsie called after him. Joe turned and set his gaze on him.

"What do you want me to say, Kelsie? What do you want me to do?"

Kelsie didn't answer.

Joe raised his hands in supplication. Kelsie looked away, frustrated.

"That's what I thought," Joe said.

It was a clean white screen, the cleanest thing in Frank Jordan's life. It had been his for so long, and now it was being taken away.

What had he done to deserve this?

He leaned back in the old front-row-center theater seat and let his gaze drift across the vast white expanse of the screen. Everything in this place was old, filthy, fading, dusty. Everything but the screen. The beautiful, gleaming white screen.

Fifty years of slaving for the thing. He had served its purpose for so long. Why was he being thrown away now?

Why?

"Why, old man?"

Frank turned suddenly. He peered up the aisle and saw, in

the gathering darkness of the theater, the one with the sledgehammer. Andy.

There was Andy, now walking down the aisle, the sledgehammer swinging slightly at his side.

"Why, old man? Why are you still here?"

"This is my place," Frank said, but his voice lacked strength.

Andy chuckled. "You don't belong here, old man."

"This is my place!"

Andy stood over him, towering like a great living god over the piteous servant. "It's mine now. I've waited, old man. I've waited for a long time. It's mine. All of this is mine."

Frank looked up, a hint of a smile on his lips. "Yours? What makes you think it's yours?"

Andy faltered a little, his eyes darting. "You said—"

"I said!" Frank huffed. "Yeah, I said a lot of things back then, didn't I? I said if your mom and dad died you'd get the Fareland. So you made sure of it, didn't you? You made sure they died so you'd get the Fareland."

Andy took the sledgehammer in both hands, holding it out in front of him. Frank chuckled.

"The Fareland's being sold, son. You don't get shit."

"No!" Andy shouted, his eyes blazing with anger. He lifted the sledgehammer high over his head.

"Go ahead," Frank said calmly. "Go ahead and kill me, it won't change a thing."

"You don't know that!"

"I don't?" Now Frank was laughing, and the look of confusion and frustration on Andy's young face made him laugh even harder.

"Don't laugh at me, old man!" Andy seethed. "Don't laugh!"

Frank stopped, took in a long breath, and held it as he gazed upon the fine young face of the manchild, barely eighteen years old. Andy was strong and handsome, with hair the color of gold and eyes like pure emeralds—a diamond-green set in a smooth young face of cream. How could someone so beautiful have such a black heart?

But that was a silly question.

Frank finally let out his breath and motioned Andy to lower the sledgehammer. Reluctantly, Andy did. He sat next to his grandfather and together they gazed at the gleaming white screen.

"I wanted it to go to you," Frank said sadly. "But the rules have changed. It'll be sold, and there's nothing either of us can do about it."

"Why, Grandpa?"

Frank sighed deeply. "We made it angry, I guess. Showed you the movie ten years ago, and it never forgot." He touched his grandson's hand. "Never should've showed you that movie, son."

"I'm glad you did," Andy said. He let his head fall back as he gazed at the screen. "I'm glad."

"And another is coming," Frank said quietly. "Another like you. Another. . . ." He closed his eyes.

"My cousin," Andy said.

Frank nodded. "And I have no brothers. No sisters." He turned to look at Andy, look into the deep emerald eyes. "But she's your cousin, because that's part of the plan too." He shook his head in a sad, beaten way. "I gave so much. So much. Now I have nothing."

They were quiet for a moment, both gazing at the screen. Then Andy said in a solemn, determined voice, "I will kill you, Grandpa. You know that, don't you?"

Frank nodded. "Yes, Andy."

"It's part of the plan."

Frank closed his eyes. "Yes, Andy. It is."

Karen had a grand dinner waiting for Joe when he got home. Fried chicken, southern style. Green beans and mashed potatoes with country gravy made just the way he liked it. Too bad he didn't feel like eating. He didn't feel like doing anything but sitting in his chair and staring off into space, trying to figure out if this time he would just cut his throat again or save it.

His wife had another surprise for him, one far more tantalizing than the magnificently humble meal she had set before him, but he didn't know this until after he had taken three bites of the spicy fried chicken and ended up with the last bite just lying in his mouth, unchewed.

There was a neatly folded newspaper at her right elbow, and from his angle he could see that it was opened to the classified pages. Karen was watching him carefully, holding her counsel, her eyes switching from him to the paper to her plate with silent patience. She spoke only when the chicken breast left Joe's hand and thudded on the plate. "What happened?"

He looked up at her. She was a tall woman, with hair the color of spun copper and skin so soft and creamy white, you'd think she'd been carved from alabaster. He had fallen in love with her the moment he saw her sitting next to him in a dead language class in college. She knew he was staring at her then, and she knew he was the one she would marry. She knew it before he did, and that was magical in a way. It was perhaps the one reason he found her so exciting. She was magical. She was a goddess.

"Richards," he said through the unchewed chicken in his mouth.

Karen nodded silently.

"Bastard makes my stomach hurt."

"Did you quit?"

Joe glanced up. "What do you think?"

Karen smiled. She sat quietly for a moment, watching him, then picked up the paper. "Do you believe in destiny, Joe?"

Puzzled, Joe could only shrug. Karen smiled again. How sweet her smile was, like the purity of a spring rain. No, not rain. A shower. Yes, a gentle spring shower.

She handed the paper to him. Circled in red, just below an ad for a thirty-year-old fixer-upper clothes shop, was a small ad with only two lines:

DESPERATE. MUST SELL BEFORE AUGUST 31
Contact: Frank Jordan   Fareland Cinema, Fareland, CA.

"I saw it today," Karen said, taking a bite of mashed potatoes.

Joe lowered the paper and looked at her. "What's this all about?"

Karen shrugged. "Seems clear to me."

There was a pause, and then Karen set her fork down and looked at Joe. "You've wanted to own a movie house ever since I first knew you. Here's your chance."

Joe stared at the ad, and a sudden feeling came over him, like a waterfall of pure warm water laced with honey. "Destiny . . ." He smiled. "You have such a way with words, Karen."

"Well, what else would you call it?" she said casually, taking up her fork. "I knew you were going to quit. I've known it for some time. Richards has been coming down hard on you for three weeks now."

"I never said I quit."

"You didn't have to," she said, scooping up potatoes with her fork.

Joe looked at the ad again, running his finger over the print.

"You were never made to work *for* someone, Joe. Here's your chance to be your own boss."

Joe set the paper down gently. "Why aren't we talking about the real problem?"

"Which is?"

He sighed.

"You feel safe, Joe. That's all." Karen tapped the paper. "There's a risk here."

Joe got up from the table and went into the living room, carrying the paper. He sat down heavily in one of the easy chairs flanking the fireplace and gazed at the ad.

There's a risk here.

He ran his hand raggedly across his eyes.

Why didn't they talk about the *real* problem?

He was scared.

Well, maybe not scared. Not exactly. Nervous, maybe. Anxious.

One thing was certain: He was not going back to his job.

"You could take Kelsie with you."

Joe jumped. He hadn't heard her move up behind him,

and when she spoke it was almost the sound of a mirror breaking. "No. No, I don't think I want to do that."

"Why not?"

"I can't explain," Joe said, feeling frustrated and a little cornered.

Karen moved to the other chair and sat down. She watched him tenderly.

"You know what bothers me the most, Karen?" he asked after a long pause. "Sometimes . . ." He closed his eyes and saw again the image of his dream. Dead bodies, wasted and decayed, their skeleton fingers crumbling as he grabbed for their pretty silver rings, some with pearls, others with diamonds, all shiny and new and untouched by the weight of age and neglect.

"Sometimes I'm not sure I'm really in command."

She tilted her head in question. "Command of what?"

"Me," he stated. "Myself. My life. It's like there's something growing inside me. Something foreign. I can't really see it. I can feel it, sometimes, when everything is quiet and dark. But I can't see it. I don't know what it is."

"It's hidden," she reflected.

Joe nodded. "Hidden from me, anyway." He looked at the paper once again. "I'm not going back to Tempac. That's for sure." He sighed, tilting his head back, and gazed at the ceiling. "It's the only thing I'm sure of."

They sat in silence for a long time. It seemed unnatural to Joe. They never did this: sitting in the darkened living room, dinner barely touched. Sitting quiet and still, waiting for unspoken thoughts to make themselves known.

"Just go check it out," Karen said finally.

More silence. It was thick as syrup.

"I'm not even sure where Fareland is," Joe whispered.

"It's just outside of Oakland. I looked it up today. It's a tiny little country town. Don't you see, Joe? It's perfect. Just what you've always wanted. This whole thing is playing like a finely tuned instrument." She smiled, rose, then knelt at his knee. "You've wanted to quit for a long time, Joe. This is your chance." She laid a hand on his thigh. "Go for it."

Fire moved up his thigh and into his pelvis. He forgot

about the newspaper, let it drop suddenly from his hand, and leaned toward her. She was there to meet him, there in his arms, loving him, kissing his neck, blowing softly in his ear. His belly was on fire now, and he realized suddenly that he had picked her up into his arms without thought, carrying her to their bed.

The memories of a child often blur with age, but when the first subtle gust of wind played with his whitened hair, Vordy Halleran's childhood memories crystallized.

Ten. I was ten. I was ten years old.

From his rocking chair on the back porch of the house he'd inherited as the last remaining member of the Halleran family, Vordy felt the wind, felt its cold, and shivered. It had been fifty years since he'd felt the cold, fifty years of hard work on a failing farm, alone in his labor, alone with the memories of when he was ten and everything was okay, until the cold came and his family was taken from him. Fifty years alone, and never quite warm.

From outside of himself the phone was ringing. He almost didn't answer it.

Almost.

By the third ring Vordy had drunk half a bottle of vodka and was looking at the cracks in his aging skin. Once he'd been strong and tan; now he was bent with age and afraid. The farm had finally failed more than ten years ago, and except for the occasional twinkle in his green eyes when he'd had just enough to drink, his poor broken body had faded with the green sweet grass of yesterday.

On the fourth ring he knew the phone would never stop except when he answered it. He pulled himself up and went into the house.

The memories were strong, but not strong enough.

Or maybe it wasn't the memories at all. Maybe it was something else; something he hadn't felt in fifty years.

The Hiding Fear.

Vordy shivered. He picked up the phone. He said nothing, only listened. When the caller was finished Vordy simply said, "Okay," and hung up. Then he finished the bottle of vodka.

The Hiding Fear.

He put on his coat and went out the back door. He walked with a bit of a sway, watching secretly as the new wind cartwheeled leaves along the edge of the dirt road. A tiny dust devil swirled about his legs, following him impishly.

The Hiding Fear.

The others were already waiting for him in front of Rozina's bar. He stopped across the street and gazed at them through the haze of the vodka. Old men. Old memories. Had he really known these men for fifty years?

Was it possible? After all these years, could the Hiding Fear seize his heart again? He hadn't believed it, not until this moment as he stood on the corner watching his old friends huddle together against the new wind.

It's come again, he thought. *Just like Andy said it would. It's come again,* and he remembered.

The Hiding Fear.

He pulled the frayed lapels of his coat close to his throat and walked across the street to join his friends.

They stood in a circle for a moment, eyeing each other suspiciously. Vordy had known these men all his life. Rudy Olsen had had a promising career in football but had chosen to stay in town and run his father's five-and-dime. John Williams there, he ran the gas station. His father had died about the same time Vordy's father had died. *Ten. I was ten. We were all ten, weren't we? Ten, when the Hiding Fear came.*

John had good grades in school and could have gone to any college he wanted, but he decided to go to St. Anthony's because it was close and he wouldn't have to move out of Fareland. Studied economics and business administration, and dropped out after the first semester.

Alan Mayhew owned Fareland's only hotel. He'd inherited it from his dad, who had died in the forties. Alan had seen it happen and had never recovered. He smiled a lot now, but his eyes were like small round ice cubes.

Vordy remembered the deaths of their fathers, but for the

life of him he couldn't remember what had happened to their mothers.

At some point in their adult life they had all had the opportunity to leave Fareland, but they had all chosen to stay. Small-town loyalty? Vordy thought so, or at least he used to think so. Now, he wasn't so sure.

Something about this town. Something about Fareland. . . .

After a few uncomfortable moments Vordy shivered and gestured toward the large oak door of Rozina's bar. "We goin' in?"

The others nodded silently.

Vordy felt the difference in temperature the moment he'd opened the door. Inside the air was still and cozy warm. There were only three people in the bar, but he wished they were anyone but these three. Jeff Baines, that businessman, always wore a suit and tie. He had the look of a trapped rabbit on his slender face, his eyes always darting, his lips fretting. He remembered the day Jeff had come to Fareland. He'd had a business partner then, but Vordy couldn't remember his name. A ponderous man with a flair about him so pompous, it was sleazy. He'd bought Jeff that large mansion on the hill overlooking downtown. Jeff had been like a hermit up there for a long time, until the accident, and then he'd started venturing into town. He would slink around town, hiding in shadows, always watchful, fearful. The man made the back of Vordy's neck itch.

Over in one corner was Janice D'Lacy. Crazy woman. She'd gone insane the night her husband and son were killed

Ten years old . . .

and always talked of the wind coming. Wind's comin', she'd say. Don't you mistake it. It came once, and it'll come again. Crazy woman.

Or was she?

Behind the bar was Rozina.

Rozina was one scary bitch.

Vordy straightened his shoulders and returned Rozina's steely gaze. "This still a public bar?"

Rozina said nothing, only stared at them in her quiet, regal way that always made Vordy nervous.

"Okay, then. Will you get us some beer?" He held her gaze a moment longer than he should have, because when he turned away he could feel her inside his head.

Vordy and his friends sat down at a table near the front door. They all sat with their arms on the table and their fingers laced. Their heads were bowed, and they remained silent until Rozina had brought them a pitcher of beer and four glasses. As she turned to leave she squeezed Vordy's shoulder.

He reeled.

Why had she done that?

Ten I was ten I was ten years old oh God my papa . . . my papa . . .

"You okay, Vordy?" It was Alan.

Vordy smiled limply. "Yeah."

Rudy Olsen poured himself a beer, downed it, and then poured another. He took a deep breath. "We know why we're here."

They all nodded silently.

"Time to choose up sides," Rudy continued. "And I know I want to be on the winnin' side. That means Andy."

They mumbled their agreement.

"We don't know that for sure," Vordy said. They looked at him. "I mean, we don't really know for sure this is all startin' up again, do we?"

Alan looked surprised. "Can't you feel it?"

Vordy shrugged. "I feel somethin'. I feel the scare. But I don't—I don't feel the—the . . ."

"Excitement," Alan said. His eyes sparkled. He focused them for the first time since their meeting outside the bar, and set a gaze on Vordy. "My dad, he took me to the movies, and I remember the excitement. I remember, don't you? You seen the movies, too, Vordy. You remember."

Vordy shuddered. "No, Alan. I don't. But I remember the horror."

"There was no horror."

"There *was*!" Vordy closed his eyes and struggled to control himself. "Look, that's not the point."

"So, what is?" John asked.

Vordy looked at him. "The point is, how do we know Andy's the one?"

They all looked at him in shocked surprise.

Vordy took a deep breath. "Come on, guys. I mean, how can we know?"

"We know," Alan said. "We've always known. Since he was a kid—"

"Things change," Vordy said. "And sometimes we remember things . . . wrong. Remember different from the way it really happened." His gaze met Rozina's, and he stared at her for a very long time before going on. "Something's—something's wrong with the memory."

"What are you talking about, Vordy?" John said coldly.

"I don't know. . . ." Vordy dragged his hand across his eyes. "Hell, I don't know, Johnny. I'm—I'm confused. And scared."

John stared at him, his face firmly set. "What are you talking about?"

Vordy returned his gaze. The tension between them was thick and humming. "John, don't you remember how it *really* was?"

John kept him in his gaze for a moment longer before his face thawed and a smile touched his lips. "Okay, Vordy. So why don't you just leave? Nothin' keepin' you here. Just leave, pack up, move to Walnut Creek or even San Francisco."

"This is my *home*!" Vordy said, slamming his fist on the table. Alan squeaked his surprise.

John opened his mouth but before he could speak, Janice D'Lacy stood, knocking her chair over. She was staring at the four of them, her eyes wide and animated. Her mouth was stretched in a humorless smile. She raised a crooked finger at ~~t~~   ~~ou~~ can't leave."

~~ghed~~ in ponderous annoyance, poured himself a

~~'t~~ leave," Janice reiterated, moving toward them

with a noticeable sway to her gait. "You can *try,* sure, but it won't happen. It won't let you leave."

John drained his glass of beer and slammed the glass down. "Shut up, old woman."

"Can't shut me up either," Janice said, her voice colored with a slight chuckle that was neither humor nor dismay. "Shut me up once, it did. Not this time. This time I got friends."

"What do you mean, Janice?" Vordy asked. "What do you mean we can't leave?"

"You can leave," John said quietly.

"Can't," Janice said.

John threw her an angry glance. "My wife left. Left with my daughter and my station wagon. She had no trouble leaving, old woman, so don't tell me we can't leave!"

Janice cocked her head, smiling in mock humor. "Did she leave, Johnny? *Did* she?" She moved slowly toward John, step by calculated step, like a cat moving in on an unsuspecting bird. "Did you *see* her leave?" Janice asked, moving in slowly. "Did you *see* her get in that station wagon with your little daughter? Did you *see* her drive out of town?"

John looked down at his hands.

"You didn't see her at all, did you, John?"

John looked to the others for support, and Vordy saw a hint of panic in the old man's eyes. His gaze darted from one man to the other, desperately searching and finding nothing. Then he drew in a breath and held it. His legs were jumping spasmodically.

Finally he looked up at Janice in firm defiance. "No, Janice. I didn't see her leave."

Janice's smile broadened. "Ah! Yes! So how did you find out?" She leaned down and put her face close to John's. "Who told you she'd left, Johnny? How did you get the news?"

John shrank from her.

"Frank Jordan, right?" Janice asked.

John was silent.

"Frank Jordan told you about your wife leaving, right?"

Alan leaned toward him. "Is that true, Johnny?" he whispered. "Is it true you never saw her leave?"

"That means she's still here," Vordy said.

"Where is she, then?" asked Rudy.

"All right!" John shouted, standing up so suddenly that the rest of them jumped. "All right, Frank told me. So what? So what? You sayin' he was lyin'?"

Janice straightened, a look of quiet triumph on her face. John stood with his fists clenched, his body shaking with anger and frustration. Finally he raised a trembling hand and pointed at Janice. "You don't scare me, old woman. You never did. I know what side's the winnin' side, and that's all that counts. I don't wanna leave. Why should I leave? Anybody wants to leave that's their business. They can leave. It don't mean nothin' to me." He sat down heavily and downed his beer.

"We can't leave," Vordy said quietly. "Janice is right. Any of you ever try?"

None of them answered.

Outside, the wind buffeted the large oak door and sent swirls of cold across the floor of the bar. Vordy felt the cold lap at his legs. He hunched his shoulders, shuddering. "Storm's comin'."

"That's right," Janice said, moving back to her own table. "Storm's comin' and you can't see it. You don't remember. Leastways, you don't remember what *really* happened. All you remember is the pleasure. The fun. Saw your folks all puffed up with power and lust. But I seen other things. I seen the blood." She fell into her chair and motioned to Rozina for another shot of liquor. Rozina brought it to her silently.

Janice took another look at them all, then downed the shot in one swallow. Without being asked Rozina poured another.

Alan turned in his chair to look at Janice. "I remember it, Jan. I remember the power. I remember the rain that fell and it was good. It was sweet!"

Janice shook her head. "You're blind, Alan. Always been blind to the real things. All of you, 'cept maybe Vordy. You been had, boys. You been played the fool and you're gonna be played the fool again."

"We can stop it," Vordy said. Janice fixed him with a stern gaze.

"You try, Vordy. You just try." She downed her jigger of whiskey.

"Maybe I will," Vordy said. He stood and crossed to Janice. "Maybe I will, this time."

Janice offered him a crooked smile. "You saw your papa die, didn't you, boy?"

Vordy closed his eyes.

"And when you were twenty-one, you tried to burn the theater down, didn't you?"

Vordy swayed a little, his legs trembling.

"What stopped you, Vordy?"

"I—"

"What stopped you?"

"I don't know. I couldn't do it." Vordy covered his face with his hands.

"Leave him alone, Janice!" John said, slamming his fist on the table.

Janice turned slowly toward him.

"I got good memories," John said. "They're good memories, every one of them. My dad, he took me to the movies, too, and it was *good*!"

"Me too," Alan said, smiling foolishly. *"Good* memories!"

"Where's your dad, Alan?" Janice asked simply.

Alan's mouth twisted in a snarl.

Janice nodded slowly. "Blind. Deaf. Dead from the neck up. When's the last time your dad looked at you and knew who you were?"

"Stop it," Alan hissed.

"When he died, Alan, when he died, did he know who you were then?"

"Shut up!"

Jeff, who had remained silent and still throughout the discussion, now leaned forward and laid a hand on Janice's arm. This seemed to quiet her, or at least put her in check for a moment. Vordy saw something pass between them; something unsaid but powerfully sad, and it made him shiver.

Suddenly Alan was up, shaking his fists at nothing. His

eyes were red and rimmed with tears. "He had it coming! Had it *coming*!"

Janice laid her hand over Jeff's, and suddenly Vordy felt alone. His memories, like photographs from an old album long forgotten, flitted in his head. *Ten I was ten I was ten years old. And my daddy . . . my daddy . . .*

"Storm's comin', can ya feel it?" Janice said. "Storm's comin' and the rain ain't sweet. I tasted it before." She looked at Vordy. "Sour rain is gonna fall."

Vordy stared at her, at Jeff, then turned and looked at Rozina. The winning side, John had said. The winning side.

His dad had been on the winning side.

Joe lay in bed with his arms wrapped around his wife, smelling their sex like a fine perfume. Her body was soft and warm, snuggling comfortably against him. Her hair smelled of roses. He was just drifting off to sleep when she spoke, her voice muffled.

"What?"

She raised her head and looked at him. "Have you decided yet?"

"Decided about what?"

She gave him a smile. "The Fareland. Are you going to check it out?"

He sighed and pulled her back into his embrace. "Maybe."

"I think it's a good idea," she said, settling back down with her head on his chest. "I think it's the best idea to come along. What have you got to lose?"

"Nothing," he said, biting his lip. "Everything."

"Everything?"

Joe stared at the ceiling. "I got some sick time coming. I'll call in sick tomorrow. Tell them I won't be in for a week. Then I'll go up there and check this place out." He kissed Karen on the head. "How's that?"

"Sounds good," Karen said. She ran her hand lightly across Joe's chest. "Sure you don't want Kelsie to go with you?"

"Yeah, I'm sure. I want to do this myself."

"You'll fall in love with the place as soon as you see it. I know it, Joe. I just know it." She moved her hand down to Joe's stomach, then across his hip. "There's nothing to be afraid of."

Joe started. "What do you mean?"

Her hand froze, lying heavily on his hip, and then it was gone and she was up on her hands looking at him. "You're afraid, aren't you? I can feel it." She touched his face. "You're scared."

Joe stared at her dumbly.

Scared?

I
THE
FARELAND

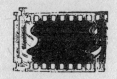

1

 Nervous, maybe. Anxious . . .

Yes. *Anxious* had crossed Joe's mind several times on his way up north to Fareland. He was itching to get going, get on the road, get there and get back.

But the nervous part, that had come later. It wasn't really anything substantial, but there was a feeling about the old Fareland Cinema that came to Joe like an undercurrent of cold seawater beneath the sun-warmed surface. There was, he would think later while alone in his hotel room wishing he hadn't sounded so guilty when he'd talked to his wife, a pervasive atmosphere about the place; a musty smell clinging to everything like an invisible gray fog. A chill, a worry, something definitely not normal but too elusive to really catch. He'd first felt it when he saw the tower of the Fareland standing out amid the tall pine trees in the tiny valley beyond the highway, and it had occurred to him then that the town of Fareland seemed to be hiding. Had it not been for that towering sign with its muddy green lettering running vertically along its flank, Joe would have missed the town completely. That's what made him nervous.

Well, partly, anyway.

There was the crowd that had gathered across the street from the Fareland Cinema when Joe first parked his car at the curb and got out to look at it. Just your normal crowd, gathering randomly, looking on with the nonchalant air that seemed forced, and they had a funny look to them, something Joe couldn't quite place. His nervousness had clicked up a notch at that, and the feeling of the undercurrent, nibbling your toes but too deep to feel with any certainty, became something more than just an afterthought. Indeed, it had forced itself into the fore of Joe's mind with such authority that he found himself thinking about it as much as he was thinking about the crowd.

And then there was Frank.

He'd emerged from the darkness of the theater as an animal might emerge from its lair, and for a second Joe thought about running. But then the old man had set his gaze on Joe with eyes alive and watchful, darting and narrowing, making mental catalogues for later reference, and Joe felt compelled to stand there, complying, because it was clear nothing got past this old man without having first gone through careful scrutiny. It was also clear, as they stood together in front of the theater while across the street the tiny crowd gathered, that Joe was not only being scrutinized, he was being judged.

So, yeah. He was nervous. And he was anxious, because he'd left L.A. early that morning without calling in sick. He'd gotten up before dawn, showered, dressed, kissed his sleeping wife gently on the cheek, and crept out of the house. Then he'd gotten into his car and saw that his hands were trembling, because he was anxious about not calling in sick, and he was anxious about getting up north, and he was nervous about why all this was happening with such fast and furious secrecy.

Why hadn't he called in sick?

"Didn't catch your name first time round, young fella," the old man said in a crisp New England accent that set him apart in this small northern California town.

Joe jumped, just barely able to catch the squeak in his throat before it had escaped. He put out his hand. "Name's Joe. Joe Moreson."

The old man smiled and took Joe's hand in a firm grasp. "Pleased to meet you, Joe. Name's Franklin Jordan. Most folks call me Frank." He held his grip longer than Joe cared for, then released it, as though something had nudged his mind and told him to let go. "Like I was sayin', once you get that projector runnin' again, you'll make a fortune. Ayuh, that's the ticket."

The projector?

"What do you mean, Frank?"

Frank shot him a sideways glance. "Got a lot on your mind, young fella. Don't ya? Ayuh. Young folks think too much for their own good." He narrowed his eyes for a moment, then curled his lips. "Projector's what's got you the fortune here, boy. You get it runnin', you got no trouble. Follow me?"

Joe nodded dumbly. "I think so." But he wasn't really sure. He'd been thinking about being anxious, and nervous, and was he scared too? Or was that just a by-product of being nervous and anxious?

Why hadn't he called in sick?

Joe shifted his weight to his other foot and scanned the front of the building. "It is worn down, isn't it?"

The old man stood with his back arched as he peered up at the large marquee that hung over the front of the movie theater. Above it was a massive neon sign proclaiming the name of the theater in green and red script. "Ayuh. Seen its prime back in the forties. Interior's a little worse for wear, but the screen's still good." He reached into his pocket and pulled out a battered stick of gum, absently unwrapped it, and popped it into his mouth. Then he turned to Joe and winked. "Won't much matter once you get the projector runnin'."

"It won't?"

Frank shot him another sideways glance, like a shark eyeing a promising dinner. "Say your name's Moreson? Any relation to John Moreson, out the Valley way?"

"No, sir."

Frank's jaw worked lazily at the gum. *Like a cow chewing cud,* Joe thought, smiling inwardly at the sparked memory of his grandfather and uncle ruminating over a broken-down tractor, chewing tobacco or gum. A lazy sun sending slants of light across their broad backs, the two of them looked like heifers out to field. Those were good times. Those were times not yet muddied by hesitation, passivity, and fear. Always ready to run from the fight, that was Joe's motto. Why stand there and get your face all bloodied? No one cared.

It was then that it occurred to Joe quite suddenly, which

surprised him more than it should have, that for some time
now he'd been unable to keep his mind from wandering. It
had begun to wander the first time he came down the slope
of highway into the small valley with its tiny hidden town,
continued to wander as he drove slowly down the main street
looking at signs and small buildings all clean and crisp and
new with white paint, people meandering on the sidewalks,
unmindful of traffic laws as they crossed the narrow main
street randomly and without looking both ways before you
cross because one of these days, Joey, you're going to get
yourself killed. People don't care about you, no one cares.
You have to learn to take care of yourself. And if that
means—

His mind was wandering again.

"Got a family, do ya?" Frank asked.

Joe blinked. "Yes . . . well, a wife. Her name's Karen."

"Any kids?"

Joe squirmed a little. "No . . . we . . . I can't . . ." he
trailed off.

Frank nodded, seemingly pleased. "Good."

"Good?"

Frank ignored him. "Your wife come with you?"

"No. She's still in L.A. That's where I'm from."

"What she doin' all the way down there?" Frank turned his
head slowly and gave Joe the kind of look a man might give
another when sitting in a bar after one too many as they
talked about wives and conventions and how the two never
mix.

Joe fidgeted. "Um . . . well . . ."

"She know you're here?"

Joe felt his face flush. "We talked about it. . . ."

Frank tilted his head and gazed at the midday sun. "You
got in your car and you came up here and didn't tell a soul
you were comin'. That the picture, Joe?"

Joe felt himself squirming and hoped it didn't show. "Listen, Mr. Jordan. I, um, don't really see where that's any of
your business."

Frank turned his head back, even slower than before.
"Ayuh."

They stood in silence for a time longer than was comfortable for Joe. His head was aching with conflict; swimming with questions and conflicts and why did he need to explain himself to *anyone*?

And for *God's* sake, why was he so fucking anxious?

Frank left him standing alone on the sidewalk, twisting and scrambling with his mind, and went to the front of the theater.

Joe watched him go, wanted to follow, wanted like hell to be let off the hook. He forced himself to focus on something else, something more tangible, and lifted his face to look at the theater's facade. On the marquee was a jumble of letters arranged in nonsensical groupings.

Oh yeah . . . that helps. That helps a hell of a lot. Yes, I'm feeling much better now, thank you very much.

That crowd over there, across the street. Watching him. Watching everything he does. . . .

Frank was at the front door of the theater, pulling out a tarnished key from his pocket and, with a hint of arrogance, slipping it into the lock. He made a grunting sound that rumbled up from his pelvis as he pulled hard on the door, swinging it open on rusty, screaming hinges. A strong musty smell floated out from a shroud of darkness within the mouth of the theater, hanging in the still air like a statement. Frank stepped inside and disappeared into the darkness, and for a second Joe had the distinctly distasteful feeling of having just seen someone being scooped up into a gaping maw and swallowed in one gulp, without chewing. One quick gulp and the old man with the intermittent yet fluent New England accent was gone forever. It gave Joe a shiver, one that he felt somewhere at the base of his spine. He stood outside, feeling strange in the silence of his aloneness now on the sidewalk; alone except for that crowd. That small crowd gathering so innocently, there across the street in front of the whitewashed grocery store with its hand-painted signs proclaiming a sale on pork. He wiped sweat from the back of his neck and reeled in a shaky, heady sigh.

It did not surprise him that, when he finally heard Frank's old crackling voice calling to him from the darkness, he felt a sense of relief like the sudden splash of hot water from the shower, washing over a body cooled to an intolerable degree from a long cold night. "You comin' in or not? Haven't got all day."

"I'm coming," Joe said, and hurried to the door. He could almost feel the stares of the crowd licking at his heels.

The strong musty smell that before hung floating in the air like a moist memory now greeted him in full force as he stepped across the threshold. He had to stop a moment, breathing in short, wary gasps. The lobby was large, almost cavernous, and had once been decorated in good taste. No . . . better than good taste. The decor was exquisite, the only problem being a strange and undecided coupling of Art Deco and rococo. It was as though the designer had been at odds with himself, attempting to satisfy two very distinct but predictably opposite desires. The result tended to set one on a slant, your eyes never really sure where to look, or why. And now, adding to the confusion, was the wear of time. The rugs and wallpaper were faded, cobwebs hung low and dusty in the corners of the ceiling. Dirt and filth were everywhere. There was a sort of sadness in the air, like grief of something lost. Something wonderful, a dream perhaps, a betrayed wish, now suddenly turned sour and forgotten. And lost.

A chill. Suddenly.

Joe turned on his heel and let the sunlight glaring through the front doors flood his body. Its warmth was not only comforting, it was liberating, and he stared at it long enough to leave a mark on his retinas before turning back to continue surveying the lobby.

Frank watched him in silence. Frank scrutinized him, in silence.

The snack bar stood to one side, and opposite the front doors were the entryways to the house. Frank was standing at the center entrance. "Feel that chill? Ayuh. A draft someplace. Old building." He turned, headed through the curtains. "Very old."

Joe stood there, by the front door, eyes blinking stupidly. He looked again through the front doors, saw the crowd again, saw the dust and debris of age, the sweet and wondrous thing gone sour. It hung in the air, enshrouded the place like smoke in the valley after a terrible forest fire.

Why were they gathering?

Joe found himself drawn to them as he leaned close to the glass door and studied them through the dusty streaks that warped them into something more like a dream. There were three—no—four old men clustered together, talking among themselves. A few kids skittered about their feet. One old woman stood at the rim of their circle, leaning in as though trying to hear what they were saying. A younger man in a business suit stood at her side, a hand on her arm as though he were trying to pull her away from them. The old woman's shoulders were so badly slumped that her oversized sweater hung around her knees. Her look was a little different from the rest—although he hadn't placed their look yet—he knew what was in that old wrinkled face of the woman with the too-big sweater. He'd had that look himself.

She was anxious. And she was scared.

Scared?

Was he scared? Joe asked himself. He thought about it for a moment but couldn't be sure. He was nervous. He was anxious. But was he scared? Really *scared*?

He just couldn't be sure.

There was another look on the old woman's face that was unmistakable. She was pissed. Her lips were drawn back to show her old brown teeth. Her eyes glinted in the sunlight, sending sparks of muddy fury at the four old men. She was yelling at them in short bursts, but Joe couldn't hear what she was saying. Each time she shouted, the young man in the business suit gave a tug on her arm. It seemed to have no effect on her.

Joe turned his attention to him, because there was something about him that seemed familiar. He had more the semblance of order about him, his hair combed back from his forehead and that business suit looking so out of place amid the casual country wear of the others. He had a fitful, darting look to his face, his brow furrowed and his mouth grimly set. He was anxious, too, but not for the same reasons as Joe.

And just why was Joe anxious? Because he'd left L.A.

without telling anyone? Because he hadn't called in sick?
Because . . .

Wandering. Always wandering. So many questions.

Suddenly he was aware of the young man in the business
suit watching him. Their eyes met, and the man looked suddenly stricken, his eyes widening and then darting away as he
tugged again on the old woman's arm, this time more urgently than before. But the old lady ignored him. And she
still looked pissed.

Why was she pissed?

Why hadn't he called in sick?

Just what the hell was going on here, anyway? Or was
anything? Was it possible he was laying upon the tiny crowd
across the street the confusion and questions crowding his
own mind? He had moved so quickly, without forethought.
Well . . . no . . . that wasn't completely true. He'd been
thinking about the Fareland Cinema ever since Karen had
shown him the ad. He'd been thinking about quitting for
months, but never had the guts to actually do it. And on that
day, when Richards lumbered into his cubicle and wheezed
out his nasty trouncing, Joe had come to a crossroads within
his own mind. He knew he couldn't take it anymore, and he
knew he couldn't do anything overtly to shut Richards up.
Oh, sure, Kelsie was right: Joe always stalked out. Joe always
made a scene and then came squirming back, using the shadows and the corners to wriggle his way to his cubicle unnoticed. But this time . . .

. . . *this* time . . .

Something was different. Something inside had snapped. It
was the rings. All those pretty rings he'd stolen from dead
fingers and put on his own living ones, admiring them. Cov-
eting them. Having them. That had been the difference.

But it wasn't enough of a difference, was it?

That's why he hadn't called in sick. That's why.

Frank's voice broke through the gathering gloom of Joe's
rumination. It was a sound so sharp and clear that it made
him jump uneasily, almost squeaking out a cry. He turned
and hurried toward the curtains of the entryways, glancing

just once over his shoulder at the crowd before entering the house through the center curtains.

The house was arranged in a spreading fan shape that curled around the screen. The seats were split into two groups with three aisles: one on either side and one down the center. The smell of stale popcorn and mildewed upholstery permeated the static air. The cushions of the two hundred and some odd seats had once been a rich ruby color, probably velvet, but now they were threadbare and torn, and very sad looking.

That feeling again; a terrible sadness, like grief. And something else. Something . . .

Anxious?

Expectation.

Joe shuddered.

"Still feelin' that chill, eh?" Frank said behind him. "Ayuh. Most folks do. Place's got a draft, like I said before. Which reminds me." He laid a hand on Joe's shoulder. "Might be a good idea for you to employ m'grandson, Andy. Knows this place inside and out. Grew up here, y'know. Knows the town good too. He can show you round. Ayuh." His grip tightened. "Be a good idea, get my message?"

Joe turned hard enough to loosen Frank's grip. "No, Frank. I'm not sure I do."

A tiny, almost frightened grin crossed Frank's face. He shrugged. "Don't take me wrong, Joe. Don't mean no harm. Don't mean no offense either. Just sayin' Andy'd make a good helper. Just sayin' you should think about it. Might be just the ticket." He moved past Joe, shooting him the kind of dark glance a kid might give an adult when he knows he's done something wrong. He stopped at the front of the house and set himself in a wide stance, his back to the seats, his arms spread wide and proud. "Look at that screen!"

Joe looked up at the screen and blinked. Then he blinked again and on the third blink he reeled. He'd heard the term *blinding white* before, but never had he truly understood the term until now. It was as though they were in some sort of time warp that split the theater into two separate eras. Here, amid the dank and muddy ambience that was the house, was this screen, so strikingly white, it seemed brand new. There was not one tear, not one spot, in its entire expanse. And it was clean, unnaturally clean. Within the old and tattered house, the screen seemed out of place.

Or was it the other way around?

Joe moved closer to Frank until they were side by side, both staring in wonder at the screen. They gazed in silence, the only sound being the slow and steady smacking of Frank's jaws against his chewing gum. The sound echoed up through the rows of empty seats and bounced off the back wall in waves of muffled clicks.

Did the crowd outside know about this screen?

Joe sighed, and from the corner of his eye saw Frank flinch as if a jolt of electricity had just gone through him. He reached out to touch Frank, to apologize, but Frank waved him off. "Just wadin' in some old memories, Joe. No need to say you're sorry."

The chill again. Sudden chill, like being nudged with ice. Frank's voice was different. Nothing distinct, nothing obvious, but Joe's mind snagged on it and the chill came. He listened carefully, hearing a deep whistling seep through the man's jagged teeth, and wondered just what it was he'd touched on.

"Well," Joe said. "That's some screen."

"Oh, ayuh. Some screen indeed. Not a mark on her. Clean too."

"So, why did you let the projector go to seed?"

Frank twitched. "Not sure I understand you, Joe."

"Well, you kept the screen up so well. I'm surprised you didn't maintain the projector as well."

The old man chewed his gum in silence for a moment, then turned and trotted up the aisle.

Joe watched him, nonplussed. As he disappeared through the doors he called over his shoulder, "You comin', Joe? Haven't got all day."

"I—" Joe stared at the screen and suddenly had the feeling the screen was staring back at him. He turned and hurried up the aisle.

The chill followed him.

Do they know? Do they know about this screen?

Frank led Joe up a curving staircase directly opposite the snack bar. As they walked, Joe examined the lobby more completely as it descended slowly below them. The entries to the house were adorned with ornate designs, probably gold leaf as the color was brilliant, free of tarnish and fade. In all its confusion of thought and planning and dreams as flimsy as an unformed thought, the Fareland Cinema had been an opulent place.

"Real gold leaf," Frank muttered. They stood now on a kind of mezzanine overlooking the lobby. Frank leaned on the railing, both hands gripping the wooden frame.

"This is oak, isn't it?" Joe asked.

"Ayuh."

Joe ran his hand along the smooth, curving surface. "Carved oak. Very nice."

"Ayuh."

"We're going to the balcony?"

Frank straightened. "Every good movie house has a balcony, that's for sure."

They slid through tattered curtains onto the balcony and stood for a moment while Frank pointed down at the screen. Joe was almost afraid to look. He turned with his eyes squinted shut, like a kid watching a horror movie, and his fear was well rewarded.

Looking down at the screen from the balcony, he could see that there was definitely something wrong with the angles at which the seating was arranged. The balcony hung way over the house, almost to the screen itself, so that those sitting in the first row were looking at the screen at a ninety-degree angle, and those at the back of the balcony barely had visible access to it at all.

"This is," he began, shaking his head, "—this is all wrong."

"How do you figure?"

Joe threw him an astonished glance, but Frank only smiled and winked.

Then he stopped, as though a cold hand of caution had touched his shoulder, squeezing it with foreboding. His face darkened, and his body swayed forward in a secretive slump.

"Don't you go onto the balcony, Joe. You stay away from it, when the movie's goin'."

"Why?"

For a second it seemed that Frank wasn't going to offer an explanation, then he finally sighed and leaned against the railing. "Can't really see the screen from here, y'see? Balconies' good for . . . you know . . . for the young folk. Up here doin' their kissin' and such. But you can't see the movie." He slumped a little, sighing.

The chill.

Funny. Suddenly I'm scared.

As quickly as his face had darkened, Frank's eyes sparkled with clarity and frivolity. "Not much movie watchin' goes on in balconies," he said, and then he was off again, waving at Joe from over his shoulder.

Against his better judgment Joe surveyed again the overall design of the house. The main house seating arrangement was as cockeyed as the balcony's. The fan of seats curled so dramatically around the screen that those viewers at each side would be looking at the screen at an extremely poor angle. It was like the distorted images of a dream, or a memory going old. You just couldn't quite put your finger on the reality of the situation.

Joe took a swipe at his forehead, not surprised to find his hand came away warm and moist. He closed his eyes, made a wish so foolish as to not be said out loud

when I open my eyes this will all be gone

then peeked one more look

damn

before following Frank across the balcony to another door framed by thick and tattered curtains.

Joe took a deep breath. "I'd like to see the projection room, Frank."

"Figured you would," Frank said. "That's where we're headed."

Just inside and to the right of the door was a small staircase, and at the head another smaller door. As Joe watched Frank ascend the stairs he saw that something had changed in the old man. His back was bent, his movements became labored and painful. His hardy old frame now sagged with each step, like that of a man being confronted by an old enemy. One that had beaten him often. When he finally reached the top of the stairs his hand went out, groping for the railing. The other hand clenched his chest in a sudden, encompassing arrest of mind and heart. In an instant Joe saw himself left to clean up matters unknown to him. Make arrangements, see the lawyers, deal with death, oh, God. . . .

Never should have come up here. Never should. It was wrong.

But Frank only stood there, his shoulders trembling with exhaustion, his hand curled tightly around the rail. A rigid moment passed and the old man straightened, slipped his hand into his back pocket, and produced a tiny silver key. Deliberately he slipped it into the keyhole.

As he did, a touch of light made the silver key flash. Its image burned itself into Joe's mind. The door creaked opened, aided by Frank's trembling hand. He motioned Joe to follow him inside.

Inside, into a tomb. That's what it was like. A tomb. Or a shrine.

It's cold in here. It's cold!

Joe followed him, allowing himself to be led by the flickering gleam in Frank's eyes and the deepening soft of the darkened room. His heart raced, flicking against his rib cage and tightening his throat to near total constriction. He probably would have reached a crescendo—a climax of anticipation in the subtle, sliding way one does when frightened slowly, methodically—but his eyes were struck and the moment lost when Frank hit the wall switch.

It wasn't anything like what Joe had expected.

There, near the center of the tiny room, lost in a mountain of dust and debris and a filigree of cobwebs, was the projector. It stood silent, inanimate.

Impotent.

Joe groaned.

As Frank watched in some kind of reverent silence, Joe moved toward the projector, circled it once, and, having taken full stock of it, rubbed his eyes distractedly. "I'm going to have to buy a new projector."

The old man whispered, "No. . . ."

"What do you mean!" Joe turned on him, and if he hadn't been so preoccupied with the absolute waste he saw before him he would have seen that Frank was decidedly stricken. "Look at it. You haven't run it in fifty years, have you? It's a mess." He examined it more closely. "Christ, the teeth are worn, the take-up's shot, and look at this." He grasped the cord between thumb and finger. Its frayed end dangled lifelessly. "You haven't run this thing in fifty years."

Frank said nothing. He just stood there, looking dazed and stupid, lost in some kind of trance. It was as though he hadn't heard a word Joe had said because he was listening to someone else, someone . . .

His face was blank, but his head was cocked to one side and his eyes sparkled with attention. Yes, he was listening to someone else.

Who?

Joe dropped the cord and sighed heavily. "Well, at least it's a thirty-five."

Frank tilted his head. "Thirty-five what?"

"Millimeter," Joe said. "The film size, Frank."

"Oh." His eyes focused again, and the blank look faded away. "Well, that don't much matter, film size and all. It'll take anything you give it. Never worried too much about size. Ayuh, she's a fine machine no matter what you stuff in her."

Joe glared at the man, both frustrated and angry, and a little shaken by his initial tension at what he might have encountered in this dark little room. By Frank's behavior he had almost expected . . . well, he wasn't sure what he'd expected. Something fantastic. Something so inexplicably terrifying that his mind would shatter like delicate crystal. Instead the simple reality of a projector too old and unusable stared at him in blatant normalcy. He glared at Frank with the anger of embarrassment, enraged by his own seduced imagination, but Frank simply grinned at him and winked. "Once you get it runnin', your troubles are over."

Joe couldn't decide if he was angry or relieved. He slammed his hand down on the projector. The sound was heavy. A breath of dust blossomed into the still air. He heard a groan and turned to see Frank swaying to one side, his eyes rolling back in their sockets, his head reeling, then flopping clumsily to his chest.

He's having a heart attack, Joe thought wildly. *Ah, Jesus . . . Christ . . . why now?* He lurched forward and caught the collapsing old man around the waist. "Frank! Are you all right?"

As swiftly as he had swooned Frank righted himself. His face was hard, deep-set lines suddenly etching across the smooth skin on his cheeks. Joe looked closer and saw the pupils dilating, a fierce twinkle of rage glimmering deep in their centers.

Joe stepped back.

"You want the theater or not?" Frank said. The New England accent was completely gone from his voice. "I haven't got all day."

"Yes . . . I mean, I'm not—"

"My price is fifty thousand," Frank said sharply. "You'll make that back in a year, if you do what I told you. Get the projector running. It'll make you a fortune."

"Okay," Joe whispered.

As Frank nodded and turned to leave, Joe reached out and touched his shoulder. "Are you sure you're all right?"

"Never better," Frank said, and left, shutting the door behind him and leaving Joe strangely alone. The afterimage of Frank's solid change, the fierce twinkle in the center of his dilating eyes, hung in the air like an echo. Joe found himself bouncing with the echo, out of control, desperately grasping at his bounding thoughts.

He stared at the projector.

Scared?

No, not scared. Nervous, maybe. Anxious. Confused.

God, that twinkle. Deep in his eyes.

For the first time since he'd left L.A., he wished Kelsie were here. Kelsie Brown had a knack of being able to make sense out of confusion, disorder, discord, tumult, uproar, hysteria . . .

. . . Panic.

Lightning . . . in his eyes. . . .

Just what had he gotten himself into?

Suddenly, completely, he felt the aloneness extend itself to encompass the whole of his life. He leaned against the wall and sighed deeply, dragging in air until his lungs ached, then released it as though to send with the air all that was hurtful and strange, all that made him feel . . .

. . . God, made him feel . . .

The air rushed out of him and he shuddered, rubbed his eyes hard, and took another breath. Slowly, painfully, his mind began to focus. Calm replaced the panic.

Nervous? Well, yes. That was okay. It was sensible. It was safe.

Scared?

He trembled.

No, not scared. Not *really* scared. Just . . .

. . . well . . . worried.

Yes.

He straightened himself.

Yes, he was worried. And that was okay too. That was sensible. After all, look at all he had done in a very short time.

Anxious?

Yes, that was okay too. Buying a theater, just like that, was enough to make any man anxious. Such an undertaking. He didn't know anything about running a theater.

He'd bought the theater.

Suddenly his heart lurched.

Just like that. He'd bought it. Just like that.

Well, that wasn't so strange, was it? That's what he'd come up here to do.

No . . . no . . . he'd come up here to check it out. Wasn't that right?

No . . . no . . .

He'd come up here to escape. He'd run in the night, not telling anyone, because he'd wanted to escape.

So what?

Joe crossed his arms across his chest, his lips tightening. So what?

He couldn't take the pressure anymore. It was hurting him,

hurting his stomach, hurting his heart. He'd had enough. He hadn't been able to change what was happening at Tempac, so he'd gotten out. And gotten out fast. So what?

Now he had a chance to run his own life. Be his own boss. He loved movies, and here was an opportunity to do just what he wanted. Follow his dream.

Wear the pretty rings.

Joe's mouth twitched.

But so what?

Always being subject to the whim of someone else. Always on his knees, taking crap, *eating* crap with a smile planted firmly on his lips. So what?

He trembled.

He looked at the projector. Old, almost ancient, and far more useful than he felt at that moment.

There was nothing wrong with trying to do something with your life instead of just staying stagnant in a hopeless situation until you fester and rupture. And die.

Nothing wrong in that. Nothing. He wasn't running away. Not running *away*. He was running toward something. Something better. Something easier.

He *did* love movies, always had. As a kid he'd spent many long, enjoyable hours at the local theater, lost in the fantasy the silver screen conjured just for him. In there, in the darkness of the house with the screen illuminating visions made just for him, things never seemed so bad. He could lose himself. He could be free. So what if it was just fantasy? For a few short hours he was master of all he surveyed.

If Joe was such a valuable asset to Tempac, they should have treated him with a little respect. They shouldn't have nudged him with a hot needle and expected him to dance.

It wasn't Tempac. It was just one man.

Joe shook his head fervently. Richards *was* Tempac.

They were sorry now. Yes. He'd spit in their collective, high-corporate faces. He'd kicked his heels and left them in the dust to come to northern California where it's cold and there are a lot of trees. He liked trees just about as much as he loved the movies.

Old movies. The classics. His own theater, where he could

screen the classics, the really good movies; the kind you just don't see anymore. The supply was infinite: *Casablanca, Key Largo, Maltese Falcon, Vertigo, North by Northwest,* and his favorite classic—albeit not a popular one—Alfred Hitchcock's *Shadow of a Doubt.* He particularly liked the symbolic portrayal of man's duality as it was presented in the bar scene midway through the movie. Joe had always harbored a secret desire to be, if not wicked, at least ruthless in his dealings with others. It was a feeling of confidence alien to him, and often the source of indignation and frustration whenever he found himself in a position of vulnerability. He was the pleaser, the smoother of ruffled feathers. Rarely did he confront the adversary in any posture other than one of compliance.

But if he had been ruthless—if he'd had at his command a sense of inflexible authority laced with the hard-core assurance of a man undaunted by political intimidation—perhaps his life would have turned out differently.

Things at Tempac would have been different. He'd still be there, for one thing. And he'd be in a position of power and influence. He would have been giving the orders instead of taking them.

Giving orders. Wearing the rings himself.

Carpe diem. Kelsie had said it often. *Carpe diem.* Nothing else mattered because life was too short.

The thought of Kelsie suddenly made him smile. What a man of rationality Kelsie was. Both feet planted firmly on the ground. Kelsie had a way about him that was both seductive and frightening. He could, with the mental dexterity of a fakir, expose your hidden intangibles. Kelsie Brown, Joe often thought, was the dream incarnate.

Without knowing it Kelsie had forced Joe to take matters into his own hands. Okay, so he'd slunk out of town under the cloak of darkness. Okay, so it was a chicken thing to do. But he'd done it. He'd *done* it! And that's all that really mattered.

Things were going to be different. No more pressure, for one thing. No more abusive authority lurking on the rim of his sanity, waiting for him to perform, to bow, to lick heels from a standing position.

He was going to start taking more decisive steps, and he wouldn't be afraid to present them to anyone within hearing distance, their responses be damned!

Things were going to be different.

He was going to stop lying to Karen, for one thing.

Well, they weren't lies, actually. They were half-truths. They were safe-truths. Like sneaking out in the early dawn, before she was awake. Things like that. They avoided confrontation. What would it prove? Joe Moreson was still the man she thought she'd married.

Almost, anyway.

But things were going to be different.

Joe touched the projector with the tip of his finger and then wiped his finger on the front of his shirt. Fifty thousand dollars was a hell of a lot of money for a broken-down theater and a useless projector.

The reflection from the overhead light played gently on the curve of the metal casing, like a silver eye staring up at him. He smiled inwardly, and he believed, for an instant, a tiny, almost imperceptible instant, that the silver eye winked at him.

He found Frank in the box office, shuffling through some old papers in a rusty file cabinet. He didn't look up as Joe walked in. Joe cleared his throat. "I'm sorry if I upset you, Frank. It's just that . . . well, I have limited funds. I was hoping that all the equipment would be in good running condition. . . ."

Without looking up Frank said, "Will be, once you get it runnin'. Make you a—"

"Fortune, yes." Joe sighed, but at the same time he felt something loosen in his chest because Frank was back to his old self, the New England accent ringing true and clear in Joe's head. He gazed out the box office window at the few people still gathered there. They were leaning forward, eyes squinting, necks stretched as they tried to peer in through the foggy glass of the box office window. He watched them wondrously, feeling a kind of captivation with their keen glances and fitful faces.

Scared? No . . . nervous, maybe. Anxious . . .

Hungry.

Joe flinched.

Hungry. Yes. They looked hungry. Strange . . .

At length Frank straightened. He was holding a large pile of old papers in his hand. He carried them to the desk opposite the file cabinet and laid them down carefully, smoothing out the crumples with a gentle caress. "Ownership papers." He grinned. "Ayuh, this is my place. I own it. But I can't afford it anymore. Can't . . ." He turned and looked at Joe. "Was going to tear it down, put up a parking lot or an office building. You know, something to bring in the money. But the town folk, they'd have nothing to do with that. Landmark, they called it. Can't tear down a landmark." His eyes lost their focus. "Can't let her die."

He stood for a long time, his face growing withered and old and his eyes, once sparkling and clear, now gazed uselessly at a time long gone. A memory grown old and sour.

He touched the papers, let his hand linger there for a moment, and as he gathered them up and held them out, Joe noticed the old man's hands were trembling.

2

 On August 27, after Joe had signed the final papers and the Fareland was his, he went to his motel room and put in a phone call to L.A. When the phone clicked Joe nearly jumped out of his seat. Karen answered the phone without saying anything more than "You bought it, didn't you?"

Joe blinked once, shifted a little, then swallowed hard. "How did you know?"

Karen laughed softly. "It wasn't difficult to figure out. You took off, Joe. Didn't tell me where you were going. You had your mind set before you even had the car door closed and the ignition key turned."

Joe smiled. "You know me so well." He bit his lip. "What do you think, Karen?"

"About what?"

"About my buying the place."

There was a slight pause, then Karen said solemnly, "I think you have to follow your dreams, Joe. You have to take some control of your life."

Joe's lips tightened. "What do you mean?"

"I—"

The image of the rings, the pretty rings stolen from dead and decaying fingers, filled the fore of his mind and made his entire body stiffen with something so inexplicable that he could only shudder. "What do you mean I have to take control?"

"What is this, Joe? What's going on? You've got that sound to your voice."

Lost for words, Joe sat in the midst of a fog of confusion and turmoil. He fought against the image, against the tightening of his body. He shook his head, rubbed his hand across his mouth, swallowed, swallowed again.

"Joe?"

Slowly, almost painfully, the sensation subsided. He drew in a deep, cleansing breath and let it out slowly, turning his face away from the mouthpiece. "I'm sorry. I'm full of . . . I don't know. . . ."

"Confusion," Karen said gently. "Excitement. Fear. Guilt. You took a big step, Joe."

"Did I? Really?"

"Sure."

"I ran away, didn't I?"

A moment, then, "Or ran toward."

Joe smiled gratefully. "I love you, babe."

"Back at you, love." He could hear her shifting in her seat and readied himself for what she was to say next. "Be your own boss. It's important. And it's scary."

"Scary?"

"Sure," Karen said easily. "And you know it. That's why you took off in the night."

"You knew, didn't you?" he said with a half-smile.

"I felt you get out of bed, I heard you get dressed. I heard you creep out of the house and I heard the car start."

"You knew . . ." Joe echoed, knowing it was true. "Why didn't you say anything?"

Karen chuckled. It was a pleasant, comforting sound. "Because you didn't want me to."

Joe smiled inwardly, his shoulders relaxing. He sat there silently, listening to her breathing as it filtered through the receiver, and knew she was smiling too.

"Are you going to call Kelsie?"

The tightness returned. "No. I'm . . . no."

"Why not?"

Joe's eyes darted about the motel room. "Not sure. I guess I'm afraid of what he'll say."

"He's on your side."

Joe said nothing.

"Call him, Joe."

"Karen, couldn't you . . ." Joe ground his teeth.

"You call him, Joe. He's on your side. Trust me."

Joe closed his eyes. "Okay."

"As soon as we get off the phone. Okay?"

"Yeah."

"You're not going to, are you?"

Joe stood up, paced a little, his eyes darting about the room as if looking for a place to hide. "I need a little time. Want to look over the town, get my bearings—"

"And figure out what you're going to say to him."

Joe huffed. "Will you stop that?"

Karen chuckled.

Joe sat down and thought for a moment, thought seriously, collating the myriad actions of the last day. "I didn't quit Tempac, you know? I really did run away. He went to work and saw I wasn't there. I don't know, Karen. I feel a little . . . wimpy. You know?"

"It'll pass."

He sighed. "Hope so."

"Call Kelsie."

"Does he know I'm up here?"

After a moment of silence, Karen said cautiously, "I told him you had to find something. You had to be alone for a while. I told him you'd call as soon as you'd found what you were looking for. He seemed to understand."

That made Joe feel a little better, but he was still reticent about calling his old friend. "I have to give myself a little time."

There was another moment of strained silence, then Karen conceded.

"I'll need you to take care of things down there, Karen. Put the house up for sale, stuff like that."

"Don't worry about it, Joe. Just get yourself settled there. I'll take care of things down here."

"Thanks, babe. Gotta go. I'm suddenly very tired."

"I'll bet."

"Call you soon."

Another thoughtful silence, then, "I love you, Joe. I love you."

Joe smiled, his heart warming. They hung up on a note that left him feeling both satisfied and anxious.

Anxious . . .

Why in hell was he so anxious?

Joe lay back on the bed and placed his hands behind his head. Why was he feeling so anxious?

The theater, the crowd. Frank. His stealthy escape in the night . . .

. . . his reluctance to call Kelsie.

Joe jerked a little. That was it, yeah. Afraid to call Kelsie. Afraid of what he'd say.

Funny thing was, he needed to talk to the man. He needed to hear Kelsie's cool, unaffected voice that always reassured him when his own voice had started to waver and crack. Karen had said that Kelsie seemed to understand, and he believed her. But something—something was stopping him.

A gentle breeze wafted through the room, barely noticeable.

"Hell with it," he said aloud, and sat up. He grabbed the phone in a tight fist, gritted his teeth, and dialed Kelsie's number.

He waited anxiously while the phone rang, almost hanging up once, then jumped when the phone clicked and Kelsie's strong tone filled the earpiece.

Joe felt himself sag, but he wasn't sure if it was from relief or the weighty sensation of impending doom. He was never really sure just how Kelsie was going to react, and sometimes that state of perpetual unpredictability put Joe on edge.

"Hey, Kels."

"Joe?" A laugh, thank God. The sag in his shoulders became more a comfort than a cumbersome burden. "Well, God damn. How are you? Okay?"

"Yeah."

"Find your dream?"

The question sent Joe into rigid silence.

"Joe?"

The rings. He never should have told Kelsie about the pretty rings.

"Joe? What's going on?"

"Nothing," Joe said forcefully. The gentle breeze that had swirled in the room suddenly grew cold. "Didn't think I'd do it, did you, Kels?"

There was a moment of silent confusion, then Kelsie asked, "Do what?"

"Didn't think I had the guts, right?"

He heard Kelsie take a deep breath. "Joe, what the hell is wrong?"

"Never mind." Joe ran his hand across his brow. "I'm sorry. Guess I'm just . . . defensive."

"Because you took off?"

"Yeah."

"Where are you?"

Joe took a deep breath. "Well, I'm in a small town called Fareland, about thirty miles east of Oakland."

"Really?"

"Yeah."

Long pause. Long, tense pause.

"I'm not coming back, Kels."

Pause. And that bitch of a sensation, that unpredictability.

"I'm"—Joe rubbed his eyes—"I'm not coming back."

Pause. Joe gritted his teeth.

"Do you understand?" he said, eyes closed, teeth clenched.

"Yeah, I do," Kelsie said without hesitation. "You want me to tell Richards?"

Feeling like a child, Joe nodded his head.

"Joe?"

"Yes. Yeah . . . I . . ."

"Relax, Joe."

Joe lay back on the bed with his eyes closed. He held the receiver tightly.

"Call me if you need me," Kelsie said gently. "Okay?"

"I will," Joe whispered, then hung up without saying good-bye.

He lay there on the bed, in the darkness, staring at nothing and at everything. Finally he closed his eyes and tried to look into his heart. Kelsie had said he understood, but did he really? Did he understand about dreams? Knowing your dreams? *Owning* your dreams? Did he understand about how you take so much? You take it and take it and take it until you are bloated with a festering boil of discontent and self-effacing indignation, until you finally have to do something, to *do* something before you bust open and all that disease and filth spills out of you, corrupting your world.

That's what he'd done, when he crept out in the night and came to Fareland. That's what he'd done when he bought the theater.

And that's what he'd done when he ran away from Tempac.

Joe placed his hands over his face. He took a deep breath and let it out forcefully through his fingers. His breath felt hot against his skin. He'd run away.

He ran away from the big bad boss. Didn't face up to him. Didn't face up to his responsibilities.

But Kelsie understood, or at least Joe *thought* he understood, and that counted for something. It did, yes. It was confirmation; a quick and easy resolution to a threatening problem. Kelsie understood the need for deliverance from his presently dangerous life situation, and he understood the need for expediency. And escape.

Desperate, the ad had said.

Desperate.

Kelsie had given his blessing, and his good wishes. "Call me if you need me," he'd said.

The gentle breeze playing with the window curtains turned chilly. Joe sighed heavily and tried to clean out the cobwebs of discord in his mind.

Okay. Okay, he thought. Where was he now?

The owner of the Fareland Cinema, for one thing. And that was good, wasn't it?

Or had he made a mistake?

Ah, Christ. It's always something. . . .

Those people, that crowd outside the theater. They were strange. It wasn't as though they'd gathered aimlessly. It was as though they'd come there under the direction of anticipation, of knowing. And that one woman, the one with the oversized sweater. There was understanding in her face, and a fire in her eyes. She was pissed. Yes, she was definitely pissed.

And the others weren't so much just casually observing. They all had expressions of their own. One with a look of wonder, a childish awe. Another with apprehension and a sense of urgency. And on like that. Solid. Knowing. And connected.

Connected.

To what? The theater?

According to Frank it hadn't been in operation in fifty years. Those people in that crowd would have been children. How could the reopening of a theater they'd never been in be of any interest now?

But the interest was real. Very real. Anticipation, awe, and that lady.

That old lady, the one with the big sweater . . . she had looked pissed. . . .

Joe jerked to a sitting position, his hand moving in reflex toward the phone while his mind simultaneously asked the question *Who are you going to call? Kelsie? And what can he tell you that you don't already know?* His hand lingered in space a moment, and then he lay back down. Okay, he thought. Okay. Let's take stock of things. First, he'd run away—

No no no . . . run toward. Yes. Run toward . . .

—then he'd gone to the theater, checked it out. Really checked it out. He made mental notes of everything needing replacement or repair. He completed the transaction with deft precision and good business sense. And he'd done all this swiftly, unhesitatingly, performing like a finely tuned instrument with every detail fitting snugly into place. Everything perfectly timed. Like part of a plan.

Then he'd called Karen, got things going on that end. That was good.

And he'd called Kelsie. That was good too.

Everything was fine. Everything was just as it should be.

And that old lady looked pissed.

The chilly breeze turned cold.

* * *

Learning the business side of theater management turned out to be a singular experience in itself. It was almost as if he'd been turned into some kind of megacomputer, and a force of superior intellect was feeding data into him at super speed. Understanding, knowledge, expertise, came to him not only with very little effort on his part, but at a pace more comparable to idle thought than extensive concentration. Only five days had passed since he'd bought the theater and already he knew how to find and order films, and since he had chosen to screen only the old ones, the ones pre-fifty, cost was decidedly within his means. He'd selected *Shadow of a Doubt* for his opening film. That symbolism of man's duality had been playing itself over and over again in his mind since he'd talked to Kelsie five days ago. Man's duality. Man's ability to be kind and ambivalent, and at the same time almost brutally hardhearted. Everyone had a dark side, didn't they? And just because Joe was not the kind of man to put his dark side to use in any profitable way didn't necessarily mean he was lacking in ferocity, did it?

Joe was aware of the now familiar crowd gathering across the street from the theater as he was setting up the marquee with the title and grand opening date, and at first he was uneasy. They just seemed to have this knowing air about them. There were really only three or four of them, but to Joe it seemed like a sizable crowd; a collective conspiracy. Strange. He thought perhaps, once he was finished with the marquee, he'd go over to them and get a better understanding of whatever it was they knew. And they knew something. Yes, they knew something, but worse than that, they knew something he himself didn't know. And if someone were to ask him what he meant by that, oh, the energy he might expend on such a conundrum was unnerving.

They looked hungry, for one thing. They looked . . . he didn't know . . . hungry, and nervous. Anxious.

Scared?

Very unnerving.

There were new faces too. A group of three, very young, had gathered near the others. They seemed cocky, puffed up, and sort of, well, sort of wicked. They chuckled a lot, rocking on their heels with that confident, pompous, belligerent way of the very young. They made Joe shudder. They had the potential of mischief, and that potential would not need much bolstering.

And then there was one. A young man with golden hair and a smooth, clean face. Very handsome, very pleasing to look at. His demeanor was casual, almost aloof, and quite separate from the rest. This young boy watched Joe with intense attention.

Joe finished with the marquee and tried to lean back on the ladder in order to see what he'd done, but he was too close. It all looked like just a jumble of letters. He climbed down the ladder, picturing in his mind what it should look like:

COMING SOON

SHADOW OF A DOUBT

and below that in slightly smaller letters:

JOSEPH COTTEN

SHOW TIMES   5   7:15   8:30   10:45

OPENS APRIL 1

But as he jumped off the ladder and looked up, his heart gave a whimper:

BONGOMG SOHEI

FOGMAOBJN

JIGBIOHF FGOMNBV

JIOANBG GVBO GVOVN A÷OBGV GVONA

HFJFNOLHNJ V

How could he have screwed up so badly? He looked around at the crowd that was peering up at the marquee and scrunched his shoulders, feeling silly. While he stood there, the fine young man crossed the street and came to stand beside him. Joe's embarrassment grew. "I feel so stupid," he said to the boy, who stood now with his hands in the back pockets of his jeans, his head tilted up to scan the marquee.

"Why?" the boy asked in a gently even tone.

"Well, just look at that mess," Joe said, pointing to the marquee. The young man turned his head and studied the jumble of letters, then shrugged.

"Looks pretty good to me," he said simply. Joe stared at him, but the boy took no notice. "You got some secret reason for screenin' that movie?"

A tiny jolt slipped through Joe's middle. "What movie?" he asked cautiously.

The boy looked back at the marquee. *"Shadow of a Doubt."*

The jolt shot through him, and Joe yanked his head around to look at the marquee.

It was no longer a jumble of letters. The words were spelled out exactly as Joe had intended them to be.

"Not many know about that movie," the boy said casually, turning his head to look at Joe. "Not many at all. You got some secret reason? Got somethin' you're tryin' to say?"

Joe shook his head in dismay. "This is crazy."

"Then why show it?" the boy asked.

"No—I mean . . ." Joe rubbed his eyes distractedly. "I could have sworn all those words were jumbled. And now"— he glanced back at the marquee timidly—"Now they're . . ." He looked back at the boy, who was watching him with a hint of interest, and noticed for the first time that the boy was smiling. But not just smiling.

Well, yes, smiling. But the smile came more from his eyes than from his mouth, making the eyes bright and penetrating, with just enough intimacy to make Joe's shoulders tighten painfully.

And then there was that chill again.

Joe cleared his throat. "You . . . uh . . . asked why I'm showing *Shadow of a Doubt.*" He smiled crookedly. "There's a reason for it."

The boy continued to watch him, continued to smile with his eyes.

"See," Joe said haltingly, "see, I want to show all the old

classics here. Giving it a sort of—I don't know—a congruence, I guess." He smiled a little, feeling his shoulders beginning to relax. "Frank, the old owner, said this theater hasn't been in operation in over fifty years, so I figured—"

"Frank's dead."

Joe's mouth went suddenly dry. "W-what?"

"He's dead," the boy said again, his eyes still bright, smiling, and Joe felt the world slanting away.

He swallowed hard. "When—how do you—"

"Died the thirtieth," the boy said casually, turning his attention back to the marquee. "You bought his house, didn't you?"

When Joe didn't answer, the boy looked at him, his bright eyes turning dark and discerning. "Well?"

Joe's head reeled. "Yes, I—well, yes. . . ."

The discerning look in the boy's eyes deepened. "Fits, don't you think?"

Frank was dead. Five days after selling the theater, and Frank was dead.

The boy smiled. "Yep, sure fits fine, you ownin' the theater *and* the house. Kinda like everything fallin' into place." He turned his attention back to the marquee. "Like part of a plan."

Had it not been for the sudden gust of a cold breeze skittering up Joe's spine, he would have stood there frozen for probably the rest of his life. He shook his head, swallowed, shook his head again, and wondered.

Wondered . . .

But the boy's news of Frank Jordan's death had helped to put a little focus on just what was happening. Like, why some lawyer had called him to wrap up the little details in the sale. After that first day Joe didn't see Frank again. He'd gone to Frank's house and found it empty and dark. Within a couple of days a for-sale sign appeared by the mailbox along the front road. He went to the real estate office and inquired. The agent's clean young face with rosy cheeks and glittering eyes went suddenly dull and gray at the mention of Frank's name. The agent rustled through her papers with shaky fingers and brought out the listing, chattering and giggling nervously while making her pitch. The house was going for a price that was decidedly below market value, which the agent explained as the usual family-wants-to-sell-quickly bit. But her eyes never left the paper. They were glued there, as if to look at Joe would probably turn her to stone.

Joe made an offer and she wrote it up. That night she called to say the family had accepted his offer, which was then again five percent below their asking price.

As Joe got off the phone he was struck again at the precision with which everything seemed to fall into place, but now it was beginning to unnerve him a little. He was beginning to feel a cold, familiar nudge between his shoulder blades. The foot on his throat. He didn't like it.

And now he knew why. The papers for the house had been signed on August 30.

The day Frank died.

Desperate. Must sell before August 31.

"Amy Joann," the boy said, "she didn't give you no trouble, did she?"

"Huh?"

The boy looked at him, his eyes still smiling. "The broker. She give you a good deal?"

Joe nodded dumbly.

The boy nodded his approval. "Figured she would. It all fits, you know? Good, to have things fit together so neat and tidy."

Joe stared at the young man through a haze of confusion and shock. The boy seemed not to notice. Rather, he just continued to gaze at the marquee, letting his eye wander from it to the front of the theater, casting a casual, attentive, and almost appreciative gaze on what he saw. The silence between them was deafening.

Frank was dead. And Joe owned his house.

"Shadow of a Doubt," the boy said finally, nodding. "Yep, that's one fine movie to be showin'. Guess I do see your point. Know what you're trying to say." He gave Joe a sideways glance, the corner of his mouth curling slightly, impishly. "Everything just fallin' right into place."

Joe took another look at the marquee, where first there

had been jumbled letters and now the words were crystal clear. He looked at the boy with the smiling eyes and the now impish grin set on his young face. He looked at the crowd still gathering about him, gazing only to a degree at the marquee but watching him . . . watching with a studious eye, and the gathering realization that indeed things were falling into place left him with a stabbing feeling in his stomach. Things were falling into place, and he wondered just how consequential his involvement in all of this was, if at all.

Was he a cog in the wheel?

Like part of a plan.

Or was he just a monkey, being made to dance?

He didn't like that. It had a familiar ring to it. A shining ring that slicks through the skull and leaves a fire trail across the brain. Wasn't that just what he had been trying to get away from?

Yes, it was.

So he should stop it.

He *should* stop it. He really should.

Joe looked at the marquee, eyes riveted to it as though it were something tremendously profound, and jabbed a fist into the knot that was growing in his stomach.

"Things are gonna happen now," the boy with the smiling eyes said. "Good things, now that you're here." He turned to Joe. "Glad to have you here, Joe. Theater's glad too."

Joe blinked. "The theater?"

The boy nodded, his impish grin expanding. "Don't take my word for it. Just look at it." He made a sweeping gesture with his hand.

The boy was right. Joe hadn't really noticed it before, but the theater was different somehow. It was . . . well . . . taller.

Cleaner. The windows, for one thing. On the day he'd first seen the theater, the windows were nearly opaque with dust and grime. But now they were sparkling clean and clear as crystal.

But Joe hadn't cleaned the windows. Joe hadn't really done anything to clean up the place, and yet it was cleaner.

But Frank might have done that, yes. Frank might have cleaned the windows.

Why would Frank clean the windows?

Maybe someone—something—wanted to look out. Maybe . . .

Joe felt the knot in his stomach finger out, gripping the bottom of his rib cage. He sank his fist deeper into the soft flesh of his abdomen. *I'm thinking crazy. It's crazy. Gotta get control. . . .*

The chilly breeze began to diminish as dusk fell. The cool colors of rose and blue infused the still air and veiled the theater in an opulent embrace. The cluster of people began to thin, but Joe lingered, looking at the marquee, the clean windows, the building that had somehow become taller as if straightening its shoulders to bear new weight.

Frank was dead, and Joe owned his theater. Frank was dead, and Joe owned his house. Everything fitting into place, like part of a plan.

To dance, to dance . . . see the monkey dance.

3

Fareland, California, hidden in the Oakland Hills thirty miles east of San Francisco, was established in 1867 and consisted at that time only of a combination grocery, drug, and dry goods store, a livery stable, and a post office. The surrounding area was farm and cattle land, and a few horse stables. Fareland's growth over the years was slow, which pleased the locals no end. They were not accustomed to strangers and preferred to keep their numbers small, familiar, and friendly. When Joe Moreson came to Fareland in the summer of 1993, the population of the town proper was just over 150. The cattle ranches had dwindled after the closing of the butcher houses in Dixon, and the farms, whose main product was feed for the cattle, had closed down one after another, falling like dominoes, until the remaining few grew only enough to sustain the families that kept their farms working for the sake of tradition and a deep-seated sense of familial connection with the land. The ranches were subdivided and sold in parcels of two-, three-, and four-acre lots to San Francisco businessmen. Custom-built homes peppered the hills surrounding Fareland, but the dwellers of these icons of financial success rarely visited the town proper, a thing for which the locals were grateful.

When Joe finally moved into Frank's old house, the summer was still in full swing. He'd heard that fall came toward the middle of October, and what with the many clusters of liquidamber trees, he was looking forward to the sunburst of color come fall. But for now the scent of pine and oak permeated the amazingly still air, and the humidity was at a degree far too overwhelming to bear. Joe had to keep tugging at his shirt to pull it free from his clammy back. His legs were sweating, too, and he hated sweaty legs. No more than an hour had passed since he'd gotten out of bed as the sun peeked through his window, when he realized he'd be wise to wear shorts and changed to them without further discussion.

Still, despite the heat and humidity, the ambience of this small town was pleasant and quietly comforting. The air was clear and clean. Birds flew lazily in an acetylene blue sky that was pleasingly free of smog. He could not remember when he'd last seen that deep a color of blue before, if he ever had, and he gazed at it for a long time, marveling at the vivid, alien color. It was not until the sound of his growling stomach wrenched him from his wonderment that he got up, stretched, and went into the house to get something to eat.

The house was large and lofty, with plenty of room. Karen would like that. It was bright, solid, and clearly very old. Joe was pretty sure it was one of the original houses in Fareland, and its claim to antiquity would gratify her love for old things. The furniture, which came with the house, was equally old but had been very well cared for. Indeed, the entire house had been given good care over the years, and it was inarguably clear that one last and very thorough cleaning had taken place before Joe moved in. Yes, a very thorough cleaning.

Too thorough.

Thorough to the point of being sterile.

This bothered Joe. It nagged at him, like a gnat flying about your head. The house was sterile, but more than that, it was void of anything having to do with Frank Jordan.

Joe had always felt that people tend to leave their mark on a house when they leave. Nothing cosmic; no ectoplasmic residue or the hint of a vapor and the scent of mimosa, but a mark. Some kind of evidence of a life lived. Yet this house held nothing of Frank. This house was a shell. A void. A vacuum.

He pulled out a skillet and set it on the gas stove. He lit the stove, then went to the refrigerator for bacon and eggs. Then he put two slices of bacon in the skillet and watched them sizzle.

Why had Frank been erased from this house?

The bacon crackled, spraying grease into the air. Joe jumped back a bit.

There had to be something left. Something missed by whoever had cleaned this house. Joe hadn't known Frank long, but he'd been acquainted with him long enough to know he would not allow himself to be completely expelled without a trace. Frank Jordan would have found a way to prove he'd been here.

A chilly breeze wafted in through the open kitchen window.

The attic, Joe thought suddenly.

Something in the attic. Something hidden.

The chilly breeze curled about his legs.

Something deliberately hidden.

Joe turned off the stove, wiped his hands on his shorts, and headed for the attic.

The chilly breeze followed him.

The attic was as surgically clean as the rest of the house, barren except for a stack of boxes along the west wall. The stack was six boxes high, six boxes wide, and three boxes deep, with perhaps two or three boxes missing from one end on the front row of the stack. Joe lifted one of the boxes and found that it was empty. He lifted another, and finding it empty as well assumed they were all empty. By the appearance of this stack Joe surmised that they had been used for packing, and whoever had done the cleaning up and clearing of the house had stored them here, taking a box at a time as it was needed. These boxes were the sole contents of the attic. There was nothing. Not even a cobweb.

But Frank had left something here: Joe knew it. He knew it in his heart. Frank had left something hidden, so that it couldn't be discarded with the rest of his life.

Joe gazed thoughtfully at the stack of empty boxes, letting his eyes move slowly and deliberately over each one. They were all the same. Same size, same dimensions, same lettering printed on the side. He pondered, and while he pondered many thoughts came to him, flitting in and out of his consciousness. He thought about Frank. He thought about the theater. He thought about the boxes, all looking the same, and he thought about Edgar Allan Poe.

As well as classic movies, Joe loved the works of Poe. His favorite story was "The Purloined Letter."

With tempered fancy Joe began to remove the boxes from the neat stack. He took them one by one, delineating their sameness with cursory mental acknowledgment. When he reached the center of the stack, a tiny spark of excitement illuminated his mind. There, hidden among the kindred boxes, was one that clearly didn't belong. Slowly, with an almost insidious feeling of triumph, Joe smiled.

The chilly breeze, nearly unnoticed while Joe was searching through the boxes, now swirled up his back and made him shiver. It distracted him for a moment, but only a moment. He took the box from its hiding place among its fellows and moved to the other side of the attic. He sat down cross-legged, the box on the floor before him, and hunched over it as a hungry man might hunch over the first bit of food he'd had in days, feeling avaricious and even a little wary.

The box was old and flimsy, sealed with tape gone yellow with age. It gave way without struggle, and as he opened the flaps the smell of age and decay drifted up into Joe's face. He sniffed at it with distaste.

In this box, this old and decaying box, was the remainder of the man he'd known for only a few hours, but in those few short hours Joe had begun to like the man. He wasn't sure why; something about the glint in his eye, so inharmonious to his elusive, secretive, and oscillating demeanor. He was a mystery, that Frank Jordan, and the mystery was enchanting. He was almost a personification of a dream, a dream Joe had kept hidden deep in his heart (or perhaps had no idea it was there at all) until now. And this old box . . . well . . . it was like the keeper of the dream. The heart of the dream. The trappings, like a magician's cloak.

Joe smiled warmly as he gazed down at the contents of the box. There wasn't much in it, but what was there gave weight to his feelings. A threadbare flannel shirt that at one time had been red in color. Three tablets of yellowed paper that crumbled when Joe handled them. A piece of soapstone. A copy of *Alice's Adventures in Wonderland* stuffed with old yellowed papers. Joe picked up the book and removed the papers.

They were old clippings that appeared to have come from the local newspaper. Most of them dealt with the construction of the Fareland Cinema and its impending grand opening. Joe smiled at the picture of construction workers laboring over the half-built theater as cows watched them passively nearby. One clipping, dated September 29, 1940, depicted the night of the grand opening. It was evident to Joe that the building had been quite a showplace in its time. The faded photograph depicted the people gathered at the entrance of the theater; women adorned with furs and diamonds *(dripping with diamonds . . . now I see the relevance of that phrase),* and men standing stiffly in creased tuxedos with backs straight as boards and their heads held high in aristocratic affectation. Ah, yes, Joe thought, this was a fashionable place, and the copy beneath the photo confirmed his assumption. It seemed a bit peculiar, San Francisco being a good thirty miles from Fareland, but the City's upper crust had entitled the Fareland as the singular in vogue locale.

The article continued with reports of locals not being too happy about their small town's newfound fame and fashion. Back in 1940 the population of Fareland proper had been fifty-two. The article finished with the news that the owner, Frank Jordan, had plans to placate the townspeople by giving "special screenings" for locals only.

Another clipping, dated a week later, showed a gathering of people undoubtedly less wealthy than those of the first clipping. They wore plain clothes, polished work boots, and frayed hats. But their smiles were broad and proud as they stood before the entrance of the Fareland cinema. This was their night, Joe thought, smiling. This was their "special screening."

But his smile swiftly turned sour as he reached for and opened another clipping. In this one there was no proud gathering of people in front of the beautiful, fashionable

Fareland Cinema. This clipping had no copy, no article about special screenings.

In this clipping there was death. Horrible, bloody death.

Joe's hand slapped against his mouth as he studied the clipping, unable to take his eyes away. The photo was as old and faded as the others, but for Joe the image was clear as a clean thought. It was the picture of a boy, maybe fifteen or sixteen years old, stretched out in a field with his wrists and feet tethered to stakes. The boy had been methodically, brutally slashed from head to foot. Blood was everywhere.

Joe closed his eyes tight and kept them shut until he began to see sparks on the insides of his lids. When he opened them again, the photo of the bloody boy came into focus.

And there was something else.

Next to the boy, all bloody and misshapened with lacerations and broken bones, was the body of a man. He knew it was a man because the body was naked. It was the only way he could know, because the body had no head.

At the bottom of the clipping was a word scribbled in pencil:

ENOUGH

Joe raked in a ragged breath and found the air was cold. He gingerly folded the yellowed paper and placed it back in the book. He silently and carefully replaced the book in the box, closed the box, and then sat there.

Night had settled many hours before he finally got up and went downstairs. The house was dark, and clean, and still large and lofty. But it was no longer sterile.

He went into the kitchen, where his bacon and eggs had been waiting for him since early morning, and looked down at the half-cooked bacon lying embedded in coagulated grease, hoping the unsavory sight would somehow nullify the memory of what he'd seen in the attic. But it didn't. The memory of that photo with the bloody boy and the decapitated body had become an afterimage imprinted on the inner folds of his brain, and nothing as lightweight as a flimsy strip of bacon lying in a little gelatinous grease was going to erase it. Indeed, it seemed only to enhance it.

There had been no story accompanying the photo. There had been no date.

Joe left the kitchen and went about the house, turning on every light. He locked both the front and back doors, checked each window to insure their latches were secure, pulled all the window shades down.

Those lacerations on the boy, they were strategic, inflicted with determined precision. Like a ritual.

He tore the covers off his bed and checked the sheets, lifted the mattress and examined the box spring and the bottom of the mattress, shook out the sheets and blankets, checked them, shook them again, then remade the bed. Then he got on his knees and checked under the bed.

Yes, a ritual. And someone had taken a picture of it.

He opened the walk-in closet and turned on the light. He took each garment off its hook, checked it inside and out, put it back on its hanger and placed it back on the clothes rack. He left the closet light on and the door open.

Someone had taken a picture, and Frank had saved it.

Joe walked downstairs and went into the living room. He took the poker from its stand by the fireplace and ran it beneath the couch and chairs. Then he pulled up each cushion and checked it thoroughly before replacing it.

And there was that word, scribbled beneath the photo. That one word. *Enough.*

Joe sat down on the couch.

When the sun slanted in through the slit between the front-room curtains, Joe was still sitting on the couch. He had not moved. He had not slept, not even for a moment. What he did while sitting there in Frank's old house with all the lights on and all the shades drawn was think.

He thought about dead, decaying people with pretty rings on their fleshless fingers, and how he had taken them, put them on, and admired them.

Suddenly he wanted out of there; out of the house and into the clean fresh morning air. He jumped up quickly, and his muscles, having been static for so long, screamed in protest.

He limped-leapt to the front door and dragged it open. The
sun hit him full in the face, bathing him with its mild, early-
morning warmth. The air was brisk and clean, smelling of
pine. Joe breathed it in as he stumbled down the front steps
and headed off down the gravel driveway to the road.

He had to get to the theater. At the theater he'd be safe.

He walked briskly down Trenton Road, one of only two
residential roads in Fareland. Branching off of Trenton was
Valley Road, which ran about three blocks before crossing
with Devil's Mountain Road, the town's main street. The
Fareland Cinema was on Devil's Mountain Road, and across
from it was John Williams's gas station, and a small junk
store claiming to sell antiques. Half a block down from the
gas station was a small gravel road. At the end of the road
was Alan Mayhew's Fareland Motel. The clerk was a jolly old
woman Joe had taken a liking to the moment he'd met her.

On the other side of the Fareland Cinema was Rudy's
combination grocery-drugstore. No pharmacist: people needing prescription drugs had to go to Walnut Creek.

Farther down Devil's Mountain Road, and nearly on the
outskirts of the town proper, was the only bar in Fareland. It
was run by a woman Joe had known in college. He'd met her
through Kelsie, and he didn't like her. She was hermetic.
That was the only word Joe could come up with to describe
her. *Hermetic.* And she knew too much. He hadn't bothered
to pay her a visit, and he had no intentions of doing so in the
future.

That was pretty much the whole of Fareland. A small
town. Quiet, picturesque, subdued.

A bloody ritual

And hiding secrets.

He quickened his steps, propelled by an urgent need to get
to the theater. He would be safe there. Safe from . . .

Safe from . . .

People watching him. Yes. People watching, studying. Not
many, but a few. As he walked down the road he could see
from the corner of his eye the movement of window curtains
being pulled aside slightly. He could feel eyes staring at him,

and when he turned his head to look the curtains quickly closed.

In the theater he'd be safe from peering eyes. Eyes without faces.

As he neared the theater he began to relax. Across the street John and Rudy sat in old folding chairs placed at the edge of the sidewalk. They waved to Joe as he passed, and Joe returned the wave.

"Goin' to the theater early today," John shouted. Joe nodded, smiling.

"It's lookin' good, Joe," John said. "Lookin' fine indeed. Can't wait for openin' night."

"Neither can I," Joe said, fishing out the key to the front door.

"Gonna be one of them special screenings?" John asked, and the tone of his voice, distinctly more probing than idle chat, made Joe feel suddenly exposed. He looked over at the two men.

They were both looking at him, studying him, their eyes keen. Joe felt a small tingle crawl up his spine, and the sensation of anxious friction began to rub at his nerves.

He drew in a deep breath and feigned diffident composure. "They're all special, John." He smiled confidently and pulled the door open. Before entering he gave the two men one last glance. They were smiling, yes, but there was consternation in those smiles. Their eyes were sharp and discerning, and for a moment Joe feared he would not be able to tear his attention away from them. He had an uncontrollable urge to yell at them, "What! What are you waiting for? What do you want?" But he didn't do it. He bit his tongue nearly hard enough to draw blood and hurried inside, pulling the door closed after him.

The interior of the theater was cool and comforting. His nerves, heated and raw, began to quiet down. The jumble of disquieting thoughts that had plagued him since he first signed the papers for this place began to fade into the background, overshadowed by the opulence of the theater and the myriad considerations of remodeling and renovation. At first he'd considered only remodeling the Fareland, but then on impulse he'd decided on complete restoration. The Fareland, after all, was a landmark. A piece of Americana. It should be restored. It was right. It felt right. And Frank would have wanted it that way.

Inexplicably, Joe knew that the theater wanted it that way too. He had calculated that restoration of the theater, including reupholstering the house seats, buying new curtains for the entryways and new glass for the snack bar, would cost well over five thousand dollars. But so far he'd spent only a fraction of that, and the restoration was nearly complete. More, he'd only been working on it for a week. Every stumbling block, every potential problem, seemed to solve itself as he worked on the restoration. The carpet, for instance. Through the filth of fifty years Joe could see that the colors had faded. Where traffic had been substantial the carpet had been worn away completely, exposing the floor beneath.

But when Joe began to clean the carpet, something strange occurred. It was subtle. Very subtle. But the carpet . . .

Well, the carpet rejuvenated itself.

He hadn't paid it much notice at first, but after a while, as he ran the steam cleaner over the old carpet surface, the change was difficult to ignore. The carpet wasn't just cleaner. Its colors had actually begun to brighten, the darker hues to deepen, the design to delineate itself. But even more disconcerting was the actual condition of the carpet. The worn areas seemed to have disappeared. Frayed corners were neatly stitched. Indeed, Joe might have argued without fear of rebuttal that the carpet was brand new.

And it wasn't just the carpet that seemed to be rejuvenating itself. There was the banister of the stairs leading to the mezzanine. When Joe had first looked at it the day Frank showed him around, he had taken note that the wood was very dry and cracked, and would need refinishing. Joe had started at the bottom of the stairs, applying a thick coat of paste wax and then buffing it out. He had anticipated having to do this procedure at least three or four times, but just the one coat seemed actually to heal the cracks, and the wood itself took on a new sheen. By the time he had reached the

top of the stairs, the entire banister gleamed with newness
. . . even the part he had not yet touched.

And another thing. Sometime during that week the
spiderweb crack in the snack bar case had gotten smaller.

It would have been easy, very easy, to consider this entire
venture to be bordering on the surreal, the supernatural, if it
hadn't been for the curtains. They were badly tattered and
torn, and Joe had watched them carefully and with fearful
anticipation of their rejuvenation, but it never happened.
They remained in poor condition and in need of being replaced.

Joe thanked God for the curtains. They, at least, were staying within the confines of reality.

But that wasn't exactly correct, and when he thought about
it, really *thought* about it, everything could be explained ra-
tionally. The carpet, for instance, could have only appeared
to be in irreparable shape due to the amount of grime and
filth. And it was possible, very possible, that he had remembered the crack in the snack bar case to have been larger
than it actually was. He had, in fact, given it only a cursory
look when he first toured the theater. And then there were
the seats in the house. The fabric was threadbare and definitely needed replacing.

Yes, if he thought about it, everything could be explained.

Everything except the projector.

A cold draft swooped in and curled around his legs. He
bent and brushed absently at his leg, then straightened, feeling foolish. It was only a draft.

The projector . . .

Just a draft. It was an old building. Drafts were to be expected.

He couldn't really explain the projector.

He walked up the stairs and crossed the balcony to the
small staircase leading to the projection room. He fished in
his pocket and pulled out the small silver key that opened the
door, remembering with fondness how Frank had first fished
out the little silver key, and had given Joe a glance and a
wink and told him, "Keep the door locked, son. Always keep
it locked, you remember that, ayuh. Things gotta be pro-

tected." Joe hadn't understood that at the time, but now he did. Something about the projection room needed protection. He couldn't really be specific; he just knew it had to be protected. So he forced himself into the habit of locking the projection-room door whenever he left, and he kept the little silver key with him at all times.

Knowing the projector was safe made him feel safe. And touching the projector, feeling its smoothness against the skin of his palm, made him think about the pretty rings.

He unlocked the door and stepped inside.

The projector had really turned out to be extraordinary. It was an unusual make, not very popular, which added to its venerability. He believed it would take him at least a week to get it cleaned up and have the worn parts replaced. The dust was encrusted in a thick layer of filth that had to be scrubbed away with steel wool. But once he had started, a sense of security, a kind of bonding, began between himself and the ancient projector. He ran the steel wool over it with more the touch of a caress than one of strenuous and rigid cleaning, and the projector had responded to him, like a cat arching its back to meet the curve of a loving hand. It responded, radiating a kind of warmth one would feel from the touch of a lover. Joe was no more cleaning the projector than he was embracing it, probing its contours, exploring its inner texture. It became a part of him, touching him in a way so intimate that he had no words to describe it. He was not at all surprised to find that, after just one hour of contact with the machine, it looked brand new.

He did not consider this to be extraordinary, and he didn't know why. But he didn't care, because when he was in here with the projector, he felt safe.

It was new to him, this feeling of security, and he wasn't about to question it. Questioning could lead to suspicion, and suspicion could lead to betrayal.

Joe started.

Betrayal? Where had that thought come from?

It was an odd thing to consider, and there was something else . . . something . . . he didn't know . . . some kind of contention. And that feeling again. The monkey, being made to dance.

The cold draft, curling about his legs.

Joe laid his hands on the surface of the projector, stroking it with loving care. "I'd never question," he said aloud. "Never." He looked around, eyes darting, feeling both foolish and vindicated for talking aloud to an inanimate object.

It could all be explained. Easily explained. This was his dream, his hope for a new life. This was his ticket out of being trapped forever in a world not of his making, where he spent every waking hour groveling and every sleeping hour agonizing over nightmares of oppression and degradation. He was his own boss now. No more running. No more excuses. He was his own boss, and the theater had given it to him, a gift, like a fine opulent pearl.

So maybe he was going overboard a little, talking to inanimate objects and such, but who cared? He was free, and he was protected. Everything had fallen into place, like part of a plan. *Destiny,* Karen had said, and why not? Why not get a little ethereal about it? After all, the projector *had* rejuvenated itself, or so it seemed.

That was it. It all seemed to be moving along of its own accord, and so what? It could be that Joe was so wrapped up in the excitement of it all that he just didn't see the fine details. He saw the overall picture; the final glimpse of the job completed. That was all, and that was natural.

He slid his hand down along the side of the projector. "Okay, so I talk to you like you can hear me. So what? Like Frank said, you're going to make me a fortune, right?" He patted the machine tenderly, then moved away and leaned against the far wall. "But tell me this: How are you going to make me a fortune in a small hick town like this one?"

It was then, from the corner of his eye, that he noticed a medium-sized white box hidden in the shadows at the far left of the room.

He stood straight, turning his full attention to it. It was bright, clean white, brand new, free of dust. Strange: he hadn't noticed it before now.

He glanced at the projector, then moved toward the box.

He stared down at it for a few moments before finally hunkering down and lifting it.

It was fairly heavy.

He sat down and removed the lid.

Inside was an eleven-minute reel of 65-millimeter camera negative film.

"Oh, my God," Joe whispered, lifting the reel out of the box. Adrenaline rushed through his veins, making his skin tingle. There was only one house that he knew of that used 65-millimeter camera negative film, and then only for special effects. Negatives were originals, never screened. And this reel was 65 millimeter, untouched, virgin, undeniably valuable.

This was it. This was the fortune Frank had left him.

Joe looked at the projector. He held the reel up before him. "This is the prize, isn't it?" he asked the projector.

The projector stood there, gleaming silently.

Joe ran his finger along the rim of the reel. It was the feeling of silk, this precious find.

Yes, oh, yes. Very precious.

His fingers began to tremble a little as he took the end of the film and paid out a foot, careful not to touch the film proper, and held it up to the light.

The draft . . . the cold draft . . .

Scared I'm scared I'm caught and I'm scared oh Jesus

He dropped the reel suddenly, his hands clamping over his heart.

Bloody ritual

He scrambled backward until his back was against the wall. Confusion, bewilderment, fear, and strange enchantment all coalesced in the splitting of a second, leaving him feeling shaky and weak, yet at the same time so turbulent, he thought his mind would shatter into fragments. The reel lay at his feet, the foot of film snaking out and lightly touching the cuff of his jeans. He scrambled away, holding his breath, afraid to let even a little air into his lungs made fragile by the severity of his sudden emotional disarray.

I'm all right everything is all right breathe, you idiot. Breathe!

He let a little air in, gulping it timidly, and when his lungs didn't splinter he let in a little more until he was sucking it in and holding it, then letting it out and sucking it in again. He hung his head, holding his hand against his chest as he struggled to control his panic.

Several minutes passed before he was able to breathe normally. He lifted his head and stared at the reel at his feet, afraid to touch it, afraid to move, and wondered if maybe the pressure might not be getting to him more seriously than he had previously thought.

No, no, no, that was crazy. It was just a reel of film. Precious film, indeed. But still just a reel of film.

Joe reached out and touched it with tentative fingers, and ice spread up through his hand.

He gasped, jerked his hand away, but it was too late. The ice was moving up his arm, and he could almost see the shimmering of frost as it cloistered his fingers, his wrist, up his arm, and moved like something alive toward his shoulder. He watched in numbing terror as his arm disappeared in the glistening brilliance of the ice, and knew there was nothing he could do to stop it. Nothing, except sit there huddled on the floor and pray the ice would stop before it spread through his body and froze his heart.

He sat there, looking at the reel, praying, feeling the thunder of terror in his fluttering heart. And the frost crept into his shoulder.

Please God please make it stop make it stop

He closed his eyes.

please God please please

Just as his collarbone began to grow cold the advancement of the ice slowed. Joe held his breath.

Yes, it had slowed. It had stopped at his collarbone.

Joe sat there, shivering, and wondered if he'd ever feel warmth in his arm again.

More time than he could measure passed, and then his fingers began to tingle with life. He opened his eyes cautiously, flexing and extending his fingers. His heart slowed a little.

Then his wrist, more supple now, and warmer still. He breathed a heady sigh of relief.

By the time his shoulder had thawed, the memory of terror was no more than an echo, and he found himself gazing once again at the reel of 65-millimeter camera negative film. It lay there on the floor, in pristine preservation, and beckoned him. He was almost surprised that he wanted to touch the film again.

Almost . . .

Instead he grasped the reel, carefully wound the length of film he'd paid out, and placed the reel back in the box.

By the time the lid was safely in place, Joe's need to touch the film again was seductively fingering his brain.

But this film was not a thing to touch or fondle. It was something to hold in reverence. That's what the ice meant. He had ventured uninvited, and he had been warned.

Next time the ice would imprison him completely, and he, too, would be perfectly preserved.

Oh, but if only he could touch it just one more time.

4

When Joe called his wife that night, he wasn't entirely sure what he expected from her. In a way, he wanted her already to know about the film, and about the way his arm had frozen when he touched it. He wanted her to know about the wondrous expeditiousness of the theater's restoration and how it made him feel both euphoric and anxious. He wanted her to know that when he touched the projector, it was like touching a lover. A responsive lover. A demanding lover.

That was something he hadn't thought of before. The projector was somehow demanding something of him, but he hadn't as yet discovered what that was. He just knew it was real. And it wasn't just the projector. It was the theater itself, the town, the people . . . all expecting something to happen. Everything, everyone, watching and waiting for him to dance.

Or was this just a remnant of his past with Tempac?

Possibly.

Yes, quite possibly. One does not lose old behaviors overnight, right?

Right.

Still, he didn't want to have to explain anything to Karen. He wanted her to know. He wanted her to understand without his having to say a word.

Karen picked up the phone on the third ring. "I'm ready to come up. You ready for me?"

Joe smiled. "I'm always ready for you, babe. The house sold already?"

"You bet," she said with a hint of wonder. "Quick as a wink, Joe. The offer couldn't be refused. And they took all the furniture as well, so we don't have to worry about selling it." She paused, then continued. "I'm all packed, Joe. I'm ready to come up now."

Joe ran a hand across his brow. "You knew, didn't you? You knew I was going to ask you to come up now, instead of after the house goes through escrow." The silence on the other end told him she was nodding. He gripped the phone gratefully. "How do you always know?"

She chuckled. It was a sweet sound. "Well, I could be conventional and say it's because I'm a woman, but the feminists of the world would probably hang me in effigy." She gave a little sigh. "I just know you. You haven't called—"

"I know," he said quickly. "And I'm sorry. It's just that . . . well, I've been so busy. . . ." He trailed off, feeling lame.

"Have you called Kelsie?"

Joe shook his head guiltily.

"Are you shaking your head, Joe?"

"Yes."

"Are you okay?"

Joe flinched. "Sure . . . yeah . . . why do you ask?"

"I don't know," she said. "You sound a little funny."

Joe rubbed his eyes hard enough to hurt. "Just tired, I guess."

"Is the house okay?"

"Sure it's okay," he said defensively. "Why wouldn't it be okay?"

"And the theater? Any problems there?"

Ice. Living ice crawling up, taking over . . .

Joe ground his teeth together. "Why are you asking me so many questions!"

" 'Cause I'm your wife. I got a right."

Another silence fell between them and Joe pressed his fist against his belly. Then Karen spoke again, her voice light and friendly. "You know I'm on your side, don't you?"

Joe nodded.

"Are you nodding your head?"

"Yes."

Silence again, this time heavy with tension.

"Kelsie says he gives you half a year before you come crawling back to L.A.," Karen said finally.

"He's on my side, too, I guess," Joe said sourly.

"Of course he is." Karen sighed deeply. "He was just kidding, Joe. You're reading in things that just aren't there. All he meant was—"

"I know what he meant!" Joe snapped.

Tense silence. Ragged silence.

"When's the last time you talked to him?" Karen asked.

"The day I bought the theater."

"That's a long time. Why don't you call him again? Tell him how things are going."

"Because I'm not—" Joe bit his lip.

"Not . . . what?" Karen asked.

"I'm not sure what he'd say. I don't need bullshit right now. You know?"

"He wouldn't bullshit you," Karen said tenderly.

"Okay, yeah," Joe said, feeling guilty. "Maybe I am reading into what he says. It's just that . . ."

"That what?"

"I don't know." Joe sighed heavily, looked at his fingers, flexed them for reassurance.

Another thoughtful pause, then Karen said forcefully, "I'm coming up tomorrow. Leaving bright and early. I should get there around three o'clock."

Joe exhaled. "I'd like that, Karen."

"Okay, then. I'll see you tomorrow. I love you, Joe."

"Yeah. . . ." He shut his eyes and rubbed his forehead. "Look, I gotta get going." He paused, then said with an urgency that surprised him, "I want you up here right away, Karen. I—I want you to start up here tonight."

"Joe?" She sounded a little frightened.

Joe took in air and held it. "I'm okay. I just . . . start up tonight."

"Okay. . . ."

"Okay . . . good." He let the air out in a trembling sigh. A light sweat had formed on his brow and he wiped it away nervously. "I'll see you soon."

He hung up the phone and stared at it.

Lonely. So alone.

It could have reached my heart. It could have frozen. . . .

He rubbed his arm roughly, then stretched out across the bed and gazed at the ceiling.

Did it really happen? Did his arm really freeze up, or was it just an illusory thing, brought on by stress? *Stress-related illness.* He'd heard that phrase at least a dozen times a day back at Tempac. *Stress-related illness.* At least three in ten suffered from conditions brought on by *stress-related illness,* and it had occurred to him that suffering from such an illness was beginning to be as fashionable as the power tie.

But now he was beginning to think there might be some validity to the diagnosis. He was under a tremendous amount of stress, and not just because he had changed life-styles so suddenly. It was a lot of things. The restoration, progressing not only at an alarming pace, but seemingly doing so with very little of his own participation. The impeccable timing of his buying the theater and Frank's death, buying Frank's house, finding that clipping . . .

Bloody ritual

. . . and that clean white box with the 65-millimeter camera negative film, so carefully preserved. So precious.

Wanting to touch it. Wanting to *fondle* it.

And something else. Something he had tried very hard not to think about, but it was forcing itself to the fore of his consciousness with every passing second.

When he'd first bought the theater, he didn't know a thing about running one. Not one damn thing. He had no idea how to get films, especially the classics. He knew nothing about renovation, knew nothing about building permits, property taxes, publicity, wholesale outlets for snack-bar supplies. He knew absolutely nothing.

But as the days passed, and just when he needed to know something specific, it came to him. Any knowledge he needed was mysteriously, extemporaneously, unconsciously provided, as though he'd known it all along.

He remembered thinking of himself as some kind of megacomputer being fed data at super speed. It had been an exhilarating thought at the time, a thought that gave him a curious sense of self-esteem in his ability to assimilate so swiftly. And it was this unprecedented sensation that had allowed him to take with a grain of salt all the strange events that had occurred from the moment he first walked out of Tempac. From that moment on, everything had seemed just to fall into place.

Destiny, Karen had said.

Destiny.

Everything had been part of a plan. Even himself.

But he didn't feel that way anymore. Creeping into his mind, pushing out that wonderful feeling of self-esteem and individuality that had given him control over his own destiny, was a feeling that was leaving a bitter taste in his mouth and a localized pain in his stomach.

I'm a monkey.

That pain, in the pit of his stomach, had started just about the time he'd learned of Frank's death. Maalox helped a little, but he was never completely free of the pain.

I'm a monkey, made to dance. And my stomach hurts.

Stress. Had to be stress.

He rolled over and opened the nightstand drawer where he kept a bottle of Maalox. The bottle was two thirds empty. He untwisted the cap and raised the bottle high, taking two large gulps of the chalky liquid, then settled back down and tried to relax by taking stock of what he had accomplished.

He owned his own theater. He owned his own house. He had a working knowledge of the theater business. The theater was nearly finished, ready to open. These were good things.

He had a wife who loved him. He had a friend he could trust.

And he had a reel of 65-millimeter camera negative film. A treasure. A precious thing.

A thing that made his arm freeze when he touched it.

The music's playing, monkey. Just for you.

It wasn't just that his arm had begun to freeze.

The film, that film, that unique piece of cinematographic treasure, had sent something into him.

punishment

He kneaded the pit of his stomach, where the pain nudged him.

That's crazy that's just crazy! Punishment for what?

A gentle wind was beginning to build outside. Joe turned his head to the window and looked out at the night. Illuminated by the full moon, the landscape glowed a bluish white.

You're asking too many questions. Questions lead to suspicion, and suspicion—

"To betrayal," Joe said aloud. He got up from the bed, pressed his fist deep into his stomach, and went to the attic.

The boxes were still where he had left them. He lifted the lid of the one containing *Alice's Adventures in Wonderland* and opened it, pulling the clipping of the slaughtered boy out and unfolding it.

Punishment?

He ran his thumb gently across the surface of the paper. "Did you ask too many questions, Frank?" he said aloud, pondering the photo's blatant horror. "Did you get suspicious?"

Betrayal

He traced his fingers over the image, exploring with his mind the surgical accuracy of every laceration. "Did you die, Frank? Did you just die?"

He sat there a moment longer, then gently folded the paper and put it in his pocket. "Or were you executed?"

A cold draft puffed and swirled about the room. Joe rubbed his arms in reflex.

I'm reading too much into this.

He went back to the bedroom and stretched out with one arm over his eyes and the other pressing into his stomach.

Retroactive response. Yeah, that was it. Like overusing a muscle, and when you stopped using it, it would shake uncontrollably. All that energy stored up inside the tissue had to go somewhere. He'd been on overdrive for so long that he'd built up a good store of adrenaline, and it had to go somewhere. What better place to go than his mind, already working overtime trying to compartmentalize everything that had happened to him since he'd crept out of bed late that night and come here to Fareland? He had spent the last month playing psychologist, carpenter, investigator, and new guy on the block being watched with silent scrutiny, while at the same time trying to make friends with the locals like John Williams and Vordy Halleran, only to find such endeavors to be physically tough and mentally taxing. And he'd done it all alone, with no one to offer him an objective view of the myriad occurrences he had been trying to collate into some kind of cohesive, rational chain of events.

But Karen would be here in about eight hours, and that would be good. That would be great. He wouldn't be left to his own devices anymore. He'd wait up for her, and then he'd make love to her and give all that adrenaline a damn good place to go.

And tomorrow he'd feel better. Tomorrow, yeah, tomorrow he'd feel a hell of a lot better.

The wind outside grew stronger, sending thin tendrils of cold air through the cracks in the windowsill. Joe turned on his side, wrapped the bedspread about him, and slipped into a light sleep. In his dreams illusory images mingled with thoughts of Karen, the theater, the precious 65-millimeter camera negative film, pretty rings taken from dead fingers, and the ghostly, flitting monkey music.

As he slept, the deep night hours slipped away unnoticed. In the fragile fabric of early morning Karen slipped into bed beside him, pulling him out of his sleep with a warm caress across his cheek. He took her into his arms and smothered her with kisses. She let her hands slip and stroke his body, tenderly at first, then more insistently as she began to tug at his clothes, stripping them off and discarding them without thought. He responded in kind, removing her clothes with elegant ease.

They moved as one, oblivious to everything not directly related to the coalescing of tender affection and tangibility they shared, giving and receiving, in unison. They saw nothing of the world outside their protective cocoon. They did not see the velvety ground fog forming on the street below, made amber by the streetlamps, which cast their glow on a slender figure as it slipped into their illumination and out

again, gliding with the grace of a cat on the prowl, coming to
a stop across the street from the Fareland Cinema.

The hard streetlight lay warm with a foggy brightness on
an uplifted young face that could only be described as beautiful; skin as fresh and gleaming as polished gold and smiling
eyes the color of emeralds. The bright eyes gazed at the marquee of the Fareland Cinema and a grin skirted across the
mouth, causing the shadowing light to bend and crease, and
change the beautiful face into something sinister. An ugly
mask, deceitful, wicked, and savage.

Early morning. The new day dawning. The new age.

5

Joe's attempt at finding normalcy and rationalizations for all that had happened to him had begun to show an inkling of success with Karen's arrival. She gave him something solid to latch on to; a secure, almost authoritative control over outward events, as well as the restoration of his faltering frame of mind. But her presence and her influence, however dynamic, could not outshine the formidable appearance of the new curtains.

His plan was to purchase new entryway curtains from the manufacturer of the original ones, but that company had gone out of business in the fifties. He went to countless fabric shops both in Oakland and across the Bay, searching for the exact color and material, and as the day wore on his hopes grew increasingly thinner until finally, at the end of a long and unwavering succession of failures, he was left with a feeling of dejection and frustration. He returned to the theater empty-handed and angry, his stomach aching.

He parked his car in front of the theater and sat there, staring at the front doors, thinking about how horrible the day had been. One fabric shop after another, storekeepers with well-meaning smiles colored by helplessness . . . it had been a horrible day.

As he gazed at the front doors of the theater, it came to him with a suddenness so severe it made his heart lurch, that his troubles had only just begun.

The front door of the theater was standing ajar.

He grasped the steering wheel hard enough to make his knuckles turn white. Maybe he'd just forgotten to lock the door.

No, no . . . he distinctly remembered having pulled it

shut, inserted the key. He had even given the door a tug to assure himself that it was locked.

Someone had broken in, God *damn* it to hell anyway!

He looked around nervously, trying to find someone to help, but the street was empty for the first time he could remember. He peered at the door, squinting his eyes, and raked a shaky hand across his mouth. With his heart lodged in his throat he opened the car door and slipped out, keeping his eyes on the door. He walked slowly, almost on tiptoe, swiping anxiously at the sweat forming on his brow. As he neared the door the pain in his stomach reached a maximum and sent a lump into his throat. He reached for the door with a trembling hand, believing for an instant that it would burn him, and as he laid his fingers against the glass, the door swung open.

He fell back, nearly stumbling over his own feet. He gulped air into his constricted lungs. The lump in his throat threatened to become something more than just a lump.

I'm going to throw up. I know it.

A young man stood in the doorway, the smile on his face a curious curve. "Had a busy day?"

Joe clutched his hands to his stomach, fighting off the cramp. "What the hell do you think you're doing?"

"Oh, come on, Joe, don't get so hot. I'm here to help you."

"Oh, really?"

"Sure." The boy stepped outside and extended his hand. "Name's Andy. Andy Jordan."

Joe blinked. He knew this boy. He'd seen him before.

Joe took a tentative step toward the boy, then raised a finger. "You're the kid I saw that day. You told me about Frank dying."

Andy grinned.

Joe narrowed his eyes. "Frank told me about you. Why didn't you tell me then you were related to him?"

Andy shrugged, the grin changing now to something a little less than a sneer. "Time wasn't right. Timing's everything, don't you think?"

Joe pulled back a little. That sneer, it seemed to change

something in the boy's face. It was a beautiful face, with smiling emerald eyes, but that sneer . . .

That sneer changed it. Marred it as the scar of a devil's claw would make ugly the face of an angel.

Joe didn't like it, and he didn't like standing there watching a beautiful young face turn ugly and sinister. It made him uneasy, and after the day he'd had the last thing he wanted was to feel uneasy.

"I don't have enough money for an assistant," Joe said flatly, pushing his way past the boy with only a little of the force he'd liked to have shown.

Andy followed him inside. "You can't afford not to hire me."

"Just what makes you so sure?"

"Had some trouble replacing the drapes?" The sneer again.

Joe eyed him suspiciously. "Yeah . . . so?"

The boy smiled, and that horrible sneer-grin disappeared. Joe felt something loosen in his chest. How a look could be so disorienting was a curious thing. Perhaps it was because the boy was so beautiful. His hair was the color of spun gold. His body was strong and lithe, well proportioned and with a posture befitting an athlete. Anything even remotely negative was amplified beyond ordinary appearance. "Your troubles are over, old man. Take a look." Andy pointed to the main entryways into the house.

Joe turned and his heart thumped heavily. The curtains hanging in the entryways were a deep, rich velvet, crimson in color, with a brilliant shine to them. They were brand new. Joe turned to Andy, his mouth gaping. "I've been all over the Bay area looking for just those curtains. Where did you find them?"

Andy's eyes closed to secretive slits. "I got connections."

Joe bit his lip. "How old are you, Andy?"

"Eighteen."

"You look sixteen."

Andy shrugged, still smiling. "You gonna hire me or not? It's your choice. You can put me on the payroll, or I can take my curtains and go."

Joe stared at him, and Andy returned the gaze. In the quiet of the lobby the sparks from their eyes hummed with electricity.

"I'll have to think about it," Joe said finally, but his voice had lost some of its punch. He moved past the boy and headed for the stairs leading to the mezzanine. As he climbed the stairs he could feel Andy's eyes on him, and knew that the sneer-grin had returned.

Joe went to the projection room, hastily unlocked the door, and went inside. He stood just inside the door and gazed at the clean white box in the corner across the room.

The box beckoned him.

He rubbed his hands on his jeans, took a tentative step, then moved rapidly and knelt beside the box.

His hand snaked out, fingers running lightly over the lid.

So precious . . .

He sat down and placed the box in his lap.

Frank said he should hire the boy. Frank said he couldn't afford not to.

Joe hugged the box.

Those curtains . . .

When he went back down to the lobby Joe found Andy at the snack bar, polishing the new glass that hadn't been there this morning.

"I suppose you replaced the glass too," Joe said, a little shakily.

Andy turned his head slowly and looked at Joe. His emerald eyes sparkled with the glow of his smile.

Frank had said it would be a good idea to hire Andy, and Joe was beginning to think Frank had been right.

Aside from his good looks, there was something about Andy Jordan that seemed ageless. Perhaps it was the way he'd just stand back, skirting along the edge of things, watching. Joe was constantly aware of those piercing green eyes staring at him, watching him, calculating. There were many occasions when he'd be deep in work, hunched over his bookkeeping, and suddenly he'd feel his concentration being rudely jarred by the feeling of being watched. When he'd look around, there would be Andy, standing there, observing, the sneer-grin marring that beautiful smooth face.

But there were other things about the boy. The way he moved, for one thing. It was with an exact fluidity, a deep grace born of quiet, almost secretive strength. It reminded Joe of the strength hidden beneath the loose skin of a cat. To look at a cat one would think it was flaccid and weak. But when you run your hand across its flank or down its back, you are met with the tight and powerful solidity of thick muscle, unyielding and quietly profound. And when the cat moves, jumping to a high place or running with the liquidity of a precision instrument, you are left with a feeling of dumb embarrassment at just how stupid humans can be, especially when that swift grace is moving rapidly right at you and there is no chance in hell that you are going to escape with your entrails intact.

It scared Joe to death.

And then there were those eyes. Deep green. Unnaturally deep green. Two emeralds plucked from the deepest shaft of an ancient mine. At first Joe thought there might be a kind of inherited wisdom in the sparkle of those eyes, but soon enough he learned the look was not one of wisdom, but rather a kind of ageless age, senseless and edging toward wicked. Sometimes they deepened with thought, but most of the time they smiled.

But that wasn't it. At first Joe thought of it that way: smiling eyes. But as he got to know the boy, as he came to be in his presence for longer periods of time, he learned with a deepening conscious fear that those eyes were not smiling so much as they were flickering, like candles. They flickered in an inhuman way, and that flicker scared Joe to death.

But the idea of having made a mistake in hiring Andy never crossed Joe's mind. The boy was good with his hands, quick and very strong. He knew the theater inside and out, even understood the wiring and superstructure. And he had amazing connections. If something was needed, however complicated or difficult to obtain, Andy acquired it sometimes within hours. If the completion of restoration had been remarkably swift before Andy came, its speed now was unfathomable, and inexplicable. Joe wasn't even needed at the theater once Andy took over, and it gave him the time he needed to work on the old Jordan house, refurbishing it and imprinting upon it his own personality. Andy was helpful in that area as well. He knew the Jordan house as intimately as he knew the Fareland, and it seemed to Joe that this young man's talents sometimes hugged the supernatural.

Joe's initial discomfort with the boy soon gave way to a genuine liking, but his affection was tempered with wariness. It couldn't be helped: The boy was a juxtaposition of beauty and grace, and sinister calculation. Everything Andy did seemed part of a twofold plan. Behind the beautiful eyes was a mind working on a split-level foundation. His loyalty seemed to rest with Joe and the restoration of the theater, yet at the same time there seemed to be another agenda forming in that young, convoluted mind. Things would happen. Strange things. Like the time Joe was cleaning the carpet while Andy worked behind the snack bar. The day had been quietly warm and Joe had lapsed into a feeling of concrete satisfaction, when suddenly a trifling gust of cool wind swirled into the lobby. In the next instant Andy yelped painfully.

When Joe looked around he found the boy on his knees, clutching his right hand to his chest. His face was pinched with pain. Joe went to him, grabbed his hand, and looked at it. There was a gash across the palm. Andy was breathing hard, shaking with the pain. He yanked his hand out of Joe's grasp.

Joe looked around, puzzled. "How did you do that?"

"Things happen," Andy said coldly.

"But how?"

Andy looked at him angrily, the emerald eyes darkening. "You ask too many questions. Anyone ever tell you that?"

Joe pulled back, surprised. "Hey, look, I'm—I'm just concerned."

Andy turned away, clutching his hand to his chest.

Joe fidgeted, feeling confused. "Maybe you should have it looked at."

"Shit! Just a little cut."

"It could get infected."

"No," Andy said, shaking his head. "What's done is all that'll be done. It's enough."

Then he looked up at Joe and the pain in his face vanished. In its place was a sort of whimsy, as if he was playing a game. It danced across his face and then disappeared.

"Theater's like a woman," Andy said. "You have to give it respect. Treat it right, and it'll drown you with affection. But if you treat it wrong"—he pointed a formidable finger at Joe —"it'll slit your throat." Then he turned away, drew inward, looked frightened, nervous, and Joe had the feeling the boy had said more than he should have.

He reached out, meaning to touch the boy's shoulder, then decided against it and turned away.

Things like that happened all the time. With Andy around, every day brought new and peculiar developments. But the boy had also brought with him the promise of the opening of the Fareland Cinema on September 29, the anniversary of its original opening. That was payment enough for putting up with Andy's strangeness.

Or was it really because of Andy?

Everything going according to some kind of plan. . . .

Was he being made to dance yet again?

Could it be that Andy's arrival was just another piece of the original plan?

Was Andy a monkey too?

Or was he the Organ Grinder, cranking out the monkey music?

No, no, no.

Joe threw the thought out of his mind. He thrust it out, as if ridding himself of some oily, stinking dirty rag, because such a thought was the kind that the old Joe Moreson would have harbored. The Joe Moreson who had let others control his actions, his thoughts, his personal code of conduct. That Joe Moreson was dead. He had killed that Joe Moreson when he walked out of Tempac for the last time, and had buried—no, cremated—that crudely manipulated replica of a man on the night he left for Fareland.

A new Joe Moreson had risen from the ashes of the pitiful

shadow of a stooge, and this new man was the master of his destiny.

It was he who had made real the possibility of opening the Fareland on the anniversary of its first opening. It was he who had made the decision to hire Andy. It was he who had summoned his wife to his side and it was he who had fashioned for himself a home from the shell of a house from which the memory of its former owner had been wiped clean.

The house. Ah, yes, the house was something to behold, now that Karen had added the finishing, refining touches to it. She had placed her own mark upon it, creating an intimate partnership between Joe's masculinity and her own femininity. It was an environment of natural harmony.

The house was set back in a small, sloping grove and was surrounded by oak trees. A wide creek flowed along its front yard. The road leading up to it was overhung by willow trees, providing a pleasing privacy to the place. It could not be seen from the main road, and at night Joe and Karen would sit on the large front porch, delighting in the serenade of a host of frogs from the creek. In the early morning, ground fog, refined and delicate, hugged the grass as deer came to graze on their front yard. Karen had gotten into the habit of leaving them trays of food the night before. She had also made acquaintances with a family of raccoons, two opossums, and a variety of birds. Waking to the sight of the early-morning gathering of the wild for breakfast had become a thing most treasured by Joe, and he never tired of the sight from his bedroom window. He would linger there for at least an hour, savoring the serenity and relishing the knowledge that this house was his house. His home. He belonged here.

But Karen remained uneasy. She never really expressed her uneasiness in words, but she was uneasy, and the reason she was uneasy was that she knew the house didn't like her. She never said this aloud. She didn't have to. Joe could feel it. It hovered in the shadows of the house like cobwebs. Karen was uneasy because she believed the house didn't like her and didn't want her there.

They never talked about it, which made it even more evident. Their shared silence about the subject shouted in Joe's ears to the point that he was almost always uncomfortable, especially during those times when he should be the most relaxed. On the porch in the evening, for instance, while listening to the frogs. He had begun to fidget in the last few days. He would get up from his chair, pace a little, lean against the post, sit down, and fidget some more. The sound of the frogs' song would seem off key to him. Annoying.

"It won't let me take a hot bath," Karen said one night, without waiting for the question.

Joe sighed deeply. "It's just a house, Karen."

A few crickets joined the frogs, serenading them in two-part harmony. It should have been pleasant. Instead it was distracting.

"I'm telling you, Joe. I go up there to take a bath, and all that comes out is a cloud of rust. Nearly chokes me to death."

"I took a shower this morning."

"Yeah, sure, the house likes you."

Joe looked at her, a crooked smile crossing his lips. "Houses don't discriminate."

"This one does."

Joe's smile soured. He had been half joking. But Karen was being fully serious. He leaned back in the chair and was silent.

"The house doesn't like me," Karen said resolutely.

Joe slapped the arms of the chair and got up. With firm conviction he went into the house.

He heard Karen following him, the screen door slamming just as he reached the top of the stairs. Quietly, calmly, he made his way to the bathroom and turned on the faucet. Clean crisp water began flowing into the tub just as Karen rounded the door. He looked up at her. "See?"

She said nothing, only scrunched her face and walked away.

"The human imagination is a tricky thing," he called after her as he turned off the faucet and got to his feet. "Leave it to its own devices, and it can—"

make your arm freeze

Joe stopped. His throat tightened.

"It can what?" Karen said from the bedroom.

Joe said nothing. His eyes felt too big for his face.

Karen's head popped out from the bedroom door. "Joe?"

"I'll have Andy check the plumbing," he said stiltedly. He fidgeted a little, then turned and walked down the stairs.

He could feel Karen watching him.

He went to the kitchen, opened the cupboard, and grabbed the bottle of Maalox. By the time he'd taken a third swallow, Karen was standing in the kitchen doorway, watching him.

He replaced the cap and put the Maalox back in the cupboard.

Karen moved to the kitchen table and sat down, her eyes on him, filled with questions. Joe sat down across from her.

"Karen," he began, taking her hand, "are you angry with me?"

She smiled and shook her head.

"Well." He began to fidget again. He squeezed her hand. Her eyes, darkening a little, looked down at their hands. "Are you—are you disappointed in me?"

"For what?"

Joe searched for the words. "Well, for giving up a secure job."

"You've got a secure job," Karen said levelly.

"Not really," Joe said. "We don't know whether we'll succeed. Our life is . . . ambiguous . . . don't you think?"

Karen shook her head.

"We're starting a new life. There's trauma in that—"

Suddenly Karen got up, crossed to him, and sat on his lap. Joe wrapped his arms about her thin waist.

"Joe, listen to me. You did what you had to do, in a way you could do it. So, maybe someone else would have done it differently. I don't care about that. All I care about is that you're happy. You are happy, aren't you?"

Joe nodded.

"Okay, then," she said, and kissed him on the forehead. "That's all that matters."

"And the rust from the plumbing?"

Her face tightened a little. "Sometimes—sometimes the

imagination can be tricky. Left unfettered, it can conjure up all sorts of fantastic things. It's like what you said about the restoration of the Fareland. Happening so quickly and all." She shrugged. "A lot has happened to us. Drastic things. It's only natural that our imaginations would . . . you know . . . go a little wild."

"You think that's all there is to it?"

She smiled. "Yes. I think that's all there is to it." She wrapped her hands around his neck. "Joe, you have inner strength. It's why I love you so much. You have your own ways, ways you can live with, and you don't have to answer to anyone. You do what you have to do, and I respect you for that."

"You love me, babe. Don't you?" Joe said, smiling impishly.

She returned the smile. "Always have. Always will."

He hugged her tight. "Thank you. Thank you for that."

She pulled him closer to her, resting his head against her breast. Warmth emanated from her, surrounding him and penetrating him, leaving him with a strange but wonderful sensation of childish security and adult sensuality. It was a very nice sensation, and he found himself letting go, sinking into its silkiness as one would sink into a tub of hot water.

"Joe?"

Absently, bemused by the splendid sensation of her encompassing embrace: "Hm?"

"Why won't you let me come to the theater?"

Like a sudden, splintering fracture in fine crystal, Joe felt the silky warm sensation shatter to let through the cold of his repressed secrets. In less than a second he had passed from security to apprehension. From apprehension to suspicion. He pulled away from her a little, looking up into her face. She'd felt the sudden tension in his body. He could see it in her eyes.

"It's not that," he began. "I just—I want you to see it. . . . I want the surprise—"

"Are you afraid to let me see the theater?"

His stomach began to churn. "No—no, I—I just . . ." Suspicion increasing, moving now into a realm more uncomfortable, Joe lifted her off his lap and stood up. He clenched his fists, trying desperately to keep from kneading the growing knot in his stomach.

"Well?" Karen asked.

Joe gritted his teeth. "I don't—I don't think I like you asking me such a question."

"Why not?"

"It's not a fair question!" Joe said forcefully, then pulled back and fought against his growing sense of . . .

. . . sense of . . .

What was it? What was going on? What had happened to that beautiful moment shared between them? What had happened to his love for her, his need for her, that sensual security that had suddenly gone sour when she'd asked him . . .

. . . asked him . . .

Questioned!

The knot in Joe's stomach tightened, and with it came the growing sense of hostility.

"You're not being fair, Karen," he said in a low, musky voice. "You're not being fair."

She sat there, unmoving, watching him keenly. So potent was her gaze that Joe couldn't return it.

She's got no right to question me. No right!

"Okay, Joe," she said finally, and left the kitchen.

But the intensity of her gaze, the magnitude of her presence, remained like cigarette smoke hanging pervasively in the air long after the smoker has left the room.

Joe rubbed his hands together and sighed heavily. What had happened? What had made things go so sour?

She came too close to the truth.

Joe gripped one hand in the other. That was it. She'd come too close. Too close to a truth he hadn't even come to terms with himself. He was afraid.

Afraid of what?

Afraid of . . . afraid of . . .

Joe slapped his hands against the sides of his face and then rubbed hard enough to hurt. The sounds of Karen preparing for bed drifted down the stairs. He listened with a kind of longing, wishing things hadn't gone so wrong, wishing she hadn't questioned him about the theater.

There were just some things that needed to be kept secret. That was all. Sure. That was all there was to it.

She'd just have to understand.

By the time he got to the bedroom Karen was already in bed, lying on her side, facing the window. Joe undressed silently and slipped between the covers without so much as an unassuming rustle of the sheets.

She'd just have to understand.

"It's okay, Joe," Karen said softly.

Joe gritted his teeth and pulled the covers up close beneath his chin.

They slept back to back.

6

 She woke him with the scent of bacon and freshly brewed coffee. Strong coffee, just the way he liked it.

He turned over on his back, breathed in the lovely odors, and lay there, trying very hard not to think about the night before.

He got up, showered, dressed, and came downstairs with a smile on his face and gave her a good-morning embrace. She kissed him on the cheek, smiling. He kissed her on the mouth. Neither of them had said anything yet, and it was Joe's guess that neither of them would. At least he hoped it would go that way. Some things were just too sensitive to discuss.

They ate in silence, and Joe left by the back door, whistling as he walked down the gravel driveway. Karen watched him through the screen door, watched as he disappeared through the tangle of overgrown branches, and wondered.

Joe had changed some, since coming to Fareland. It wasn't much of a change, but enough to make her wonder if her wary, abstract, and quite nonsensical feelings about the house weren't altogether unfounded. She couldn't put her finger on it, but there was something . . . oh, she didn't know . . . something . . . weird about it.

There was something weird about Fareland too. And it was her guess that there was something weird about the theater. Something Joe didn't want her to know about.

The house definitely didn't like her. Call it intuition. Call it cosmic, metaphysical bullshit. Call it anything you like. The house didn't like her.

And it was her guess—inarguably—that the theater didn't like her either.

Was Joe trying to protect her? Or was he trying to protect himself?

It was a question she didn't like to consider. Joe was a good man, and a good husband. His loyalty was seated deep in his gut and the few people he had chosen as friends were like him. People like Kelsie Brown, a man he had known since childhood. Nothing short of death could come between them, and she wondered if even that could quell their relationship. Like attracts like, she supposed, and Kelsie was every bit as handsome as her husband. He stood maybe two inches taller than Joe, crowned with a healthy crop of premature gray hair, offsetting his youthful face in pleasing contradiction. Joe had not said much about the day he'd left Tempac, but it was her guess that, either by providence or by design, Kelsie had most likely been a deciding factor in Joe's leaving. He respected Joe's tenacity, admired his determination. Kelsie was the kind of friend most people can only dream about.

She was more than glad that Kelsie was his friend. She was relieved, because right now Joe needed a friend more than anything. She couldn't shake the feeling that the difference in Joe was not altogether a good one. Indeed, she sometimes felt there was something very wrong.

The idea of calling Kelsie had crossed her mind more than once since she'd come to Fareland, but something always stopped her. Perhaps it was because Joe hadn't called him at all, except that one time. For some reason Joe didn't want Kelsie around.

Maybe that was a good reason to *have* him around.

Karen turned away from the kitchen door and went upstairs. She went into the bathroom and looked in the mirror, wiping strands of hair away from her face.

"Gotta get a grip on things," she told her reflection. But the reflection didn't seem to think such a thing was achievable. It stared back at her with eyes shaded in worry and concern. Joe never seemed all right these days. Sometimes he was a little okay, but never completely all right. There was always something . . . the tension in his voice, his defeated posture. He'd begin his day looking refreshed and happy. A little nervous, but that was okay. But when he'd come back from the theater, he was always—*always* drained, in one way or another, and almost always irritable, suspicious. It was as though the theater was draining him of strength. Maybe it was.

Well, of course it was. He was working at light-speed, trying to get it ready. Of course he'd be tired and irritable when he got home.

But suspicious?

Karen slipped off her robe, went to the tub, and turned on the faucet for her shower.

Maybe she should call Kelsie.

The plumbing rumbled, the faucet sputtered, and from the shower head came a rusty plume of dust.

Karen sank to the edge of the tub. "God damn it."

This night was no different from the others. Joe came down the gravel driveway looking haggard and frayed. His face had pulled down in a heavy frown and his shoulders drooped wearily. He came in through the back door, letting it swing shut with a snap, went past her silently to the cupboard above the sink, and pulled out the bottle of Maalox. He took two long swallows, then replaced the bottle and slumped groaning into a kitchen chair.

"Hard day?" Karen asked as she poured him a glass of milk.

He wrapped his hands around the glass and lifted it to his face, pressing it gratefully to his cheek. "Yeah. Rough. Really tired." He took a swallow of milk. "Theater's almost ready."

Karen arched her eyebrows. "You're kidding!"

"Why would I kid about a thing like that?"

Karen glanced at him. The edge to his voice was matched only by the strain in his face. She ladled a plate of stew from the pot on the stove and placed it before him. He looked at it silently, then picked up his fork and began to eat.

The tension mounted.

She sat down next to him, and an uncomfortable silence

settled over them while Joe ate his stew. He seemed to be on automatic, scooping up the stew with a spoon and shoveling it into his mouth. He chewed unconsciously, like an after-thought.

Karen took a deep breath and braced herself. "So, when do you think you can open?" she asked.

"September twenty-ninth," Joe mumbled, his mouth full of half-chewed meat and potatoes. Gravy dripped from the cor-ner of his mouth.

"Really?"

He looked at her sharply. "Yeah. What's wrong with that?"

"Nothing. I just . . . didn't realize it would be so soon."

"You got a problem with that?"

"Of course not, Joe." She reached out to touch his cheek, but he pulled away. "What's wrong?"

"Nothing's wrong!" he snapped, standing suddenly. Karen flinched. "Why do you keep asking me if anything's wrong?"

Karen sat there, her mouth half open in bewilderment.

"Get off my back, Karen! There's a lot of pressure on me, I don't need you fucking with me when I come home!" He turned away from her, slamming his fists on the counter.

Karen sat there a moment longer, measuring her anger. Finally she stood. "To hell with you, Joe."

She could see by the sway of his body that she had struck home. He turned, tried to reach out for her, but she pulled away. "To hell with you."

She turned and left the kitchen.

Joe sat at the table, the sight of the cooling stew coagulat-ing in its own juices making him feel sick. It wasn't supposed to have been like this.

He closed his eyes tightly, rubbing them with his knuckles. Oh, God, if he could just get through this until the theater opened. Then everything would be all right. He'd be able to relax then, let Andy run the theater and he could take some time off. They'd take a little vacation. He could take Karen to San Francisco for the weekend.

He rubbed his eyes harder.

They'd check into one of those plush hotels, like the Hyatt

Regency . . . one of those three-hundred-dollar-a-night jobs with the room service and the linen napkins and the real rose on the tray. Eight bucks for a glass of milk, for crying out loud. But the milk was like fine wine. Anything costing eight bucks a pop was like fine wine, or at least it had better be.

So they'd check into one of those fancy plush hotels and they'd lie around on their three-hundred-dollar king-size bed and make love all day. He felt a little surge of excitement well up inside him as he pictured Karen lying naked on that three-hundred-dollar king-size bed. No, wait, not naked. No, she'd be draped in satin. Brown satin to offset the alabaster of her skin.

Ah, yes.

And then they'd order room service. Steak and lobster, and a baked potato smothered in butter and sour cream.

Then the brown satin again, only now her smooth silky skin would be sheathed in a fine, pearly sweat and she would smell of honeysuckle and pine, refined to a cresting sensuality by the clandestine scent of musk.

Joe opened his eyes. He looked around the kitchen, appreciating its cleanliness, then got up and went to the living room.

He found Karen sitting on the couch with her legs tucked neatly beneath her. She was reading a book, her face almost void of expression, but in her eyes he saw her anger, her righteous indignation, and consciously shrank from it. He squirmed for a moment, then cleared his throat. "Babe?"

She acknowledged him only with a subtle shift of her legs.

"I'm sorry."

Karen looked at him, and Joe could see by the animation in her eyes that she was seriously considering not letting him off the hook. He offered her a timid smile.

That softened her glare a little. She sighed. "Why don't you trust me, Joe?"

"It's not that, Karen. I'm just . . . I'm tired." He took a step toward her. "I'm so tired all the time."

"I know you are," Karen said, placing the book down and

leaning forward. "But that's no excuse. I'm sorry, but it isn't."

Joe nodded guiltily.

"You've been trying to do this thing all on your own, you know?" Karen said gently. "You've been secretive, even evasive. You've pretty much pushed me out of the picture, and that's not fair. I have a stake in this too."

Joe tried to look at her, but found he couldn't. After only a few seconds he gave up trying.

"You think I don't worry about you?" Karen persisted. "You think I don't see how much Maalox you're downing every day? You think I don't see how tired and haggard you are when you come home from working at the Fareland? And what am I supposed to do? Just sit back and let you fall apart without trying to do something about it?"

"What could you do?" Joe said in a weak voice.

"Be here for you," Karen said. "Be here for you, Joe, if you let me. But it's your decision. You have to decide who's on your side, and who isn't. You have to decide who your friends are."

"It's hard," Joe whispered.

"Why?"

Joe grappled inwardly with the question, and found it to be more complex than he thought it should be.

"It's more than just a change," he said finally, forcing the words out, forcing inexplicable emotion to verbal translation. "Things have been happening—"

He stopped suddenly, feeling cold.

"What things?" Karen asked.

The cold stole up his spine. "I can't explain," he said, feeling miserably impotent.

Karen leaned back on the couch, regarding him sternly.

For a second, as fleeting and elusive as an indecipherable whisper, Joe wanted to run.

Instead he went to her, sat down next to her, and put his arms about her. He buried his face in the curve of her neck.

Karen responded immediately and unconditionally. She embraced him, comforted him, accepted him without further question.

But the echo of her earlier words had set his heart to trembling. He knew she was right, and knowing it frightened him. He tightened his embrace.

Then suddenly, without warning, Joe began to cry.

Karen rocked him gently and stroked the back of his head. He could feel the warmth of her love, her caring, and he pulled it around himself like a blanket. He fell into her, hid there from the prying eyes of those deceptive and cunningly cruel, and wept like a child.

When the last of his sobbing was spent, he sighed heavily and pulled away to look at her. He touched her cheek, ran his hand gently across her copper hair. Not red; copper, like fine burnished plateware. Streaks of silver ran through the soft strands. Light glistened and sparkled in the curls when she spoke or laughed, and the copper flecks in her brown eyes made her seem more like a dream than waking reality. He loved her, more than anyone could love another. He loved her so much, it almost hurt.

With his fingers he probed every curve and line of her face, her neck. He touched her eyelids, traced her eyebrows, explored every part of her as though seeing her for the first time.

It was more on his part an attempt to erase the confrontation than it was an act of love, and Joe knew this deep in his heart. But he excused it.

He ignored it to the point of negating it.

At least, that was his hope.

When he kissed her, she responded, and the trembling in his heart abated. The negation was complete.

She let her hand slip to his groin and his passion engulfed him. He let it flood out of him, let it merge with hers in an igniting of sensual intimacy and sexual exploit. They moved as one on the couch, exploring each other as if for the first time, pressing and stroking in unison as their passion engulfed them and sent them soaring to inexplicable heights of desire. Their bodies joined, and together they kept time with the timbre of their intimate symphony.

Joe didn't know it, but it was the last time he would ever make love to her.

It was not the last time he would use her.

7

 For as long as he could remember, Andy Jordan had spent many hours sitting quietly in the darkened house of the Fareland Cinema, but he could not, in recent times, remember being as reflective as he was on this night. The closest he had come to feeling so in concert with the theater was the time when, as a child, he had learned of the varying powers within the Hiding Fear.

He remembered now, as he sat with his chin resting on laced fingers and his eyes focused on the screen, blinding white even in this darkness, that it had not been what he had expected it to be. He had heard of the Hiding Fear, and he had seen with his own eyes, as well as through the eyes of his grandfather, what the Hiding Fear had invoked in those favored with the revelation of it, and yet not once had he ever believed it could invoke in him the trueness of ultimate power now so closely within his grasp.

Could it be, then, that his grandfather had private plans of his own? Could it be that he had, in his way, prepared his grandson for something other than the part of the player in the perpetual ritual of replenishing what had been depleted? The scheme of things had kept him in childhood for so long that his sudden transition to young adulthood had been cumbersome and confusing. His personal needs, the needs of a child and subsequently an adolescent, had paled in the sunless conspiracy of the scheme of things. It was only logical, then, for him to assume his role as the player.

His grandfather had taught him well. Frank Jordan had, in action and deed, shown him the pitfalls of being merely a player, and Andy had heeded what he learned. The Hiding

Fear had not devoured him. Rather, it had catapulted him to heights previously unimaginable as he waited through the endless, illusory years from childhood to the age of reason, when he knew he would not have to settle for the part of being merely a player. He would, at this time, become the Game Master, and the spiraling of memory in the years of waiting and interminable forced patience would finally, resolutely, be rewarded.

A stiff pain in his hand nudged him from the inner workings of his reflection and he turned his attention to the laceration in his palm. It was deep and thick, and as he opened and closed his fist it gaped and shut, gaped and shut, like a blood-red mouth gasping for air.

Andy's lips tightened to a contemptuous straight line. "Back off," he whispered. "Back off me. I know the scheme of things."

The brilliant white screen glowed in the darkness, marking distinctively the place of power. It was a warning Andy heeded well.

He heeded it, but he was not afraid of it. Unlike the others —even his grandfather—Andy had learned the lessons of the Hiding Fear.

Intimidation: that was the key. Scare the shit out of them and they'd cut off their right arm for you. Anything you say, Andy ol' pal. Just don't hurt me, okay?

Okay?

Ah, yes . . . he'd wedged himself into the scheme of things with slick exactness. He was slick, oh, yes.

Andy flinched suddenly as the twinge in his palm flared. He looked up at the screen, his beautiful face bathed in its rich brilliance. "No reason there can't be cooperation, you know?" He smiled wickedly, that sneer-grin momentarily subverting the angelic handsomeness of his face. "You have your agenda, and I have mine. No need for mutual exclusivity, right?"

"Your speech betrays you, cousin."

The words sliced through the thick silence of the theater with such clarity, they made Andy jump in surprise. He rose from his seat in the first row and stood in the aisle, feet spread apart, fists clenched. The unexpectedness of the voice filled him not so much with fear as with embarrassment at having allowed himself to be caught off guard. He'd thought himself better prepared. The brilliance of the screen did not extend beyond the first three or four rows of seats. The back of the theater was dark as pitch, and the voice came from the depths of it.

"Since when do eighteen-year-olds use words like *mutual exclusivity*?"

Movement, quietly arrogant, shifted the pitch and separated it. Pitch turned to a shape in the darkness, and a shape in the darkness to solid form.

A cat. Large. Opulent black coat shimmering with highlights of iridescent blue. Eyes the color of a midmorning sky; powdery blue.

Andy watched, outwardly impassive, inwardly impressed, as the cat moved with sinewy elegance. Each step brought it closer to him, and as it came within the glow of the brilliant screen its form began to change, imperceptibly at first. Every aspect of the cat began fluidly to vacillate among conflicting configurations. It rose from its forepaws; the claws, long and black, began to retract. The pointed, exacting snout of the animal mellowed and flattened, the ears shortened as they disappeared into long, flowing hair. It rose up, and as it stood awkwardly on its hind legs the body maneuvered slowly and deliberately in a dimension somewhere between animal and human, allowing the mind no opportunity of witnessing its final reconfiguration. Andy could only stand with eyes fixed on the woman before him, all attributes of the cat delegated to obscure memory, except for the powdery blue eyes.

They stood there in silence, regarding one another. Finally she moved toward him, stopping about three feet in front of him.

"Neat trick," Andy said coolly.

"Thank you," the woman said in a low, melodic, sinister voice. "Want to see another?"

Andy stiffened. He could feel her, standing more than three feet away. He *felt* her caress, the seductive stroking of her fingers as they moved in a whispery way, like the touch of a feather, neither hot nor cold but increasingly imposing, sending electric shivers through his nervous system. He fell into the sensation, losing himself in the sensuality of her touch, then cursed himself as the torture of steel blades sliced through his skin. He cursed the trembling of his body at the suggestion of her, the want of her, the supplication to affliction at the mercy of her savagery, and he fought against his own arousal because her touch, even as seductive as it was, had the sinister edge of evil.

Then the pressure was gone, but wounds remained like fire on his back, between his legs. Against his will his body strained for her but she ignored it, turning away, leaving him to ache.

"Funny thing about arrogance," she said over her shoulder. "It can leave you feeling a little . . . achy. Can't it?"

"My grandpa told me about you," Andy said, trying to hide the breathlessness in his voice. "You're my cousin, from siblings he never had."

"And you're his grandson, from children he never had," she answered.

"I've always been his grandson," Andy said. "But you haven't always been my cousin." He narrowed his eyes. "Remember that."

The woman crooked an eyebrow. "Such arrogance. Be careful, Andy. Arrogance can be a virtue, but sometimes"—her hand whipped out and grasped his, the fingernails digging into the laceration in his palm—"it can be quite painful."

Andy hid his pain carefully behind a sullen face. "Let me go."

"Ask me nice."

Andy clenched his teeth and stared into her powdery blue eyes with firm defiance. "Let me go."

She did.

Andy stood with his back straight, determined not to show his pain. He let the silence move in between them again as he regarded her with measured tolerance.

And she studied him, but with the glittery eyes of amusement.

"I'm not a kid anymore," Andy said. "I'm grown up now."
She smiled, nodding.

"And I know the plan. I know how to run things."

Another nod.

Andy narrowed his eyes. "Then why are you here?"

"To serve. As are you, cousin." She turned to face the screen, scanning it with reverence. "There is a great hunger, and patience wears thin. Satiation is long overdue." She turned to him, her face dark with foreboding. "Watch yourself, cousin. You'd be wise to measure your power and know its limits."

Andy seethed. She was crafty, this woman, but she was not what she claimed to be and he knew it. He knew his power. How could he not? He had been cultivating it for timeless, measureless years.

He turned his head and lifted his eyes to a pinpoint of light that flickered at the back of the theater where the projection room was. He looked deep into the light, felt its warmth spread through him as he raised his hand and invoked the power therein.

He heard a tiny cry, and when he turned he saw the back of the woman's head, her shoulders scrunching up suddenly as though someone had grabbed her around the neck. He stood frozen, let the power pulse through him, and watched her squirm.

"You don't want to touch me like that again, bitch," he hissed. "Understand?"

"Okay!" she cried. "Okay, come on, cousin. Just playing around."

"We've got no time for that," Andy said. His hand still raised to the light, he clenched his fist. The woman cried out in sudden pain. "I've got no time for your bullshit. You remember your place. You remember who's in charge."

"And you remember as well!" The woman screamed through her pain. "There's no gain in this test of wills, cousin. Let me go."

Andy hesitated.

"Let me go!"

Slowly, cautiously, he relaxed his hand. The flicker of light shuddered, then dimmed, and the woman fell forward, whipping her head around, her eyes now shiny black like hematite, and for a moment Andy thought they would battle again.

But the darkness faded, her face relaxed, her eyes, once again powdery blue, avoided his.

Andy smiled. "Okay. We got problems with his wife. She's strong, got a will of her own. And some guy named Kelsie. Friend of his. That bitch wife is thinking about calling him and I don't think I can stop it."

The woman raised her eyebrows. "Why not just send her to the balcony?"

Andy shook his head, his brow furrowing. "Too much static. Too much conduction. . . . I don't know. She's got a connection I'm having trouble figuring out, and so does that fucker Kelsie. We have to deal with them on our own, and that's where you come in. You'll have to take care of it, and that means staying with Joe all the time. Not just here. All the time."

The woman gathered herself up, glaring for a moment. "You've got this all figured out, haven't you, cousin?" She leaned close to him, her blue eyes sending sparks as thin as thread. "Remember the lesson, cousin. Remember, there is only one scheme. There is only the whole."

"And you serve the whole, right?" Andy said tightly.

"Don't you? Or do you have plans of your own?"

"I'm trusted," Andy said evenly, straightening his shoulders. "And I'm not afraid of you, cousin. You remember that. You remember who has been here longer. I give the orders."

She regarded him with careful wariness, then smiled sweetly and turned to move up the aisle.

"You have your orders!" Andy called after her, but she ignored him, moving up the aisle with liquid grace. As she moved her body changed, and Andy found himself caught in that netherworld of conflicting configuration, helpless to stop the appearance of yet another being. By the time the woman had reached the rim of light from the brilliant screen, every aspect of the human was gone. There in the aisle stood a large German shepherd.

"Do you have a plan?" Andy shouted.

The dog turned, setting its powdery blue eyes on him, and in his mind he heard the echoing memory of the woman's voice: *We all have plans.*

Then it was gone, moving swiftly through the curtains with barely a sound except the whisper of fabric, and Andy was alone.

He went to the front of the theater and sat in the front-row seat.

This new one, this cousin . . . he had no memory of her; not even in the remote and fabricated memories of his childhood. She was new, and her power possessed a capacity for potential. Her power was derived from the whole, as was his, but her designs were singular and motivated by the whole, and his were not.

It occurred to Andy, as he sat alone in the darkness, that it was time to assess the situation anew. Things had changed. Things were not as they had been when he first came to the age of reason, and he resented the fact that the whole had decided, without his knowledge, that he needed to be watched. It could be said that the goals of the whole were not necessarily identical to his own, but that didn't mean he was ready to break off on his own, nor was he attempting to position his own needs above the need of the whole. He knew his place. He knew his responsibilities, and he would not betray the whole, the giver of the power he possessed.

But he did have plans of his own, and it was only fair that he be allowed, within the parameters of the whole, to carve for himself a sizable territory of his own. Such a thing would not diminish the whole. He had no desire to do that. He sought only coexistence.

She had come without a past, not even a fabricated one. He had no memory of her. She had not yet been fashioned by the whole at the time Andy's own development had begun, as a child, as an entity unto himself.

But this one, this cousin, had come without memory. She had come to watch over Andy, to observe and catalogue, and possibly subvert. This new one, this cousin, was wholly the product of the whole, and that made her a threat to that which he sought. He needed to reinforce his exclusivity, and the locals were not sufficient, not even with the power of the Hiding Fear.

He was going to need allies.

8

The morning sun has a subtle, sliding way about it, peeking over the horizon like a child rounding the corner of the stairs and catching a look at Christmas morning. It caresses the land in quiet determination. The promise of blasting heat later in the day is clear.

But now, in the early-morning hours, its touch is gentle and suggestive, never demanding. It invites you to pause and consider, relishing its kindness before the abrasive heat boils the sweat on your back. The air softly pulsates with whispers as the world awakens, rested and strong again.

The morning hours were Joe's only refuge, and he endeavored to make them last. In the night he'd gather strength, used up too quickly as the morning progressed. He'd rise early when the world was dark and young again and go to the theater, hoping to reach its cloistered safety before his meager strength was spent.

On this morning he felt stronger than usual, in control, and that was something. Probably it had to do with the nearness of the theater's grand opening. Something about that day was revitalizing. He walked slowly, listening to the sounds of the still morning, his mind working over plans that seemed to have connected themselves into a string of preordained events, as though someone had found him clinging precariously to a crumbling cliff, had thrown him a rope, and then had threatened to cut the rope and send him plummeting into oblivion.

The thought had slammed against him, dragging a scratch across his canvas of certainty. He tried to ignore it.

Tried to. But it lingered. It followed him, as a thief follows his victim, until he finally reached the theater and ran inside.

The lobby was dark and still. From the pit of the house Joe could hear muffled sounds like a rumbling; no doubt Andy was working on the seats. The upholstery needed some finishing touches; some polishing and replacing of the numbers. "Andy?"

The rumbling stopped. "That you, Joe?"

"Yeah." Joe moved toward the entry to the main house and pulled the curtain aside. "You been here long?"

"Not long. Almost finished." Andy dropped his hammer and walked up the aisle, watching Joe closely. "You talk to your wife?"

"About what?"

"You were going to ask her about working the snack bar."

Joe rubbed his forehead absently. "Oh. Yeah. . . ." He'd forgotten all about it. That tight scene in the kitchen had wiped his memory clean.

Andy smiled. "No problem, really. I was sorta gonna talk to you about it, anyway. I have this cousin . . . she's been away at school a couple years now. But she's back in town and she needs a job. What do you think?"

Joe glanced at him sharply. "The snack bar?"

"Sure," Andy said casually, but his eyes stayed fixed to Joe's. "Why not? Come on, Joe. You don't want your wife slavin' over a hot popcorn machine, do you? Hell, man, keep her at home where she belongs."

Joe's eyes shifted momentarily to the silver screen that blazed behind Andy's back. "Maybe—maybe so. Okay, Andy. Have her come in this afternoon and I'll talk to her."

"Great!" Andy clapped his hands together, wincing briefly.

Christ, even casual talk with Andy was always shaded with tension. That slice on Andy's palm was significant, he knew, but he was afraid to mention it. It would only add to the tension. He didn't need that. Not now. The two of them were like cats, circling one another, watching their backs, and Joe always came away feeling drained.

And now, a cousin? Another Jordan? The place was infested with them. That's just what it felt like, an infestation.

A taking over of his precious theater by the Jordan family of rats. Joe turned away from Andy and started back up the aisle, calling over his shoulder. "What's her name?"

"Nancy. Nancy Macullough."

"Not Jordan?"

"No. She's from my mom's side of the family. She's a good worker, Joe. You won't be disappointed."

"Yeah," Joe said hollowly, and left the house.

Sitting at her dressing table, Karen brushed her hair with thoughtful strokes. The air outside was warm and still, and although the beads of water still clinging to her skin were soothing, it was not quite enough to calm her troubled mind. Alone in this hateful house, brushing her hair and letting her gaze settle on nothing important, her mind wrestled with past events. That urgent call from Joe in early September, his growing impatience with the theater's progress . . . it all seemed to connect, somehow, with his preoccupation and brooding. And his stomach problems were like an exclamation mark at the end of an already formidable sentence.

Joe had always brought his headaches home with him, often taking them to bed but never allowing them to tarnish their relationship. Karen had been a refuge for him; their marriage the soothing balm for a troubled existence.

Until now.

It hurt her to see his boyish face scarred so terribly by what was going on with him. And just what was going on? Where was the innocence she had so often relished as she gazed upon his face, his dark eyes reaching out for her and tugging on her heart, making her love for him flood out and wash over both of them? Where had he gone? And who was taking him away?

The Fareland. That was who.

She shook her head distractedly. That was *what* . . . not who. . . .

The Fareland was changing him, pulling him in and pushing her away, shutting her out. You always hear about people who draw inward and close up, and no one can reach them. No one. . . .

The image of Kelsie Brown suddenly came to her. If anyone could get through to Joe, it was Kelsie.

She gazed out the window at the warm morning. The dew had been burned away and a dusty swirl of leaves swept across the backyard outside her window.

Maybe she was jumping the gun. Joe wasn't all that different. He hadn't been different in bed last night. It had been the same old Joe, the same man she had fallen in love with more than ten years ago.

The same old Joe. Yeah . . . except for the crying.

The shaking, and the crying.

Oh, hell, what could it hurt, calling Kelsie? He was a friend. It was time for a visit. The theater was going to open soon. Surely Joe would want Kelsie there. Surely he'd want to gloat about how fast restoration had gone. One month. Record time. Surely he'd want to gloat.

Kelsie wouldn't come up here unless he was invited. That's just the way he was. She'd call him. Yes. She'd call him that afternoon.

She didn't call him.

The eleven reels of Alfred Hitchcock's *Shadow of a Doubt* were waiting for Joe when he reached the theater that morning. Andy had carted them upstairs to the projection room and had left them in two neat stacks outside the door. Seeing them there gave Joe a new vitality. Things were coming together. The film was here and now he could really get things going. He unlocked the projection-room door and pushed the cans of film inside.

The room was unusually cold. He flicked the switch and the light blinked on for an instant before it sputtered and cracked, then went out completely, leaving the room in darkness except for a sliver of dim light that filtered through the projection window. Joe cursed under his breath and groped around for the flashlight he kept in a drawer near the projector. His fingers touched something warm and soft.

His breath caught in his chest.

He yanked his hand back and his eyes strained against the darkness until he clamped them shut.

Subtle pressure nudged him in the back.

He whirled around, muscles tensing.

A whisper of breath brushed his cheek.

Christ . . .

There was someone else in the room.

He searched wildly in the darkness but found nothing,

oh, Jesus

no one he could see.

But he could feel it: a lingering, a memory of touch. His stomach coiled.

Someone was there.

Someone had crept inside, someone had crept inside to wait for him. To . . .

His hands groped for the projector. "Who's here?"

A shift, like a second thought. Then nothing again. Watching him. Watching, and waiting.

He shuddered, planted his fist deep into his belly, but the sour liquid flooded his throat and gagged him.

"God damn it! Who's in here?"

Pressure, like radiant cold. Pressure swayed against him, caressing him with frigid fingers. His body trembled beneath its silent intensity. He was afraid to move.

Then it left him.

Still afraid, still sick, he reached out and found the door, felt for the doorknob and it's just like when you're a kid, oh, God . . . you reach out for the doorknob, for safety, and something comes down on you and . . .

His insides erupted. He threw open the door and stumbled down the stairs, crashing headlong with a thud at the bottom.

Something in the room. Something waiting for him.

He groaned, shivered, and prayed he wouldn't throw up.

"What's wrong?" It was Andy. He was standing over Joe, looking puzzled.

Joe shook his head. "Nothing. Just—just slipped. That's all."

"Hell, man. You look like you saw a ghost."

Joe got up, pushing Andy aside. "You look like the son of one, so what?" He marched down the length of the mezzanine with his head held high with indignation, glancing back only once as he descended the stairs and marched to the box office. When he closed the door he slammed it, and listened to the sound of his anger bouncing off the theater walls. It sounded good. It sounded strong.

Once inside, he leaned against the counter as his indignation and strength gave way to his fear. He shuddered a little, determined not to give in and wipe the cold beads of sweat forming on his brow. He stood there, supporting himself against the counter, and tried to calm his fear. He liked the box office almost as much as he liked the projection room. More, in fact, because the box office felt more his own. He was the soul of it. He was the forethought, the countenance that gave the room its flavor. It was larger than conventional box offices, the kind you see in the center front of a theater, as this one was set to one side much like the box office of a stage theater. On one wall, adjacent to the box office window, was a set of cubbyholes used to place reserved tickets in alphabetical order. Beneath it was a counter, which moved along the wall to the corner and ran under the window. Behind him was a filing cabinet and to his right was the door. Fifteen-hundred-dollar-a-month New York apartments were smaller than this room.

He smiled a little. Normal thoughts, yes, think about normal things. Relax. Be normal and it'll go away. Remember why you came in here.

He shuffled papers around distractedly and the memory came back,

Pressure, like radiant cold, snuggling up to him, oh, God Jesus . . .

stealing in through the cracks in his mind.

A sting behind him stabbed at the base of his spine. He whirled around.

A cat it's a cat how the hell—?

In silhouette the figure swayed, slender and feminine.

A cat . . . it was a cat and now . . .

Joe cleared his throat. "Who are you?"

"Nancy Macullough," the woman said as she stepped inside the door, closing it shut behind her. "I'm your new counter lady."

Joe stepped back instinctively. The woman's eyes were taking him in, moving slowly across the curves of his body, assaulting him. His hand crept slowly to his chest. "I'm . . . not ready for you yet." He turned away, trying to look busy, but all the while he was keenly aware of her gaze. It was unmanning, knowing she was looking at him, touching him

Pressure . . . like radiant cold

with her eyes in a way that made him swear she had her hand on him, pressing against the small of his back, an imperceptible feeling that was almost comforting until the pressure moved, sliding gently down his right buttock and across his hip to the inside of his thigh. His muscles tensed. He wanted it to stop. He reached for the hand to push it away, but there was nothing there.

Nothing there.

Sound. Fire . . .

. . . fire, inside. Sweet fire . . .

. . . the hand . . .

. . . not there, but there, between his legs, pushing hard, cupping . . .

. . . stroking . . .

. . . making him throb, blanketing him in oily sweat . . . it hurt . . .

. . . hot breath against him . . .

. . . nothing there!

"You're ready for me," she whispered. "Yes . . . I can *feel* you ready for me."

Pressure,

radiant cold, it's cold!

between his legs, surging, intensifying, falling into it . . . please . . . yes. . . .

Then it was gone.

Joe slumped forward, catching himself clumsily with shaky hands, his body aching so viciously, he could only tremble. It was madness.

Madness.

He turned slowly, wanting to look at her, to see her again because the sight of her would bring back the awful pressure, the fire.

But he was alone.

Slowly, like the dawning of a putrid thought, sickness seized him. He clutched at his stomach, groaning.

She'd had her hands on him.

Christ . . . her hands.

She was a cat, a big cat, she crept inside and then she changed. . . .

He dug his fist into the pit of his stomach, felt the bile rise in his throat.

Hands on me, her hands on me making me . . . making me . . .

His body flushed in a rage so furious, he thought he would explode in fire.

hands on me, her hands on me

In his fever he found the image of Karen and gripped it. He stumbled out of the box office, walking like a crippled man to his car, getting in, all the while clinging to the thought of Karen, the vision of her, using it as a shield against the cat that wasn't a cat that had its *hands* on him!

He drove with his fist gripping the steering wheel, shoulders hunched forward, mind set on the image of Karen. Real image. Something real. Something tangible. Not that

radiant cold

awful feeling of being touched when nothing was there.

Nothing was there!

He wheeled into the driveway and slammed on the brakes. The car swerved to one side, sending a spray of gravel against the side of the house.

Radiant cold

And he was on fire. He was on fucking fire!

Karen came to the side door, her face pinched with concern. "Joe?"

He clambered out of the car, falling to his knees.

Karen ran to him, grabbed him by the arms, and began to pull him to his feet. Without thought he embraced her hard, trying desperately to shield himself from the fire raging within.

Sweet Karen. Sweet and clean. Oh, Jesus, Karen, please . . .

hands on him hands that weren't there
The pressure, the radiant cold . . .
And he was on *fire*!
So clean, so sweet, standing there in his embrace.
Jaded fire, dirty, but it swelled in him, flowed out of him.
"Joe, what's wrong?"
In utter desperation he embraced her, kissed her, tried so hard to lose himself in her and dispel the vision, the memory of that bitch's touch, the swelling fire. The radiant cold. He felt Karen move with him, matching her breath with his, her hips pulling upward, her silky legs wrapping around him. He pulled her into his arms and carried her into the house.
And used her.

9

 September 29.
　　It could have been everything Joe wanted,
but somewhere he'd lost it. Somewhere he'd
felt his grip break free, cleanly, like a pinecone from a dry
branch. He didn't know exactly how it had happened, and he
wasn't even sure he wanted to know.

But he knew *when* it had happened, and knowing that was
just about as much as he could take.

It had happened the day he'd walked out of Tempac.

At the time, he'd thought he was taking charge, for the
first time in his life. And for a long time he'd believed this,
but as the days wore on, as the events occurred in such exacting sequence, he slowly found himself being tugged and
pulled, maneuvered, used.

The monkey, being made to dance.

And the bitch of it was, he allowed it. He actually allowed
it.

Why?

It was that film. That 65-millimeter camera negative film
tucked safely away in the projection room.

And it was the projector too. He spent a lot of time with
that projector, talking to it, touching it, marveling at how it
seemed to clean itself and rejuvenate itself, all on its own.

No. No, not on its own.

Over the days, as the restoration continued, Joe found
himself becoming more and more attached to the projector.
There was a kinship growing between himself and that inanimate object. There was a brotherhood, an attachment, a coupling.

Joe not only had a hand in its rejuvenation; Joe was, indeed, the cause of it.

That singular thing, amid the array of circumstances unfolding around him, made him feel more a part of the restoration, rather than just the observer, or the cause. Joe, too, was being restored. Not only did Joe own the Fareland Cinema. He *was* the Fareland Cinema. They were inseparable. They were one.

Karen couldn't understand that. She had asked the night before if he was going to let her come to the grand opening, and he had put her off.

It didn't seem right. She asked for explanation, but he had none. It just didn't seem right. She told him that was stupid, and that had made him mad.

"You're blocking me out again, Joe," she'd said. "Why do you do that? Why do you treat that theater like a mistress?"

He'd turned on her then, enraged. "Why do you make everything into something more than it is?" he'd screamed at her. "A house that doesn't like you. A theater like a mistress." He stomped back and forth, hands balled into fists, mouth so tightly clenched that his jaw was beginning to ache.

"And why are you so angry," she countered, "if part of what I'm saying isn't just a little bit true?"

He had no answer for that, so he turned his back on her.

"You do what you want, Joe," she said evenly. "You don't want me there, then fine. I won't go. It's your theater. Your life. You want to exclude me, go ahead. But by God, don't keep coming to me when things get out of hand."

He turned, opening his mouth, but she stopped him with a raised hand. "Don't try to deny it. I'm not stupid. I know when I'm being used."

And that had been the end of it. She turned, went upstairs to their bedroom, slamming the door shut. Joe spent the night on the couch.

Fuming, restless, every muscle taut from the rage he felt in the wake of their fight, Joe turned his thoughts to the theater, the projector, and the camera negative film. Like a soothing balm the images calmed him and he fell asleep almost instantly.

In the morning there was no breakfast waiting for him. The house was unusually quiet. He went upstairs, saw that their bedroom door was still closed, then went into the bathroom to take a shower.

The hot water woke and refreshed him. Karen had laid out clothes for him in the bathroom. He dressed quickly and went downstairs.

In the kitchen he found a note from Karen attached to the refrigerator door. *Gone for the day* was all it said.

Good, then, he thought. *Good. She's out of my hair.*

He stepped out into the early-morning air, and for the most part it was as it always had been. Morning dew laced the air with a beady kind of moistness that hitched a ride on your shoulders. A morning ground fog hugged the gravel driveway, and the quiet was broken only by the distant sound of birds.

This was Friday. This was September 29.

The grand opening. The Fareland, come alive again.

Joe Moreson, come alive for the first time in his life.

He walked down the driveway and made his way to the theater.

But as he neared it he began to feel a kind of foreboding. An uneasiness, seated somewhere in the pit of him and fingering out slowly, like the roots of a tiny plant. He ignored it at first, assuming it was just the excitement of anticipation, but as he drew closer to the theater, the feeling grew to proportions too great to be ignored. It began to weigh on his shoulders.

When he reached the theater he cupped his hands against the glass front doors and peered in. The lobby was dark and quiet, and when he tried the doors he found them solidly locked. He cupped his hands again. Silly, really. Why didn't he just unlock the door and go in?

Something was different. He couldn't pin it down, but he could feel it bristling the hair on the back of his neck. A tiny tingling scurrying down his spine.

Something was different. Something was *wrong*.

So he just stood there, hands cupped to the window, looking like a kid snatching a peek through a hole in the wall of

the girls' showers. He peered into the darkness of the lobby
and scanned it with hesitant eyes. No one there. No one in
there and why did he feel so guilty? Where was that sensation coming from . . . guilty, going to get caught. Going to
blow your fucking head off if you don't get away from that
window, you bastard—

Joe pulled back quickly, cold air catching in his throat. He
stuffed his hands in his pockets and glanced nervously about
him, trying to breathe easily and shake that feeling. That
scary, anxious feeling of something wrong.

He took a couple shuffling, aimless steps, then pulled out
his key and inserted it with feigned nonchalance.

The door moved easily now, having been brushed clean of
rust and well oiled, but still the hinges screamed at him, in
protest, in defiance of violation. Joe raised his arms in frightened reflex, realizing with a kind of despair that his heart was
striking his breastbone with frightful fluttering force like the
skip of a rock on the smooth surface of a pond. It would skip
so lightly and then without argument plunge into the cold,
dark water. And being here in this place, alone, he was as
weak as the rock of his own heart.

He wished he knew where Andy was.

And why wasn't he here?

He waited all day, fooling with supplies in the box office
and behind the snack bar, measuring and then measuring
again the syrup for the soft drinks, filling, emptying, and then
refilling the saltshakers, counting and recounting the hot
dogs, snitching Junior Mints then recounting the supply and
where the hell was Andy? He ambled up and down the aisles,
glancing repeatedly at the small square hole at the back of
the house where the projector was.

Glancing, but not really looking.

That was it. That was the problem. The projection room,
his sanctuary. Until that night.

And by the way, where the *hell* was Andy?

He'd been in the projection room a thousand times and
he'd felt safe, secure. It was his place and no one else could
go in there. At least, no one was supposed to go in there, but
all that was changed now, wasn't it? It had changed when the

lights were out and the cold soft pressure had leaned against him.

Why had that happened?

Was it a threat? A warning? He didn't know.

God damn it, Andy. Why don't you come?

Come and make things okay. Come and tell me it's just nerves. Just the pressure. Nothing there, not really. Nothing there but you felt it, didn't you? You felt it. And you liked it.

"No . . ."

He jumped, his own voice, wispy and lame, frightening him.

Andy, please come. Don't leave me here alone.

But Andy didn't come. Andy was not here. Joe was alone in the big dark theater. Alone, except for that thing, that pressure lying just beyond the shadows, waiting for him to screw up, just as his boss had always done. Big guy. Tough guy sitting up there in his penthouse office just waiting for Joe to screw up so he could lower the boom and change Joe from a rooster to a hen in one easy swipe.

He clenched his fists.

Fuck you, Andy.

Just like the little bastard to be late. He knew how important this day was. He knew how much Joe needed him to be here.

Deep afternoon sunlight was slanting through the slits in the entryway curtains, sending shafts of white in laser beam patterns across the seats. It was almost time. The box office was to open at seven P.M. and people would be arriving soon. Joe shook himself inwardly to steady his nerves and marched up the center aisle.

Everything was okay. Everything was just fine. His film was ready to go and just needed to be threaded and set up. He'd locked the cans of film in the projection room for safekeeping. No one had a key except himself. No one could have gotten in there. No one except . . .

Dread flooded in.

No.

No one had gotten in there. That pressure, that radiant cold . . .

It was already there. It was there before he had gone in that night. It was there, waiting for him.

No, oh, no . . .

Nothing was wrong please don't let anything be wrong.

Joe turned slowly, heading up the aisle. Fear was coming in waves now.

Please please please don't let anything be wrong.

He moved, trying desperately to walk slowly, calmly, but the adrenaline was rushing through his system like a renegade jet stream. It devoured his nerve endings, sending them into sporadic tremors. His throat had gone tight and dry, and he held back a gripping scream as he walked up the stairs, across the balcony to the projection room.

When he grasped the doorknob and found it locked he breathed a little easier.

Nothing to be afraid of. Jesus, this was crazy. Anxiety attack, that's what it was. Brought on by nervous exhaustion. Brought on by things in the shadows touching, pushing, shoving . . .

"No!"

He wrenched the door open and went inside.

He groped for the light switch but he didn't need any light to know what had happened. He knew it the moment he smelled that acidic, rusty air.

"Oh, God . . ." But then it was gone, a wisp of cool air brushed his cheek and the acidic smell swept past him, out into the hall, and down the stairs. It was gone, and only the dusty air of age remained.

He stood there, confused.

He stood there for a long time.

Finally he breathed, pressed against the knot growing in his stomach, and moved toward the ten cans of film stacked neatly in the corner.

Ten cans.

Ten cans. Ten reels.

He uttered a tiny cry.

He went to the stacked reels and lifted the top one. Fingers shaking, he opened it, pulled on the film, and looked at it in the light.

Panic grew, slowly, like a festering wound.

He dived at the remaining cans and opened each one, yanking on the film and looking at it through the light.

The first reel, the title, the first eleven minutes of the film, were not among them.

The first reel was gone.

He looked up at the projector on its flimsy metal stand in innocent repose.

In the lobby, people were beginning to stream in. The sound of their light chatting floated up to him, making him cringe. He fell back against the wall and sank slowly to the floor. The opened cans of film lay about him in a tangled mess.

What the hell was he going to do now?

As he stood across the street, watching the crowd of people as they filed into the theater, Andy's heart was pounding heavily in his chest. His legs ached with excitement. He'd waited so long. How cold it is; existing between the flicker of an eye. It's like having an itch you can't scratch.

He didn't notice the old woman who had shuffled up next to him until she spoke. "Not this time, bastard."

Andy jumped.

"Caught you off guard, huh?" The old woman smiled. "Yer losin' yer touch."

"Get away from me, old woman."

"I'm not afraid of you, Andy. Not anymore. You hurt me once, but not this time. I'm stronger now."

Andy's lips curled back in a snarl. "What are you talking about, bitch? I don't know you."

"You know me," Janice D'Lacy said. "You know me well enough. Think I don't know who you are?"

Andy glared at her silently.

Janice swiped at her nose, then pointed a crooked finger at him. "Think I don't know *what* you are?"

Andy said nothing.

The old woman glanced across the street at the people streaming in through the front doors of the theater. Her eyes were pale and watery, but held determination. "Think yer gonna start up again?" She shook her head slowly. "I'm gonna stop you. This time, I'll stop you." She held him in her angry glare for a second longer, then her tired shoulders sagged. Her head hunched forward and she turned and shuffled away.

Andy thought about going after her. She might mean what she'd said, but probably not. She was old, worn out, and crazy. No threat. No real threat. Let her have her moment. It wouldn't last long.

He watched her huddled frame until she disappeared around a corner, then turned and trotted across the street, entering the theater through a side door.

As he came into the lobby he saw Nancy behind the snack-bar counter, removing her sweater. She turned to him and smiled, winking.

He scanned the lobby. Everyone was there. Rudy Olsen. Vordy Halleran, who might prove to be a problem. John Williams. Alan Mayhew. All natives of Fareland. The old men passed by Andy, averting their eyes, studying their hands or looking at their feet. Only Alan Mayhew looked him straight in the eye, but Alan was special. Alan was charmed. The Hiding Fear had driven him crazy.

All these men were the children of those who'd been there in the beginning. Now they would provide the means for completing the whole, just as their parents had done.

But they could not be his allies.

He glanced at the front doors of the theater. At the threshold stood three young men dressed in dirty clothes, their hair sloppy and unclean. He knew them, from his illusory memory. Childhood buddies. Crow, Stricker, and Harley the Runt. Crow was strong and impulsive. Stricker had a mean streak in him that could be exploited. And Harley . . . well, Harley was crazy.

A thought came to Andy. A clean, comprehensive thought. He filed it away.

There were others with a past connected to the theater, but many of them had found ways to repress the Hiding Fear. Some of them had forgotten it altogether, except in their dreams.

That was enough.

The scheme of things was as complete as it needed to be. Nothing would stop what was meant to be. Nothing could stop it.

Everything going according to plan.

Dennis McWade was another from his illusory memory. Andy saw him enter the theater and felt a tightening in his throat. He'd known Dennis since grammar school and he had always been a hitch in Andy's side. His nemesis. Dennis was always fighting him, and although he may have believed the rumors that spread like a disease about Andy's peculiar preoccupations, Dennis was rarely intimidated by them, or by Andy. Had it not been for what Andy knew would eventually come to pass, he would have wasted the son of a bitch before they finished junior high. But timing was everything, and Andy's time would come soon enough. So he waited. He put a lid on his rage, and like the cat sitting like stone before the gopher hole, he waited.

Dennis stood a good four inches taller than Andy. He had that clear-eyed, clean-haired look about him that made Andy's nerves itch. Dennis was a jock, captain of the high-school football team. And this new girl he was with was almost as athletic looking as he was, with a tan so deep and rich, it could have been painted on. Looking at the two of them as they stood arm in arm in front of him was like looking at a Norman Rockwell painting. Small-town shit. It made him sick.

Dennis hit Andy's shoulder with a friendly slap. "Hear you manage the place, Andy. Good money in it?"

"More than money, pal," Andy said through clenched teeth. He didn't like having Dennis touch him. "There's a lot of satisfaction in this kind of work."

Dennis laughed heartily. "Really!"

Andy let his eyes wander to Dennis's girlfriend. She squirmed. "Your girl's not from around here, is she?"

Dennis's smile soured. "No. No, Sheila's transferred out, from Modesto."

Andy offered her a friendly smile. "Well, Sheila, I'm sure you'll fit right in."

The girl nodded, smiling timidly, and gripped Dennis's hand. Dennis pulled her close to him.

"She's not from around here, Andy. She's not local."

Andy offered a perplexed look, but the twinkle in his eyes betrayed his understanding. Dennis glared at him, then wrapped his arm firmly around the girl's shoulder and pulled her away. "Remember that. Remember, she's not local."

Andy grinned. "Dennis, where'd you ever get the idea that mattered?"

Dennis glowered at him and Andy matched it. Sparks flew between them, the air alive with electricity.

Then Andy smiled his sweetest smile, his face lighting with an angelic glow. He waved his hands in a sweeping gesture. "Everyone's welcome here. Sit anywhere you want." He turned his gracious, congenial look on the girlfriend, who was now cowering behind Dennis. "Maybe even the balcony. You'd like that, wouldn't you?"

The girl nodded timidly.

"Of course you would," Dennis said kindly. He gestured toward the entry curtains. "You go in now. Have a nice time."

She looked at Dennis, clung to him, and Dennis took her away. Andy smiled, and as they disappeared through the curtains his angelic smile soured into something more sinister, but it was still a smile.

He walked up the stairs and stood on the mezzanine, hands resting lightly on the railing as he took one long sweeping look at the lobby below. Ah, yes, master of all he surveyed. But as the thought settled comfortingly in his mind his glance caught Nancy. She was looking directly into his eyes.

I know my place, bitch. He glared at her. *I don't need you dogging me.*

Why had she been brought in, anyway? Wasn't he trusted? Hadn't he suffered enough to be trusted?

Fuck her.

He continued to scan the lobby nonchalantly, pretending not to notice her, but damned if her stare didn't lie on his skin like a dirty film.

He looked again at the three in the corner; rotten grapes on an otherwise perfect stem. Stricker, Crow, and Harley the Runt.

A new age, he thought, and sighed. *Oh, I've waited so long.*

After one more scan of what lay below, he left the mezzanine, heading for the projection room.

The room was dim, lit only by the filtered light of the small stairway landing. From the depths below he could hear someone sniffling, chuffing, like a child who has been badly beaten and left in the schoolyard all alone with only his broken toys to give him solace.

Andy switched on the projection-room light. From his place in the corner Joe flinched, cringing, and curled into a small ball with his knees to his chest. The sniffling, chuffing sound became quick, breathy sobs. He glanced at Andy once, then buried his head in his folded arms.

Andy took a step forward. "What the hell are you doing?"

"Look at this!" Joe bellowed, then nearly sobbed again and swept his arm across the floor of the room where the cans lay tossed in disarray. "It's useless!"

"Why?"

Joe glowered at him. "The first reel is missing, you asshole. It's *missing*!"

"So what?"

Joe's head snapped up, his eyes wide with disbelief. "Don't you understand? We can't screen this movie. Not without the first reel."

"Sure you can."

Joe slammed his fists against his knees. "Not without the first reel!"

Andy crossed to the other side of the room, bent down, and lifted the top of the box that held the 65-millimeter camera negative film. He held the reel out to Joe. "Screen this."

Joe stiffened. The look of despair turned solidly to fear. "How did you know about that film?"

Andy shook his head. "Old man, how much brainpower does it take? I know everything about this theater." He held the reel out to Joe. "Screen it."

Joe shook his head. "No. No I can't. It—it won't fit."

"It'll fit." Andy held it out to him. "Thread it up."

Joe took the reel in a shaky hand, pulling it close to his chest. "I don't want to."

Andy rested his hands on his knees and clicked his teeth. "Since when does what you want matter?"

"Andy . . . don't make me—"

"Make you?" Andy straightened. "I don't make you do anything you don't want to do, Joe. It's your theater. You want to show that film. You know you do." He fixed Joe with a wicked gaze, and Joe saw a flicker, a dazzle of green light at the center of those eyes. "You know how it'll make you feel."

Transfixed, Joe nodded.

"Tell me, then," Andy said. "Tell me how it makes you feel."

Joe swallowed. Unable to take his eyes away from the flicker of green in the center of the young man's beautiful eyes, Joe swallowed hard, feeling desperate, enraged, frightened, and impotent. How could he separate the emotions? They were all mixed up, like the ingredients of a witch's brew; all mixed up and coalescing into something far more powerful than the individual parts of the whole. Andy taunted him, coerced him, made him feel inadequate and used. And the theater, both full and hollow, both empty and gorged, filled him with righteousness, great strength, enormous purpose.

How could he explain, in just a few words?

"How does it make you feel?" Andy asked again.

Joe looked at the reel of film he held in his hand, felt it pulse beneath his touch, and pressed it lovingly against his chest. "Hungry," he said.

"Good, then," Andy said. "You thread it up, and you show it. And listen, Joe. Don't ever call me asshole again. Okay?"

Joe nodded dumbly, the reel still pressed close against his chest.

When Andy left it was like being released from a choke hold. It had frightened Joe, that friendly young face with the burning eyes. He felt useless and sick, used up. Used.

A monkey. Made to dance.

He held the reel before his eyes.

And at the same time, powerful, righteous, in control.

He hugged the reel to his chest. "It won't fit. It'll ruin the film."

A monkey.

Numb, frightened, he touched the film. His fingers turned to ice.

"It won't fit!" he pleaded.

Hand numb now, shrouded with sparkling frost.

He got up, moved to the projector, and put the reel in place.

Arm now, moving to his shoulder, moving to his heart.

"Too fast!" he pleaded. "It's happening too fast!"

With his frozen fingers he stuffed the end of the film into the first thread.

The house lights were dimming. The soft chatter of voices stilled.

The projector hummed.

Air, cold air, a blast of it, struck hard against his chest, sending him staggering back against the wall. His breath left him in one long abrasive gush as he slid a little before he could catch his balance. The projector purred with power, electricity glowing around it in a veil of soft yellow light. As he watched in terror the film threaded itself, making soft wet sounds. He braced his back against the wall and thought about leaving. He thought about Karen. He thought about Tempac and computers and Kelsie and how much he wanted to go back to L.A. and maybe try again at his old life because no matter how rotten it was, it wasn't cold. And he was cold. The ice lay on him like a shroud and he was very cold.

He thought about all of that and then he let himself slide to the floor, his hands pressed firmly against his trembling lips, and tried very hard not to scream.

If he could reach up, turn the projector off.

But he was just too cold.

The projector hummed, its light streaming out through the lens casting distorted shadows on the walls. The shadows danced, taking swipes at Joe as he sat in a hunched ball, hands clamped firmly to his mouth. They danced, mocking him, and the projector continued to hum.

In that moment, when the film began and shadows danced, Joe realized he would never be warm again.

And something else . . . like a thread of himself, from his soul, from the heart core of him, something seemed to stream out. He saw it, like a gossamer thing floating loftily on the air, streaming out of him, and into the humming, dancing projector.

Slowly, almost as slow as glass flows, a smile crept across Joe's face.

10

 The screen lit up with a shadowy gray glow. Sheila shifted uneasily. "What is this?" And when she saw the look on Dennis's face, her blood chilled. He grabbed her by the hand and pulled her roughly into the aisle. "Hey! Dennis, what's wrong?"

"We're getting out." Dennis pulled her along the aisle. At the top, just before the door, he stopped. Across the row of seats she could see Andy's slender silhouette in the center aisle. Dennis was looking at him, his shoulders rising and falling. He clenched her hand hard enough to make her cry out.

Andy's head turned toward them; he acknowledged them with a tilt and the touch of his fingers to his brow. His eyes were twinkling in the soft gray light.

Dennis tugged on his girlfriend's arm and pulled her out of the theater.

But as they reached the front doors, they found Andy waiting for them. He was smiling, his eyes twinkling with a kind of fiery elation that belied the perplexed, concerned look on his face.

"Don't like the movie, Dennis?" Andy said, the concern in his voice as counterfeit as the look on his face.

Dennis was breathing heavily, shaking. He shook his finger at Andy. "I'm not going to be a part of this, you bastard. You can't make me be a part of this!"

Andy shrugged innocently, but the twinkle remained in his eyes. Dennis tugged on his girlfriend's arm, pulling her out of the theater.

Andy watched them go, smiling. He went back into the

theater and stood at the threshold of the middle aisle entry. He was calm, in control, and very much aware of the diversity of reaction in the audience to what they were seeing on the brilliant screen. Some of the people were mumbling their bewilderment and displeasure, but that was to be expected on this first screening. Not all of these people were natives and therefore had no real connection with the theater's past, but it didn't matter. What they saw would dictate, as it always did, what they felt inside, depending on the degree of their own convictions.

Everyone had the Hiding Fear. It was manifested in many ways, as diverse as those who sat here in this darkened theater made to glow and dance with the multifariousness of light and shadow, substance and conjecture, that danced across the screen. And each reaction, each multifold emotion, was being seeded, cultivated, and molded into the instrument of satiation, the ultimate element in the scheme of things.

On Andy's right Vordy Halleran had begun to squirm. His usually ruddy complexion had become waxy and pale. His jaw was working furiously as he watched the screen with painful consternation. Andy reached out and touched his shoulder.

"Settle down, Vordy," he said in a quietly commanding voice.

Vordy looked up at him. His face was wildly animated. He started to rise, but Andy's hand kept him in his chair.

"I don't have to take this," Vordy whispered harshly. "I don't have to be a part of it, not if I don't want to." He looked at the screen. "I remember. I remember!"

"Don't blow it," Andy said.

Vordy looked at him again, his eyes liquid with rage. "You think I don't remember it right, don't you? You think—"

"Shut up, Vordy." Andy said it calmly. Quietly. Vordy's mouth worked furiously, but no words came out. He turned his attention back to the screen, but the anger continued to make him squirm and shudder. "You're a monster," he rasped. "You are a fucking monster."

Andy did not ignore him, but he did let him get away with

it. Timing was everything, and the time would come according to plan. He turned his attention back to the rest of the
house.

They watched, some frightened, some silent and confused,
some losing themselves in a turmoil of emotion as the Hiding
Fear broke through the confines of their inner core. A jagged
edge of terror and confusion ripped the fabric of what they
saw and how what they saw made them feel, until finally the
screen went dim, and the houselights came on.

Andy walked down the aisle with deliberate arrogance.
The people bowed their heads as he passed, not wanting to
look him in the eyes. He stood in front of the screen and
watched them as some squirmed and fidgeted in their seats
while others sat quietly, immersed in the deep well of their
inner selves.

He smiled, and scanned them with a directness that made
them tremble as one. Then he raised his arms.

"Scared?" he asked them. They answered as one with a
small, depleted groan.

Andy lowered his arms and fixed them with a controlling
gaze. "But you're not hungry anymore. Are you?"

The crowd didn't answer, but as Andy opened his mouth
to speak, a tall man with a rugged, strong face suddenly leapt
to his feet from the center of the theater. He pointed a finger
at Andy. "I ain't scared, Andy. And I sure as hell ain't hungry!"

A hushed murmuring came from the audience.

Andy regarded him silently. The man rubbed his hands
hard against his thighs. "This is all bullshit."

"You saw your daddy when he got caught in that mulcher,
didn't you, Tom?"

The strong, angry look on the man's face faltered. Andy
went on. "You saw it when his legs went down inside, didn't
you?"

"That ain't got nothin' to do with this!" he screamed. "All
this—this bullshit, it's a sideshow!"

"No!" It was Vordy, now standing at the back of the theater. All heads turned to him. He moved from his chair and
started down the aisle. "It's no sideshow. Some of you, you

don't know. You don't remember. Or you do, but you don't remember right. I was there." He looked at Andy angrily, pointing a shaky finger. "He was there!"

"That's impossible," Tom said.

"It's not!" Vordy yelled. "He was there. Maybe not the way he is now, but he was there!" Vordy scanned the audience. "Try to remember. Try to remember the way it really was! Don't let it happen again!" He pointed again at Andy. "Don't let him make it happen again!"

The audience settled into an uncomfortable silence. Vordy looked at them, saw the confusion melded with quiet, fearful surrender, and felt the heartache of defeat fill him with horrible frustration and fear.

He turned to Andy, and spoke in a quiet voice, both defiant and shaky with fear. "I won't be a part of this, Andy. I won't."

Andy smiled at him. "Your choice, Vordy." Then he cocked his head. "Or is it?"

Vordy clenched his fists. He scanned the theater, looking desperately for support, and found none.

He backed away slowly, watching Andy, then turned and bolted for the exit.

Andy returned his attention to the man standing in the center of the theater. He could see by the look on the man's face that he had not been swayed by what he saw on the screen. He was an alien, disconnected, unaffected by the whole.

The man's wife was sitting next to him. She sat quietly, outwardly passive. But inside . . .

inside . . .

Andy smiled. "You go home now, Tom. You take your wife, and you go home."

"Damn right I'm goin' home," Tom said angrily, grabbing his wife's arm. "And I ain't comin' back. Not ever!" He pulled his wife up and made his way to the aisle. As they reached the aisle, before they turned their backs on Andy and moved to the exit, Tom's wife glanced at Andy.

The knowledge in her eyes made Andy tingle with excitement.

Andy returned his attention to the rest of the audience. The tension had left some of them decidedly drained. There was a strange blend of relief, discontent, confusion, and pain in their appearance. The air had grown heavy and moist.

"Go home now," Andy said, his arms raised. "Go home."

Silently, submissively, they filed out.

But a few remained. Andy beckoned them to the front-row seats. They got up and came down the aisle, sitting in the seats Andy selected for them.

Alan Mayhew. Rudy Olsen. John Williams.

Andy smiled at them. "Chosen," he said.

John took a deep breath. "You know we're on your side, Andy. You know we know what the winning side is."

"All but one," Andy said.

John looked away. "But there's another. Ed Wilson." He pointed to a young man hovering halfway down the aisle, rubbing his hands together. "He wants in."

"He's in," Andy said.

Ed smiled nervously, and moved to join the rest.

"There's business tonight," Andy said. "Business that can't wait. You know what it is. You saw it."

They all nodded.

"Anyone against what needs to be done?"

No one moved.

"It must be done," Andy said. His voice was tinged with a kind of urgency the men hadn't expected. It made them squirm a little. "It must be done, until there is enough."

They sat in silence for a moment, then Andy motioned to them and they got up as one, moving quietly up the aisle. Andy followed them.

As he reached the back of the theater, he found Stricker, Crow, and Harley the Runt still sitting in their chairs. Their faces were round and pale, eyes wide with wonder, and it occurred to Andy that his plan had been propagated with almost no effort of his own. He wasn't sure how to take this, but decided against challenging the ultimate purpose of the whole, from which he got his power.

"You three," he said, pointing to them. "You go to the balcony."

As one they stood without question and moved out of the house. Andy followed them, watched them enter the balcony, and as the brilliance began to increase he averted his eyes.

Tom Farrell rushed through his back door, letting it slam the wall and bounce back, nearly hitting his wife, who was coming in behind him. He went to the kitchen cupboard, got out a bottle of bourbon, and took it to the kitchen table. He sat there for a moment, seething, shaking, then took a long drag on the bottle. He slammed it down and rubbed his face hard.

His wife opened the back door slowly and looked passively at her husband. She went quietly to one of the kitchen drawers, opened it, and pulled out a carving knife.

As Tom took another swig from the bottle, his wife stood behind him, carving knife in hand, and contemplated the back of his neck.

Vordy Halleran slammed his front door and locked it. His heart was pounding too fast and his hands trembled. Had to calm down. Wouldn't do him any good to have a heart attack. Had to stay calm. Alert. Watchful.

He kept a healthy stock of vodka in the pantry for the winter and he went there now, pulling a bottle from one of the ten cases he stored there.

Now was as good a time as any to start warming up.

Vordy sat down in the easy chair he had placed in front of the fireplace. It was a comfortable old chair with a wide back. He took a long pull on the bottle and let the fiery liquid slide down his throat. As it blanketed his stomach with heat he began to feel a little better.

God damn that Andy anyway, who the hell did he think he was? Did he really think he could frighten Vordy into supplication? No. No! He remembered. He remembered when he was ten and his father died.

Andy had done it. Vordy knew. Vordy remembered it was Andy who had killed his father.

Maybe not the same Andy. Maybe not the same, but it was him.

"Not him," Vordy said aloud, and took another swallow. "Not him. That theater. That fucking theater and the—"

The Hiding Fear.

His father had told him about it, and he'd told him something else. He'd told him how to fight it. And fight it he would.

He took another swallow and heaved a long, shuddering sigh. Footsteps on the porch. Four, maybe five men. Vordy's heart fluttered.

"I can fight it. I know how!"

They wouldn't bust his door down, would they?

No . . . come on!

They were his neighbors. His friends, for Christ's sake! They wouldn't—

Three sharp raps.

"Vordy?"

It was Andy.

"Get the fuck off my property!" Vordy screamed, and took another long swallow of vodka.

"Open the door, Vordy."

"You go to hell!"

They wouldn't bust down his door. If they were going to do that, they would have done it already. He leaned forward. "You're slime, you know that? You're fucking sli—"

The boards in the door swelled inward. As Vordy watched, the boards heaved. The hinges screamed.

They weren't going to bust his door down. They didn't have to.

Andy was with them. They didn't have to do a thing. Just stand there and let it happen. Let everything happen according to plan. He'd seen it before, oh, yes. The Hiding Fear, come alive. Come alive and bust your door down with a single thought.

The straining boards of the door suddenly splintered in a resounding crash. Vordy yelped in spite of himself.

Andy stood in the doorway, flanked by four men, neighbors, his friends . . . God, he'd known them since childhood—

Ten years old we were ten years old we were all ten . . .

Andy stood there, feet placed firmly, hands laced elegantly together. "Saw a good movie tonight, Vordy. Did you like what you saw?"

"I ain't scared of you!" Vordy shouted.

Andy took a step toward him. "But you're scared, aren't you?"

Ten I was ten I was ten years old

"No!"

"You're scared," Andy said, taking another step. "Can't help but be scared. That's the way things go."

Instantly Vordy bolted for the kitchen and rough hands grabbed him, pulling him back to the chair. His arms were wrenched around its wide back and pinned there. Andy stepped up to him, planting his feet firmly on Vordy's and leaning over, resting his hands on the arms of the chair.

Vordy glared at him, baring his teeth. He shook with fear but his heart pounded and his blood was fire with the memory of being ten years old.

"I saw what you did to my dad," Vordy said. "I saw, and I remember!"

"I wasn't even born then, Vordy," Andy said calmly.

"You were there!" Vordy screamed.

Andy closed his eyes for a moment, as if deep in thought. When he opened them, Vordy saw a flicker of sickly green light emanate from their centers. Suddenly the strength of his anger melted away, and he was left only with the growing fear, the Hiding Fear, so deep within the center, now dragged so close to the surface as to be suddenly raw. He groaned in defeat. *I remember I remember. . . . Pa said to be strong. . . .*

Andy gazed at him thoughtfully, his beautiful young face marred only by the sickly green light. "When you slaughtered your pigs today, did you remember to hone your knives?"

I'm sorry, Pa. I'm sorry

"Andy . . . don't—"

Andy reached into his back pocket, producing a knife with a thin blade. He held it up to Vordy's face. "Wouldn't want to leave a jagged edge."

"Don't do this!"

Andy cocked his head. "Don't do what, Vordy?"

"K-kill me." Vordy gasped. His arms had begun to ache. He squirmed helplessly.

Andy frowned in mock disappointment. "Ah, Vordy . . . I thought you were paying attention. We're not gonna kill you. Didn't you see? Didn't you watch?" He leaned closer. "Didn't you feel anything?"

"I felt it," Vordy said in a small voice. "I felt it . . . God help me. . . ."

"God?" Andy scowled.

Vordy squirmed a little, trying to lessen the pain in his arms. "What are you gonna do, Andy?"

Andy took a deep breath. "Everything goes according to plan, Vordy. You don't want to be in this, but you've got no choice. Your daddy should've taught you that. Too bad he didn't." He waved the blade under Vordy's nose, lightly touching the skin and making a trace over Vordy's face. "We still need you. So we're not gonna kill you. But there's gonna be a little accident." He turned the blade a little. Light glinted off its edge. "You were out there today, see? Slaughtering your pigs, and the phone rang. You never were too smart, ol' buddy. You went running for the phone with the knife still in your hand, and you tripped. Fell. Facedown." He laid the tip of the blade against Vordy's left eye.

"Oh, my God, please!" Spittle sprayed from Vordy's mouth. His body convulsed against the hold on him. "Please, Andy . . . my God, please don't do this to me! Don't cut out my eyes!"

Andy held the knife against Vordy's eye a second longer, watching his victim squirm and blubber, delighting in it, then straightened. He looked at the men holding Vordy's arms, then at the other two huddling in the shadows. He turned back to Vordy. "It's got to be done. Sorry."

"Please . . ."

Andy laid the knife against Vordy's left eye. He leaned in close, whispering in his ear. "You want me to do it, Vordy. You want me to be the one, because I'm fast."

Vordy was crying uncontrollably now, his body quivering. "You can do anything else . . . anything you want, I won't fight you, I promise. I *promise*! Only please don't cut out my eyes. Anything else . . . not my eyes!"

Andy arched his eyebrows. He pulled the knife away. "Anything?"

Vordy nodded frantically. Andy stepped away from him, turning his back, thinking. Vordy watched him fitfully until Andy finally turned back. He looked different, as if a shadow had passed over him, distorting his features. Only his eyes were unchanged. They flickered with a green flame deep in their centers.

"Strip him," he said to the men. "And lay him out on the kitchen table."

The two men holding Vordy grabbed his arms and hauled him up. Andy watched as they dragged him into the kitchen. "I don't want him to suffer," he said.

As Tom took another swallow of bourbon, his wife raised the carving knife and brought it down in a swooping gesture, slicing through the flesh of Tom's back.

Tom howled, jumping to his feet. He swaggered, clutching the table, and fell to one side.

As he lay on the floor writhing, his wife knelt down beside him, carving knife held aloft. "Are you scared, Tom?"

Tom looked at her, eyes wide with terror and pain. She smiled and brought the carving knife down again. This time it cut a bloody swath across his right thigh.

Tom's back arched as he screamed. He flailed his arms uselessly, trying to get at the knife.

"Are you scared, Tom?" his wife said, smiling, eyes dancing.

"Mary . . ." Tom whispered.

She brought the knife down again. It sliced through his hand, cutting it in half. The severed fingers wriggled on the floor.

"Are you scared, Tom?" his wife intoned again.

Tom writhed helplessly, terror etching deep grooves in his face.

"I'm not scared," Mary said in a seductively sinister voice, "but I'm hungry." She brought the knife up again. "I'm hungry, Tom."

Tom watched in horror as she raised the blade and brought it swooping down, slicing it across his face. She raised it again as he screamed, and brought it down into his gaping mouth. She felt the tip hit home in the floor beneath.

Mary sat back, breathing evenly, staring at the knife protruding from her dead husband's mouth. She flicked it a couple times and watched it shudder. "I'm not hungry now, Tom," she whispered. "It's enough." She wiped blood from his face with her fingers, raised them, looked at them and smiled. "It's enough."

When the men had completed the task Andy had given them, Vordy was stretched out naked on the kitchen table, his head, shoulders, and legs hanging over the edges at painful angles, his wrists and ankles bound to the table legs with tape from the first-aid kit Vordy kept below the kitchen sink. He was strangely calm now, partly from relief at not having had his eyes gouged out, but mostly because he was drunk, more drunk than he had ever been in his life. Before they had bound him to the table they had forced two bottles of Absolut down his throat. He'd thrown up some of it, but most of it stayed down and now he was lost in a drunken stupor.

Andy moved to the table with small, gliding steps and ran his hands over Vordy's distended belly. If Vordy had been fully conscious, Andy's caress would have sickened him. Andy lifted a bottle of vodka over him and let the liquid pour out, splashing on Vordy's chest and stomach. Then he lit a candle.

He moved to the edge of the table so Vordy could see him and asked in soft, seductive tones, "How long do you think it'll take for the alcohol to burn? Huh, Vordy? How long before the fire reaches you?"

Vordy didn't answer. His mouth was sealed with tape.

"You said I could do anything. Anything, as long as I saved your eyes. I promise you, Vordy. The fire won't touch your eyes."

Andy touched the candle to Vordy's chest, and the alcohol exploded silently into flames.

Joe woke up screaming.

The sound had come from deep inside, harsh and guttural. He sat upright, clutching the covers close to his chest. He had a sudden urge to suck his thumb.

Karen came out of her sleep and dragged on the light. "Jesus, Joe! What's wrong?"

"I'm sick!" Joe rocked forward, grabbing his stomach. "Oh, God, I'm going to be sick!" He scrambled out of the bed and stumbled into the bathroom, slamming the door behind him.

II
COMES
KELSIE

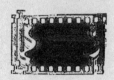

1

 Kelsie Brown was leaning back in his chair waiting patiently for the computer to load his ponderous program, wondering offhandedly if he had enough memory. To work on a program in bits and pieces, as he had done for the last several months, was dangerous at best. He had filled at least three microdisks, and even with the new motherboard he'd installed he wasn't completely satisfied that enough memory was available. So he sat there, listened to the faint whirring of the computer's innards, watched the lights flicker from the A drive to the B drive, and waited.

Finally the computer finished its loading, and the B prompt blinked.

Kelsie straightened in his chair and rested his hands on the keyboard. Disconnected thoughts ran through his mind at varying speeds. Cathode ray tubes. Color versus monochrome. Was a program designed to play out the generations of selective genetic design so outlandish? He was doing it on his own time, after all. Using his own money. What's to hurt?

And what if the results were groundbreaking?

And how about the implications? Had he weighed the implications?

Yes, he had.

The undoing of evolution. Or the rewriting of it at least. In a few moments he would know exactly what to expect in a society devoid of ignorance.

Some call it genetic cleansing. An apt phrase, Kelsie thought. But how PC.

"A master race?" he thought aloud.

Yes. Perhaps. His program would provide proof.

Kelsie took a breath, then typed in the command, "Execute Life."

First there was silence, as though the computer were contemplating the possible outcomes of such an endeavor. Kelsie narrowed his gaze, his eyes fixed on the screen.

Then suddenly a loud warning buzzer sounded. The dark screen turned white. Kelsie leaned back.

"Uh-oh."

The white light exploded, filling the room with its blinding brilliance, bathing Kelsie with its numbing radiance until he was aware only slightly of a sensation of flying as he moved swiftly through a tunnel too narrow at first and then expanding, letting in the light, the shadows, the sound of a buzzer, and the buzzer focused until the sound transformed itself into a tangible, audible sound. A phone ringing. Yes, the phone was ringing, and then it stopped.

A hand came down on his shoulder.

"I need more power," he mumbled groggily.

"What?"

Kelsie dragged open his eyes and as they focused he saw Shari standing over him, the phone nestled in her palm. Her usually smooth face was etched with lines of irritation. Her crystal eyes flashed.

Kelsie blinked once, then again, and pulled himself up on one elbow. Shari thrust the phone into his face. "It's a woman." She turned sharply on her heel and glided swiftly out of the room.

Kelsie hoisted his body into a sitting position and spoke into the phone. "Yeah—"

"Kelsie? Did I wake you?"

"Karen?" Kelsie yawned.

"Oh, shit, Kels, I'm sorry. I didn't realize how early it was. You want me to call back?"

"No. No, it's okay." His eyes moved to the bathroom door where Shari had retreated. Her anger should have sent the door slamming shut, but it stood ajar. Her shadow played seductively on its surface. "I'm awake now. What's up?"

"Kels . . . I—" She was struggling with words. Kelsie knew immediately that something was wrong, and his senses sharpened. He swung his legs over the side of the bed and sat up.

"Are you okay?" he asked.

"Yes." She paused. "Kels, I wasn't going to make a big deal out of this, I mean, I didn't want to worry you. But I never was any good at bullshit. Could you come up here?"

"Now?" He looked again at the bathroom door. Shari was standing in it, watching him.

"Yes," Karen said. "I wouldn't ask this if it weren't . . ." She sighed deeply. "It's important, Kelsie. It's Joe. Something's wrong with him."

"Is he sick?"

"No—I mean, I don't think so. He had this dream last night. Real bad one. It made him throw up."

"You're kidding!"

Shari had moved from the bathroom to his side. She sat next to him, silently, her soft hand resting on his thigh. A trickle of warmth crept into his belly.

"No, I'm not." Karen's voice had begun to tremble. "He woke up screaming, sort of clutching the covers. I've never seen him like that. But he wouldn't tell me what was wrong. He just got up and went to the bathroom. The next thing I know, he's throwing up. But not just throwing up, Kels. I thought he was gonna choke. His body was . . . jerking. Like a seizure. Could you come up?"

"Sounds more like he needs a doctor."

"I tried that. He won't have anything to do with it." Karen was on the verge of tears.

"I had a feeling something was going on," Kelsie said. "But I'm not sure I'm the one he should see. He's been sort of short with me. Ever since he bought the theater."

Karen sighed. "Yeah, well, that's when it started. When he bought the theater. Kels, there's other things. He's different, somehow. Rougher . . . a little weird . . . I don't know. Now it sounds . . . hell, this sounds stupid."

"What does?"

He heard her take a deep breath, as if to muster strength. "He says there's something inside him." She paused, and silence fell between them. But the silence was heavy, laden with fear. Kelsie felt it in his spine; a sudden tingle that spirited down his back and into his legs.

"He says it's growing," Karen said finally.

Sounds like he's flipped, Kelsie thought, but said nothing.

"Kelsie?"

He jerked. "Sorry. I was just thinking."

"Kelsie, I'm scared. I mean really scared. Can you come?"

Kelsie squirmed. He had two months' vacation coming and had planned to take Shari on a world cruise. Now he'd have to put her off, and she'd be pissed. Oh, yes, pissed to the hilt. Shari didn't take kindly to playing second.

He shot a glance at her. She returned the look, and her hand rubbed lightly against his thigh.

"I'll get back to you, okay?" Kelsie said.

There was a strained pause, then, "Yeah . . . okay, Kels. See if you can make it."

"I'll get back to you," he assured her. "Promise. Today. Karen, just hang on, okay?"

"Okay, Kels," Karen said quietly, then hung up.

Kelsie replaced the phone gently and turned to Shari. The morning sun sifted through her hair, highlighting it with streaks of silver. God, she was beautiful.

And she was going to be pissed.

"What's going on?" she asked. "Who was that?"

"Karen," Kelsie said, looking just over her shoulder, into space. "Joe's wife—you remember Joe?"

Shari nodded.

"She says something's wrong with him. Sounds like maybe he's sick." He laid his hand on hers, felt the tiny muscles in her fingers twitch. "She wants me to come up."

"Now?"

Kelsie looked at her. "Yeah."

"How long are you going to be gone?"

Kelsie took in air and held it. "Not sure."

She looked away, her expression sagging. Then she stood silently and crossed to his bureau. Without a word to him she opened one of the drawers, then closed it and laid her hands on the top, her head bowed.

"I'm sorry," Kelsie said lamely.

"I've known you for three years," she said, head still bowed, eyes closed. "Been living with you for one. I know you, Kelsie." She looked at him then, and he felt his shoulders tense under the weight of her direct gaze. "The only thing that comes before your friends is your job. I knew that when I hooked up with you." She sighed.

Kelsie smiled awkwardly. "You're letting me off easy."

"Not really," she said, crossing to him. She looked down at him, traced her finger gently along the fine line of his jaw. "I'll get you for screwing up my vacation." She smiled, bent low, and kissed him hard on the lips. He moved to caress her cheek, but she pulled away and stood straight, looking down again. Looking down on him.

"In my own time," she said.

Travel was easy, taking Interstate 5 out of L.A. and passing through the San Joaquin Valley on a straight ribbon of highway. There was very little traffic; most tourists took the highway 101 route along the California shoreline. The weather was typical for the beginning of October, cool and crisp. The morning sun winked at him from across the flat plains to his right. As he drove his mind wandered through memories of what had brought Joe to him a few weeks before leaving Tempac. There had been an uproar and Joe had been thrown into the eye of it. But intolerance had begun long before then, both in Joe and in his bosses. Joe had been getting more headaches, each one more severe than the last. His nerves had been wearing thin and his productivity suffered for it. Funny thing about Tempac's higher echelon, but maybe it was like that everywhere. They're your buddies as long as you can produce and guarantee them future profit. It can all be summed up in dollars. Accountability, quality, productivity, all pivoting on the central theme of money. But let your value slip a little, just enough to show up on even the most obscure level, and they'll hang you by your ankles, slit your throat, and drain you of every last drop. They'll squeeze it out of you, and then toss you away like a spent lemon.

Business, after all, is business.

And it was such a waste. Joe Moreson was what some

would call a hidden asset. His mind was a precious gem, rough perhaps but ready for the cutter. He had in his possession the talent to produce millions of dollars' worth of software; it seemed logical, and even beneficial financially, to afford him his few eccentricities. Humor him. Give him some time off, let him regroup and regenerate. What's so bad about that?

But it hadn't happened that way. They'd seen in him an avenue of expense, and that was not acceptable. But instead of just confronting him with it, giving him a warning, anything to maybe frighten him into buckling down and shaping up, they had contrived to get rid of him.

Getting rid of him was an easy task. Joe had often stormed out of Tempac, only to crawl back a few days later, beaten, weaker, supplicated.

Then the blow-up came, and the stage was set. Richards bore down on him hard, giving him no time to breathe.

The whole thing had been a plan of strategic subterfuge. They could have shot him at point-blank range and done less damage. And the worst of it was, even though it bore all the earmarks of premeditation, Joe had never seen it coming. Probably he was too trusting for that. Too naive. Or maybe he was just too singular in purpose. Joe believed, honestly and innocently, that hard work, quality work, was enough. Kelsie doubted if Joe was able to see anything shady in human behavior. He'd probably believe a thief when he asked for the time.

Richards had ridden him and ridden him, piling on the humiliation, the degradation, until finally Joe broke. Something sharp and finely honed had snapped in two.

Kelsie remembered that day as if it had been yesterday, and he remembered his own impotence. He had known, as Joe walked away from him, that he would not be coming back. And there was nothing Kelsie could do about it.

They never talked about it. They never had the chance. The next time he talked to Joe the rift between them was so severe, Kelsie could do little more than try to convince Joe that he was still a friend.

With a feeling of personal dishonor, he believed he had

failed in this. They'd talked only once after Joe had left, and Kelsie believed any further talk was beyond the realm of possibility.

He remembered once, a long time ago, when they had talked about their dreams over a bottle of tequila gold, when Joe mentioned always having wanted to own a theater. Kelsie had prodded him to do it, but Joe only laughed it off. Said he couldn't afford it. Too much risk, being his own boss.

There was more truth to that than Kelsie had wanted to say, and when he spoke he spoke gently. "You're just not a fighter. You're a follower, and if you're following the wrong kind you end up getting wasted."

"So you think I should quit? Start my own business?"

Kelsie raised his hands concedingly. "I just think you should do what you want to do, and fuck everything else."

That night had been only two months before Joe left Tempac for the last time, and bought himself a theater.

That was in August. Now it was the beginning of October and Karen was talking about nightmares and sickness and things growing inside. It was beginning to sound like that last blowup at Tempac had done more damage than Kelsie had suspected. Stress is retroactive. It digs a hole inside you and lays eggs. The eggs grow, feeding off your guts, until they have gained enough strength to crack open and spread throughout to poison your whole system.

The sun hung high over his head and as he neared the turn onto Highway 50 Kelsie wondered just what he could do to help. He'd seen the shadow on Joe's face. He'd seen the rage, the bitterness of pain. Pain like that, it lingers. It never really goes away.

And there had been that dream. The one about the pretty rings on dead fingers. Kelsie had not been able to forget that dream.

He was so deep in his thoughts that he nearly missed the turnoff for Fareland. If it hadn't been for a sudden cramp in his back that wrenched him out of his reverie he would have gone right past the sign that read DEVIL'S MOUNTAIN ROAD. CENTRAL FARELAND and probably wouldn't have realized he'd missed the turn until he was well into Oakland. He slammed on his brakes and swerved the car onto the off-ramp.

The road veered left, then down a gentle grade and emptied onto Devil's Mountain Road. The scent of pine and oak floated gently through the open window of his car. Those smells always had a profound effect on him. First they rushed through his nerves like a stimulant. Then they hit his brain, relaxing him in a way that could not, in any form, be duplicated.

How, in the *world*, had he ever become an urbanite?

There was one small side street about halfway down Devil's Mountain Road. On one side was a small grocery store, and across from it was the Fareland Cinema. He turned into the parking lot of the grocery store and shut down the engine.

He got out of the car and stretched. He made a cursory scan of the area, then crossed the small side street and went up to the front doors of the theater. It was dark inside, seemingly empty of activity. Kelsie cupped his hands against the glass and instantly, with a jerk and a gasp of surprise, pulled his hands away.

The glass was unusually cold.

He brought his face close to the glass. A bubble of cold seemed to radiate from it. Kelsie could feel it as much as three inches from the glass.

He reached out to try the door, then decided against it. He stepped back, then turned away.

Across Devil's Mountain Road was a gas station. Two men sat in chairs leaning back against the station wall. They were watching him. He waved.

Apparently that didn't sit well, because the two men slammed their chairs upright and looked at each other, their lips moving. Kelsie bent his head, feeling a little uneasy. This was a small town. Damn small. You just didn't go horning in until you'd been invited. Locals didn't like strangers, particularly city folk, and Kelsie no doubt had the word *citified* emblazoned on his brow. He drove a BMW, for Christ's sake, and it was probably the first Beamer these guys had ever seen.

He looked up at them again and shouted, "You folks know where I can find Joe Moreson's house?"

They looked at him. "You a friend of Joe's?"

Kelsie nodded.

"Come on over," one of them said, waving his hand. Kelsie sprinted across the street.

There was an empty seat next to them but they never offered it. Indeed, the look on their faces dared him to ask, but he'd been driving a long time and needed to stretch. Good excuse. He felt their eyes on him, studying him. He shifted a little, looking down the street. "Nice town."

"We like it," one of them replied. Kelsie looked at him. "My name's Kelsie Brown."

"Rudy Olsen," Rudy said, nodding. "This here's John Williams. Runs this gas station here. You say you got business with Joe?"

"I'm a friend of his," Kelsie said. "From L.A. We used to work for the same company."

"You a yuppie?"

Kelsie smiled tightly. "I'm a systems analyst. I write computer programs."

"A yuppie." Rudy scowled.

Kelsie took a deep breath, feeling his anger rising. "Can you tell me where Joe lives?"

"What's your business with him?" John asked, eyeing Kelsie suspiciously.

"Just here for a visit."

"You don't know where he lives?"

Kelsie gritted his teeth. "I got his address, but I don't know the town. I just want directions."

Rudy nodded tightly. "It's just we don't like strangers comin' in here and askin' a lot of questions. You understand."

"I told you I was a friend of Joe's. Is he in some kind of trouble?"

"Didn't say that," Rudy deflected.

Kelsie felt his patience slipping away. "Look, if you don't want to tell me what I need to know, that's okay. Just say so."

Rudy and John exchanged a glance, then leaned back simultaneously and regarded Kelsie with vacant eyes.

Kelsie took a step forward so that he was nearly standing over them. "You shit on people too much, you're bound to step in it yourself. Get me?"

The confident look on the men's eyes faltered a little. They hid it well, but Kelsie was savvy enough to see it. He'd made his point.

He stepped back, staring at them until they averted their eyes. "We'll meet again, I'm sure," Kelsie said in a friendly voice tinged with a touch of intimidation. "Maybe have a beer. Talk shit. Stuff like that, you know. Stuff guys like you find entertaining."

The two men glared at him. Kelsie ignored it, turned on his heel, and walked back across the street.

But his heart was beating fast. He was angry, and it wasn't always easy for him to silence his anger quickly. No doubt he'd fume about that little scenario for some time.

But once he'd gotten across the street he realized that it was more than just anger. He was unnerved, and he wasn't exactly sure why.

Something about the look in their eyes. A twinkle, or something. A flicker that didn't fit the scenario. An alien thing, glittering in the depths of their eyes.

He looked at the grocery store. Inside, people were milling around, studying canned goods and produce. A large woman with steel-gray hair was at the check stand. He decided to go in and try his luck.

The woman greeted him with a warm smile that pinched her pudgy face, making her look like a Pekingese. She wore a simple cotton dress too small for her ample size. Hairpins stuck out of her bound hair at crazy angles. She smelled of roast beef and honeysuckle. "Can I help you?" she asked pleasantly.

"I hope so," Kelsie said. "I'm looking for Joe Moreson."

Her smile withered. "What business do you have with him?"

Kelsie felt his stomach muscles tighten. *Oh, Christ . . . here we go again. . . .*

"I'm a friend of his, from L.A. Maybe he mentioned me? I'm Kelsie Brown."

She squinted her eyes, then suddenly her face relaxed. "Oh, yes! Karen's mentioned you many times. She's very fond of you."

Kelsie exhaled. He hadn't realized he'd been holding his breath.

"Joe never mentioned you," she said in a voice decidedly darker. Kelsie's stomach tightened again.

"I've got their address," he said, forcing himself to sound pleasant. "But I don't know my way around town. Can you give me directions?"

She nodded, pointing out the front door. "Just take this road down to the end, turn left, then up three blocks till you hit Trenton. Take a right. Their house's third one from the end. Can't miss it. Big front porch. Creek shoots right through the front yard."

Kelsie smiled. "Thanks."

She nodded again, her Pekingese smile etched warmly on her face.

But Kelsie wasn't really looking at her face; not really. He was looking at her eyes. They had that same flicker.

He forced his smile to stay in place as he nodded to her, turned, and left.

As he got back into his car he caught sight of an old woman shuffling along the sidewalk across the street. He probably wouldn't have noticed her if it hadn't been for Rudy and John. Rudy had stuck his foot out in front of her, tripping her. She stumbled forward, nearly caught herself, then went slamming face first into the pavement. Rudy and John laughed.

Kelsie shook his head. Even in the small towns they had bag ladies. You couldn't get away from them. By-products of a world too fast and too cold, they seeped into the fabric and made a stain that would never come out. He watched her pull herself up and wrap her too-large sweater close around her frail body. Her head turned slightly, then moved as if she was saying something to the men. They laughed again.

He watched her, captivated, but he wasn't really sure why.

Then, suddenly, she turned her head and looked at him. He could see a burning concentration in her eyes; a sign of recognition. So intense was her look that he had to turn away.

This is one fucking weird town, he thought to himself as he turned the ignition, put the car in gear, and drove off.

John and Rudy watched in silence as the BMW moved into the street and disappeared around the corner. They listened to the sound of its engine as it faded into the distance, then leaned back in their chairs.

"S'pose Andy knows about this guy?" John asked.

"How could he not know?" Rudy answered in a quiet, apprehensive voice.

"Andy knows," came a scratchy voice off to their left, and they both cringed. Afraid to look, they knew who was coming. Like three rotten grapes on an otherwise perfect stem. The smell of them came on the cold wind, and there was a time when John and Rudy would have gone inside to avoid them.

But things had changed.

There was no avoiding Stricker, Crow, and Harley the Runt. They were charmed now.

And they were connected, in a way John and Rudy fought desperately not to understand. Some things were just too dangerous to understand.

So they sat there, stiffly, and waited for the three boys to join them.

Crow came first, hands in pockets. Then Stricker came up beside him. Harley held back a little. The look in his eyes was wickedly stupid. But the look in Crow's and Stricker's eyes was exact, foreboding, and dangerous.

Charmed

Rudy leaned back in his chair and crossed his arms over his chest, trying to appear relaxed, but John betrayed his feelings by swallowing too often. "Any news?"

Stricker spat. "Not yet."

"How long do we wait?"

Crow turned a slitted eye toward him. "As long as it takes, pal."

"Just askin'.'"

"Yeah, well, don't ask too much, see?"

Rudy's face went dark.

"Andy's gonna be pissed," Harley said, scratching his belly. John turned to him, his face scrunched up distastefully.

"Hell, man, don't you ever take a bath?"

Stricker spat.

John turned to Crow, trying to avoid looking directly into those dangerous eyes. It made him think of myths, of looking into the eyes of Medusa, and being turned to stone. "That guy Brown's gonna be trouble. Andy know's he's gonna be trouble, doesn't he?"

Crow's wicked eyes narrowed to a fine point. "You ask the wrong questions, Williams. You always have." He leaned down, bringing his face very close to John's. "You got a problem with the way Andy's handlin' things?"

"Oh, hey . . ." John chuckled nervously. "I'm happy, don't get me wrong. I'm happy the way things are."

Crow smiled, displaying a row of brown, rotting teeth. "Sure, as long as they keep playin' the same movie. But the movie can change. You ever think about that?" He turned, caught John's avoiding gaze. "Ever think about change, old man?"

John swallowed.

"You scared?" Crow asked him. John nodded.

Crow straightened, smiling. "That's good, Johnny. 'Cause you don't want to know what's inside, do you?"

John closed his eyes, swallowed again.

Crow clicked his teeth. "You don't wanna know what's way . . . deep . . . *down* inside."

John said nothing, but continued to swallow. Very hard. Very fast.

2

 The decision to keep Kelsie's arrival from Joe was not an easy one. Karen wasn't even sure why she'd made it, except to say that telling Joe just didn't feel right, which was really dumb considering the affection the two men felt for each other. But when she imagined it in her head, it felt wrong. It felt dangerous.

She was going to tell him as they sat at the table that morning. Joe looked so tired and beaten, clutching his coffee mug with both hands. His shoulders sagged over the table, his back so terribly bowed, he looked broken. She thought the knowledge of Kelsie's impending arrival might cheer him up, but when she opened her mouth to take a breath, Joe looked up at her and she shut her mouth with a snap.

There was something in his eyes. Something alien. Something incongruous to his beaten, haggard appearance. In his eyes there was something flickering, lively, and wicked.

She kept her mouth shut.

They sat in silence, Joe listlessly eating his breakfast and Karen watching the cream blend into the blackness of her coffee, her mind struggling with that horrible alien flicker in Joe's eyes, until finally Joe finished his breakfast and left without saying a word.

Something inside him, she thought as she washed the dishes. *Something growing.*

She finished the dishes, cleaned the kitchen.

A flicker, light, deep in the center, like it was coming from his soul.

She dusted the living room and then went upstairs to make the bed.

Something growing in his soul.

Then she ran out of things to do. She sat down on the couch to wait for Kelsie.

From outside she could hear the deer crunching over the dry leaves as they made their way to the creek, and she wondered if she'd put out their food. She thought about getting up to check. She thought about putting water on for tea. She thought about Kelsie, and Joe, and the Fareland Cinema.

Something hiding. A hidden thing.

The thought made her shiver.

She'd sat down on the couch at ten o'clock. At one she began to cry.

At one-thirty she heard a car turning into their driveway and bolted upright, her heart pounding so fiercely, it made her chest hurt. She went to the window and peered out.

Kelsie was just climbing out of his BMW when she pulled the curtains back. As she watched him stretch and scan the front yard, she felt a sudden sense of relief. It struck her with such force that she swayed to one side and had to grab the curtains for support. Kelsie looked clean. That was the only word for it. He wore his customary blue jeans topped with button-down shirt, tie, sleeves rolled up to the elbows, and a suit vest. The ensemble always made Karen think of a split-screen image. Kelsie called it the desk-job uniform. No one could see you from the waist down, so you only had to appear businesslike from the waist up. To Karen there was a certain sensuality attached to his apparel. It accentuated both his broad shoulders and his narrow hips. Top the whole thing off with a crown of gray hair, and you had one hell of a good-looking man.

But above all, he looked clean.

Unusually clean, and that bothered her. If he looked so clean, it could only mean that everything else was dirty.

As he came to the front door, Karen stifled an urge to run away and hide.

The doorbell chimed, cutting through the sickly silence of the empty house, and Karen jumped, almost lurched. She walked numbly to the front door and opened it.

Kelsie's warming smile melted what strength she had left and she fell into his arms, sobbing.

The great thing about Kelsie Brown, the beautiful thing, was that he never pushed. He said nothing to her, just held her tightly until her catching sobs had quieted, then led her into the living room and sat her down. Then he waited.

She looked at him. "Sorry."

"Okay. You want to tell me what's going on?"

Karen wiped tears from her face with the heel of her hand. "Joe's sick."

"That much I know," Kelsie said, leaning back.

Karen steeled herself for a lengthy, unbelievable explanation laced with doubt and obscurity. She wasn't really sure where to start, and Kelsie seemed to sense this. She felt his warm hand on hers and her strength melted again.

"Everything was fine," she began haltingly, "until he bought that damned theater."

"It's not working out?"

"Well, yes . . . it is . . . but something's not right. He's got a boy working for him, Frank Jordan's grandson, I think. He's creepy, you know? Kind of . . . sleazy."

Kelsie cocked his head questioningly.

"I mean," Karen struggled, "he just has a kind of look about him that scares me. He's sly . . . I don't know how to explain it." She bit her lip. "You've heard that expression about the devil being disguised as a well-dressed, good-looking young man?"

"You think he's doing something underhanded?"

Karen sighed. "Not just underhanded. Dangerous."

Kelsie's brow knitted. His gaze wandered about the room as his mind worked. Karen sat with her hands folded neatly in her lap, feeling suddenly the foolishness of the situation. She'd placed some of the newspaper clippings Joe had hidden in their dresser drawer on the coffee table, and reached for them now. "Look at these."

Kelsie took them from her and studied them in silence. Among them was the picture of the brutally slain boy in the field. Kelsie looked at this one for a long time, turning it over in his hand. "That's pretty gruesome."

"It was taken about fifty years ago," Karen said. "I found it in a shoe box in the dresser. I think Joe was trying to hide it from me."

Kelsie set the clipping on the table and leaned back. "Why?"

"I don't know why. But he hides a lot of things. Did he tell you about Rozina?"

Kelsie stiffened a little. "No. He didn't." He rubbed his mouth distractedly. "Rozina's here?"

Karen nodded. "She runs a small saloon. Joe told me he'd call and tell you she was here. He knows how close you two were in college. But he wasn't too happy about her being here."

"She's a little . . ." Kelsie sighed, looking troubled.

"I think Joe considers her to be trouble," Karen said flatly.

Kelsie glanced at her. Now he looked more than troubled. He looked frightened.

"You're scared now, aren't you?" Karen said. "It goes with the territory. It's in the air." She reached for another clipping. "Now look at this."

Almost reluctantly Kelsie took it from her and studied it. "This is recent," he said quietly.

Karen nodded. "His name's Vordy Halleran. He's a local."

"He's been burned."

"Yeah," Karen said tightly. "It was in the local paper, the day after the Fareland opened." She took the clipping from Kelsie and placed it on the table, next to the older clipping. "I think these two incidents are related."

Kelsie looked at her. "They're fifty years apart."

"I know, but"—she looked around suddenly, then lowered her voice—"I think they are related and . . . I think—I think Joe's involved. I'm not sure how, but I know he's in on it."

"In on what?"

Karen's chest tightened. Now came the real test, the ultimate challenge of her mettle. She had called him here, had based her need for his help on an intangible fear for Joe's safety and sanity. Could she, in the face of all that was rational and normal, convince Kelsie that evil was more than a paltry notion lurking in the warm wet recesses of an unsound mind? Or was she going to simply fall apart, degenerate into a raving thing bent, in the name of pride, on her own self-destruction?

But it wasn't just pride. She could see the fear in Kelsie's eyes, and in that fear she saw confirmed her own credibility. And there were other things. Scary, dirty things. Things like Joe throwing up so violently that there had been blood to clean up the next day. Things like the shadow on his face, the slump in his usually strong shoulders, and his constant digging and kneading at his belly, mumbling about things growing inside there.

And the flicker, deep in his eyes. Something hiding. . . .

Karen straightened her shoulders, took a breath, and set a resolute gaze on Kelsie. "There's something going on. Some kind of . . . conspiracy." Kelsie looked at her incredulously and she grated her teeth. "These two incidents—the boy in the field and Vordy Halleran—they're related. I know they are. Look at the date on the picture. Vordy Halleran was burned the same night the theater opened."

Kelsie looked. "What's this?" He pointed to the scribbled word above the date.

Just as she opened her mouth to speak, a metallic clinking sound floated in from the kitchen. Both their heads turned toward the sound just in time to see the kitchen door swing open and an enormous German shepherd pad in. Karen heard a short gasp catch in Kelsie's throat as the beast ambled toward them, head low, eyes intense and watchful.

"Jesus," Kelsie whispered.

"It's Joe's dog," Karen said distastefully. "Name's Razor."

He breathed again. "Where'd he come from?"

Razor moved in between them and sat on her haunches. Her large tongue lolled out as she breathed, and Kelsie rubbed her nose.

"Actually, it's a she," Karen said. "Joe came home with her one night, soon after I got here. I don't like her. She watches me all the time."

"Big dog."

Karen nodded. "And creepy. Look at the eyes. . . ." As

she spoke the dog turned her head, and the powdery blue eyes settled on her. She shuddered. "I hate those eyes. They're unreal. Whoever heard of a dog with blue eyes?"

"It's rare," Kelsie said, "but not unnatural. She's probably got a little Samoyed in her." He put out his hand and Razor nudged it with her muzzle. The massive tail thumped happily on the carpet. Kelsie smiled, but it made Karen nervous to have Kelsie's hand so close to those large white teeth.

Karen led Kelsie into the kitchen to fix him something to eat. As she worked at the stove she told him about some of the other things she'd noticed in Joe's behavior. He'd gotten into the habit of calling his opening night a "special screening." He'd even decided that would be the only time he'd screen movies. Friday night "special screening." The rest of the week would be dark. Friday night. Only Friday night. And after the first night, the first "special screening," a man was nearly burned to death.

Kelsie listened quietly, absently scratching Razor behind the ears. When she'd finally exhausted her store of information, she sat down across from Kelsie and watched him.

He said nothing, but his eyes drifted thoughtfully. It made Karen uneasy, because she knew he was deciding whether or not his trip up to Fareland had been a fool's run. Anxiety welled inside her, pulled on her spine.

At length, and after drawing in a long, preparatory breath, Kelsie spoke. "I don't see anything wrong with 'special screenings.' Sort of goes along with Joe's whole plan, doesn't it?"

"*Someone's* plan, anyway." Karen gritted her teeth. "No, Kelsie. There's nothing wrong with them. Nothing at all. Except they happen to be the only time anything's shown in that place."

Kelsie blinked.

"I told you that," Karen said.

"It didn't register." Kelsie leaned forward. "He only screens movies on Friday night?"

Karen nodded.

"How do you live? I mean, where's the money coming from?"

Karen hitched a breath. "You know, I hadn't thought of that." She looked at him. "I don't know, Kelsie. I honestly don't know. But we have plenty. There's always plenty in the bank when I go to make withdrawals."

Kelsie nodded absently, deep in thought.

"I admit this all sounds foolish," Karen said, "maybe even paranoid. But all you have to do is see Joe for yourself. You'll see the change. Can't miss it. All I'm asking is you look into it. If I'm wrong, nobody gets hurt. I'll shut up. But if I'm *right* . . ." She bit her lip, trying desperately to hold back the stinging tears because they were the last thing she needed right now.

She pulled herself up straight and looked Kelsie directly in the eyes. "Just talk to him, Kelsie."

He was thinking again, considering. He looked again at the clippings he'd brought in from the living room and suddenly his face relaxed with decision. When he looked at her she saw that his usually bright gray eyes had gone a shade darker. "Where is he?"

"At the Fareland."

Kelsie straightened. "I was just there. It's dark, locked up."

Karen nodded. "He's there. And so's Andy."

Kelsie stared at her.

"You don't want to talk to him there anyway," Karen continued.

"Why not?"

Karen sagged. "Kelsie, please . . ."

"Okay . . . yeah. . . ." He looked at the clippings again. "Okay."

Karen gave him directions to the Fareland Hotel. She'd invited him to stay with them, but Kelsie was not one to go in for staying at someone's house. He liked the freedom and privacy of having his own room. Karen knew that, but had offered anyway, out of courtesy. The only time Kelsie had stayed at their house in L.A. was the time he had been too drunk to drive, and the morning hangover was too vicious to endure in a standing position. He'd slept nearly half the day, then dragged himself out to his car in a heap of wrinkled clothes, muttering his thanks through a mouthful of cotton. His condition had endeared him to Karen, and for the first time, watching him stumble down the walk to his car, she wondered what would have happened if she'd met Kelsie first.

Watching him now, walking straight and strong, his broad shoulders set high over a slim body, was the second time.

She headed back into the house, calling Razor as she crossed the living room and went into the kitchen. She pulled a large can of dog food from the cupboard, opened it, and shoveled its contents into Razor's bowl. Then she called the dog again.

Then again.

But she didn't call a fourth time. Feeling stupid and angry, she knew she was alone.

"No dinner for you then, bitch," she muttered as she threw the dog food into the wastebasket.

The Fareland Hotel wasn't really what one would call a hotel. Seven individual bungalows set in a U shape around a small, cracked birdbath. They were clean looking, freshly painted, but old. Kelsie parked his car in front of the bungalow farthest from the street, got out, and trotted up to the office.

The office was modest, clean, and airy. Behind a mahogany desk sat a plump little man with fat cheeks and a rosebud mouth. He lifted his round head and smiled as Kelsie walked in. "Yessir! What can I do for you?"

Kelsie nodded, smiling. "I'd like a room, please."

"Sure thing." The little man reached under the counter and pulled out a small piece of paper. "Cost you ten bucks a night. Good TV reception, and the phone's hooked up. How long you staying?"

"Long as it takes," Kelsie muttered.

"Pardon me?"

Kelsie smiled. "I'm not sure. Can I pay by the week?"

The man's friendly smile faded. "Sure. Why not?" He glanced down at the piece of paper Kelsie had scribbled on and pushed forward. "From L.A., I see, Mr. Brown."

"That's right."

"Here on business?"

"Not really." Kelsie shifted his weight onto one foot. "I'm a friend of Joe Moreson's."

The man's fading grin went completely sour. "Oh! Well, any friend of Joe's . . ." He turned slowly and reached for the mailboxes.

"I'd like number five, if that's all right."

"Sure," the man said stiffly, reaching for the key. He plopped it down in front of Kelsie. "Be seventy bucks in advance, Mr. Brown."

Kelsie nodded again, reaching into his back pocket. He produced a fifty and a twenty and presented it to the man with a smile. "Thanks."

The man nodded politely. Kelsie took the key and left.

"Say hi to Joe for me, will you?" the man called after him, and Kelsie acknowledged him with a wave of the hand.

As the door slammed shut the man's scowling face melted into a gleeful, crazy leer. "You scared, Mr. Brown? Huh? You scared yet?"

The man giggled.

Opening doors to hotel rooms was pretty much a common event for Kelsie. As a computer engineer he had been obliged to make several trips out into the field, troubleshooting and teaching. Sometimes it got to be a bit much, being called in the middle of the afternoon from some remote part of the United States by a haggard clerk whose computer "just wouldn't work." Off would go Kelsie on the next flight to Sandbox, USA, and once he got there and inspected the computer he'd discover that he'd just flown five hundred miles to plug the damn thing in.

But mostly, he spent his time teaching. He was second only to Joe Moreson in the whiz kid department, designing programs and then going with them into the field to teach them to Tempac staff across the country. Hotel rooms were more his home than anything else.

This one was no different, except perhaps in style. He usually stayed at all the best places. He was accustomed to classy suites with new carpet and freshly painted walls. And room service. He loved room service. But he didn't think this place knew the term.

Still, it was nice. It was clean and bright, a typical prewar room with fabric lamp shades and crystal light fixtures. Flimsy chiffon curtains swayed lazily in an afternoon wind. In the center of the west wall stood a double bed with nightstand, and on the stand was an old telephone.

Kelsie crossed to the bed, dropping his suitcase midway, and sat down. He pulled out the slip of paper with the Fareland Cinema's telephone number and stared at it. Beneath the number Karen had written, *Please be careful.*

She was really spooked, Kelsie thought, his gaze wandering to the tiled bathroom adjacent to the bed. The rusty stains streaming down from the shower head jarred him for a moment, reminiscent, in that moment, of blood. She was really scared and that was not like her. But that wasn't what had decided him. It had helped, maybe, but it hadn't been the final thing. It was those clippings.

Making a connection between the two—the slain boy and the burning man—well, that would take some imagination. It would take a hell of a lot of kneading and stroking of the mind to plant that kind of conjecture into an otherwise rational self. But he had seen something else. Something at the top corner of the news clipping that had clearly been scribbled in Joe's handwriting, and bore a frightening similarity to what had been scribbled on the picture of the boy, fifty years ago.

A single word.

He picked up the phone and dialed the Fareland.

It rang twice, and a young voice answered. "Fareland Cinema."

"Joe Moreson, please."

"Who's calling?"

"A friend."

Long pause.

Just as Kelsie opened his mouth to ask if anyone was there he heard the phone being clunked down angrily. He loosened his tie and slipped it over his head while he waited.

After a moment another voice came on the phone, this one much older and rough, and for a moment Kelsie's skin twitched.

It's Joe. It's Joe, but it isn't.

"Joe?"

"Who is this?" the old voice demanded.

"Kelsie." His own voice cracked. "Kelsie Brown."

"Kelsie!" The voice changed, sounding friendly, young. Sounding like Joe. Kelsie felt a shiver down his spine. "Why, you old bastard, where are you?"

Kelsie breathed. "I'm here, you jerk. Here in Fareland."

"Jesus, I don't believe it. Really? You *dog*! How'd you get the time off?"

"You kidding?" Kelsie laughed, but it was a timid and trembling laugh. He tried to ignore it. "They owe me the world, you know."

Joe returned the laugh. "That's true enough. How much did you save Tempac on that Pluto program?"

"Fifty million, give or take."

Joe whistled. "So, where are you? At home? Have you seen Karen?"

Kelsie bit his lip. "Not yet. Just got in. I'm at the Fareland Hotel. Say, how come everything in small towns is named after the town? Fareland Hotel, Fareland Grocery." He paused. "Fareland Cinema."

No answer.

Kelsie could feel a coldness developing, like ice, a barrier being formed. He breathed in and nearly shouted into the phone. "So! When do I get to see the place?" While waiting for an answer, Kelsie also waited for a change in the voice. A stiffness, perhaps. A tightness.

"Why not now?"

"Okay, great. See you in a few minutes."

"Good, Kelsie." There was a pause. "I'm—"

"You're what?"

Another pause, tight and unyielding. "I'll see you in a few minutes."

Joe hung up without saying good-bye.

Kelsie stared at the silent phone for a moment, then replaced it in the cradle.

He looked around the room, thinking. He could wait and unpack later. Yes. No need to freshen up. He wanted to get out there, get to the theater, see Joe. Make sure Joe was all right.

A single word.

One written fifty years ago. One written by Joe.

A gust of wind moved the curtains in turmoil. Kelsie went to the window and closed it, noticing distractedly how cold the breeze had become.

When he got to the theater he stood outside, studying the facade. It looked great, really great. Joe had done a marvelous job restoring it. The old Art Deco had been recaptured, which had both its virtues and its faults. Art Deco was a part of American architectural history, but it was ugly. Damn ugly. Its only plus was that it reminded Kelsie of *The Wizard of Oz*. For that, he'd forgive the cold lines and awkward bulges.

But this place was really a masterpiece in design. If not for the empty marquee it would have been the perfect picture of a successful theater.

Kelsie stared for a long time at the marquee. He stared at it and wondered, and didn't stop wondering until a movement to his left caught his attention and he turned just in time to see an old, withered lady watching him from across the street. He crooked his head around sharply, met her eyes. It was the old woman he'd seen with Rudy and John.

Her stare was determined. For a moment Kelsie thought about going over to her, but suddenly she let her gaze drop. She turned and began to shuffle away, but not before she had succeeded in giving Kelsie a chill.

She had been staring right at him. She had been staring, as if she knew who he was. As if she knew . . .

"Kelsie!"

Kelsie jumped, not realizing how tense he'd become while watching the old woman. He hitched his shoulders as though trying to discard an unwanted coat, and turned and saw Joe

at the front of the theater, waving wildly. Kelsie waved back
and Joe stepped out from the theater. He was tilted slightly,
walking the way a man would if one leg were shorter than the
other. His left arm hung down past his thigh, and for a fleeting second Kelsie was reminded of Igor, Dr. Frankenstein's
faithful, deformed, insane assistant. He shook the image
away before Joe reached him.

Kelsie smiled and extended his hand. Joe stared at it.

Another pause, and the barrier of cold that had begun to
form earlier magnified. Kelsie let his hand drop slowly.

"God damn, it's good to see you," Joe said shakily.

"Same here."

Why didn't Joe want to shake his hand? They always shook
hands. Some friends hugged, some slapped each other on the
back. But Joe and Kelsie *always* shook hands.

Why not now?

Joe sighed deeply, his eyes catching Kelsie's. There was a
smile on his face, but it didn't touch his eyes. Those eyes
were cold and watchful, making Kelsie uneasy. He wanted
very much to look away but he kept the gaze until Joe finally
looked away himself, and when he did, Kelsie felt himself
shudder.

Joe took a deep breath and made a sweeping gesture with
his hands. "So! What do you think?"

"Looks great, Joe," Kelsie said.

"Want to see the inside?"

From over Joe's shoulder Kelsie caught a glimpse of a
figure standing in the darkened doorway of the theater. It
was slim, willowy, and very dark. He felt suspicious, suddenly, afraid to move or say anything that might be over-
heard.

Don't talk to him there.

It was a warning.

"Let's go somewhere. Take a walk."

Joe glanced at him sharply. "I guess you city folk don't get
out in the country much. Come on, I know a great place."

But instead of moving off, heading toward the car, they
both stood there, facing each other, and over Joe's shoulder
he could still see the dark figure. He tried not to let his eyes

shift, tried to keep them on Joe, but it was difficult, because the figure had changed shape. He felt his heart quicken and struggled to keep his eyes on Joe, but it had *changed*!

Darkness in the threshold, cutting out a line of something broad and low. A woman at first, he was sure of it. But now . . .

If something didn't happen soon, he was going to explode.

Joe watched him, their eyes locked, as though neither of them wanted to say anything about that thing in the threshold of the theater. That thing changing. . . .

Kelsie felt a whimper and stifled it, nearly wrenching his chest.

They both turned, Joe leading Kelsie to the curb. Suddenly the car became a refuge, an escape from the changing thing, and Kelsie stumbled toward it.

But as he got in behind the wheel the thing in the threshold moved. It swayed out

it's coming for me!

and ambled toward the car. Joe turned to it, slapping his thigh with an open hand.

Long legs ambled as the head rocked back and forth with the motion, its tongue lolling out in a lazy fashion, but the powdery blue eyes were sharp and piercing, and fixed on Kelsie.

Joe smiled sheepishly. "My dog."

"I gathered," Kelsie said, trying to sound normal. He had begun to shake with a fine tremor.

The dog jumped up into the backseat and sat down.

"Name's Razor," Joe said.

"Where'd you get a name like that?"

Razor sat quietly, breathing in that way a dog has, and Kelsie knew her eyes were on him.

"Well," Joe said, "she's a smart dog, you know . . . sharp . . . like a razor's edge." He gave a halfhearted, almost apologetic shrug.

The dog was still watching him. Watching him, and now he was getting angry. He craned his neck to look at Razor, meet her gaze.

Her eyes lost their focus, and she shut her muzzle with a snap.

"You mind if she comes along?" Joe asked.

"Course not, long as she stays put. Can you do that, Razor? Be a good dog?"

Fuck you

Kelsie jumped.

He'd heard it, in his head, but it was as if the dog had said it out loud, and she was watching him again, pupils down to a pinpoint and then dilating.

Fuck you

He heard it.

Hands gripping the steering wheel, Kelsie faced forward.

Couldn't be. Dogs can't talk. Couldn't be.

But he'd heard it.

Okay, okay . . . enough of this. Let's stop with the horror show antics, okay?

Okay?

3

 Joe directed Kelsie out of town and up a winding mountainlike road. They rode in silence, Razor's muzzle up against Kelsie's left ear as she strained into the passing wind, and Kelsie wondered if having the beast ride in the back, behind him, the maw full of long sharp teeth so strategically close to his carotid artery, was such a good idea. The feel of the dog's hot breath against his neck was nerve racking, especially when she'd lick her chops and swallow, reminding him of something wild and very large rending and slurping down a tasty morsel of meat. Every time it happened he would cringe and suck in air through clenched teeth. Joe would glance at him briefly, and Kelsie thought the glance a little too dark, too . . . proprietary.

At the summit was a small dirt road snaking up a short hill. Joe pointed to it and Kelsie turned the car onto it. They drove around the hill and up the back side.

At the top they stopped and got out, Razor first. She'd made a striding jump right through the car window before they had come to a complete stop, and on her way she thumped Kelsie's head with her back paw. He cursed, his hand rubbing the side of his head where a hot bruise had already begun to form. Razor turned once as he glared at her, and he thought he saw a sinister grin on the dripping muzzle. He'd expected that, but not Joe's reaction: that dark look again, but this time there was the hint of a smile. When Kelsie turned to him the smile quickly winked out. He got out of the car without saying a word.

Kelsie rubbed his head absently, the burning pain now subsiding to a dull ache, and wondered if Joe realized that kick in the back of the head had been purposeful.

Probably he did. There was that smile. That hint of amusement skirting across Joe's face like the flicker of candlelight.

"That's crazy," Kelsie muttered, and got out of the car.

From the hill the view of Fareland was a hazy panorama, very subdued, the kind of scene you'd commission an artist to capture in oil. The hill itself was a kind of grassy knoll, the grass short and feathery. In the center of the peak stood an old oak tree. Joe moved toward the tree while Kelsie chose to stand on the incline, looking out at the town. Razor sat between them. He could feel her at his back.

"This is really something, Joe. How'd you find this place?"

When Joe didn't answer Kelsie turned around and a cold spike of disquiet butted against his spine.

Joe was sitting Indian style beneath the tree, absently chewing a stem of grass. He was in the background and Razor sat in the fore, watching Kelsie. The icy barrier was back again, this time made flesh. Razor watched Kelsie carefully, her head bowed and her eyes intelligent and shrewd. Over her shoulder he could see Joe, looking out of focus, like the inconsequential background filler of a photograph. He looked old; worn out and defeated. Kelsie had to look hard to see anything familiar in the drooping shoulders and bony hands. His face was so very pale and placid, and looking at this faded semblance of the man he had once known so well frightened him.

It was during this moment that Kelsie's mind began to catalogue what had happened since he'd left Joe's house, the foremost being that the dog, friendly at first while he sat scratching it behind the ears, had seemed to him something other than animal in the cold darkness of the theater, and now seemed a sinister, sentient being, determined not only to encroach upon the bond between Joe and himself, but possibly to undermine it, even destroy it.

But worse, and infinitely more distressing, was the out-of-focus image of Joe, depleted in the presence of the dog's authoritarian countenance.

Finally, mercifully, the moment passed and Joe came back

into focus. Kelsie stepped toward Razor and hesitated. He wanted to stare that damn dog down, but it didn't seem like a good idea, or even possible. Razor looked directly at him, following his movements, narrowing her gaze with the acuity of a hunter. She had a bead on him, and it was disturbingly clear to Kelsie that this was not the time for confrontation. What do they say? Don't look a dog straight in the eye because it means you want to fight, and the last thing Kelsie wanted to do on top of this lonely hill was fight a large German shepherd. There was no doubt in his mind that, in the end, he would be lying in the grass a bloody mess.

He lowered his head and moved past the dog swiftly, half expecting Razor to take a chunk out of his leg. His foot came down next to her.

Her head inclined.

She's going to do it she's going to take my foot off

But then he was past her and sitting down next to Joe. He sat with a heavy thump and breathed a heady sigh, surprised and a little embarrassed by his own quaking. *I'm no good at crap like this,* he thought grimly. *I'm being played with. Or am I just going crazy?*

Razor watched him.

He turned to Joe. There was a distant look in Joe's eyes; one of indifference, or preoccupation—Kelsie wasn't sure which.

"Are you here?" he asked.

Joe's head snapped up. "What?"

Kelsie made himself comfortable. "This is a great place. How'd you find it?"

Joe shrugged. "Don't know. Just did."

"Are you okay?"

"Yes," Joe said vacantly, and then silence fell between them as Razor moved to join them, lying down next to Joe and putting her head on his knee. Her eyes were just beginning to close.

Joe scratched the top of her head. "I'm a little confused."

"About what?" Kelsie asked.

"About why you're here."

"Well," Kelsie said, "I've asked myself the same question.

I mean, last time I heard from you wasn't exactly . . . pleasant."

Joe shrugged. "I was tired."

"Working hard on the theater?" Kelsie asked, and Joe nodded. It was a sullen nod. The kind of nod given by a crook who knows his game won't work anymore.

Kelsie watched him for a while, watched his face as it sagged with something more than just fatigue. Then he ventured, "Maybe too hard. I mean, I thought you told me the theater wouldn't open till April. Now Karen tells me you've already had—"

"Karen?" Joe's eyes went sharp, giving off sparks.

"Well, yeah," Kelsie said, fidgeting. "She called—"

"She *called* you!"

Razor's eyes were open again, watching. Dilating.

"What's wrong with that?" Kelsie said tightly. "Why do I all of a sudden feel like I've done something wrong? My best friend has his opening-night gala and he doesn't invite me. Who did the wrong thing, here? Huh?"

Joe continued to glare, but the sharpness had abated.

"So I came up here to see my best friend and my best friend's wife and my best friend's theater, and I get the third degree because my best friend's wife—who also happens to be a good friend of mine—calls me and invites me up . . . a little late, but what the hell? What are friends for, anyway?"

Joe looked down, patted Razor.

Kelsie asked softly, "Are you really okay?"

Joe's mouth worked painfully. He looked away, at the sky, down at Razor, who met his gaze, and Kelsie thought there was something he wanted to say. Something he needed to say. Something he'd needed to say for a very long time.

When Joe finally spoke, his voice was just barely above a whisper. "I'm tired, that's all. You know, I've been working. Hard. It's been . . . hard." He fell into another silence.

"Any problems with the decision you made?"

"No," Joe said quickly. "I'm really happy. It's a great place, the Fareland. Great place. Practically restored itself. And I've got this great projector. God, you should see it,

Kelsie!" His eyes shone with sudden excitement. "It's great! Mint condition. And I've got some good help. . . ."

"Why didn't you tell me Rozina was here?"

Joe's excitement deflated. "What?"

"Rozina. Karen says she runs a bar here. Why didn't you tell me?"

Joe looked away, his hand grasping the back of Razor's thick neck. "I didn't . . . I . . . hell, I didn't think it was that important." He looked at Kelsie guiltily.

Kelsie felt the tension, but didn't know what to do with it. He cleared his throat. "So, you've got some good help."

"Yeah," Joe said, but his voice lacked the excitement it had held before. "Old Frank's grandson, name's Andy Jordan. He's been like my right hand. That's why I was able to open so soon." Joe hesitated, his mouth working again. "Look, I'm sorry I didn't tell you."

"It's okay."

"It's just that—well . . . it hasn't been . . . it hasn't . . . there are some things going on—"

Razor nudged Joe's crotch.

It happened so quickly, Kelsie almost didn't believe he'd seen it. Joe let out a whooping yelp that came from deep down in his guts and slapped at Razor's muzzle. "Razor! Son of a bitch!"

"Dogs have no tact." Kelsie chuckled, but the chuckle was feigned, Kelsie disturbed by the way Razor had nuzzled Joe's groin. "What were you saying?"

Joe waved his hand. "Nothing. Not important. I'm glad you're here." He smiled, and Kelsie saw that it was only painted on. No, the smile was real, but the look in Joe's eyes had moved down his face to cover the smile like a glacier.

Kelsie asked, "So, when do I get to see the thing in operation?"

"Oh, not until"—his hand went down reflexively as Razor's muzzle made a move toward him again—"well, you could come tonight, I guess. . . ."

Kelsie shivered.

Jesus . . . everything he said, every move he made, was

done with caution, with fear. And if he said the wrong thing . . .

"Where are you staying?" Joe asked uneasily.

"The Fareland Hotel."

Joe nodded. "Nice place."

"Just like home," Kelsie said, and thought, *Any more of this careful conversation and I'm going to explode.*

"Hope you're comfortable," Joe said lamely.

Why don't you just talk to me, Joe?

The worst of it was knowing Joe wanted to talk, needed to talk, but was afraid to. And there was nothing he could do about it. He felt as if there were a clamp around Joe's head, tightening whenever he made an attempt to draw Joe out.

And then there was Razor. Ever present, ever watching. Guarding. Warning.

That nudge. That little nudge. So routine, so very much like a dog to do that. Right?

So routine. And so perfectly timed.

"Karen says you only show movies on Fridays."

Joe glanced at him tightly. The suspicion was back in his eyes. "So what?"

"Well, don't you think that's a little . . . strange?"

"No."

"Okay."

Silence reigned. Jagged silence. Razor looking at him, eyes trained on him.

That nudge. Deliberate. Perfectly timed.

Watch it, big man. Watch it, or you're next.

Kelsie smiled. "It's your theater."

Joe nodded, but feebly. He stared out into space, looking at something so horrible, it made him tremble.

That *nudge.*

He didn't like Razor.

He looked down at the dog. She raised her head from where it rested on Joe's knee, and her powdery blue eyes rolled toward him, focusing in, narrowing.

Is it understood, big man? You want to understand. You want to understand real good. And there's something else you should understand. Being dead is no big deal, but dying is a ball-breaker.

Kelsie rubbed his hands together in an effort to stop them from trembling.

Kelsie dropped Joe off at the theater and promised he'd be in time for dinner. There was something Kelsie had to do. There was someone he wanted to see.

He drove slowly, thinking, but thinking was hard and it made his head ache. He tried to buffer the terrible thoughts bouncing around by watching the tiny town drift by as he drove, but it didn't do much good. It was a tedious place, with everything named after the town. God, why did they do that? No sense of individualism. No personality. Everything the same. Fareland Groceries, Fareland Garage, Fareland Trust and Savings.

Fareland fucking Five and Dime.

He needed a drink.

And he needed to talk with someone. Someone he knew would give him answers, because her being here in this tiny town was not a coincidence.

On his right, down near the end of the block, he saw the familiar trappings of a saloon and his heart fluttered. As he drew near, the sign on the front of the old building came into his line of sight. It was amazing; the faded sign sticking out in the tapestry of sameness like the proverbial sore thumb.

ROZINA'S

He'd met her in college, so many years ago he cared not to count. She was taking the same physics class, and sat near the back in an unassuming position, but the professor knew she was there and it made him decidedly nervous.

Kelsie and Rozina formed a friendship through a mutual love of logic. Rozina could have become as successful as Kelsie, had she furthered her studies in computer arts. But she chose a different route, and Kelsie had known she would. She chose to draw inward, and left Los Angeles in a cloud of mysterious events. Kelsie was never really sure just exactly when he'd begun to miss her. It just came, one day, as gently as a summer breeze. He missed her. She hadn't been around for a while, and he felt the emptiness she'd left.

He knew she had some royal blood in her, but maybe there was a little bit of the witch doctor in her as well, because she knew. She always knew, and she always had answers, if you could get past the displacing smile and her cryptic, mystical speech enough to understand. Rozina's words were euphemistic, double edged, but she always knew.

And if it really was her, if the name on the sign outside the weather-worn building belonged to the one he'd known before, its blatant revolt against town tradition was clear.

He entered the bar through a double door. Instantly the musty smell of incense and beer caressed him. It was a familiar smell, laced with warm memories.

It was the kind of room you'd expect to see in a Bogart movie. Dim lights, smoky air giving the room a kind of diffused glow. Warmth radiating from somewhere just beyond the senses. A few people huddling around a corner table, and across from them on the left wall a small jukebox, its light filtering in friendly swirls through the smoky air. A simple blues tune wafted with the light.

Atmosphere, one used to say, was everything.

But it was the familiarity of the room that made Kelsie smile, perhaps for the first time since he'd arrived in this sickly town. *Sickly,* yes, that was a good word for it. Like a festering boil, the sickness lay upon the town and stank up the air with a gassy smell. But in here, in this quiet dim place, the air had a shielding of its own that repelled the foul air outside. This was more than just a bar. This was shelter.

Before he saw her, standing regally behind the heavy oak bar and emanating a power subdued by wisdom, Kelsie felt Rozina in the essence of the room. It was always that way with Rozina. So complete within herself; the surroundings reflected her essence.

She hadn't seen him yet, but she must know he was there because nothing got past Rozina. She had eyes in the back of her head. She stood no more than five feet two, midnight in her ebony face and moonlight shimmering in her black hair.

Her mouth pursed powerfully beneath watchful, knowing eyes. Those eyes, Kelsie thought, could slit a man's throat with a single subtle twitch.

The eyes shifted a little, acknowledging but not quite giving way to the new person invading her domain. But still she did not look at him.

Kelsie waited for permission.

Finally, her head moved with an arrogant but graceful nod. "Took you long enough."

Kelsie smiled inwardly. He always liked the way Rozina talked, accentuating every other word with a self-proclaimed importance, her head bobbing gracefully with each accentuation. So animated were her features that one never got tired of looking at her. It was like looking at a kaleidoscope. Always changing. Always new. He moved toward the bar and sat down in front of her. "Good to see you, Rozina."

Rozina graced him with a glance from half-closed eyes, but her lips were smiling. "Of course. Your hair went gray."

"It sure did."

"I told you it would."

"That's right. You did."

"That's right." She watched him with half-closed eyes and an easy, knowing smile. "Told you a lot of things. Sometimes you didn't catch on. Sometimes you didn't listen at all."

"So you left," he said quietly. He kept his eyes on her, but it was hard, because even a glance from her was like being blasted with a blowtorch. She knew so much. And she was so elusive.

She watched him silently.

Kelsie laced his fingers together, studied them. "You didn't have to do that. I could've taken care of myself. When you left, I got to missing you."

She looked at him evenly. "You were vulnerable, Kelsie. And you didn't know what you were fooling with. Your hair wasn't always gray."

In the dark pool of her eyes he saw the truth of what she had said, and nodded somberly.

"You're too logical, Kelsie," she said in a low, reproachful voice. "Too logical then, and too logical now. You got to lose some of that, if you're going to survive here."

She continued to watch him, holding him captive in the depths of her sagacious, solemn gaze. It was disconcerting, even a little unmanning, the way Rozina could look right through him. She was the only woman, the only person, who could do that, but sometimes Kelsie thought maybe she wasn't all that human.

Finding her here, after all these years . . . it just wasn't a coincidence.

Finally she released him, turning away and reaching for a bottle of golden tequila. She poured him a shot and silently set it before him.

"You know I can't handle that stuff," Kelsie said, fingering the shot.

"I know you reach a point where you don't care."

Kelsie lowered his eyes. True. Very true.

He took the shot and upended it, letting the tequila race down his throat without swallowing, then slammed the shot down on the bar, upside down, in a gesture of victory. His eyes were watering.

Rozina shook her head disgustedly. "You always forget the lime and salt."

Kelsie closed his eyes.

She drew a glass of draft and set it next to the empty shot glass. "What do you want to do, Kelsie?"

He groped for the beer, allowing himself time to think, but he also needed a moment to let his throat loosen. A buzz had begun in his head. "Well . . . I guess you could say I'm here to help a friend in need."

"Joe Moreson." She poured another shot.

"I'd say I'm surprised," Kelsie said, looking at the shot with a little apprehension, "but I'd be lying. I guess you know that too."

"And what do you want from me?"

"A little information, maybe." Kelsie fingered the shot. "Think you can help me?"

"Depends."

"On what?"

"On whether or not you listen."

He reached for the beer, took a swallow. "I'm listening," he said carefully.

Rozina looked at him levelly, her gaze so direct and forbidding that it made his stomach flutter. "Kelsie, you can look a man straight in the eye and not really see him, because he's just not there anymore."

Kelsie took a breath, trying to calm the fear that was growing steadily in his heart. "I have to help Joe. I have to do what I can. But first I have to find out as much as I can about the Fareland Cinema."

Rozina said nothing, but her eyes flashed with sudden rancor.

"Will you help me?" Kelsie implored.

"I don't go to movies."

"So, you don't know what's going on."

"I didn't say that. I just said I don't go to movies."

Kelsie took a breath, gearing up, then asked, "Is there anything you can tell me?"

"Yes, Kelsie." She fixed him with a critical gaze. "You turn around, and you leave. And don't look back."

Kelsie clicked his teeth. "Can't do that."

Her dark eyes flashed. "Come to complicate my life with this bullshit? Hell with you." She sighed disgustedly, losing patience, and turned her back on him. It was a gesture as unyielding and impenetrable as a brick wall.

Kelsie grasped the glass of beer with both hands. "Rozina, do you remember what you said about my animal spirit?"

Without turning she nodded. "I told you your animal spirit was a saber-toothed tiger. You thought that meant dangerous." She turned her head a little. "But you were wrong."

"I know," he said quietly. She turned to face him, surprised. "I didn't know it then, but I do now. I knew when my hair went gray, and I realized why you left." Kelsie drew himself up. "You left to save me, because my animal spirit, the saber-toothed tiger, isn't dangerous."

"What is it?" she asked softly, eyeing him.

He looked at her solemnly. "Extinct."

She placed her hands flat on the bar and looked at him. Her face was fierce and firmly set.

"You tried to save me from the soul-eaters," Kelsie said.

"But you didn't believe in the soul-eaters," she said sullenly.

"So you left. And you took them with you."

Her eyes shifted a little, losing some of their fierceness.

Kelsie smiled. "You see, Rozina? I *did* listen."

She lowered her eyes, her face softening to a look of both sorrow and fondness.

"You helped me then," Kelsie said. "And I'm asking you to help me again. Because I listened. And I'm listening now."

She glanced at him, and he gave her his most enchanting smile. "What do you say? For old times' sake?"

A hint of a smile flitted through. "Shit. You tickle me. And when I'm tickled my hands get weak."

Kelsie laughed.

"They do," Rozina insisted, and the smile came through. She regarded him affectionately. "I knew you'd come. Knew it the day Joe showed up. Knew it when the Fareland opened, and enough was no longer enough."

Kelsie's stomach tightened, his blood chilling. It wasn't a very strong sensation and it didn't last long, but the connection was made in his mind.

Enough. Scribbled on those clippings.

Enough.

"What do you know?" he said, this time his voice cracking a little.

Rozina straightened, her face darkening, and she looked away from him, past him, in a way that made Kelsie feel as though he were intruding somehow, on a private place where he had no business. "People get wrapped up in their troubles and look for answers in the wrong places. Can't see the forest for the trees. Remember that, Kelsie, if you remember anything. There are forests. And there are trees."

Kelsie nodded timidly. He didn't really understand.

"You know what linear thinking is?" she went on. "Yes, I think you do. Say, a magnet on a bulletin board falls behind a metal desk. You, with your computer logic and convoluted walls inside that brain of yours, you think about trajectory, logical course of events, action and reaction. If the magnet hits the floor at a certain velocity on a certain edge of its structure, it has x number of trajectories in which it can go. So you plot those trajectories, each one, and you follow them to their logical conclusion. But do you find the magnet?"

Kelsie stared blankly.

"No!" Rozina said sharply. "You don't. Because you don't know how to think linearly. The magnet"—she smiled arrogantly—"is stuck to the back of the metal desk."

Kelsie blinked, and Rozina shook her head. "Fool."

"I'm assuming all this is leading up to something," Kelsie said.

"Everything leads somewhere," Rozina said. Then her hand went out and touched his. He could feel her body heat warm the spot where her fingers lingered. "Everything's connected."

Impulsively he thought of grabbing her, pulling her close to him, and holding on. The source of the desire was unknown to him; perhaps he had loved her in a way few men would ever know in a lifetime, the kind of love that bites and rips, and at the same time brings salvation. But he didn't grab her. He fought the urge, because it was not her way.

"I've got answers for you," Rozina said, "but only if you know the right questions."

"Okay." Kelsie drew in a breath. "First question. Am I going to be able to help Joe out of this mess?"

"How can you help him *out* of it, when you don't know what *it* is?"

"Do you know?"

"Of course. But I don't know what you want to hear."

His lips tightened. "What don't I want to hear?"

"That Joe has made his own bed. He pulled the covers down and hopped right in. You pull those covers off, and he's going to get cold."

"What should I do?"

Rozina paused, considering the question. Then she said, "You should talk to Janice D'Lacy."

"Who's she?"

Rozina's eyes shifted, her gaze skirting the length of the bar. "Bag ladies is everywhere. Comes with people getting together and making a society."

Kelsie stared at her with disbelief. "You're kidding! That old woman?"

"Age has a lot to do with it. Bag ladies get that way because of what they know, and what they can't tolerate anymore in a normal way. D'Lacy is crazy. Crazy as they come, so don't listen too hard. Take what you can, and then get the hell away from her. She'll drag you down with her if you're not watching very closely."

"Where does she live?"

"Out on the end of Broken Hollow Road. Old farmhouse. Go easy, Kelsie. Go slow."

Kelsie looked down into the shot glass. He sat quietly, gazing into the clearness, peering at the bottom of the glass distorted by the gold liquid, wanting to see something there that would help him to understand, and Rozina stood behind the bar, watching him, giving him time.

When he finally looked up it was into those dark, discriminating eyes. He breathed deep, and noticed the air coming out of him was hot.

"One more thing," Rozina said. "Don't go to the theater. And don't go to the movies on Friday night."

"Friday night?"

Rozina nodded.

"It seems to me that Friday night is the one night I should go."

Her eyes flashed again, giving a warning, admonishing him for being so obstinate. *You're not listening again, Kelsie. The soul-eaters are hovering above you and you're just not listening.*

Outside the sun was fading behind the hills. The jukebox had long since fallen silent and the room had emptied. But still the smoke and odors remained, and the warmth inside laid light on Kelsie's mind, but it didn't comfort him. A chill from inside was seeping out, cloaking him in cold.

"Are you scared?" Rozina asked suddenly.

Kelsie nodded. "Yeah. Yeah, I think so."

She poured him another beer. "Ever think about what's inside, Kelsie? Ever think about what's hiding there, inside?"

The question sent a jolt through his middle.

She slid the beer over to him. "You think about it, Kelsie. Think hard, then cover your head because there's a storm coming, and the rain is sour."

Kelsie took the beer in a shaky hand and as he did she leaned close to him. "There is another like you."

"Like me?"

Rozina nodded. "Logical. Skeptical." She straightened and began scrubbing the bar methodically. "Business type. Wears a suit all the time." She squeezed the cloth between her fists, wringing it slowly, almost ritualistically. "Very skeptical, like you, until the day when he stopped being warm."

Kelsie blinked. "I'm . . . not sure I understand you."

"Of course not," she said, looking at him with narrow eyes. "But you remember it, just the same."

Kelsie downed the beer and stood, preparing to leave, then hesitated. "Rozina, one more question."

She looked at him.

Kelsie took a deep breath. "What are my chances?"

She didn't answer.

4

The week had not been an easy one. Kelsie spent the days and early evenings at Joe's house having dinner, chatting, wasting time, and never really getting anywhere. Every time Kelsie tried to draw Joe out, Joe would pull away, pull inward, and become more suspicious of him. Every time Kelsie broached the subject of the Fareland Cinema, a barrier would form, as though Joe was spinning a cocoon around himself, a protective shield that deflected any and all questions. And whenever Kelsie managed to slice through the cocoon and Joe's defenses began to falter, Razor intervened. She would grab Joe's hand in her massive jaws, tug on him urgently, and lead him off to the backyard or upstairs, or out the front door. If Kelsie tried to follow, Razor would be there, just outside the door, her powdery blue eyes trained on him with a stare of impending retribution. It was a look that made Kelsie's skin crawl, because it wasn't quite animal. An animal can give you that look and you know you'd better back off. But what he saw in Razor's eyes was more than that. There was intelligence. There was a beckoning, a daring, as though Razor almost hoped he'd challenge the boundaries of her territory. And that territory was singular and absolute. That territory was Joe.

As Friday drew near, Joe spent more time at the theater, leaving the house as soon as Kelsie had left for the night, staying out late. One time Kelsie waited down the road, in the shadows and away from the moonlight, and saw Joe coming, looking beaten, dragging his feet as though carrying a great weight. He thought about calling to him, thought about confronting him there, in the darkness when no one was

around, but he didn't do it. He *couldn't* do it, but he didn't
know why.

Friday night came and Joe left early, without dinner. He'd
come home just as Kelsie and Karen sat down to eat, went
upstairs to shower, and then came down again and was going
to leave without having said a word. But Kelsie stopped him
at the door.

They looked at each other.

"I'd really like to see the Fareland, Joe. What do you say?"

Joe squirmed.

"You've been holding me off all week. Seems like you
don't want me to see it."

"Don't be crazy."

"So, how about it, then?"

Joe looked around, as though desperately searching for
something. Or someone. When he looked back at Kelsie he
was gritting his teeth. "Not tonight."

"Why not?"

Joe's face pulled down in a fitful, angry grimace. His arm
went back and his fist clenched. Kelsie saw the fist coming, in
slow motion, looping down as Joe's face twisted with rage.
He caught Joe's wrist with one hand, and suddenly every
joint in his body locked.

Joe's skin was ice cold.

He peered at Joe with amazement and fear, because what
he saw wasn't Joe.

You can look a man right in the eye and never see him.

"My God, Joe," Kelsie whispered. "Your skin is freezing.
What the hell's wrong with you?"

Their eyes locked, and there was a moment of sick tension,
the kind that always happens when two friends breach the
border of their relationship. Kelsie felt it in the pit of his
stomach, and it filled him with a sense of loss.

Because he's just not there anymore.

Joe tried to twist free, but Kelsie held on. He held on to
what he remembered was between them. He held on to that
part of Joe he'd grown to respect and love. He held on,
desperately, and hoped the ugliness masking Joe's face
would break apart, and after a while it did. It came slowly,

the rage melting into fear and fatigue. Joe looked pleadingly at Kelsie, pain now straining that poor familiar face, and for a moment Kelsie believed he'd broken through.

"Evening, Joe."

Joe's eyes cut to a place just over Kelsie's shoulder, and the hardness returned. Kelsie craned his neck to see what Joe was looking at, and in that instant, that momentary lack of concentration, Joe broke free of Kelsie's grasp.

Three men stood on the porch. Kelsie recognized all of them: Rudy Olsen and John Williams, the two who had played with him the first day he'd arrived in Fareland. The third was the owner of the Fareland Hotel.

Their smiles were cool and easy, but their eyes burned.

Joe pushed passed Kelsie and went out onto the porch to stand with the three men. They moved around him, forming a kind of circle about him, an impenetrable circle that held Kelsie at bay.

"Thought maybe we'd walk with you to the Fareland," Rudy said, his eyes still burning into Kelsie.

Joe nodded silently.

Rudy gave Kelsie a cursory nod. "Night." They moved off as one, with Joe in the center of them, looking weak and passive. It was as though they were carrying him.

Kelsie decided to give it one more try. "Joe, don't you think—" He was cut off short when Joe turned to look at him.

In the center of Joe's eyes was a flicker of red that hadn't been there before. It not only put a clamp on Kelsie's mouth, it put one on his heart.

Joe stared at him a moment longer, until the group moved as one and left the house.

Once they had gone, Kelsie began to shake.

Karen was sitting on the couch, hands in her lap, her lips tight. "They protect him."

"They do a hell of a lot more than that," Kelsie said, joining her on the couch.

Karen shook her head. "It's ugly."

"No . . . what it is, is weird." Karen looked at him questioningly. "No secrecy. Haven't you noticed? There's no real secrecy. Everything's so blatant, so obvious. I mean, seems to me if something bad . . . evil . . . were going on, there'd be a hell of a lot of secrecy. But even Joe's unwillingness to talk is saying a hell of a lot more than if he were to just come out with it. I feel like we're being played with." He sighed. "God, I hate being played with."

"We're being set up," Karen said hollowly.

"No," Kelsie said sullenly. "We're being used."

"Used?"

"Yeah." He shifted a little and faced her. "It's being made to look like we're being shut out, but that's not it. That's just a cover for something else. We're being used, just as much as Joe is. There's just enough being kept from us to prevent us from fighting back. Ignorance, you know, is a lethal weapon for your enemies."

"But how can we find out what's going on if Joe won't talk to us?"

"Well, a good place to start would be the Fareland."

Karen bit her lip. "They wouldn't let us in."

"So what?"

Karen looked at him, suddenly excited. "Sneak in?"

"Sure! Why not?"

Without another word they stood in unison, and headed for Kelsie's car.

It was a pleasant feeling, really, all this cloak-and-dagger stuff. It reminded Kelsie of his childhood when his friends would smuggle themselves in to the drive-in with one of them in the trunk and the others laid out flat on the floor. Here go Karen and Kelsie, sneaking into the Fareland Cinema on a clear, cold Friday night.

Kelsie rounded another corner and drove past the Fareland. Outside people were gathering, some in clumps and some alone, all moving slowly into the theater.

"There's Dennis," Karen said, pointing to a young tall man with his arm around a girl. They were standing at the corner. Karen rolled down her window as Kelsie pulled up.

The boy bent down and stuck his head in through the window. "Hey, Karen. How goes?"

"Going to the movies?" Karen asked, and Dennis nodded.

"Nothing else to do."

"You were here opening night, weren't you?"

The boy's friendly smile soured. "So what?"

"And you're coming again tonight?"

He straightened, looked around sharply. "So what, Karen?"

"Dennis, come on—"

"Gotta go," he said tightly, and was off, his arm wrapped firmly around the girl.

Karen threw the door open and climbed out, calling after him. He stopped, rocking fitfully on his heels.

"You want to tell me what's going on with my husband?" Karen asked.

"Don't know what you're talking about."

Kelsie joined her, but she seemed unaware of him. Her eyes burned into Dennis's back. "Sure you do. You know. You're a part of it, aren't you?"

Dennis rounded on her, and the fury in his face made Karen step back. "Don't *say* that! *Never* say that!"

"Dennis—"

"I'm not a part of it!" He was shaking badly, his teeth chattering, glistening. He looked insane.

Kelsie put a hand on Karen's arm. He was going to pull her away, but she stood frozen.

"There's Andy," she whispered.

Dennis whirled around, pulled his girlfriend close to him. He threw a tight look at Karen, then moved away quickly.

At first Kelsie only glanced at Andy, but then a shiver went through him, and he found himself strangely compelled to stare at the handsome young man with the angelic face. It confused him, but more than that, it frightened him.

Andy stood there, watching. Smiling. Even with twenty feet of space between them Kelsie could feel the vacuum; a compression of air, a sucking. He felt it pulling on him, seductively, drawing him forward. His heart fluttered.

Get away. Get away from him. He's not what he appears to be.

Hidden. A hiding thing.

Fear rode high in his chest, burning his lungs, and the heat swept through his body. He tugged on Karen's arm. "Let's go."

"I want to talk to him."

"Not now." Kelsie tugged again, this time more urgently. "Let's go."

He pulled her away, shoving her down the street in front of him, glancing over his shoulder swiftly, not wanting to, having to, because what he had seen when he first looked at the boy was going to still be there. But it would be worse, as in a dream, it would grow and distort into something wickedly unreal.

Hey . . .

The eyes.

Ever think about what's inside?

The boy's eyes.

He glanced over his shoulder and knew only after he'd done it that he shouldn't have because it happened, just as he knew it would, and he couldn't look away then, because the eyes, the boy's eyes, were larger, cartoonish, too large for the face, leaking out at the edges. Round glass eyes with black liquid swimming in the centers. And then the smile grew, too, flopping over the edges like the eyes, and the mouth and eyes floating off the face and coming toward him.

His fingers dug deep into Karen's arm. She winced, yelped, but Kelsie ignored her as he shoved her ahead of him, wanting now to run. Run fast and hard, and don't look anymore at the nightmare cartoon eyes and smile that were floating along a windless stream, heading for him. Heading directly for him.

Ever think about what's hidden? Way deep down?

They rounded the corner and Kelsie finally let go of Karen's arm as he fell against the side of the building. His heart was pounding painfully against his breastbone. Karen touched his shoulder and he flinched.

"Kelsie?"

He was breathing too hard. Had to slow down. Had to.

"What's wrong?"

He took in a deep breath, held it, then let it out slowly. His body shuddered. "Not sure. I think . . ."

Hey . . .

He closed his eyes. "I'm not sure."

Karen looked around nervously. "Andy knows what we're up to."

"Oh, yeah."

"Maybe we should forget it?"

Kelsie looked at his hands. Stretched out in front of him, fingers splayed, they shook uncontrollably.

"Are you okay?"

"Yeah. . . ."

"You don't sound okay, Kels. You sound bad." Karen looked around again, shifting her weight from one foot to the other. "Let's just forget it."

"Oh, no. . . ." He stuffed his hands in his pockets to hide the shaking. "It's getting too good to back out now."

Dennis paid quickly and tugged Sheila into the theater. As they reached the entry curtains, Sheila pulled loose and stopped, crossing her arms defiantly across her chest.

"Dennis, what the hell is wrong with you?"

"Nothing." He grabbed for her, but she pulled away. "Sheila, come on!"

"I'm not going in there with you if you don't—"

"Anything wrong?" The voice was like ice against Dennis's back. He could see who it was by the look in Sheila's eyes.

"Nothing's wrong," Dennis said, turning to face Andy. "So why don't you just back off?"

"Touchy," Andy chided.

"Fuck you."

What was once a friendly smile turned suddenly sour on Andy's face. "You know why you're here, don't you, pal?"

Dennis said nothing.

"You're here for the same reason everybody else in this shithole town is here. Because it's never enough." He smiled a little, his eyes twinkling, but his face seemed foul. "Sometimes, we just don't get enough."

Dennis trembled, his rage welling up and nearly flooding out of him. He wanted to throttle Andy and it took all his

strength to keep from doing it. He grabbed Sheila, who had
suddenly become acquiescent, and started for the house.

"And something else too," Andy said. Dennis stopped.
"Something hidden, and it has to come out."

Dennis turned, the muscles in his face working hard.

"You can't escape what's hiding inside you, pal," Andy
said. "Don't try."

Dennis turned and stormed into the house.

The backstage door was ajar, and Karen let Kelsie go in
first. They found themselves in the dark wings to the right
and in back of the screen. From a curtain at the side they
could look out into the house. This was their first glimpse of
the Fareland Cinema.

It bothered Kelsie.

He studied the house in silence for a long time, pondering
the strange positioning of the balcony. The people were meandering about, some already sitting, and others just finding
their seats. It looked, on the surface, like just another Friday
night at the movies. But there was something else, something
he could see in their eyes.

They looked hungry.

At the head of each aisle stood a figure, and Kelsie
thought of sentinels, like gargoyles perched on the corners of
a mansion, set there to guard that which dwelled within.
They stood with their arms across their chests, smug looks set
deep in greasy faces. In the center aisle stood the boy who
only a few minutes before had set his sanity on so dangerous
a slant that he thought he would never find his balance, but
now Andy looked abnormally normal, almost contrived. He
was young, muscular, neatly dressed, and cleanly washed. He
made the other three look like garbage thrown together in a
hasty mockery of humanity. Andy was scanning the theater,
his head moving slowly, almost mechanically, and as his gaze
crossed the screen and the curtain where Karen and Kelsie
were hiding, Kelsie looked down at the floor. He didn't want
to look into those eyes again.

He caught sight of Dennis. He was sitting in the third row,
his throat working hard, his chest rising and falling too fast.

The girl next to him sat hunched over, frightened and confused. She leaned over and said something, but Dennis didn't answer. He just kept staring straight ahead.

The lights dimmed, and a dark silence fell over the house as the screen lit up.

Terror struck at him, sudden and yet secretive, like a foul whisper brushing the ear. Kelsie felt a trickle of electricity finger his spine. The room slanted away from him and he caught his balance only when Karen spoke, her voice a hissing whisper.

"Look at the people."

He looked, and saw in the faces of the crowd a distorting horror. Some writhed in their seats, some choked and sputtered, as if waves of nausea were rushing through them. A few people sat numbly with wide white eyes. Others sat with freakish grins on their faces.

"They see something," Kelsie said, and stepped back to look at the screen. Again the terror swept over him, but it was gone as quickly as it had come. On the screen were shapes and shadows, but nothing really concrete. "What the hell is that?"

Karen looked, squinting her eyes and shaking her head. "You know that garbage you see at the beginning of the film sometimes? Looks like that."

Like white noise, Kelsie thought, and looked back through the curtain. "Those people are—I don't know—they're reacting. Everyone's reacting in some way." He looked at Karen. "What the hell do they see?"

He turned his attention back to the audience just as Dennis was getting up. The boy's face was on fire. He grabbed the girl and dragged her up the aisle.

"Something's going on."

"Huh?" Karen was still watching the screen.

"That boy who came up to the car, Dennis—he just took off up the aisle like his ass was on fire."

Karen peered out through the curtain. "I wonder what's wrong."

Kelsie watched the boy as he stormed out through the entry curtains. "I don't think he liked what he saw."

* * *

Dennis slammed the car into second gear and swung it around the corner. Sheila touched his arm. "What's wrong, Dennis? You're scaring me."

He shook his head. "The Hiding Fear. The Hiding Fear!"

She frowned. "What does that mean?"

"I knew about it. I've known a long time. I thought I could face it, control it. But I can't. I can't!"

Sheila shook her head. "I don't understand."

Dennis looked at her, and in his eyes she saw a flicker that hadn't been there before. It was a burning, cold and very deep, but burning. She shrank away.

"Dennis, what's wrong? Tell me! Why are you so scared?"

"I have to be!" he screamed. "I have to be, because it was hidden and now it's—"

He never had a chance to finish his sentence. His body lurched back as his foot slammed on the brakes. Sheila went forward, striking the windshield. She saw the black spokes of a tractor wheel, thought how silly it was to leave the cat in the middle of the street, then in the instant before she died she saw a white and silent explosion web out from the center of her vision, melting away as the ceiling of the car swept past her.

"We have to get back home before Joe does," Karen said, and Kelsie agreed, but he was having trouble pulling himself away. He was having trouble with a lot of things, like breathing, and keeping himself awake. The air had gone stale and cold. It sliced through him painfully, but still he wanted to stay, wanted to watch the screen although he didn't know what was there.

Then something happened. Somewhere, in the depths of him, in a place he'd never seen, never even knew about, something came to life.

Karen tugged on his sleeve, then grabbed him fully by the arm and pulled hard. "Kelsie!"

Kelsie moaned. Karen pulled again, harder. "Kelsie, God damn it!"

He looked at her, and for a moment that was as fleeting as

the horror, he couldn't see her. He couldn't see anything
except color, and light, and flashes of something thick and
suffocating that had grabbed hold of him, dragging him
down, pushing him into a blackness thick with disease and
unearthly terror. And at its center, in that place deep down
where he'd never been before, that thing, that living light,
was growing.

He looked at her, a monster-thing, and he wanted to grab
the monster-thing that held him, held his face in the filth,
grab it and squeeze it until it ruptured, its foul sickness spew-
ing out and splattering, bringing back the light, the air . . .

. . . put his hands around her neck and squeeze until her
face turned blue and then he wanted to squeeze harder . . .
bones crushing . . . splintering in his fingers . . .

"Kelsie, *please*!"

Kelsie moaned again, slumping forward, clutching the
monster-thing. "Stop," he whimpered. "Stop, stop, make it
stop."

Strange hands, rough hands, grabbed Dennis by the shoulders and pulled him from the driver's seat. His mind was
clouded and his ears rang with shrill siren sounds. As his
vision cleared he craned his neck to look back at the wreck-
age that had once been his car. Sheila was there, sitting upright in the passenger seat, hands folded neatly on her red
jumpsuit.

No, no . . . she hadn't worn a red jumpsuit. She had
worn a white one, a pretty one with eyelet lace at the collar,
and sometime between leaving the Fareland and now, she
had dyed it red.

It was red, all red. Wet . . .

Dennis screamed.

Her head was gone.

The hands tightened their grip and dragged him away
across the street and into a field where Andy stood waiting.

His arms were pulled behind his back and pinned there.
He struggled, but his head was yanked back and held at a
sharp angle.

Sheila was dead.

Her head was gone.

He tried to scream again, but his throat had closed shut and it took everything he had just to breathe.

Andy was standing at the rim of a small hole, maybe two feet in diameter, that had been dug in the ground. Seven men stood by wheelbarrows filled with something wet and solid looking. The wheelbarrows were arranged in a semicircle around the hole. Four of the men stood with their heads down, but three of them, younger, jumped and swayed, giggling, their faces dancing with an inner light. Dennis knew them, knew them well. They were classmates. Stricker, Crow, and Harley the Runt. Stupid boys, worthless. But now they were different.

They were alive with something that glowed from the center of them. They were alive, and powerfully connected to that thing in the center, the hidden thing that Dennis had tried to escape.

Andy was standing apart from the seven, his head erect, a smile spanning the width of his face. He was holding a shovel.

Dennis squirmed against the hands that held him, and the grasp tightened. His head was jerked back even farther. He strained to look Andy in the face. "She wasn't supposed to die!"

Andy tapped him on the chest with the handle of the shovel. "Why did you run, Dennis? All this"—he waved the shovel in a sweeping gesture—"all of it, could have been avoided if you hadn't run."

"She wasn't supposed to die!" Dennis screamed.

Andy looked at him. "You did it, pal. You ran. You changed the rules."

"Bullshit!" Dennis rasped. "You killed her. You planned it that way. Don't think I don't know you, Jordan. You can fool these assholes but you can't fool me, 'cause I grew up with you, remember? I grew up with you. I know what you are."

Andy stood silently listening, the grin on his young face never faltering.

"I've seen what you do." Dennis was crying now. His throat had begun to ache. "Remember that cat you got for

Christmas? Long time ago. It got run over and you sat there in the street and just looked at it. You kept picking at it, seeing how much more you could ruin it. You pulled out its guts, its eyes, and you *loved* it. And how about football practice? That time when Randy Jenkins dislocated his shoulder and the coach put it back in place right there on the field. You watched. While everyone else turned away, you watched. Fuck, man, you were getting off on his pain, I could see it in your face. You got off on his pain. You were fucking wet with it!"

"You're blubbering, pal," Andy said quietly.

"I know what you are!" Dennis screamed.

Slowly and precisely Andy grabbed the shovel in both hands and laid the handle horizontally against Dennis's throat. The pressure bore in on his windpipe. He closed his eyes briefly, then opened them again. Andy's face was close to his and he could feel Andy's rancid breath against his cheeks. "I'm not afraid of you, Jordan. I'm not afraid of what you'll do to me. But you gotta pay for killing Sheila. That wasn't part of the plan and you know it. *You* killed her. All by yourself. You really think you can get away with that without paying for it?"

"Why did you run?" Andy whispered, sounding wistful. "We could have been brothers."

Dennis spat in his face.

Andy's expression never changed, but his eyes, once glowing only in a shadowy way, began to flicker with green, piercing light.

He pistoned his arms out, crushing the handle of the shovel against Dennis's throat. The blow sent Dennis and the men holding him backward in a staggering bundle. The men broke away and Dennis toppled to the ground. He got himself up on his elbows and looked up just in time to see the shovel suspended high in the air. There was no pain as it made contact with the left side of his face. He heard a cracking sound, then a warm wetness against his face as if someone had splashed him with water. The ground came up suddenly, and he put out his hands to keep his head from crashing against the ground, but the ground had done a flip-

flop and was above him now, sliding off to the left. The ringing in his ears grew stronger, more intense. He was dimly
aware of a hot pain in his lower belly and realized someone
had kicked him, probably Andy. Another pain in his back
joined the first, but it was muted and disjointed, like a dream.

Then the pain became a reality. His hand groped to the
left side of his face and was met by something solid and
sharp. His eye was gone. He felt something small like pebbles
in his mouth and realized they were his teeth. He spit them
out in a spray of blood, then fell over on his back and peered
up at Andy with his one remaining eye.

Andy was standing over him, and something was not right.

The confidence was gone. Andy's smooth young face had
gone old and wrinkled. The pupils of his eyes had dilated,
and the green flicker of light had turned to fire. His entire
body was shaking.

He's losing control, Dennis thought, and smiled.

Andy howled, enraged by the smile, and brought his foot
back to kick Dennis again. The pain shot through him like a
lance.

Men were grabbing Andy, pulling him away, talking to him
in hushed whispers. Andy shook them off and pointed to
Dennis. The men knelt beside him and flopped him over on
his stomach. His wrists were crossed and something cold and
thin was wrapped around them, pulling them together. The
thin, cold wire bit into his skin. Then he was being pulled to
his feet, but his legs wouldn't hold him. The men held on to
his arms, trying to support him, the pressure screaming in his
shoulders. His head lolled clumsily and as it fell against his
left shoulder another piece of bone was snapped off. The
men dragged him to the hole and began to lower him into it.

"Upside down." It was Andy. His voice rasped with his
fury.

Stunned silence, followed by nervous whispers among
them, then Andy's voice again, sharp and threatening:

"You don't want to argue with me. Not now! Upside down!
And stake his feet."

Dennis felt himself being lowered to the ground next to
the hole, and his head fell back into the mouth of the hole as

he was shoved in. His legs bent at the knees and his feet were being tied down at ground level. He tried to pull himself up, bending at the waist, but the hole was too narrow and his head crashed into its curving wall. What little strength he had left was finally expended and he hung there helplessly, blood dripping from his shattered face, trickling down and slipping off him in large drops that plunked on the bottom of the hole. *Like a deer hung from the ceiling,* he thought, *its throat slit. They're bleeding me. They're going to kill me.*

He tried again to pull himself up, but it was useless. *If only I had been stronger . . .*

Andy stood over the hole and peered in. "We could have been brothers!"

If I had been stronger, I could have beat him.

Andy motioned to the men that stood skulking behind him. Silently, shovels in hand, they began filling up the hole. Slowly.

Darkness came, in relief, dispelling the pain. In the distance, like a gentle swirl of dust held in a silent breeze, Dennis heard one last thing before his life was smothered away: "Enough!"

From behind, in a softness as subtle and seductive as a woman's caress, Kelsie felt himself being tugged. He could see the monster-thing receding into a thickening haze, and from the haze Karen slowly emerged. Her body was tilting backward, easing away from him. He groped for her in desperation, found her, pulled her back. A pressure struck him full in the chest. He fell back.

"Something here," he whispered.

"Kelsie—"

Pressure, radiant cold, closing in on him, surrounding him, engulfing him. Radiant. "Something living here. . . ."

"Kelsie, let's go."

He tried to take in air but the pressure was too great. It crept in through his ears, mouth, suffocating. "Breathing . . ."

He strained against the pressure, tried to turn his head, and it was like being suspended in syrup. He looked at the screen and saw it billow with the radiance of the pressure, the cold.

And the thing, deep down, hiding, growing . . .

Horrible pain. He cried out.

Growing, deep inside, coming out . . .

He cried again.

"Kelsie! God damn it, let's *go!*"

Cobwebby confusion wrapping itself around him. He could see only a few sparse images through it. The line of Karen's jaw, the sharpness of her eyes.

Pressure. Oh, God the pressure, it's too much. . . .

"Wants me. . . ." He groaned. "Breathing . . . wants me . . ."

Sound, in darkness, pitch oozing down on him, smothering him. He searched for Karen but his eyes had been sealed shut. He reached out one hand, hoping Karen could see it through the pitch, grab it, pull him up out of it. . . .

Then he was moving, or being made to move, and his vision cleared enough to allow him a glimpse of the door to the alley. He felt himself being shoved toward it, but it pulled away, the distance lengthening by itself.

The breathing, now at his back, quickened.

"Karen—"

In an instant, like the sharp moment of hesitation before an explosion, he felt Karen behind him. Her hands were planted firmly against his back. They were warm, giving a small area of relief against the cold pitch. Then it was gone, and the pressure, the radiant cold, enfolded him again.

5

 No matter how close he got to the four-log fire Karen had built, Kelsie couldn't get warm. He was sitting in a tight ball no more than two feet from the fire, knees drawn up close to his chest and a blanket wrapped and held tightly about his shoulders. He could feel the heat from the fire, but it was a detached, objective kind of sensation, as though he were watching only a movie of the fire. The cold was cutting into him, leaving a path of ice through his body. He stared into the flames, tried to move himself closer as if to crawl into them and wrap them around him.

Karen came from the kitchen with a cup she held by its handle. Kelsie wordlessly took the cup and drank. The liquid was sweet and warm, and he gulped it down without taking a breath. The sound of Karen gasping made him look at her. Her face was drawn and scared.

"Kelsie, that tea was boiling."

Kelsie looked into the empty cup. It had felt tepid, but definitely not boiling. Not even hot. He heaved a weighty sigh.

Karen knelt beside him, pulling her long legs beneath her and resting one arm on his thigh. "You okay?" she asked.

Kelsie nodded. "When does Joe get home?"

Karen gazed into the fire. "Late. He's always late on Friday nights." She turned to him. "Kelsie, what happened?"

"I was going to ask you that. Last thing I remember clearly was something . . . living. Organic." He moved a little closer to the fire. "Scared the hell out of me."

"You said it wanted you."

"Did I?"

Karen nodded. "What was it? What wanted you?"

A shudder passed through him as he remembered the pressure. The radiance. . . .

And that thing, living, deep inside. . . .

He pulled the blanket close around himself. "I can't get warm."

Karen got up and went to the hall closet, where she got another blanket. "I'm really sorry about this, but I'm afraid I didn't see anything. I just don't know what happened."

Kelsie glanced at her, surprised. "You're kidding!"

"No."

"You didn't feel it?"

She draped the extra blanket around his shoulders. "Feel what?"

He shivered with the memory of it. The pressure . . . reaching out from the depths and laying hands on him. "Something . . . touched me. God, I think it was trying to get inside me." He shuddered again. "Maybe it did."

Karen knelt beside him, her arm resting again on his thigh, and this time he felt her need.

"Listen, Karen. If something happens to me, I want you to find Rozina."

"What are you talking about?"

"If anything happens, you've got to find her. She can—she can protect you." He took her by the shoulders and looked at her sternly. "You go to Rozina, and you *stay* with her!"

Karen closed her eyes. "Oh, God . . . ." She wrapped her arm tighter around his leg, sending Kelsie's mind in two different directions. Fear, so intimate and explicit, was now confused by desire and muddied by confusion. That squeeze of her arm, the length of it sliding along the inner part of his thigh, was a wordless plea, a plea he wasn't sure he could answer.

His mind volleyed between the two conflicting emotions until finally his will gave out. He couldn't handle this, not now. He couldn't get warm, probably never would be warm again, and he didn't want her hand on him. Not like that. Not now.

She was sitting a little bit away from him, crying softly.

Not now, please.

He said, as gently as he could, "I'm sorry."

She looked up. "Sorry for what?"

"I thought you—" He stopped. Clear confusion showed on her face.

He turned away, feeling foolish.

"Kelsie, what are we going to do?"

"Got to learn more about this. Got to know the game plan. Ever hear of a woman named D'Lacy?"

Karen shook her head.

"She's a crazy woman, lives on a farm by herself. Rozina says she might know something. Maybe"—he closed his eyes—"I don't know. Christ, I wish I could get warm."

"What about Joe?"

He hesitated. "I don't—I'm not even sure it *is* Joe."

"Yes. It is." She had moved closer again, but she wasn't touching him the same way, and it occurred to him that he had imagined the whole thing.

Or was made to imagine it.

He shook his head. "I think I'm losing control."

"Then you'd better get it back," Karen stated. Her face was stern and strong, the firelight dancing on her cheeks. He reached out and touched her.

Karen gasped. "Kelsie, you're cold. Like ice."

"I know."

"What happened? What happened in the theater? What did you see?" She squeezed his hand. "What did you *feel*?"

Kelsie breathed deeply. "Something inside. Deep down inside. Growing." He shuddered.

"Like Joe," Karen said. "Something growing inside."

"Can you remember when it started? I mean, when exactly did he start getting sick?"

Karen stared up at the ceiling, thinking. "When he called to tell me he'd bought the Fareland. Yeah. I noticed it in his voice. Something different. And then, when he called about the house, there was something else, something beneath the excitement. I can't really put my finger on it. It just didn't sound like him. That's when I started getting worried. I figured, maybe it's just because he's doing so many new things so fast. Once I got up here he was okay." Her eyes shifted. "Well, sometimes he was okay. But other times he just seemed so tired. Exhausted. Short tempered . . . hell, I don't know . . . angry, I guess. And the stomach problems. He was eating twenty, thirty pills a day. Then, when he switched to the liquid Maalox, he was drinking four and five bottles a day. Then one night he came home and I swear he looked like the devil was on his tail. We made love, but I felt like I was saving a drowning man. That's when it all went sour." She tilted her head up to Kelsie. "It's no good between us. Not now. When he makes love to me he's . . ."

"What?"

Karen took a deep breath. "He's raping me."

Kelsie flinched at the words.

"To tell you the truth, Kelsie, I think it started way before he bought the Fareland. I just think buying that damned place has brought it all to a head."

"What do you mean?"

"Well"—she rubbed her face as though to wipe away a film of muddy water—"how can something as simple as buying a theater make someone change like that? There has to be something underneath, something sick underneath that's just been waiting to come out."

Kelsie stood, wrapping the blankets closely around himself, and started to wander aimlessly. Karen followed him with her eyes.

"I'd like to believe that," he said. "I'd like to believe it. I'm just not one to go in for all this cosmic stuff. I'm a man of logic. It's my work. My job. I don't like unexplainable things." He paused, then shook himself as if to shake off a bit of ash fallen heavy on his shoulders. "Whatever it is, it has a hell of a lot of power."

He looked out the window. The moon was spilling slants of silver light across the dirt road. The air was vibrant and electric. In the distance he saw a darkened figure, limping in the now familiar slump. It rambled up the road like someone just coming out of a three-day binge. "Joe's coming."

Karen pulled herself up. "I don't want to talk to him. I'm

going to bed." She gave Kelsie one last look, a look that went deep inside him, pleading.

"Maybe I'll stay here tonight."

Karen's face relaxed with relief. She nodded silently and hurried up the stairs.

Kelsie turned back to the window. As he watched Joe struggle up the road, his heart filled with heavy sadness. They had been friends, so close, and this thing, this whatever-it-was, with a power so wicked as to tear the frail fabric of a man's dignity, had wedged itself between them, setting them apart. At odds.

Strangers now, Kelsie thought. Strangers.

Crow pulled open a cupboard door. His face twitched distastefully. "No food. Shit."

From the living room came Stricker's croaking voice. "Get your fucking face outta there, asshole. Andy's bringin' somethin' home wid 'im."

Crow slammed the door shut and went into the living room, where Stricker and Harley were lounging, sprawled out in easy chairs. "Andy goin' for groceries? Not like him." He plopped himself down on the couch, grabbing a beer from the coffee table as he descended. He popped the tab and sprayed a foam of beer that hit him square in the chest. "Shit!"

Harley laughed, a high, squealing sound that hurt the ears. Crow glared at him.

"Shut up, cunt face."

"Don't like the way Andy's actin'," Stricker said.

Harley looked up. "Yeah? What ya mean?"

"He means Andy's getting too fucking big-assed," Crow hissed. "Thinks he can call all the shots. You see the way he acted tonight. Fucking crazy. He was gettin' off on it. Yes, sir, sure as shit that fucking asshole's gonna get us all in trouble."

"I say we waste him." Harley giggled. Crow shot him a warning glance and Harley fell silent.

"Think we should talk to Nancy?" Stricker asked. Crow shrugged.

"She's a bitch," Harley said.

Stricker leaned forward, pointing his finger at Harley and wiggling it. "You gonna get yourself in a hell of a lot of trouble, talkin' like that. Don't mess with that woman, Harley. She'll cut your fucking balls off."

Harley puffed out his lower lip. "Shit, I can handle her."

"Think so?" The voice came from behind them, cutting through the air and making them all jump. They whirled around to find Andy standing at the door with a bag of groceries in one arm. He was staring at them, his eyes moving from one to the next with a slow, seething burn.

Andy settled on Harley. "You think so? Think you can handle Nancy?"

"Yeah," Harley said defiantly, looking to Crow and Stricker for support, but they were both looking away, unwilling to get involved.

Andy moved with ease across the room to the dining table and set down the bag of groceries. "She's upstairs, you know," he said, and Harley's head whirled around with a snap. "Why don't you go on up there and show her who's boss?"

"Can't be upstairs." Harley was visibly shaken, his fingers digging into the arms of the chair. "Didn't hear her come in, Andy, didn't hear her, and we been here all night, ever since the job. Would have heard her." He looked again at the stairs, his mouth working frantically. "No, would've heard her."

Stricker busied himself with the filth under his fingernails while Crow drank his beer, a little of it catching in his throat and making him choke. The air was heavy with fear. Andy leaned against the table, regarding Harley with confident, daring eyes. "Then why don't you go on upstairs and prove me wrong? You'd like that, wouldn't you, Harley? Go on up there, go on."

Harley tried to swallow but found his throat dry.

"Go on up."

"Andy—"

"Now."

Harley pulled himself up slowly, looking at Andy entreatingly but finding no absolution. He took a deep breath and headed slowly for the stairs.

Once he was out of sight the atmosphere eased. Andy walked to the couch and sat down.

"She gonna fuck him?" Crow asked timidly.

Andy reached for a beer. "She's going to do things you've never even dreamed about." He took a swallow.

Stricker sighed.

"Andy—" Crow started, then swallowed hard before continuing. "We wanna talk to you."

"About what?"

Crow shot a glance at Stricker. "About this guy Kelsie."

"No need to worry about him."

"He's a smart guy," Crow offered.

"He'll be taken care of," Andy said. "The plan is already down."

Crow looked at him, surprised. "When?"

"After the job. Got full instructions."

Crow and Stricker looked at each other, and Andy caught the look. "Okay, boys. Something wrong?"

"You got instructions?"

"Yes."

"By yourself?"

Andy narrowed his eyes. "You're surprised?"

"No," Crow said. "Guess not. Andy, there's something else. About the job tonight. About Dennis."

"What about him?"

"Well, we was thinkin'," Crow said. "We was thinkin' maybe things didn't go off as planned. We was thinkin'—"

Andy's eyes flared, pinning Crow against the back of the couch. Crow shut his mouth with a snap.

"You think too much, Crow. It's not good for you. It's not healthy, know what I mean?"

"Come on, Andy," Stricker pleaded. "It's just that . . . well . . . it wasn't supposed to come off the way it did. You know? Burying him like that. He was supposed to be—"

"He ran," Andy said quietly. "He planned his own death." He looked at Crow. "You didn't run, Crow. Up there, in the balcony. You didn't run when the Hiding Fear took you. So what do you think? You better off now?"

Crow let his mind wander. . . .

Back there, in the balcony. The blinding white light piercing him, penetrating, making the thing deep inside come to life, and grow.

He remembered it devouring him, remembered its power. Felt it. Felt the power. . . .

He looked at Andy, saw the flicker of light in the center of his eyes, and knew that he had a flicker of his own.

"Yeah," he said, nodding. "I'm better off."

Andy smiled. "Brothers now, right?"

Crow nodded, but didn't return the smile. "But we don't think maybe everything's going down the way it's supposed to. We think maybe . . . well . . . maybe you're takin' on too much. Maybe you—"

Instantly, like the tongue of a snake, Andy lashed out at Crow with one hand, catching him tightly about the throat. He lifted Crow into the air and held him there. Crow's eyes bulged. He clawed fruitlessly at Andy's hand while Andy watched him quietly, calmly.

Stricker moved away from them. "You're killin' him, Andy. Fucking Christ . . ."

Andy lowered him, slowly, until his face was very close to Crow's. "Don't cross me," he said pleasantly. "Don't ever cross me. Now, you know what I can do, don't you?"

Crow squealed. His tongue had begun to loll out, looking blue and dry.

"So, you don't cross me, and you do what I say. And maybe, just maybe, you'll be okay. How does that sound?"

Crow's eyes rolled back in their sockets, his tongue now hanging out and flopping back and forth. In another instant he would have been dead, but Andy let him go before that happened and Crow fell in a heap at his feet.

Andy looked at Stricker, who was now hunched in the corner. He shook his head slowly, then stepped over Crow's limp body and sat down on the couch. "How does it sound, boys?"

Crow pulled himself to his knees, rubbing his throat. "It

sounds good, Andy," he croaked. "It sounds just fine, don't it, Stricker?"

Stricker nodded frantically.

"Good." Andy smiled and leaned back against the couch. "Now let's talk about tomorrow night."

Kelsie waited at the window, watching Joe as he pulled himself up the front steps. His hand went out for the doorknob, and then he stopped. His head turned a little, as if he was trying to catch a fleeting sound on the wind. Then his shoulders turned, and Kelsie knew Joe was looking at him, peering at him through the darkness.

The tableau continued, both of them staring at each other but not really seeing because it was too dark. But each knew the other was there, and in the safety of cloaking darkness they exchanged a glance, dangerously, and spoke with their eyes. It didn't last long, but it was enough for Kelsie to understand the horrible fear.

Help me can't you help me?

Joe shivered a little, then opened the door and went inside.

They met in the living room, and Kelsie could see that Joe wanted to talk as much as he did, but neither knew how to begin. They stood like two men met in a desolate place, lonely and weary and void of life. Kelsie pulled the blanket a little closer around him.

"Cold?" Joe asked feebly.

Kelsie nodded. "Have a good night?"

Joe nodded wordlessly. He went to the fireplace and piled on two more logs. He stood there, resting against the mantel, virtually clinging to it for support. His fist pushed against his belly.

"Stomach bothering you?"

"Yeah."

"You take something for it?"

Joe's lips went tight, making him look old and ugly. "There something you want to say, Kelsie? Because if there isn't, if all you want to do is make with polite bullshit, I'm really not interested."

"Okay."

Joe turned to leave, and as he did Kelsie caught sight of his eyes and saw the despair

help me can't you. . . .

etched so deeply, struggling behind the rigidity, that Kelsie felt it tug on him painfully. He reached out, but his hand froze and he stood there feeling helpless and foolish and very cold.

Joe went past him to the stairs, then stopped about halfway up. Not looking at Kelsie, he said in a low, shaky voice, "Don't go out tomorrow night, okay?"

"Why not?"

"Just don't go out. And don't go to your hotel. Stay here."

"Joe—"

"Just stay here!" Joe whipped around, and even in the darkness Kelsie could see something that hadn't been there before. Something in Joe's eyes. A flicker. A terrible red flicker deep in the center. "You don't know. You just don't know."

"So, tell me, then." He waited, hoping, but Joe was fighting a losing battle. He could see it: a slack jaw, a face without expression, and that horrible, alien flicker in the eyes.

Kelsie took a step toward him, saw Joe twist and strain. The flicker began to fade, and Kelsie felt a sense of hope. "Talk to me."

But then it returned, and Joe's face became set, hard, defeated. "I'm tired."

"So am I. Really tired, Joe."

"Then let's just go to bed, okay? We'll talk tomorrow."

"Will we?"

Joe's head snapped around suddenly. "Stop this. Please."

"I'm scared for you. I've got this crazy feeling. I feel like I'm watching an animal, like an elephant, you know? Elephants go off somewhere and no one has ever seen them go. But they go off, and they die."

"No!" Joe screamed, nearing hysteria. "I'm alive! I'm alive now, for the first time in my life, I'm really living! You want to put a stop to it—that's right! You want me to go back to

Tempac and shuffle papers and kiss ass, that's right, isn't it? Isn't it?"

"Joe—"

"You want me to fail!"

"That's not true," Kelsie said desperately.

Joe clenched his fists, his lips tightening to a firm, angry line. "You've always wanted me to fail. You always wanted to be the best. I tell you what, Kels. You go out tomorrow night. Yeah. You go on out and see who's really the best. See who has control of the situation. You go out and you have a really good time! And then you'll see! You'll see who's best!" He turned on his heel and clambered up the stairs.

For a moment Kelsie didn't know what to do. The words, the suddenness of Joe's explosive anger, had jarred him, and now he stood alone in the middle of the dark living room, feeling cold, bewildered, and frightened. He thought about going after Joe, thought about phrases devised specifically for this kind of situation. Phrases like *butting up against a wall, reaching a stalemate, concluding a problem with no positive resolution.* Joe had plate-glass armor built around him that could probably be shattered, but Joe would get cut in the process.

Walking on eggshells. Standing on shaky ground.

In one evening Kelsie had experienced an influx of indirect data, bits and pieces of an enormous puzzle, and all the pieces were white.

And at the center of the puzzle something waited for him, called to him, beckoned him from inside.

At length he went to the chair by the fire and settled into it, trying to pull it around him. The fire crackled and sputtered, sending sparks fleetingly up the chimney. He watched them in his mind, floating up through the darkness of the flue, breaking out and flying off into space. He wanted to go with them.

So many pieces still missing.

He thought about Janice D'Lacy, the crazy woman, the bag lady. She'd seen the puzzle complete, no doubt, and Kelsie wondered if that was what had made her mad.

He knew he could get some answers from her, or at least a few more pieces to the puzzle.

He'd go see her, probably tomorrow. But for now he'd sit here, huddled within the circle of comforting light, and try to get warm.

God, would he ever be warm again?

6

 Farmland, land not yet touched by concrete and neon light, has its own kind of splendor. Silence in the night is full of promise, the land glowing in moonlight, a kind of secret place of power. You can travel there, but you are a visitor, like an alien from a distant planet. Nothing familiar there.

And it was worse tonight, because the land, refusing to hold the moon's reflection, drew it into the soil, leaving darkness. The silence was thick and syrupy. It was difficult to breathe.

Kelsie caught himself snatching looks over his shoulder as he drove down Broken Hollow Road, expecting to see some kind of sucking monster, pulling in the air through large, gaping nostrils. Eating up the sound, licking up the light.

That morning, the morning after Joe's explosion in the living room, had been shaded with silence. They all sat at the kitchen table eating silently, like the condemned eating their last meal. Joe spent the day in his room, refusing to answer Kelsie's knock, refusing to answer when Kelsie called for him. When Joe left for the theater that evening it was without a word. Only the slam of the front door acknowledged his departure.

Kelsie left the house only a few minutes after, and there on the front yard, slouched in the shadows like a thief, Joe waited for him, waited for Karen to close the front door, waited for Kelsie to move to his car and pause long enough to get his keys out of his pocket. With his head bent and his mind on other things, Kelsie did not see Joe or hear him until he spoke into the back of Kelsie's neck. A thin vein of electricity ran down his spine with cold fingers. It was a sickly, seductive sensation, Joe's voice a hiss. "You'll go out, then, won't you, Kels? Go out, then. And see if I care."

"What's going to happen to me?" Kelsie asked, afraid to turn, afraid to look in Joe's eyes because he didn't want to see that flickering red light he knew was there.

"You just go out, Kels ol' buddy, and you'll see."

"Is that really you?"

The breathing, before so confident and frosty, now halted. "What do you mean?"

And then Kelsie had the courage to turn and look Joe in the eye. The burning was there, but not as vibrant as he suspected it had been before. "Who am I really talking to?"

Joe slunk away, and Kelsie followed him with his rising voice.

"Why are you going to the theater, Joe?"

Joe kept walking.

"You don't show movies any night except Friday. So why go now? What do you do, all alone up there in your private castle?"

Joe stopped, turned. Anger smoldered on his face.

Kelsie bared his teeth. "I'm not afraid, follow me? I'm not afraid of anything you think you can do to me."

For a moment Joe's anger flickered. Then he turned and moved into the shadows, into the night.

The turnoff to the D'Lacy farm loomed up on the left and he nearly missed it. It was a small dirt road, badly neglected. He turned onto it and continued on slowly until he reached an open area just in front of the farmhouse. The house was dark. He parked his car beneath a massive oak tree and turned off the engine.

The cold was returning, rushing out through him from some secret place where it had buried itself, deep inside him. It had been waiting there to radiate at the proper time, to suffocate him again. Now it came, as he watched the lonely house, searched for some sign of life, and found none. He wished he'd brought his coat.

The woman probably wasn't even home, and probably that was a godsend since he didn't even know what he was going to say to her. He had only the speculation of a woman he'd known and loved, and knew her wisdom to be solid. But what would Janice D'Lacy care of these things?

He opened the car door and slid out.

He went up to the front door and knocked.

Nothing.

He knocked again.

From his left he heard a small rustling sound. "Mrs. D'Lacy?"

Nothing.

Kelsie moved off the porch and headed toward the sound. It took him around the side of the house to the back, where he found a large yard. There were no real boundaries to the property: On his left was a stand of pine trees. On the right was a massive, lonely field. A large oak tree snuggled against the side of the house. His feet crunched in the dead leaves from the tree, the sound echoing in the darkness. Across the backyard was an old barn in desperate need of repair. It swayed laboriously to one side as if it had slumped from fatigue over decades of weight. There was no indication of livestock having been there for years, which he thought strange. There should at least have been some chickens, or maybe the sound of a cow from inside the sagging barn. He moved slowly toward the large double doors of the barn, his head jerking cautiously from left to right as he walked.

From behind, a shotgun barrel being snapped into place. He stopped, his foot still in midair. He lowered it slowly and began to turn his head.

"Don't move." The voice was cold and rough, but tinged slightly with fear. He faced forward.

"Put your hands on your head." It was a woman's voice. He obeyed.

There was a rustling of leaves as the woman shifted her weight. "You move and I'll kill you."

"I won't move," Kelsie said firmly. If the woman training the shotgun on his back was D'Lacy, and if D'Lacy was the maniac Rozina and the locals claimed her to be, he was a dead man. He felt his knees threatening to buckle and thought abstractedly that the old saying about your knees knocking did have some validity.

Silence fell between them. Kelsie could feel her studying him, deciding whether to learn more about this intruder or just kill him and be done with it. She was within her rights. He was trespassing. A small trickle of sweat crept into his eye. He waited.

At length the woman demanded in a gruff voice that he move into the barn. He didn't want to do that. Once she got him inside that barn she would kill him instantly.

"Are you Janice D'Lacy?"

"Shut up!" She jammed the shotgun into the small of his back, hitting him just right, at the curve of the spine. A needle of pain wedged between the bones, and he clenched his teeth.

"You came here to kill me, you bastard," she said bitterly.

"No . . . that's not true. I just wanted to talk to you. Uh . . . Rozina sent me. You know Rozina? She owns the bar down on—"

"Shut up!" The barrel again, this time lower. The pain shot down his legs.

"Please . . . I don't mean you any harm. You've got to believe me."

"Why should I believe you?"

Kelsie hesitated, struggling for the right answer. "My name is Kelsie Brown. I—"

"I know who you are!" the woman said angrily. "Think I don't know who you are? Think I don't know why you're here?"

A pause, then, "You been to the theater?"

"Yes."

"Saw the movie, did you?"

"Well, yeah. . . ." Kelsie shifted a little. "I think so."

"Tell me, Mr. Brown," the woman said in an almost sarcastic tone, "are you cold?"

Kelsie sighed deeply. "Yeah. Yeah, I am."

"Then that's why I'm gonna kill you, Mr. Brown."

Now the barrel was at the base of his skull. He heard the

trigger being cocked, and the world flashed white. "Please! Why? Why would you do this?"

"You know why."

"I don't. I swear it! I . . . ." His knees finally gave way, and he slipped to the ground. A computer hack from L.A. just wasn't equipped for this kind of stress, that's all there was to it. The cold shotgun barrel went down with him, planted in his flesh.

He had his eyes clamped firmly shut, and against his eyelids he saw swirls of bright color, flashing images of red and blue. His mind merged with them, flying out from him as he lost what was left of his sanity. Disjointed thoughts raced without direction. His upstairs bathroom was only half painted, and the backyard partly mowed. *My God*, he thought, *I'm leaving my life in a shambles, everything left undone.* She was going to kill him. She was really going to spread him all over her yard. That project still sitting in disarray on his desk back at Tempac, three quarters completed. Had he remembered to shut down the computer? Oh, hell, just one glitch in the electricity and the whole file would be wiped away. Just like that. Things can get wiped away with just one little half-second glitch. A small whimper escaped from his throat and added to his feeling of helplessness. Out here, turned to dog food on a cold October night, spread out over the courtyard in small, nondescript pieces. Blood. Everywhere. His blood.

His blood.

Time dragged.

Pressure against the base of his skull. Cold steel penetrating, God . . . would he ever get warm again?

"Don't move."

He tried to speak, but his tongue had cleaved to the roof of his mouth and how many times had he read that? He had never believed your tongue could actually get stuck to the roof of your mouth. He believed it now.

He could feel her watching him. Watching his agony.

His bladder cramped. He doubled a little, his hands coming down to clutch his lower belly.

"Don't move."

Wait . . .

. . . Wait a minute, God damn it. . . .

. . . What the hell was she doing?

He opened his eyes, slowly, and ventured turning his head. The hard steel slammed against his neck, and this time he groaned, but the groan was tinged with anger.

"What do you want me to do?" His voice surprised him; a little shaky, yes, but forceful, full of anger. "What do you want, lady? Want me to grovel in the dirt? Want me to piss myself? Is that what you want?"

The pressure against his skull eased.

"Why don't you come around here, lady? Watch my eyes bulge, okay? Watch me cry, you'd like that! Jesus, are all you people crazy with this crap?"

The barrel left him, leaving a small circle of cold on his skin. He heard her shuffling indecisively, then walking, and then she was in front of him, the barrel bent at an angle toward the ground. He could see into it. It was very dark inside that barrel.

October was a lousy time to die. October has such a good smell to it. The air changes in October.

Kelsie shook his head. "Hell, no, lady. You do it, go ahead. Just do it because that's it for me. I'm through putting on a show for you."

The shotgun moved, the barrel bending up into repose as she cradled it in her arms. With the sharp angle of the barrel out of his vision he could see the woman more clearly. The muscles in her jaw were relaxed, but there was keen suspicion in her eyes.

With a kind of sadness she said, "It's cold out here. Get up."

Kelsie meant to stand but instead fell forward, a gush of air bursting from his lungs in a short, painful "Uh!" His dinner was making plans to travel, and it took a great deal of effort, more than he'd thought he had in him, to keep from throwing up. Icy sweat bathed him cruelly. He was cold again. Goddamn, he was cold all over, again.

The woman bent down and grabbed him by the arm, lifting him awkwardly. He leaned on her, desperately searching for

balance, but she moved away once he was on his feet, stepping back and leveling the shotgun at his chest.

"I won't trust you just yet, Mr. Brown," she said evenly.
She motioned to the back door of the house. "In there."

He fell into a chair at the kitchen table, his body shaking
badly from the cold now blanketing him from within, and
there was a sour taste in his mouth. He wrapped his arms
tightly around himself. The woman stood across the kitchen
by the refrigerator, her shotgun still aimed at him. He was
surprised by her frailty. The oversized sweater was the one
he had seen her wear in town. Her graying hair was pulled
back in a tight ponytail.

"You are Mrs. D'Lacy, aren't you?" he asked.

D'Lacy nodded, then her mouth twisted in an awkward
grin. "I just go by Jan. Never did go in for that 'Mrs.' crap.
What do you want from me, Mr. Brown?"

She was the bag lady, but that hunched, tired look to her
shoulders was gone. Her body didn't shuffle awkwardly as it
had done when he saw her on the street. Her face was as
rugged as the land she lived on. Deep lines mapped her
cheeks and brow, darkened by sun and hard work. Her jaw
was strong and set, and the muscles of her neck sagged a
little with age. Her eyes were a striking blue that glistened in
contrast to her ruddy complexion. Despite the fact that she
had planned to kill him only a few minutes before, he could
see there had been a time in her life when she was friendly,
the kind of friendliness that was born of hard work and simple living. To have had such unique qualities crushed out of
existence so brutally was tragic.

"I'm trying to help Joe. Something's wrong with him.
Something's wrong all over, and I get the feeling you know
about it. That's right, isn't it?"

D'Lacy looked away, and for a moment Kelsie's attention
was caught by the room they were in. It was old, worn out,
and in need of much repair, but it was airy and clean, a
cleanliness that went deep into its heart. It was like the lady
who owned it, simple and rugged, and it made Kelsie feel a
little sad that, but for the two of them, it was empty. Once, a

long time ago, it had been filled with the sounds of family. If he closed his eyes he could hear them in the echoes, hiding flimsy and forgotten in the corners. The room was empty now.

"I've got nothing to tell you," she said.

"You're lying."

She looked at him sharply. "It's dangerous, you being here. Dangerous for me, and you. Don't think the theater don't know you're here. And don't you think it ain't makin' plans."

Kelsie stared at her. "What do you mean, the theater?"

Her mouth twisted, responding to some inner conflict. "Just what I said. The Fareland . . . it's got power."

The cold stabbed him. "How?"

"Some things just can't be explained, Mr. Brown. People always got to have answers. They got to have something solid they can lay their hands on, or they can't believe it. But some things just can't be explained. And they don't have to be. They're real. Stuff happens when that theater is in operation. Livestock stolen. Fields burned up. Families . . . driven out of town or killed. And there's a lot more. The theater tells them what to do and they do it. And they don't ask questions."

"But why?" Kelsie asked fitfully. "Why do these things happen?"

Janice looked away. The words whispered across his neck. "The Hiding Fear."

Kelsie shivered. "The what?"

When Janice turned back to him, her eyes were large and cold. "Ever think about what's deep inside, Mr. Brown? Way down inside, where you've never been 'cause it's too cold and it's too alien, even though it's a part of you? Ever think about that?"

Kelsie stared at her, transfixed.

Janice threw him a knowing glance. "You show someone what's deep down inside, something they could never look at, and it devours them. Makes them do things they wouldn't normally do. Makes them puppets, 'cause if they don't do it, they get shown it again."

Kelsie remembered the images on the screen moving, pulling him in. *Hiding Fear.*

He pulled the slip of paper, the fifty-year-old clipping, out of his breast pocket and placed it on the kitchen table. He motioned to it with a nod. "You know about this? You know who this is?"

She leaned forward, and he saw the recognition in her eyes. Her mouth worked with the memory.

"You know the boy?" Kelsie asked gently.

Her mouth pulled down in a hate-filled grimace. "My son. . . ."

Kelsie closed his eyes. He hadn't bargained for that.

"Tried to stop the theater, him and his dad."

"I'm sorry."

"They got in the way," she said, her voice rising with pain. "And so they were killed." She rubbed her eyes with the heel of her hand. "That's what you came here to find out? That's what you came to do? Torture me with this? You're a hateful man, Mr. Brown."

"No," he whispered, feeling sick and cold and very ashamed. "I'm trying to stop it from happening again."

She uttered a bitter laugh. "You can't." She made a lunge toward the table and for a moment Kelsie thought she was going to attack him, but instead she sat down next to him. She was trembling, her breath coming in short gasps. "Let me tell you about it. You want to hear it, yes? That's what you came for. You want all the details. So I'll tell you, Mr. Brown. I'll tell you, and then you let it seep inside you and make you colder than you are now. Think I didn't notice? You're cold. And I tell you now, you'll never be warm again. It touched you, didn't it?"

Her closeness was making him uneasy. Her eyes were unbearably intense, fear and hate raging beneath the surface. Her face was distorted with the pain, made ugly with insanity. She spoke in a halting, raspy voice.

"That theater, that power, it made an example of my husband and my boy. It does that, you know. Makes examples. My husband and my son were dragged into the field out there. They cut off my husband's head, and my son"—she stopped, her hands clenching each other tight—"he was seventeen years old, just beginning to live, you know? He was a good boy, never gave me any trouble and oh! he was so strong. . . .

"They dragged him out of his bed one night and hauled him off to that field. They made him watch while they killed his dad, then they stretched him out on the ground and they cut into him, slow. There were six of 'em, all with hunting knives. They just kept cutting into him and he screamed! He screamed for such a long time and then he just stopped. He just . . . stopped. . . ." Her head drooped, the trembling fading into hitches as she sobbed.

The terror of watching her family being brutalized and murdered was something beyond Kelsie's comprehension. Seeing now the madness, the terror gone cold and planted like seeds in fertile soil, made him tremble with foreboding. The closeness of her, the unexacting, frightening emotion, made him feel sick. But still he sat there, listening, trying to understand. She struggled to stifle her sobs, and as she raised her head Kelsie saw the whirling, intense glare in her eyes that marked her insanity. They darted, watching things he could never see. She flinched, hearing things he hoped he'd never hear. Then she looked at him, her pinwheel eyes settling on him. He fought the urge to run.

"It was a long time ago," she whispered, "and it happened yesterday. It will happen tomorrow, because that's the way it is with power. Not revolution, no, oh, no, no, no . . . not revolution. Convolution. Do you see it? Can you hear it beckoning you?"

"Yes—"

"It's on the wind, and the wind is constant here." Her face went blank.

Kelsie shifted a little, clearing his throat, hoping his voice would be steady. "Why weren't you killed?"

She stared at him, frozen, her eyes frosted over. "Enough."

Kelsie's blood chilled. "What does that mean?"

She shrugged, and her face came back to life.

"It's on the clipping. Here," he pointed. She glanced at it

distantly and shrugged again. "It's hungry . . . then it's had enough. That's all."

He sat back, rubbed his chin. "I understand the Fareland hasn't been in operation in over fifty years."

D'Lacy nodded.

"Why is that?"

"Frank Jordan was the owner back then," D'Lacy answered. Her voice was trembling, but it'd lost the strangeness. She was more lucid now, her words considered and exact and well defined. Kelsie felt a shudder of relief pass through him. "He was a rich man. Very rich. He built the Fareland from scratch, made it into a real showplace. People came up from San Francisco to watch the movies. Everything was just fine until one night, he had this 'private screening.' That's when it all began. The next day a family was found in their beds, slaughtered."

"Weren't the police brought in?"

"Oh, sure," she said cynically. "They were brought in. And then they were invited to a 'private screening.' That stopped their meddling real fast." She eyed him suspiciously. "You're not thinking of bringing the police in on this, are you?"

"No."

"Because if you do, you'll pay. The wind is constant." Her face was beginning to go slack again.

"I never thought of it," he said, his voice urgent.

Then she went on, as if nothing had interrupted, and as she did she sat with her hands tightly laced together. Her expression was intense, interrupted occasionally by a flicker of pain. "It got worse. Regular showings got to be less and less, until all that was left were the 'private screenings.' That theater, it showed people things. Told them things. Things only they could understand. And then it gave orders, and the people obeyed."

"That's hard to believe," Kelsie said.

She looked at him, her eyes growing secretive and sly. "People do desperate things, to keep from having to look too deep down inside. And what if someone else, someone bad, knew what was there? Knew what your Hiding Fear was.

Knew how to pull it out and make it devour you. Wouldn't you do just about anything to make him happy?"

Kelsie nodded numbly.

"Then it's not so hard to believe, is it?"

"Guess not," Kelsie whispered.

She heaved a troubled sigh and studied her hands. "It's not only that . . . I mean, not only trying to stop the Hiding Fear. Some people, they had the streak in them, you know? The evil was already there. And the Hiding Fear, it just brought it to life. They turned ugly. Turned evil. They needed it, made them hungry. So it went on like that, people being too scared not to do what they were told to do, and people being charmed into doing it. Loving it. And the theater . . ."

She stopped.

"What about the theater, Mrs. D'Lacy?"

She looked at him keenly. "That theater, Mr. Brown. It feeds. Feeds on the evil and the fear, until it's had enough."

She leaned back and sighed. "Then one day it all just stopped."

"What do you mean?"

"Just what I said," she answered dryly. "The projector just stopped running. Frank tried everything in his power to get it going again. I got the feeling he was getting some sort of kick out of the whole thing. I mean, like a drug. He needed that theater. It was like it was sustaining him. But it just stopped. One day. All of a sudden."

"Maybe Frank couldn't please it anymore," Kelsie guessed.

"No," she countered. "No, I don't think that's what it was. I think maybe Frank started to get cocky . . . sort of. Like maybe he thought he was the one with the power. And maybe he was, in a way. I mean, he was something concrete, something the people could identify with. I don't think they ever really believed it was the theater controlling them. It was Frank. He was kinda like . . . oh, hell, I can't think of the word."

"The dominant force?" Kelsie offered.

"Yeah! And the theater was the tool he used to control the

town. I don't think it liked that. It tolerated him for a while, then it wrote him off."

"And left him to care for it while it waited for new blood." Kelsie leaned back in his chair, frowning. "Must have been one hell of a blow to his ego."

"Yeah. He put it up for sale quick."

"Did he have many offers?"

She shook her head. "Lots of possibles, no takes. I think the theater was scaring them away. I remember one night, real late. I couldn't sleep so I took a walk. I found Frank standing outside the theater and he looked really pissed . . . shaking his fists at it and shouting, "What do you want! What the hell do you want from me!""

"So it was waiting for just the right person to come along." Kelsie thought about Joe. "Someone young."

"Yeah," D'Lacy said, nodding solemnly. "And not too cocky."

That was Joe, Kelsie thought. Young, strong, but not all that confident. He was easily intimidated. You could get him off balance with an awkward nod, subtle look, the passing innuendo. Then he was your slave.

A slave.

Kelsie shuddered.

"There's got to be some way of stopping it."

"I'm not sure you can," D'Lacy said. "It's powerful. It's got a whole town full of people doing what it tells them to do. How can you fight that?"

Kelsie leaned back, closing his eyes, and let what D'Lacy had told him sink in. This thing—this power—had Joe by the throat. Hell, it had the whole town by the throat, because somehow, possibly by virtue of its own existence, it knew what really scared them.

It had to be stopped.

When he looked again at D'Lacy she was sitting placidly, smiling, nodding her head in a way that made him feel dizzy.

"All right now," she said evenly, her eyes taking on a sheen of sanity that surprised him. "Listen to me, and listen well. Power is what it is, and the wind is constant. Go looking for it, and it will find you. Taps into you, fills you up, and empties you out. That theater knows you're here, don't think you're safe from it. No one's safe, 'cause there's always something—always something deep down, where nobody else can see, and you can't hide from it forever. Follow me?"

Kelsie remembered the blackness, the breathing, the radiant cold pressing against his back. He shivered.

"One more thing, Mr. Brown." D'Lacy leaned forward. "If they catch you, they'll kill you."

Kelsie nodded.

D'Lacy sat back, looking satisfied. "You go on now, go home."

Kelsie rose stiffly, moved to the kitchen door, and then stopped. "Am I going to be able to save Joe?"

"Are you even sure it's Joe anymore?"

The cold bit at him, bit deep.

7

Even with the car heater on full blast Kelsie couldn't get warm.

It wasn't like him to be so shaken by the words of a crazy woman, but it wasn't just her words. And it wasn't just that awful blank look on her face. Those things were part of something bigger, something he'd kept hidden, from himself as well as everyone else, because it had been too disturbing to think about. It was like getting yourself involved with something sick; a group, a situation, a morbid thought that everyone has but no one cops to it because there's too much to deal with when the spirit is weak.

He was a man of logic, God damn it. All this surrealism, all this mindplay, was getting on his nerves.

He wheeled into the parking space in front of his bungalow and shut down the engine. He sat there quietly, listening to the ticking sound of the cooling engine, and tried to sort out what he'd felt, and was feeling now, when asked so simple a question. Simple, and yet loaded with gunshot.

What's down there, deep down inside, where you've never looked before?

When he'd looked at the screen, with its geometric shapes and splashes of light and shadow, he had been terrified. But when Karen looked at it, she saw nothing. Felt nothing.

Why not?

She wasn't a local. And maybe only locals were affected.

But he wasn't a local either. So why had he been so scared? Why was it that he couldn't get warm?

You're vulnerable, Kelsie. Your hair wasn't always gray.

Kelsie gripped the steering wheel.

He hadn't bargained for this. Not this.

At length he slipped out from behind the wheel and went into his motel room.

Still shaking with the cold, he needed to do something to calm himself, dispel the sickly thoughts still pounding against the door he'd shut in his mind. Mind play. That's what it was. That D'Lacy had done a number on him. Rozina had warned him. Don't listen too closely, she'd said. Don't listen.

Because the mind is full of loopholes easily slipped. Weak knots, easily untied.

Except, there was that pressure, that radiant cold. There was that beckoning from something unseen, molding to the darkness of the theater.

No, he hadn't bargained for this.

He went to the bathroom and turned the shower on full blast. Steam rose in soft white billows and plumed against the ceiling. He undressed and slipped inside the stall.

He felt his muscles relax a little as the steaming water splashed against his back. He hadn't realized how tense he was until the heat penetrated, dispelling the cold that had been in him for what seemed like forever. He tilted his head back and let the warmth blanket his head.

He didn't even have time to scream when the light went out and they yanked him from the stall.

Five men, lifting him off the floor and propelling him into the bedroom. Rage came, full and colorful, as he struggled against them, lashing out with his feet. One foot hit a man square in the groin and he fell away, but another took his place.

The man stood in front of him, and Kelsie saw the eyes; sullen and dark except for the center, where that familiar flicker burned. He saw the clenched fist draw back, saw it in slow motion on a trajectory to his face, and he knew it would hurt.

His cheek exploded in fire and pain.

Kelsie tried again to kick at the man in front of him, but the man was too quick. He stepped back, and Kelsie's foot swung through empty air.

Another fist, in slow motion, this time ramming into his belly. The force of it took his strength.

He would have gone to the floor, but the two men holding
his arms kept him aloft as his legs went limp and he hung
there, strengthless, trying to breathe. The room grayed a little, the men blurred out of focus.

He was aware of their hands on him, dragging him across
the room, letting him fall in a heap to the floor. He tried to
roll on his side but they were on him, grabbing his wrists and
ankles, stretching him out. They stretched his arms until he
thought they would snap off at the shoulders, and heavy
weight pressed down on his wrists.

He felt his legs being forced apart, stretching, too, until his
groin screamed, and the weight again, this time on his ankles.

A trickle of strength crept into him and he grappled, trying
to break free. A heavy boot floated above him. Before he
realized what was happening the boot came down hard,
smashing into his belly. The impact sent a sick pain up into
his throat. He cried out, gagging on the sound.

The carpet felt warm and scratchy against his skin. He
craned his neck to see who was holding him pinned to the
floor. He knew them. Locals. He knew them, except for the
greasy lizard smiles on their stupid faces. And there were
three others, ones he recognized as being those who stood at
the entries to the theater on Friday night. The sentinels.
They were gathered now in a sloppy group by the door. One
of them made sickly giggling sounds deep in his throat, and
had a look that floated somewhere between delight and rancid lust.

He took in air, held it, then let it out in a sudden rush of
panic. "Why?"

A low, sinister voice sliced through the darkness from the
shadows near the door. "Orders, Mr. Brown. You know
about orders, don't you?"

Kelsie craned his neck again, this time to look at the slender figure by the door, leaning casually against the jamb.

Andy.

He walked with grace, moving to Kelsie's side, looking
down on him. Then he straddled Kelsie's hips and sat down
hard. Kelsie stifled a groan.

Andy was holding something cylindrical in his hand that glinted in the moonlight as he waved it back and forth.

It was a cattle prod.

"I'd tell you not to take this personal, Brown. But I'd be lying," Andy said. "It ain't my plan, you know? I had better plans for you. But we all got orders. We all dance, in one form or another."

"Are you going to kill me?"

Andy shook his head. "This world is treacherous, Mr. Brown—can I call you Kelsie?" He grinned. "It's a treacherous world, and if you're gonna survive, you gotta have a plan. And once you get it, you gotta stick to it." He leaned close, his mouth twisting. "I wanna kill you. I wanna watch the life come out of you, a little at a time. But it just ain't part of the plan."

"So what is?" Kelsie rasped. "Torture?"

Andy laughed. "What's torture for one man is just a walk in the park for another." He held his smile a moment longer, then let his mouth twist into an angry grimace. "We don't like strangers butting in where they're not wanted. You've been a bad boy. You need to learn some manners."

Kelsie thought about yelling for help, but he was sure no one would come. They were all too scared. And too hungry.

And something else occurred to him. Something that was so obvious, he was a little embarrassed he hadn't seen it before.

They were scared, yes. Hungry, yes. But they were also relieved, because they hadn't been the ones chosen.

Enough.

It was an important revelation, and he cursed the fact that he didn't have time to consider it further.

The cattle prod floated above him, moonlight delicately glinting off its smooth surface. Andy laid his hand on Kelsie's belly. "You're shaking, Mr. Brown. You're cold? Huh? Let me warm you up." He touched the cattle prod to Kelsie's middle.

White heat, like a shock wave, flashed through him. He felt his body convulse, lashing in protest. Air hissed through his clenched teeth.

"How long?" Andy whispered, fingering the square of burnt flesh on Kelsie's belly. "How long will it take before you scream?" He held the prod aloft, then brought it down swiftly, this time letting it skip along the inside of Kelsie's left arm. The pain snaked, following like a shadow as the prod traced a path down his left side.

Kelsie twisted away from it, moaning deeply as the agony streaked through him like a bullet. He closed his eyes against the pain, against the sound of his flesh crackling and burning, against everything.

The pain lingered. He moaned again, and heard a soft sigh of satisfaction from Andy. When he looked, he saw the animation on Andy's young face. He saw the flicker, and saw that it was different from the others', more powerful, more brilliant. Unlike the others', Andy's eyes were dancing.

The prod touched him again, this time on his chest, and the pain sent him into heavy convulsions, his back arching and twisting. The scream, stuffed down inside, now came in full force, ripping up through his chest and tearing his throat. His heart slammed hard, then fluttered, and the world went gray.

Fingers against his throat, probing. Gentle breathing in his ear. Someone talking in hushed whispers.

"He can't take another shock to the heart. It'll kill him."

"Well, then," Andy chided, "I'll just have to find another place."

The pressure on his hips lessened, then came again, pressing against his inner thighs. He slitted his eyes open and saw Andy, wedged between his thighs, looking down. He held the prod just a foot above Kelsie's groin.

Kelsie stared in horror. "No . . ."

The prod descended.

Kelsie shut his eyes.

Andy touched the prod to Kelsie's groin and let it linger.

A web of fire exploded from his groin, shooting sparks of fire up through his body, coiling, twisting in his belly. He howled, screamed, and his body jerked and writhed. His stomach wrenched free its gorge and sent it rising into his throat. He felt his head being turned and the vomit spewed out.

They wouldn't let him die. Someone had turned his head to keep him from choking. God damn them, they wouldn't let him die.

It didn't stop. The pain became a part of him, of his life, his memory. There was nothing else. No men, no one holding him down, pinned like a butterfly against a white card, no town, no cold, the cold was gone. There was nothing, except the pain. The *pain*.

All he could hear was his screaming. All he could see was the color of the scream. It was clean and clear, iridescent in the deep dark reaches of his mind. He could feel the color, could reach out and touch it, white hot, burning the lining of his psyche.

Then Andy was there, his body lying across Kelsie's like a lover's, his face very close. "Next time . . . I'll cut you open. Make you eat your guts. Hear me? Huh?" He grabbed Kelsie by the jaw and yanked his head around. "Do you hear me?"

"Yes—"

He never heard them leave. The pain was still everything. Only vaguely did he realize he was no longer being held down.

It took every ounce of strength left to him to roll over, pulling his knees up protectively to his chest. The pain had begun to subside enough to let in the rage. His body shook with it.

He tried to pull himself up, just enough to get to the phone, but his strength was gone. He'd used it up when he rolled over. He crooked a finger around the phone cord and gave it a feeble tug. The phone fell with a clunk and a short ring next to his head.

Fingers shaking, he dialed Karen's number.

As the phone rang, panic rose. What if she wasn't home? There was no one else to call. No one would help him. They'd just let him lie there on the floor, shaking, engulfed in pain, until it took away everything and left him a lifeless shell. Loneliness seeped in and gripped him with crippling force.

Then the phone clicked and he heard Karen's voice. "Karen—"

"Kelsie? My God, what's wrong? Are you all right?"

"They got to me," he said, then his body fell into uncontrolled shudders. He held on to the phone, clutching it desperately.

"Where are you?" Karen asked. She was frightened, but her voice held a certain command to it that was comforting.

"My motel . . . number five . . . hurry!"

"I'm on my way," she said, and hung up.

Kelsie let the phone drop from his hand. He thought about just lying there until she got to him. It would be so easy to just lie there, lie very still, and maybe it wouldn't hurt as much. Instead he dragged himself up on his hands and knees and crawled into the bathroom.

The sound of the shower was comforting. He drew himself toward it, let it drown out the pain. He crawled, whimpering, until he was inside the stall. He crouched in one corner. And then he wept.

Sadists, that's what they were. Monsters, horrible, ugly monsters that would do this to him.

Ah, no, but it wasn't the people, was it? No—oh, God, no. It was the Fareland.

And it was Andy. That young boy with the smooth, clean face and dancing eyes. Andy had done this to him. Andy, and that fucking theater.

A little more of the real world filtered in through the web of pain. He looked down at his body, saw the charred square of skin on his abdomen, and then quickly looked away. He didn't want to look further, not yet. He couldn't handle that yet.

Rage, bright and blade thin, flooded the pain with fresh light. He'd get back at Andy. Yes, he'd get him for doing this. And he'd get that damned theater too.

Andy for revenge. The Fareland for Joe.

8

Karen found Kelsie huddled in one corner of the shower stall, the water cascading from the shower head now cold. He was shivering, his skin a deadly shade of white. She pulled him from the stall and got him to his feet. With her arm around his waist she guided him clumsily out of the bathroom. Halfway to the bed his moaning turned to long, harsh sobs and he stumbled once, then fell sprawling just before she could get him onto the bed. It was then that she saw the burns on his chest and stomach, and only fleetingly did she see the burn on his groin. The first glimpse of it told her she would have to prepare before looking at it more closely. Already there was a thin wire coiling in her stomach.

She ripped the blanket from the bed and quickly covered him. He didn't seem to be aware of her until she pulled the blanket back gently, examining him.

"Down there," he said, choking on the words. Karen took a deep breath and lifted the blanket. Nausea welled in her throat. She closed her eyes and slapped her hand over her mouth to keep from throwing up.

She could feel Kelsie looking at her, imploring her. "Am I . . . did they . . . ?"

She reached for another blanket and ripped it off the bed, crying out as she did more in anger and despair than anything else.

"Karen!"

"No!" she almost shouted, but it came out in a sob. She laid the second blanket over the first, tucking it around his shoulders. "No, Kelsie. They didn't . . . it's all right. The burn . . . it's on your groin." She rubbed her face hard.

Kelsie's body shook as he let out a labored sigh of relief. Then he began to cry.

Karen watched him, feeling helpless and scared. He had a funny color to him; not quite gray, not quite white. Somewhere in between. In a movie she'd once seen, a woman was drowning. Right at the end of her death throes the special effects department had made her eyes white. It didn't last more than a moment on the screen, but it was long enough for you to realize that something about the woman had changed. You knew, without really understanding how you knew, that she was dying.

Karen believed that if Kelsie opened his eyes just now, they would be white.

"Kelsie."

The air caught in his chest as he tried to rake it into his constricted lungs. A cold settled in on them both, moving like a breeze, draping itself like a shroud. From somewhere she had first thought was outside came the sound of something droning, like bees. Then she realized it was coming from inside of her.

"Kelsie, we have to leave."

He didn't respond, only made that terrible shivering, catching sound deep in his chest. She thought, for a single, horrible moment, that his heart was going to just stop. He'd rake in air one more time, his chest would rise in that awful constricted way, and then he'd let it out and his body would grow still. She grabbed him by the shoulders and pulled him into a sitting position. "Kelsie, we are leaving now." She got to her feet and tugged hard, pulling him up.

Getting him into the car had been easier than she'd expected. He still had some of his strength, and some of his mind. He hadn't yet fallen into that endless, soundless well of pain and utter despair. But getting him up the stairs in Frank Jordan's house (and it *was* Frank Jordan's house, wasn't it?) proved more difficult. He'd fallen twice, the last incident almost ending in disaster as her foot slipped and her hold on him broke loose. He'd tumbled down three steps, screaming, and only his hand reaching out to grab at her, and her subsequent grab for him, saved him from crashing all the way down to the entry-hall floor. It would have broken his neck, yes, and then she'd have been alone in Frank Jordan's house. Alone with a dead man.

When she finally got him into bed he was white all over, his body bathed in sweat. The sheets were soaked just seconds after she'd gotten the covers up over him, and the wounds now had a hectic, flaming look to them that intensified her fear. She had begged him to let her take him to a hospital, but each time she mentioned it his eyes would widen in terror and he'd shake his head frantically. Finally she stopped asking, stopped entreating him, because it frightened her to see him so hysterical and not understand why. She put him in bed and set about cleaning the wounds herself.

She swabbed the burns with Silvadene ointment she'd gotten last summer for a severe sunburn. The wounds on his chest and stomach were severe but not as bad as the one that skidded down his left side, which had already blistered and was now weeping something that looked like carob syrup. Healing the wounds would be difficult but not impossible, as long as infection didn't set in. She cursed herself for having thrown away nearly a full bottle of Amoxicillin while packing to move to Fareland. Still, she was relatively confident the wounds would heal if she kept them clean.

The wound on his groin was far more serious. It lay in the fold between his leg and hip, about the size of her fist, and the outer layer of skin was completely burned away. The flesh beneath had a sickly blue-black hue to it, weeping a thick red slime. Despite her gentleness Kelsie screamed and writhed when she touched it. His screaming made her heart hurt.

Andy had done this; she was certain. And Andy had enjoyed it while he burned holes in Kelsie's body.

But why hadn't Andy castrated him? Why hadn't Andy just killed him?

A warning? Hurt him, but don't damage him permanently? A warning—or an example.

When she was nearly done Kelsie's screaming had diminished to a low groan. He seemed clearer, maybe even a little stronger. He was watching her as she worked, and she decided to try one more time to get him to a hospital. He only shook his head.

"You don't understand," he said, clenching his teeth as she touched the wound. "Next time they'll kill me."

"Then that's why we should leave," Karen said. "We should just get the hell out of here, Kelsie."

Kelsie shook his head. "I'm not leaving. Not now. Now, it's personal."

Karen fell silent. She knew exactly what he meant.

"I tried to warn you."

Karen turned at the voice, and something hot and moist gripped her spine when she saw the man standing at the door.

At first she didn't know who it was. Then she saw the face change, like a double exposure. She blinked.

"Joe?"

Joe moved past her as if she weren't there and sat down on the bed. Slowly, breathing evenly, he pulled the blanket down to look at Kelsie's wounds.

He straightened, his face slack and nearly empty of expression. "I tried to warn you, and you wouldn't listen." He chuckled in a wry, disgruntled way. "You never thought I was very smart, did you?"

"What are you saying?" Karen asked, unnerved by Joe's lack of response to what he had seen beneath the covers.

"You knew," Kelsie said, eyes widening. "You knew."

Joe nodded. "I'm sorry, Kels. I'm truly very sorry. But you shouldn't have butted in."

"D'Lacy's right, isn't she?" Kelsie said. "Next time they kill me."

Joe nodded, then leaned forward and looked deep into Kelsie's eyes. "But there doesn't have to be a next time. Not if you stay here, stay put. Do what you're told."

"By who?" Kelsie yelled. "You? Christ, you *knew* they were going to do this! You're dangerous, Joe. Dangerous to me."

"I'm not dangerous!" Joe shouted, baring his teeth. *"I'm*

not dangerous! I tried to warn you! I tried to *save* you! But you wouldn't listen! You *never* listen to me! No one ever listens to me! So I get the blame. I get the fucking blame and it's *not my fault!*"

Kelsie started to rise.

"What are you doing?" Joe asked shakily.

"I'm getting out." Kelsie's arms trembled with his weight, but he continued to struggle to a sitting position. "Getting the hell away from you."

With a swiftness that both scared and awed Karen, Joe drove his fists into Kelsie's shoulders, ramming him down and pinning him to the bed. Kelsie cried out, but Karen could see by the look on his face that it was more in fear than pain.

"Karen!" Joe shouted over his shoulder. "Get some neckties from the closet."

"Why?"

"Just *do it!*"

Karen jumped, suddenly frightened. At first she was going to protest, but the sound of Joe's voice stopped her. He was angry, and so strong—stronger than she would ever have expected. The power in his arms as he bore down on Kelsie was so forceful as to drive Kelsie halfway into the mattress. She turned on her heel and went to the closet.

"What are you going to do?" Kelsie asked shakily.

"Keep you here," Joe said, "any way I can."

Karen saw Kelsie stiffen. He shook his head slowly. "No . . . Joe, don't—don't do this."

"Shut up!" Joe bellowed. "God damn you anyway, you son of a bitch! Who told you to come here? Who told you to butt in? You're ruining *everything!*"

Karen returned with the neckties and Joe snatched them from her hands with such speed and fury, they left burn marks on her palms. She backed up a little.

Kelsie was shaking horribly now, turning his head from side to side. He pleaded with Joe, but Joe ignored him. The rage in his face distorted him, made him look inhuman. "You'll stay here," he breathed, "and do what you're told."

He rose, and brought his left knee down on Kelsie's chest, directly into the wound.

This time Kelsie screamed with a pain so severe, it wrenched his body and left him helpless. Joe grabbed his left arm, wrapped the tie around his wrist, and then tied it to the bedstead. Kelsie lay powerless as he did the same with his right wrist, pulling the necktie tight, and then went to the foot of the bed and tethered his feet in the same fashion. When he was done he stood straight, breathing hard, his fists clenching.

He turned and looked at Karen. She felt her heart skip. "You don't want to untie him," he said in a low, menacing voice. "Unless you want his blood on your hands."

Karen swallowed hard. "I'm not afraid of you, Joe. I'll take him out of here. I'll take him away where you can't get to him."

Joe bared his teeth at her. He reached out, grabbed her arm, and pulled her to the window. He shoved her against it, mashing her face into the glass.

"Look out there," he bellowed. "Look out there!"

Karen struggled to look out. There were dark shadows dotting the ground, some moving, some standing still. Clearly they were people, lots of them, all looking up at her.

"You try to leave," Joe whispered, "and they'll kill you both before you get the front door open." He released her and moved away.

Karen stood there for a moment, watching the people watch her. Then she turned. "Don't leave, Joe."

"I got nothing to keep me here," he said coldly.

She reached out for him. "Joe, please—"

Suddenly his fist came up in a wide swing, and Karen knew with all her heart that he was going to strike her. The look on his face, in his *eyes,* was so alien, so threatening. She brought her arm up protectively.

But something stayed his hand, and it hung in the air uselessly, without direction. Slowly he lowered it, and Karen saw, in the center of his eyes, a shadow of something familiar. It was something very old, and very tired, but it was familiar.

"Joe?"

"I just run the projector," he said pitifully. "You have to believe that. I don't have anything to do with what they see."

"It's killing people, Joe," Karen said. "It's killing."

Joe covered his face with his hands.

She reached out, grabbed his arms, and pulled his hands away. His face was flushed and wet with tears. "Come back to me, Joe. Why don't you just come back to me?"

"It's too late," he said sorrowfully. "It's inside me now. Breathing. Growing. I can't—it's just too strong."

He turned, walked to the door, then stopped and glanced over his shoulder. "And you know what?" he said. "I think—I think I like it."

He went through the threshold.

"You did this to Kelsie!" Karen yelled. "You did it, because you gave Andy the power to do it!"

Joe turned. His body was trembling. He opened his mouth, struggled, but nothing came out. Finally he slumped, leaving the room in a flood of defeat.

Karen went to Kelsie. His eyes were liquid with horror. He was struggling weakly, working at the ties around his wrists. When she came to him he looked pleadingly into her eyes. "Karen . . . please—please let me go."

She stood there, hugging herself and chewing fitfully on the inside of her lip, looking down on the man she'd known and loved for longer than she could admit to anyone, even herself. She looked at him now, spread-eagle and wounded, helpless. She saw the terror in his eyes and believed she could never know completely what it must be like. That kind of terror, it could kill as readily as any wound. Should she let him go? Yes, yes, there was no question. She couldn't leave him like this. She couldn't bear to see him tied down, hurting, begging for his life.

But, if she let him go, would it be true what Joe had said? Kelsie's blood on her hands. Kelsie's blood.

"Untie me."

She looked at him sorrowfully. "I can't."

"Please!"

"We have to do what Joe says."

He let out a desperate sob, soaked in pain. Karen pulled the blankets up under his chin, trying to cover him as best she could. Kelsie had turned away from her, struggling within himself now, fighting to keep his sanity.

She touched his cheek and he jerked away. That little movement went deep to the center of her. "Kelsie . . ."

"Untie me."

She shook her head, feeling useless and helpless and very much alone. "They're out there, Kelsie, watching the house. If we try to leave, they'll kill us. And if I let you go. If I untie you, I know you'll try to leave."

"I won't," he said, sounding like a child begging to be let out to play just before dark. "I promise I won't."

"You will. I can see it in your eyes." Karen sat down on the bed. "I have to be in charge now. I have to take care of this myself. You could die, and I have to do what I can to stop it."

He laughed then, a sorrowful, contemptuous sound that turned quickly into another sob. Karen slapped her hands against her ears. Now she was sobbing, too, her heart heavy with fear and terrible guilt at what she was doing . . . or not doing. But she believed, even if just a little bit, that what she was allowing to happen was somehow right. She couldn't live with Kelsie's blood on her hands.

She slid off the bed, landing on her knees.

Joe hit the front porch steps without really seeing them and felt himself sprawl before he could correct his footing. He went headfirst, his face sliding along the dirt. He lay there, breathing hard, then pulled himself up and staggered down the driveway. Before he reached the road he doubled over, sank to his knees, and threw up.

If he could just get to the Fareland. He'd be safe then. He'd be safe.

He dragged himself to his feet and stumbled down the road.

Joe saw the theater as he rounded the corner. Its lights glittered in the night fog. The front doors were open. He made a dash for them and threw himself inside.

Down the aisle, to the screen. The screen would warm him. He knew it. The screen. . . .

He sank to his knees before it, raising his hands until another cramp forced him to double over again.

From behind him he heard breathing. He turned his head and saw Andy halfway up the aisle. His body was silhouetted in the light slanting through the curtains. Joe raised a hand to him.

Andy moved slowly toward him.

"You burned him," Joe said, crying.

"I made him understand," Andy said softly.

Tears, hot and salty, had started down Joe's dirty cheeks. "Why did you do that? Why did you have to do that?"

"Hey," Andy said, smiling. "You run the projector. You know the answer."

Joe rubbed his hands together frantically. "You gotta help me."

"Help you?"

"It's not my fault!" Joe doubled over again, groaning. "Listen, you gotta help me, man. And you know it. I did everything I was supposed to, but it's coming down on me. On *me*. And that's not fair. It's not fair and you gotta protect me." He slumped forward, his voice trailing off to a raspy, wilted whimper. "Tell it to protect me . . . please. . . ."

Andy laid a hand on Joe's shoulder. The hand was ice, and it seeped through Joe's skin and into his muscle, searing it, on its way to the bone.

"Yeah," Andy whispered. "I'll help you. I'll protect you."

He reached down, lifting Joe with very little effort, bringing him up onto his knees. He cupped his hands under Joe's chin and directed his face to the back of the theater. "I'll take good care of you," he cooed. "You just trust me, okay? You do trust me, don't you, Joe?"

Joe nodded weakly.

"That's good. That's real good. Because I'm gonna take real good care of you. I'm gonna take away the pain."

"And the cold." Joe sniffed, like a child after a long, lonely sobbing. "Tell it to take away the cold."

Keeping one hand under Joe's chin, Andy raised the other

toward the back of the theater. Instantly a thread of light appeared, the beam lancing the darkness, and a tiny pinpoint of light struck Joe's forehead.

It felt like a skewer of ice, and in a fog, somewhere unreachable, he heard Andy singing to him. "It's a constant thing, old man. It is as constant as the wind."

The skewer of ice pierced his brain, fused it, then sprinted to his eyes and turned them to stone.

He screamed only once.

9

It was not until the wound had festered and Kelsie was deep in fever that Karen began to feel a little better about keeping him tied down. He was thrashing and writhing, and she never would have been able to handle him by herself. His struggling would have caused him further injury. As it was, the ties at his wrists were beginning to chafe the skin. Karen thought about cushioning them with cotton, but that would mean having to untie them and she didn't dare do that. Not even for just a second.

Sometimes he lay there quietly, making soft moaning sounds deep in his throat while his body was bathed in sweat, and Karen assumed that was the time when his fever broke. Thank God for those momentary breaks, because most of the time Kelsie was writhing, his skin so feverish that she could feel the heat coming off in waves. When he screamed Karen could feel it in her gut, and she would cringe and close her eyes and wait for the screaming to stop. Sometimes it went on for hours.

Outside, a steady wind was rising. It was whistling through the pine trees, whining and swirling, caressing the sides of the house and creeping into the cracks.

The wind was cold. Very cold.

Three days after she'd dragged him from the shower stall, Kelsie was still lost in delirium. Late at night, when Karen would just be drifting off to sleep, Kelsie would lurch against his restraints and scream. Karen would rush to him, try to hold him, soothe him, but he didn't seem to hear. One time he opened his eyes and looked at her. He cried to her, begged her to stop the snakes, the snakes that were eating him alive, eating him from the inside out. And he shouted at something just over her shoulder, something with seven eyes. She would hold on to him, caress him, coo in his ear and tell him he was all right, he was safe, and then the fever would break and his body would tremble as sweat soaked him. He would calm, slowly, and then he would sleep.

But the sleep never lasted long. Eventually he would begin again, first moaning softly, then building to a crescendo of terrified screams to let him go, stop the pain, the sickness. "NO!" he would scream, coming up off the bed, straining against the ties. "Please . . . please . . . seven eyes! Making me sick . . . you're making me sick . . . put it back!"

Karen would put her hands on his shoulders and push him back down, soothing and assuring him even though she knew he couldn't hear her. Sweat ran off his body in rivulets. He looked at her, right through her with terrified eyes. "They're making me sick, they're holding me down . . . please let me up, please . . . it's not true. . . . Oh, God, please!" He fell back, sobbing. The sweat ran, pouring off him, soaking the bed. His fever had broken again.

But Karen was not relieved. It had broken, then risen again, ten times in the last three days. His agony was tearing her apart.

She wiped his body dry with a clean cloth, and as he grew still and his breathing slowed, she relaxed a little.

This time his sleep was deeper than before, and Karen allowed herself to believe it might be over. She even went so far as to untie his bonds. He stirred a little as she did, and a little more as she changed the bed linens. But once she had finished he calmed again and his breathing fell into a deep, steady rhythm. She looked at the deep red marks on his wrists where the neckties had bound him to the bedposts and her heart thudded with the memory of his being tied there, his body writhing, and knew she could not bear to witness that again. It would be okay, she told herself. Even if he did manage to get out of bed, he was too weak to get any farther than the door before he collapsed. She was sure of it.

She nodded silently, convinced, and decided not to tie him up again. She'd take the chance.

She stood there a moment longer, then knelt beside the bed to examine his wounds. The burn on his groin had begun to swell no less than three hours after Joe had left. She'd hoped it would have ruptured by now, but it hadn't, and she feared it would have to be lanced. That would mean bringing in a doctor, and there was no way the people gathered outside would let that happen. She would have to lance the wound herself.

The thought sickened her.

She went to the bathroom to soak a towel in hot water. She'd heard somewhere that heat might draw out the poison of infection. As she waited for the water to get hot she felt her knees begin to tremble. The trembling traveled swiftly up her legs until she collapsed on the floor and cried in long, grievous moans.

She wished Joe were here.

Fool's wish, she thought sourly, then pulled herself up and went back to the bedroom.

Kelsie was lying quietly, his breathing mercifully slow. She watched his chest rise and fall steadily and breathed a calming sigh. Perhaps it was over. Perhaps it was finally over and he'd get better now. The wound would rupture, the poison would drain out of him, and he would go back to being Kelsie Brown instead of this wasted, dead-white caricature of a man.

Karen slipped under the covers and lay beside him. As she draped her arms about him and laid her head against his chest, she listened to the sound beating of his heart and knew, not for the first time, that she would have loved him if such an act were possible.

Rozina poured Janice a third shot of bourbon. She watched silently as Janice threw her head back and downed it in one swallow. Beside her Jeff sat with his head bowed.

Janice slammed the glass down on the bar. "He came. Didn't listen."

Rozina sighed. "It's hard for him. Knew it would be." She

turned to look at Jeff, saw him fidget as her gaze settled on him. His eyes were red and weepy.

"You couldn't have helped him, Jeff," Rozina said tenderly. "It was not the time."

Jeff rubbed his eyes. A small whimper escaped from deep inside his chest. Rozina reached out and grabbed his hands, pulling them down sharply. "Now's not the time for guilt. Now's not the time to let the hidden thing devour, hear me? Stop this. Stop it now, cuz time's runnin' out and you got to make your decision."

Jeff pulled in a fitful breath. "I know."

"Can't do nothin' now," Janice said.

Rozina nodded. "They hurt him. Hurt him bad. Hurt his spirit too." She turned away from the two sitting at the bar and stared into space. Deep sorrow lined her face. "It'll be a while before Kelsie's strong enough. But when the time comes, he's going to need allies."

"I'll help," Janice said quickly. Rozina turned an understanding eye on her.

"Janice, your time has passed. Any more you do now is a waste of spirit."

"I'm strong," Janice said defiantly, straightening her shoulders.

Rozina reached out and laid a gentle hand on Janice's shoulder. "Not strong enough, sister."

The words were like blades, cutting into Janice's soul. Her shoulders drooped, and she leaned onto the bar. All that was left of her defiance was the firm set of her jaw. She pointed to the shot glass, and Rozina filled it a fourth time.

Rozina then turned her attention to Jeff. He had begun to twist his hands. He looked up at her, almost pleadingly. "Am I strong enough, Rozina? Am I?"

"Only you know that for sure," Rozina said. "You have the cold in you. Use it. Use it, Jeff, because it's not just Kelsie, and it's not just the town, and it's not just Joe. It's you."

Jeff looked at her sharply.

She leaned forward and touched his face. "It's you."

III
POWER
PLAY

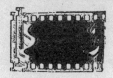

1

By the end of the fifth day Kelsie had begun to drift toward consciousness. As Karen went about the task of changing his bed linens, she became aware of him watching her, and for the first time in five days she saw clarity in his eyes. He was looking directly at her, not past her, as he'd been doing. She finished her task and straightened, offering him a smile. "Feeling better?"

He nodded. "How long?"

"Five days."

This made him close his eyes. "I'm thirsty."

"I'll bet," she said, reaching for the washcloth she'd left soaking in a bowl of cold water. She lifted the cloth so he could see it. "I've been giving you water with this. Letting water drip into your mouth. Not much, I know, but . . ." She sighed, dropped the cloth back into the bowl.

"There's still pain," Kelsie said, moving his legs.

Karen wiped tears from her eyes. "The infection's still pretty bad. I think I might have to lance the wound myself if it doesn't break. Kelsie, it'll hurt. Bad."

He nodded. "Do it, then. I want this to be over."

She brought him tea to drink, holding his head while he did so. At first he choked, but then he was able to get it down by taking small sips. When he was finished she eased him back on the pillows and went to the bathroom to get a hot washcloth. She decided to try the hot soak one more time to see if that wouldn't rupture the wound. As she worked, she thought about how much it was going to hurt him. Before, he'd been lost in delirium, not really there. But now he was fully awake. The pain would be exquisite.

She went back into the bedroom. Kelsie watched her as she came through the door. *He keeps looking at me. Like it's the first time he's ever seen me.* She knelt down and pulled the covers aside. "Kelsie, I want you to grab the headboard. Hold on to it real tight, okay?"

Without saying anything Kelsie grabbed the headboard with both hands. As she lowered the washcloth he closed his eyes.

He sucked in air and pulled hard on the headboard when she brought the washcloth down on the wound, but he didn't scream, and Karen was thankful. She pressed her hand against the washcloth.

It came suddenly, the thick rancid fluid gushing out in a kind of sickly drool. She tried to capture it in the washcloth, but there was too much of it. She bunched up the sheet and cupped it over the wound, pressing it and gently swabbing it, until the flow finally ebbed.

Kelsie was holding his breath, trying not to scream, and now his face was beginning to flush.

"Breathe, Kelsie." She rolled up the sheet, threw it on the floor, then went to the bathroom and got two more washcloths and another sheet.

As she gently swabbed the area she was again aware of him watching her.

She worked silently, packing the area with squares of torn sheet. When she had finished she took a deep breath and looked at him.

"A part of you is broken," she said, "isn't it?"

Kelsie nodded.

"Do you think it'll mend, Kelsie? Do you think you can be whole again?"

Kelsie looked at the ceiling. "Depends."

"On what?"

He closed his eyes. "On whether or not I can ever remember what it was like to be warm." He took a deep breath, then turned his head and looked at her. "I have to sleep now."

She nodded, got up, and left him alone.

* * *

More than a month passed before Kelsie was strong enough to sit up in bed and feed himself. Yet another month came and went before he could walk again, but still he was too weak to travel far and had to be satisfied with the short walk from the upstairs bedroom to the easy chair by the fireplace. Getting back up the stairs proved to be intolerable and he had to have help. He could manage it only once in the day, so he saved it until bedtime, as he was finding himself becoming stir crazy staring at the lonely four walls of the bedroom. Sitting in the easy chair all day long fatigued him, but it was better than counting the cracks in the bedroom ceiling. His one consolation was that the dreams had finally stopped; dreams spawned by fever, they'd continued long after the fever had subsided. Toward the end the dreams had become more substantial, the memory of them lingering in his mind for hours. In each one Andy was the focus, his face changing and distorting, his fingers growing long and spindly like tendrils. In one dream Andy didn't even appear to be human, but he knew it was Andy, because the eyes of the creature were fiery red and dancing, as they had been the night Andy had brutalized him.

The burn on his groin healed slowly and painfully. After a month it had begun to itch so offensively that he lay awake nights tossing and groaning. Karen had tried everything from cold packs to forcing large quantities of whiskey down his throat, but nothing seemed to help.

As March came, the winds blew up in strong gusts that sent billows of dust in swirling miniature tornadoes. The sun streaked down through a scattering of thick cloud clusters and warmed the earth in spurts. Kelsie had begun to sit out on the porch. His groin had completely healed by the middle of the month and his strength was returning at a swift and grateful speed, but the massive amount of scar tissue had left him with a permanent limp. Sitting was difficult, and bending at the waist or squatting was virtually impossible.

He wondered what it would be like to make love.

His thoughts turned immediately to Shari. Karen had called her soon after the attack in the hotel room, but Kelsie didn't find out about it until the beginning of March, and when he learned of it a tiny shiver of fear went through him. Shari was a determined, willful soul. That she might come up here was not as remote a possibility as Kelsie hoped. He called her himself and made her promise not to come.

Of course, she refused to promise.

"It's dangerous, honey," Kelsie had pleaded. "I've got enough to do without worrying about you too."

There had been a long pause, and then Shari had said, "You keep me posted, Kelsie. You keep me posted, and I won't come up there."

Kelsie had promised he would. But he had a feeling she was only placating him. Humoring him. One of these days she was going to show up. He knew it. He just knew it.

And what if Andy got hold of her too? What if she went to the theater, and felt the cold seep into her? Would she turn out like the rest of them? Like him? Would she even survive at all?

Kelsie shook his head ruefully. So many convolutions . . . why did life have to be so complicated? It seemed to him that one horrible episode of treachery, brutality, evil, and cosmic catastrophe was enough for one lifetime. Shit like this only happened in movies, didn't it? Or because of a movie.

But so far Shari had been true to her word, and Kelsie felt relatively safe in relegating foreboding thoughts of things that might be to the recesses of his mind. He needed to keep his mind focused. Only with focus could he deal with the problems at hand.

Joe.

The Fareland and what it did to people.

Andy.

The inescapable fact that he couldn't get warm.

These things, the smell and taste of them, hurled him headlong into the remembrance of the warnings.

You fool with things you don't understand.

Rozina had warned him. D'Lacy had spelled out the dangers of trying to battle a power that had no name, no concrete substance, and still he had ventured, blindly, into the realm of corruption and violence.

Sometimes you don't catch on. And sometimes you don't listen at all.

Oh, Rozina . . . I listened, but I just didn't hear. . . .

Blind. Blind and stupid, with wax in his ears.

He had been a prisoner of his injury since October, had missed the fall months that usually gave him so much pleasure, trapped in a cycle of dreams and recurrent infection. The wound had festered and ruptured three times from November to January. For him Christmas never came.

But then again, had Christmas come to Fareland at all?

For some, maybe. For those who had seen what was hidden deep down inside and were made hungry, or scared. Such strange things going on in this small town. Illogical things. People brutalizing each other. Complacency, as though this life, this existence of feeding the beast until it had had enough, was an axiom not to be contested. Such power. Such inexplicable, profound power.

It had to have a name.

He was only just now beginning to feel some of his independence returning. He spent the afternoons sitting on the porch, watching the family of deer timidly testing the water or sniffing around the plate of food Karen faithfully set out for them. The spring breeze was cool against his face, and he would have felt pretty good, if it weren't for the nagging feeling of something missing, something incomplete.

In all this time, from October to mid-March, he hadn't seen Joe. Joe was at the theater. He was always at the theater.

It made him cringe to think how Joe must look now, being trapped, as Kelsie had been, in the clutches of something so powerful, so sick with rage and betrayal. And he wasn't really sure what to do about it. Things had changed, he was sure, and not for the better. God only knew what it was like out there now.

But something else had happened while Kelsie was fighting for survival in his own personal pit of torment.

You're vulnerable, Kelsie. Your hair wasn't always gray.

He'd been touched, yes, and the cold lingered still. But the torture Andy had inflicted on him, and the ensuing torture of his struggle to return from the dementia and sickness, had made him stronger.

At least his hair hadn't gone from gray to white. It could have. In the deepest part of his mind, the part that still held on to the few threads of his personal understanding of what he was, he knew his hair could have gone white.

But it hadn't, and that gave him hope. He'd groped in the blackness and had come out the other side still sane. If he could do it himself, he could teach Joe how to do it. He could take Joe by the hand and lead him toward the light.

Lead, or drag.

Joe was keeping himself out of the picture, and hopefully that would work to Kelsie's advantage. Hopefully, it would be enough to save him.

But first things first. And first thing was revenge.

Andy.

There was a connection between the two: Andy and Joe. And the theater was the heavy twine that bound them. All very neatly packed. A nice little bundle of corruption. Christ.

Kelsie shifted a little, taking the pressure off his left leg.

Horrible sounds in the night. Sounds of despair. Sounds of hunger sated in sickly, bloody ways. And it was always worse on Friday nights.

The Fareland.

People going to the movies. People scared, too scared not to do what they were told to do.

People hungry, too hungry not to do what was deep down inside them, brought out and made real by what they saw on the brilliant white screen of the Fareland.

Hunters, and the hunted. It was operative, functional. It happened because it was natural.

And in the middle of it all was Andy. Andy ran the show.

But Joe ran the projector.

Kelsie's mind clicked.

The projector

It came full circle. Everything. Making a one-point landing on the same, solid thing. The projector. That projector.

He shuddered.

Karen stepped through the screen door carrying a coffee-pot. She poured him a fresh cup. "How are you feeling?"

"Pretty good."

"Any pain?"

Kelsie shrugged. "Some." Karen sank into a chair next to him. "What's it like out there?"

She shook her head. "Not good. People walking around in a daze, like zombies. Except at night—" She cut herself off.

"Tell me."

She looked away.

"I hear the sounds, Karen." He leaned forward, touched her arm. "I need to know."

She looked at him anxiously, then rose and went quickly into the house. When she returned she had a small stack of newspaper clippings in her trembling hands.

She sat down hard and thrust them at Kelsie. "See for yourself."

Kelsie took them, a little reluctantly, and began leafing through them.

Carnage.

"Joe saves them," Karen said tightly. "He cuts them out of the paper and saves them. And they all have that same word at the bottom." She pointed.

ENOUGH

Kelsie looked at the word for a long time, grinding his teeth, breathing deeply. "It's a wonder there's anyone left in the town."

"Not everyone is killed," Karen said. "Some are just . . . maimed. Fingers cut off. Teeth knocked out. Cuts and bruises . . ." Her voice caught on a sob. "Oh, Kelsie . . . what are we going to do?"

Kelsie folded the clippings and set them on the table next to his chair. He didn't like touching them. "Did you see Joe today?"

"No. He was gone before I got up." She stared off into space. "I'm glad when he leaves. Sometimes I wish"—she closed her eyes. Tears squeezed from the corners—"sometimes I wish he'd never come back."

Kelsie felt a tug on his heart as he saw the frightened, helpless gleam in her tearing eyes. He touched her cheek gently, capturing a shimmering tear. "Karen, do you remember the time Joe got mixed up with those guys from Granger Electronics?"

Karen nodded. "Tempac's main competitor."

"That's right," Kelsie said. "They'd been trying to buy out Tempac for years. When they couldn't do it legally, they decided to try something a little illegal. Joe was the top programmer then, and they knew if they could get to him, get him to plant a virus, they could ruin Tempac."

Karen's eyes glistened with the memory. "He was sick for weeks."

"Sure he was, and why not? They bullied him into creating the virus, and then they threatened him with exposure if he didn't plant it. But it was more than that, Karen. It was more than just bullying and threatening. They had Joe convinced it was the right thing to do. Right for him. They promised him a big promotion. Top-notch exec stuff at Granger, if he sabotaged Tempac's system."

Karen looked up, surprised. "I didn't know that."

"He was frightened," Kelsie said. "And confused. That's an explosive combination. He didn't know who to believe, or who to trust."

"But he trusted you."

Kelsie sighed. "Not at first. It took a hell of a lot of persuasive argument on my part. Days, weeks . . ." He shook his head. "I almost didn't get through."

Karen leaned forward, touched his knee. Her eyes sparkled with new hope. "But you did get through."

Kelsie nodded. "Yeah. I did." He placed his hand over hers. "And I'll get through this time too."

"Promise?"

"Promise." He smiled.

Karen bit her lip. "We're playing with dynamite this time, Kels. It's not just his reputation, or the risk of jail. It's his life." She fixed him with a dark, foreboding gaze. "It's your life too."

Kelsie took both her hands in his. "No. Next time I'll be ready for them."

Karen offered him a weak smile. "I love Joe. God, I love him so much. But I'm torn . . . and I don't know what to do about it." The last came out as a strangled sob.

He pulled her close to him and she came without hesitation. He held her, felt her hair brush against his cheek, and knew that sooner or later he was going to have to deal with his own feelings as well.

At length, after calming herself and drying her tears, she pulled away and looked at him. "Do you know what you're going to do?"

He smiled grimly. "I'm working on it."

"Is there anything I can do?"

Kelsie leaned back in the chair. "Yes. I need you to go to the library."

She nodded.

Daylight had faded to shadowed hues of russet by the time Joe came walking up the front road, his head hung low and his thoughts so jumbled and bewildered that he didn't notice Kelsie on the front porch until he had his hand on the screen door and was pulling it open. Kelsie said something he couldn't hear distinctly; it was much like the sound of gravel being thrown against something metal. It was jarring and intrusive, making him grind his teeth. When he turned to look at Kelsie he was painfully aware of the grimace tightening his lips and tried in vain to smile. "Didn't know you were out here, Kels. You okay?"

"Yeah. You?"

Joe shrugged. "Little tired."

"I can see that."

Joe glanced at him tightly. "Can you?"

"Joe . . . what do you say to being friends again?"

"Oh, yeah—yeah, that's the way it always is, isn't it? Kelsie the big peacemaker. The big man of diplomacy and arbitration." Joe could feel his resentment like bile in his throat. He turned away, peered out at the front yard. A deer had come down from the hill and was drinking from the stream. Its fine brown coat was visible through the dappled shadows of the trees. It was a quiet, serene kind of thing, that deer just standing there, drinking, looking up occasionally and then lowering its head to drink again. No problems on this quiet evening. No enemies to worry about. Just out for an evening constitutional and a little drink to wet the whistle. Then home again, home again, where everything was okay. . . .

"Joe?"

Joe closed his eyes, fighting the tension building up inside him. "I'm sorry. Just . . . sorry. I don't know what else to say." He braved a look at Kelsie and instantly regretted it. He'd hoped to see a little compassion, but Kelsie's face held none. Instead all Joe could see was strident confrontation.

Kelsie stared at him a moment past being comfortable, then clicked his teeth. "Not good enough."

"What are you talking about?"

"I need your help, Joe. What do you say?"

Joe fought back the sob in his chest. *Not now, not now. I can't deal with this now.* "I say you're crazy." He reached for the door.

"Don't walk away from me!"

That was the trigger. Joe's anger blasted out of him in an explosion of white. He rounded on Kelsie, really rounded on him this time, enough to see his anger reflected in the fearful expression on Kelsie's face. "You don't tell me what to do! *No one* tells me what to do, especially *you*! Who the hell do you think you are!"

"I thought I was your friend," Kelsie said quietly.

Joe laughed. "My friend. . . ."

Kelsie leaned back and set a hard gaze on Joe. "Remember all those projects we worked on? Remember how you'd come to me with only partial solutions? You needed me to work out the specifics for you, fill in the missing pieces, solidify uncertain conjectures. There were a lot of times when, if you'd tried standing on your own, the big guys would have eaten you alive. So we worked together and it made us strong. Remember that?"

Joe nodded, feeling wary.

"It's the same thing now," Kelsie said. "I'll do this by my-self if I have to. If you make me stand on my own. And there's a good chance I'll go down. What will you do if they kill me, Joe? How will you live with that?"

"I won't have to," Joe said sharply. "It's on your head."

"No—no, it's on yours, and you know it."

"Bullshit!"

"I want to see the projector," Kelsie said. He was leaning forward now, trembling, but Joe could see that his concentration was focused and his fear under control.

Joe laughed again, angrily, feeling it build and blossom inside him. "Are you crazy?"

"Maybe."

"Oh, good. That's good, Kelsie. That's a real fine answer." He was full of cynicism and contempt, but there was fear now. He felt it like a tremor as he wiped sweat from his brow. "There's some things you don't understand. Like how close you came to dying. Next time they're going to feed you to yourself."

"There won't be a next time."

Everything—the fear, the contempt, terrible anger and re-sentment, feelings of betrayal—everything suddenly came to-gether and Joe lost control. He pulled his lips back in an angry snarl and whirled around. Without further thought he grabbed Kelsie by the robe and yanked him up out of the chair. Their faces were very close; close enough for Joe to feel the heat of Kelsie's pain. He sucked on it hungrily. "You leave me alone, Kelsie. You fucking leave me *alone*!"

Kelsie was grinding his teeth against pain, fighting it with every breath he took. But he was still in control, still focused, and that made Joe wild.

"What are you going to do?" Kelsie said, keeping his eyes on Joe. "Kill me? That's it, yeah? You've been chosen to put me away, is that it? Well, come on then, come on, bastard. Put me away!"

Joe was breathing hard, his teeth glistening, his body shak-ing so badly, he thought he might fall apart. "Why are you doing this? Don't do this, Kelsie. Please . . . don't—"

"Is there anything left of you?"

Joe clamped his eyes shut. "I don't know what you're talking about."

"Oh, yeah," Kelsie snarled. "You know."

Joe let him go and turned away. He had the screen door halfway open when he felt Kelsie's hand on his shoulder, yanking him back with such force that Joe nearly lost his footing. He stared at Kelsie, and for an instant all those emotions, the fear and anger, the sense of betrayal, faded into a shadow of something he hadn't felt in a long time. Something came out, squeaking its way through the ugliness and the horrible power of hunger and rage. Suddenly, he was very sad.

Affliction. Yes. He felt afflicted. It was eating his soul.

Kelsie must have seen his expression change, because now his face was gentle and filled with concern. He could feel Kelsie reaching out to him, with his heart, with all that was love and brotherhood between them. All the years of loyalty and facing adversity together. Joe grasped for it, but it flitted just out of reach, and in another moment the anger was back, flooding in, drowning out the sadness. Drowning out the hope.

With the anger came the hunger, and with hunger came new strength. Joe pushed him away brutally. "I said I don't know what you're talking about."

"Joe—"

"I'm warning you, Kels. Leave me alone. There are a lot worse things then having your balls burned off, believe me. You stay out of this. It's none of your business." He turned and reached for the screen door.

"I'm getting into the theater," Kelsie said, and Joe stopped, his hand lingering on the doorknob. He swiveled his head slightly, in a kind of inhuman, mechanical swerve. He felt like an insect feeling for the light. Then he turned, facing Kelsie full, and let his fury go.

Kelsie stepped back, but Joe was too quick for him. He grabbed Kelsie by the collar and jerked him forward, pulling Kelsie's face close to his own. The heat of his fury bounced off Kelsie's face and bathed him with its radiance. It felt good. Damn good. "You come anywhere near my theater and I'll kill you." He said it quietly, with conviction.

Kelsie was watching Joe carefully, but Joe could see the man was definitely frightened and confused. He let Kelsie go with a rough push, sending him falling into the chair, wincing as he landed awkwardly on his right hip. He stared at Kelsie, daring him to speak, but Kelsie kept silent with his eyes averted. Then he stomped into the house, slamming the door shut behind him.

He hadn't seen Kelsie in five months. It was one hell of a reunion.

2

 On a warm afternoon in April a visit from one of the locals was the last thing Kelsie needed. From his vantage point on the front porch he could see the man coming up the dirt path from the main street, walking with a weary gait, his eyes darting nervously until they found Kelsie, then came to rest on him, his shoulders straightening some. Kelsie gripped the arms of the chair. His first impulse was to run into the house and lock the door. He was not in any mood to deal with one of those monsters.

But there was something about the way the man looked, drawing in air with a labored, almost painful effort, that inclined Kelsie to sit there and wait to see what the man would do.

What he did was stand a few feet from the porch, waiting to see what Kelsie would do. They eyed each other like two tomcats.

Finally, after another painful breath and a hitch of his shoulders, the stranger spoke. "Had to see you, Mr. Brown."

Again Kelsie thought of running inside, but realized that wouldn't do any good if this man meant to hurt him. Kelsie was stronger now, but still not completely up to snuff. The man could overtake him with very little effort. Better to sit out here and hope for the best. Somehow, he felt less vulnerable sitting outside in the open air rather than inside, trapped, as if in a cage.

Kelsie motioned to the chair next to him. The man hesitated, biting his lip, then moved quickly, like a rabbit running for cover.

They sat for a while, neither of them speaking, and Kelsie

regarded him keenly. He was dressed in a business suit, looking very much out of place. His hair was combed back from his face, a little too long. He was tall and slender, gentle looking, and except for the red splotches under his eyes he was pleasant to look at. Beneath the weariness there was a spark Kelsie couldn't quite place. It was erratic and cold, but smacked of intelligence. Rare intelligence, the kind often challenged.

"Uh, have we met?" Kelsie said finally, but the man seemed not to hear. He was fidgeting with his hands, rubbing the knuckles and stretching the fingers. His body had a fine, almost imperceptible tremor to it, but Kelsie saw it. He could almost feel it.

"Are you all right?" he asked, and the man jumped.

"Yes . . . Mr. Brown—Kelsie, I—I have something to tell you."

Kelsie waited.

When the man started to squirm, Kelsie reached out and touched his arm. He flinched and pulled away. His face had a drawn, tired look to it, the face of someone who'd been beaten, both physically and spiritually. There was a kind of tormented struggle going on behind that face, giving it the sheen of confusion and despair. Kelsie believed the man was inwardly weeping.

Suddenly he rose and began to pace. Kelsie watched him, not really knowing what to say. The man's body had begun to shake miserably, and it looked as though he was going to collapse, but instead he leaned against the porch railing and sighed resolutely.

"I came to—to apologize," he said finally.

Kelsie shifted uneasily. "I'm afraid you have me at a disadvantage."

The man blinked, then his mouth opened in surprise. "Oh! My name is Baines. Jeff Baines. I'm sorry I—I forgot we'd never met. You see, I know you."

"Yeah," Kelsie said. "I'm very popular."

"It's a small town, Mr. Brown. Word gets around. Especially when the word is bad."

Jeff fought for control, then finally lost and began to sob.

"Oh, Jesus, there's no easy way to tell you this. I was there. I heard you."

"Where?"

"At the motel, the night Andy—" Jeff slumped into a chair. "I was outside, walking. I take long walks at night, try to clear my head. There's been a lot going on lately. I can't concentrate. I have dreams, bad dreams. That night, Mr. Brown, the night you and Karen hid behind the screen."

Kelsie felt his chest tighten. "You knew I was there?"

Jeff laughed coldly. "Everyone knew it. Like I said, word gets around. But that's not the point. I think you felt something that night. But you didn't see anything, did you? On the screen?"

"What should I have seen?"

Jeff's mouth twisted as though he'd tasted something gassy and rotten. "Horrible things. Filthy things. But not really there on the screen." His face twisted with confusion as he struggled for the proper words. "The screen is . . . sort of . . . shapeless. I mean, well, it's a sort of . . . vortex."

"To what?"

"To what's inside." His head dropped forward.

Kelsie waited for the man to calm down before prodding him to continue. He remembered the night at the Fareland; watching the people squirming, breathing in a raspy, weighted way. He remembered the terror in the straining faces.

And the pressure. The radiant cold. . . .

Jeff lifted his head wearily. His face was red and blotchy, his eyes swollen and moist. He breathed deeply and shook his head. "I'm sorry. I haven't had much control lately. I'm really very sorry, for everything."

"You said you were at the motel?"

His face sagged again, twisting on itself desperately. "After that night I started having bad dreams. Hideous, but . . . God help me, they excited me. I think that's what was so bad. I was dreaming about torture, rape. I saw people being ripped apart, eyes gouged out, guts being pulled out and stuffed down their throats. And it excited me! I thought I was going mad."

Kelsie's stomach roiled. He came close to excusing himself, explaining that he was weak, too weak to be—

"You know Rozina," Jeff stated.

Kelsie started. "You know her too?"

Jeff nodded. "She's what keeps me sane."

Kelsie nodded his head slowly. He understood.

"She thinks we can help each other, Mr. Brown. She thinks we can beat this thing, if we work together. So I went to your motel. When I came up to the door, I heard you . . . in there . . . in trouble." He sobbed. "God help me, I was scared! I just stood out there, listening. . . . I'm sorry. . . ." His voice fell into a trailing whimper.

As Kelsie waited for the man to collect himself, he remembered Rozina had told him about another man like him. Logical. Intelligent. He realized suddenly that this was the man.

"I wasn't ready," Jeff said lamely. "I wasn't strong enough." He shook his head. "I'm so sorry."

"What makes you think you're strong enough now?" Kelsie asked.

"Have to be," Jeff said, "because you can't do this alone. You're closer to the problem, because you're Joe's friend. But you're an outsider. You know only what it wants you to know."

"It?"

Jeff's face went dark. "The beast."

A subtle breeze swayed the trees. Kelsie felt its chill penetrate his robe. "Beast?"

Jeff nodded. "I know it sounds crazy. Listen, I was just as skeptical as you. But I figure if you're going to fight something, it's best you know what it is you're fighting. It's the beast, Kelsie. Pure and simple. It feeds off fear." He looked around once, as though expecting to be suddenly silenced by an invisible hand.

"Where does it come from?"

Jeff shrugged. "Who knows? Where did Jack the Ripper come from? Where did Charles Manson come from?" He paused, giving weight to his next question. "Where did Joe come from?"

Kelsie's anger flamed. "Are you saying Joe's the beast?"

"Of course not. He's just a man, like you and me. But he's under its power. It's got inside him, works him like a toy puppet. Half the time he isn't even aware of it. And then there's Andy."

Kelsie's mind flashed with the boy, on the sidewalk outside the theater, cartoon eyes and mouth floating toward him. In the motel room, mauling and violating. In his dreams. Seven eyes. . . .

Kelsie breathed deeply. His hands were trembling.

"He's dangerous, that Andy," Jeff continued. "I'm not really sure he's even human. He's got some goons working for him too. Two guys named Crow and Stricker, and a little weasel named Harley."

They were there, in the motel room, standing by the door. He could still smell them.

"And then there's Nancy," Jeff whispered. "She's worse, even more powerful than Andy. Don't let her touch you, ever."

"Why not?"

"It would be bad." Jeff shivered.

Kelsie shifted uncomfortably. "Look"—he struggled inwardly, trying to find the words—"Listen . . . this is all pretty . . . well, it's hard for me to swallow."

"After all that's happened?" Jeff said incredulously. "After all you've seen? All you've been through?" He laughed, shaking his head. "What more do you need?"

Kelsie shifted again.

Sometimes you don't catch on . . . and sometimes . . .

He looked at Jeff, feeling ashamed. "Sorry."

"It's okay." Jeff smiled weakly. "I know it sounds crazy. I wouldn't believe it myself if . . ." He fell silent.

Kelsie thought about pushing the man to finish his sentence, then decided against it. There was a shady, secretive look to Jeff's eyes, tinged with something Kelsie couldn't quite place.

"There's a heart to all of this," Kelsie said. "I think it's the projector, but I can't get in there to find out."

"You've tried?"

Kelsie shook his head. "But I know I couldn't. Joe won't

let me near the place. He never wanted me near it, not from the start. But I think if I can get in there, into the projector room, it'll answer a lot of questions."

"Andy's got a key," Jeff said. "And I know where he lives. We could go over there, sneak in, steal it."

"How do you propose we do that?"

"Simple, really. We just wait for Friday night. Andy and his goons will be at the theater. Everyone will be at the theater. All we have to do is walk in."

"And if the key isn't there?"

"Let's cross that bridge when we come to it, shall we?"

Kelsie regarded the man before him. "Just what's in this for you?"

Jeff slumped, his body trembling, his eyes staring inward. "I'm like Joe, I guess. I mean, you don't have to be a regular patron of the Fareland to be under its power. The Fareland, that's just a house for it. Its power stems from there. But it's everywhere. It touched me. Changed me." He gritted his teeth. "Made me ugly."

They sat quietly for a moment, then Kelsie ventured, "Do you think I can still save Joe?"

Jeff wouldn't look at him. "I don't know. That place . . . it's got a powerful hold on him."

Kelsie sighed deeply.

"So what do you think?" Jeff asked, eyeing Kelsie warily. "Think I'm crazy?"

Kelsie smiled, shook his head.

"Do you want to work with me?"

"I don't think I really have a choice. I sure as hell can't do this alone."

Jeff nodded somberly. "I'm sorry I didn't try to help you that night."

Kelsie waved his hand. "There were too many of them. You would just have ended up like me. Besides, it taught me a few things. Taught me to keep my guard up, watch for signs . . . listen." He paused. "It took a lot of guts for you to come here today. And it takes a lot of guts to defy the beast."

Jeff smiled briefly, but the smile didn't touch his eyes.

They sat in silence again, Kelsie wondering just how deep the wound in Jeff's heart went, and if it would ever heal.

"When do you think you'll be able to get around?" Jeff asked finally.

"Oh, not too long now. I'm really doing better than I look." He gave Jeff a crooked smile.

"So, when do you want to go to Andy's house?"

Kelsie thought for a moment. "Soon. But there's something I have to do first."

"Which is?"

Kelsie felt a wave of hate wash over him, then subside. "Settle an old score," he said.

That evening Kelsie plunged into the first of four books Karen had brought him from the library in Walnut Creek, a neighboring town about ten miles from Fareland. He had specifically requested four books, writing their names down on a piece of paper and instructing her to throw the paper away before returning home. The first book he opened was a heavy volume with the title *Greek Myths*.

He scanned this one with only minimal interest, taking in and cataloging certain passages pertaining to Thesbos. Next, he leafed through the book titled *Legends and Ancient Demons*. In this one he learned of the minions; strange subcreatures created for the sole purpose of protecting and maintaining the dominion of their masters. He figured this was where Andy had come into the picture, being a minion of whatever the beast was, and Nancy, perhaps Andy's consort.

But more important was what he didn't find. In the entire book there was nothing even remotely resembling the power of the theater. This disturbed him greatly. He had hoped for a name, an identity, a clarification of what he was dealing with. But there was none.

Evil, without a name. Pure dominant force, with no boundary. Oh, hell . . . this was bad.

The third book dealt with incantations, and the fourth, general witchcraft. These last two books were of no help at all.

Kelsie met with Jeff two days later to discuss his findings.

They sat on the front porch of Joe's house, while Karen stayed nearby. Kelsie had invited her to join them; she declined, yet stayed within earshot. He'd catch her occasionally moving close to them, listening, then moving away and busying herself with simple chores. At one point she brought them something to drink and lingered for a few minutes. Her eyes were swollen and dark, and her fingers trembled as she poured tea.

Kelsie told Jeff about what he had learned. After careful consideration of all possibilities, he was convinced that the living force of the beast emanated from the projector, since things started happening only after there had been a "special screening."

But Jeff was undecided. "I think it's Andy. He's got a hell of a lot of power. I think he's the real head of this whole thing."

"No, I don't think so," Kelsie said. "He's arrogant, but he's still a slave. And slaves have fallibility. I can use that. I can uses his arrogance as well."

Jeff's eyes widened. "Are you crazy? You've already found out firsthand what he's capable of."

"But I know what I'm up against now," Kelsie said. "I'll be careful."

"What are you going to do?"

Kelsie let the question hang in the air while he took another sip of tea.

"Beat him at his own game," he said.

"I don't know," Jeff said warily. "I think you're rushing. You really don't know everything you're up against. Why don't you just go talk to him?"

"Oh, we'll talk. Yes, indeed."

Jeff watched him warily. "Go easy, Kelsie. Be careful."

"I'll be careful."

"No, I mean really careful. Vengeance is a dangerous thing. It clouds your judgment."

"I'll be careful," he repeated, but Jeff wasn't convinced.

They spoke again three days later, and Jeff questioned Kelsie about what he'd say to Andy, but Kelsie kept his own counsel. "It's personal" was all he'd say, but he agreed to meet Jeff later at Jeff's house in the Fareland hills north of town. The sun had already set by the time Jeff left and Kelsie went inside for dinner. Joe had not come home from the Fareland, and he and Karen ate alone, in silence.

After dinner they sat in the living room, the same tight silence following them there and settling in for a long night. Kelsie sat deep in thought, only vaguely aware of Karen's presence until she began to cry.

He moved to her, sat down next to her. When she finally looked up into his eyes he saw the terror behind the sorrow and his heart fluttered. He wrapped his arms around her and she fell into them wholly and completely. He soothed her, whispering comforts to her until her sobbing lessened.

"I'm scared for you, Kelsie," she whimpered.

"I'm a little scared for myself," Kelsie said, stroking the back of her head.

"I think we should just leave."

"No," Kelsie said. "No, not now. It's personal now." He pulled away and sat with his hands clasped together. "Joe isn't gone. He's still there, inside, fighting to get out. I can save him, I know I can. And I can beat Andy."

"Nancy is more powerful," Karen said in a quiet, thoughtful voice.

"They're both powerful, but they aren't detached. They get their power from the theater." He looked at Karen. "They *are* the theater."

Karen frowned, confused. Kelsie moved a little closer to her. "It's been hard for me, you know? Hard to accept all this cosmic crap. But I've seen enough, felt enough, to know there's something cosmic going on. A dominant force inside that theater, creating subforces. Andy and Nancy aren't human. They are only extensions of the theater."

Karen's eyes widened with surprise. Kelsie gave her a wry grin. "I've had a lot of time to think about this. And I've had a lot of time to consider my own need for logic. I can apply it here as well. It's only logical, if you stay within the realm of possibility, that these things, this theater, the beast Jeff speaks of, can and do exist. And because they exist, they can be destroyed." He leaned back.

Karen shook her head in disbelief. "I never thought you'd come around. I thought—"

Kelsie smiled. "Yeah, I know. Usually I try to find a logical, rational explanation. But you know, in a way, this *is* logical and rational." He paused, biting his lip. "If I'm going to beat this thing, beat Andy, I have to play by its rules."

They sat in silence for a moment, listening to the crackling of the fire. When Karen spoke again, her voice was stronger. "We can beat it. I know we can."

Kelsie nodded. "Yeah. Long as we know the game plan." He looked at her keenly. "And I know the game plan."

Karen smiled. For the first time since she'd come to Fareland, she felt a tingling sense of hope. "What's your first step?"

"Andy," Kelsie said in a low voice. "First, Andy. Then I get into that projection room."

Karen nodded. "I can help." She took a deep breath. "I don't know how yet, but I know I can help."

They both fell into a thoughtful silence, each contemplating the implications of their actions.

Neither of them saw Razor sitting by the stairs, watching them with powdery blue eyes.

Daylight peeked in through the living-room curtains and fell across them in a blanket of warmth. It felt good against Kelsie's skin. Beside him on the couch Karen lay sleeping. They had been so deep in thought the night before that they had fallen asleep on the couch. He watched her gentle breathing with a sense of both love and anguish. He had been through hell, but it occurred to him as he watched her now, so peaceful in her sleep, that her hell was far worse. He loved Joe, but not in the way a woman could love him; he was not as deeply and profoundly bonded to him as a wife to her husband. If Joe didn't come out of this—if he didn't survive—then a part of Karen would die with him. The thought brought into crystal clarity the gravity of this situation. It wasn't just Joe he had to save. It was Karen as well.

He got up and went to the window. Outside, the deer were gathering at the stream—the scene so peaceful, yet slick with an invisible, oily malignancy.

He had talked with great strength the night before, strength and assurance, but in the daylight, where there are no shadows in which to hide, fear began to whisper in his ear.

Was he strong enough? Did he really know what he was up against?

Could he really do anything at all to end this nightmare? Or was he just fooling himself?

It was like watching a friend sink beneath the surface of a deep pool. You reach out and your fingers touch his, and you get a feeling of hope so frail that when the grip loosens and slips away, it wrenches your heart. Then he's gone, slipping into the strangeness of liquid darkness, and you're alone.

The aloneness, the reality of it, came down heavy on him.

3

Kelsie knew if he sat outside the Fareland long enough, Andy would come out. So he sat, hunched behind the wheel of his car. He waited.

Andy emerged, dressed in buff-colored Levi's and a blue shirt. His long hair swayed in the slight breeze that followed him as the door swung open and shut. His eyes were a startling green—something Kelsie hadn't noticed before—and set in a fixed, confident gaze on Kelsie.

Andy took a few steps, then stood with his feet spread slightly apart, his hands in his back pockets.

Adrenaline flowed, and Kelsie began to shake. His brain was drenched in a sudden squall of rage. He hadn't expected it. It took him by surprise, frightened him. He tried to ignore it, stifle it, and he somehow got it under control, but it left him feeling used up. He got out of the car slowly and stood on trembling legs.

He stood face to face with Andy, a little surprised to find the boy shorter than himself. Andy kept his tight gaze fixed, his mouth set in defiant arrogance. "Want something?"

"Yeah," Kelsie began. "Thought we'd have a little talk. How's Joe?"

"Fine."

"And Nancy?"

Andy's pupils dilated.

"Haven't had the pleasure of meeting her," Kelsie went on.

"I can arrange that," Andy said, "if you think you've got the balls for it." His face split in a hideous grin.

The rage surged forward and Kelsie fought it down. But he

could see in the boy's eyes that it had come to the surface a
little. The hideous slit of a grin had widened.

"Well, let's forget all this small talk and get down to business, shall we?"

Andy held his gaze a while longer, then turned to leave.
"We've got no business, Mr. Brown."

"The hell we don't." Kelsie grabbed the boy by one shoulder to pull him back, but Andy shook free with one sudden
whip of his body. He turned on Kelsie, his green eyes flashing
with contempt.

"You don't want to touch me," he said evenly. "You *never*
want to touch me."

Kelsie stepped back a little. "I learned something from
you, Andy. I learned something about power."

"Oh, yeah? What's that?"

"I learned that power is only as strong as its slaves."

The burning in the eyes flickered a little.

"That's all you are, isn't it?" Kelsie said, his voice rising.
"You're just a fucking slave."

Andy stared wordlessly.

"You don't like that, do you?" Kelsie said. "You like to
think you're the big boss. There's a real problem with that,
you know."

Andy said nothing, but his face twitched a little. Kelsie
stepped forward.

"It's kind of like Lucifer," Kelsie went on. "He was an
archangel, you know. Right up there at the right hand of
God. Then he got cocky. Too big for his breeches. Thought
he could do things on his own. And God got pissed."

Andy turned to leave.

"So God put him in his place," Kelsie called after him.
"God put him out of commission. Gave him a stinking hole
where he could play around all he wanted. So what? So fucking what? No matter what Lucifer tried to make of it, no
matter how much power he threw around, it was still just a
shithole."

Andy turned back. His chest was heaving, hands clenched
into fists. "Man, I could blow you away with a single thought.
You know that."

"I know your name."

Andy hesitated. "You what?"

"Your *name,* pal. Don't you know your mythology? I know your name, and that diminishes you. Right?"

"How could you—" Andy looked around. For the first time Kelsie saw fear in those confident green eyes.

"You marked me. And when you did that, you gave me your name." Kelsie chuckled. "You're not too smart."

Andy took a step back, his hand reaching behind him, searching for the door of the theater. "What do you want?"

"I want a look at the projector. Just one look, that's all."

Andy's face worked as he fought with a decision, then finally nodded. "Come inside." He stepped into the darkness of the theater lobby.

Kelsie followed.

The lobby was darker than Kelsie had expected. And the pressure . . . radiant cold. . . .

Oh, shit . . .

He'd walked into it. Walked right into it like a lamb to slaughter.

Darkness thickened. He reached for the snack-bar counter, but it slid away.

Andy in front of him, a few feet away. Turning. Smiling. "Met my cousin?"

His head turned stiffly and there, behind the counter, the soft curves and gentle outline of a woman. His mind was caught by her beauty.

Thickening, syrupy darkness. It clogged his nostrils, filled his mouth. He looked at the woman, and she smiled.

He trembled.

"Her name's Nancy," Andy said, some distance away.

Nancy's lips parted slowly. She ran her tongue across her teeth, and Kelsie tried to back away but she was there, gliding swiftly from behind the counter, moving on air, and she was beside him. She kissed him softly on the neck; her hands ran down his sides, stopping at his hips and moving inward, pressing against his groin.

She stroked him, and the world exploded.

He tried to pull in air, but it was too cold, too dense. She was against him, holding him, her hands sliding, cupping, pulling. . . .

His lust mingled with terror, sweet pain washing over him, making his head ache. He sank to his knees, and she followed him down.

Andy watched, his eyes dancing.

A terrible pain. Sweet fire . . . but the *pain*!

She lay across him, undulating her body, forcing herself between his legs. Pulling. Stroking.

Mouth on his, warm tongue snaking in, darting, moving across his skin, down his throat.

The sweet pain . . . his soul ripping apart. Kelsie began to cry.

A streak of fire tore through his throat so suddenly that for a moment he couldn't remember anything. His mind reeled with the pain, then focused in and as he strained his eyes he saw Nancy's head, thick hair falling over him, softness and sharpness pressing against his throat.

Kelsie howled as hot wires of pain seared into his throat, tearing it wide open. He felt his blood gush out in spurts, washing over the floor in a warm puddle. In the distance he could hear Andy laughing.

The laughter mingled with his own screams, each forming a ribbon of light that swirled and swayed, forming a crazy quilt pattern above him. Then it faded, and just as his world grew dark he thought he heard a growl.

When his senses returned, so did the pain.

He was sprawled over two seats in the back of the theater. The house was dark and silent, and painfully cold.

He tried to sit up, but the pain in his throat and chest held him in place. He looked around cautiously, and as his eyes slowly focused he saw Andy sitting next to him. He was sitting low in the seat, gazing keenly at the screen.

Kelsie groaned.

Andy sighed. "Come around, have you? Poor old man, you don't learn good, do you?"

"Let me up."

Andy waved his arms. "Hey, you know my name. Use it. Come on, you prick, you spineless bastard. Use it. *Use* it!"

Kelsie bared his teeth.

Andy leaned forward, bringing his face very close to Kelsie's. "I don't have a name, asshole."

Frightened, feeling the weight of his defeat lying heavy on him, Kelsie wondered how a man with a master's degree in computer arts could be so stupid.

Andy laughed, then rose and stretched. "I'll give you this. You're fun. You're a really good time. I told you the next time I'd rip your guts out. But you don't listen. You're a poor learner, pal." He leaned down, patted Kelsie on the head. "You just keep coming back for more. And every time you do, I'll take a little more of you. Pretty soon there won't be enough left to feed the rats." He stood straight. "Cold in here, isn't it?"

Numbness came.

"Yeah," Andy said, looking around. "Real cold. Feel it?" He leaned down again. "Can you feel it, Kelsie Brown? It's inside you. It's a part of you. You'll never be free of it."

Kelsie gasped, and the cold sliced into his lungs. "Why don't you kill me?"

Andy shook his head. "Like I said. You're too much fun. Besides, Nancy's laid claim on you. She owns you too. If I were you, pal, I wouldn't let her touch you again."

Kelsie felt his groin swell. He gritted his teeth against revulsion.

Andy moved a few steps up the aisle. "Well, I got work to do. We'll meet again." The curtains made a wispy sound as he moved through them.

Kelsie let out a long, hellish sigh. He tried sitting up, and this time he made it.

He moved into the aisle, and blue eyes glared at him, the mouth curling into an abhorrent snarl.

Don't look don't let her touch you don't

He backed away.

Razor watched him.

He moved slowly, stepping backward and stumbling once on the seats. Razor watched silently, her mouth curling and showing white teeth. A low growl emanating from deep in her throat.

Finally he reached the other aisle. He fell into it, crying out, and clambered up through the curtains.

Cold.

In the lobby, standing alone near the center, Joe blocked his way.

His heart skipped. He peered at Joe, searching, trying to scrape away the veil that had draped itself over the man. The face. So black and obscure, lined in contempt. Hard eyes. Hateful eyes. An eclipsing of cold.

You can look a man right in the eye and still not see him
That's not Joe it is and it isn't

"Joe?"

Kelsie felt as though he were in some enormous wind tunnel with Joe—the *suggestion* of Joe—standing at the opening, obscured by the massive fan spinning at a blurring velocity, buffeting Kelsie with a wind so cold

The wind is constant here

it cut through him with unrelenting suppression.

"Joe!"

And the figure, the suggestion, the *mockery* of Joe standing at the opening, watching passively, watching as Kelsie was driven back by the cold and brutal wind.

The wind is constant

"Joe!"

You can look a man right in the eye and still not see him, because he's just not there anymore

"JOE!"

"What are you doing here?"

The vision passed, blasted out of existence with Joe's quiet, cold, contemptuous voice. His eyes still held that hateful gaze. Not glaring. Not angry. Loathsome.

Kelsie stood shivering, confused and frightened. He tried to sidestep and Joe matched him. Hateful eyes. Knowing, hateful eyes. "Sneaking around my theater, who the hell do you think you are?"

Kelsie raised his arms entreatingly.

"Get out." There was no quiver to his voice, no shake of

anger or rage, or even indignation. It was controlled, and maddeningly even. "Get out of here, get out of my house."

Kelsie touched his throat. "I'm hurt. . . ."

"Not half as bad as you will be. Get out."

Kelsie took a step forward, searching the alien face, trying to strip away the veil. "Who *are* you?"

"An old friend," Joe said coldly. *"Old* friend. You know me. You should. You screwed me enough to know me very well."

"That's not true."

"Oh, really? Why did you come here? Come to ruin my dream, take my theater. Come to claim the pretty rings for yourself. But I found out about you. I found out soon enough, and your ass is dead meat now."

"Joe—"

"Shut up!" Joe said threateningly, his voice still controlled, still in command. "You must be very careful."

"Listen to me!"

Joe looked at him and the hate came out in waves. "You'll die. You're a bastard and you'll die slow, die hard. And I'm going to watch." He put his hands on his hips and regarded Kelsie, a wicked grin stretching across his alien face. "I think I'm going to like it." He pointed to the double doors at the front of the theater. "Get out."

Feeling helpless and diluted, Kelsie nodded slowly. "Okay . . ." He cut his eyes to the lobby doors. "Okay, yeah." He moved slowly, giving Joe a wide berth. Joe followed him with a frosty glare.

As he reached the door the pressure hit him, surging like a wave, buffeting him hard enough to throw him into the doors. He gasped, grabbed for balance, and turned to look behind him, but something stopped him. Something cold and dead raked its fingers down his back and pushed him brutally out through the doors.

Outside, the sun struck him hard, hurting his eyes. He covered them for a moment, then squeezed his eyes shut until the pain subsided. As he opened them slowly he saw a crowd standing on the sidewalk. They were watching him.

Suddenly his rage came in full force, and he threw it at

them. "You let this happen!" he screamed, his voice croaking. "Why! Why, God damn you! Don't you see what's going on? Why do you let this happen!"

Rudy Olsen stepped forward. Rudy Olsen, who had toyed with him his first day in town, and who had held him down while Andy seared his skin with a cattle prod. Kelsie's rage exploded.

"What are you afraid of?" Rudy asked calmly.

Kelsie stopped, looking at him with disbelief. Rudy's eyes shone brightly. "Ever think about what's inside? You know, deep down. . . ."

Kelsie stared at the crowd numbly, his rage falling back on itself. The crowd moved on him, slowly, painting pictures in his mind. He backed away, then turned and ran.

He ran to the Fareland Motel and fell on his door. It was locked. He slammed against it.

"No rooms," came a voice from behind him. Kelsie whirled around.

The clerk stood a few feet away, that same brightness in his eyes. "No rooms, Mr. Brown."

"I need a place to stay."

"No, you don't," Alan Mayhew said evenly. "What you need to do is think about what's inside. Deep down inside." The man giggled maniacally. "Are you scared yet, city boy? Huh? Are you scared yet?"

Kelsie stepped back a little. "You can't get rid of me. Not that easy."

Alan stared at him, and Kelsie saw that flicker, the red fiery flicker in the center of the man's eyes. He stepped back again, suddenly frightened.

Alan giggled again: a vicious sound, filled with disease. "Seen any good movies lately?" Alan asked.

Kelsie staggered back, hitting the door.

"What's inside there, city boy? What's deep down inside? Want to find out? Huh? Want to see it? Want to see it?"

Kelsie covered his eyes. "No—"

When Jeff opened the door Kelsie nearly fell into his arms. He let out a gush of breath as he pulled Kelsie inside and led him to the living room. Halfway there he stopped, pulled a handkerchief out of his pocket, and pressed it against Kelsie's throat. "Who did this?" he kept saying in a fretful, angry voice as he led Kelsie to a chair and eased him into it. "Who did this to your throat? What happened? Are you okay?"

Kelsie nodded. He brought the handkerchief away but slapped it back against his throat when he saw how much blood had soaked it. "I'm bleeding a lot."

"I'll say. Who did this?"

Kelsie shook his head. "My own fault. I stepped right into it." He took a deep breath and tried to calm his quaking.

Jeff brought him a glass of wine and insisted he drink it. Kelsie didn't resist. He finished the glass off in three swallows. "I forgot about Nancy."

Jeff closed his eyes. "Oh, Jesus."

Kelsie leaned against the back of the chair and braved a feel of his throat. It was tight and hot. He put the handkerchief back and sighed deeply.

"This is bad," Jeff said, shaking his head. "This is really not good at all."

"I'm not altogether sure Nancy did this," Kelsie said. "I'm not . . . it all got confused, or something. Shit, I walked right into it. How could I be so stupid?"

"It was Nancy," Jeff said solemnly. "You've got to be careful, Kelsie. You've just got to be more careful. She's powerful. Special powers. There's a part of her in you now."

Kelsie shuddered.

Jeff poured him another glass of wine, then went to light a fire.

"They want me out of here. All of them." Kelsie closed his eyes. "Even Joe. I'm pretty sure he's setting up a movie just for me."

Jeff straightened suddenly, the burning match still in his hand. "Really?"

"Yeah."

Jeff threw the match into the fireplace, his gaze still trained on Kelsie. "Then you better start thinking about the Hiding Fear."

Kelsie bristled. "What's all this shit about a Hiding Fear?"

"It's what's inside," Jeff said forcefully. "Deep down inside you, where you've never been before. Don't you get it, Kelsie? That's what the theater uses. It's what the theater feeds on."

He threw another match into the fireplace, lighting the fire, then threw a log on and went to the chair. He sat down easily, a thoughtful look on his face. "I think you're right about the projector being the heart of the beast. Get to it, and we get to the heart. Put a stake in it, and we kill the power." He grinned. "Pull the plug on the damn thing."

"But how do we get to it?" Kelsie asked.

"Do you know anything about Andy's goons?"

"Not much. They're slime."

"They're also stupid. I think we can use that."

"Really?"

"Yeah. They're nothing. Just three blank faces. Cowards. Easily duped." He studied his hands. "I can get past them. I know it."

"What do you want to do?"

"I know where they live. I can go there, throw my weight around and scare the hell out of them. I'll get the key from them, or at least find out where it is."

Kelsie pondered. "Why don't we just wait until night? You know, when no one's around. We'll just break in."

Jeff shook his head. "We can break into the theater, but not the projection room. I've tried."

Kelsie looked surprised. "Really? What happened?"

Jeff sat quietly for a moment, a shadow passing over his face. "I went up there, up to that room. Had an ax with me and I was going to just bust down the door. But I—I couldn't. I couldn't do it."

"Why not?"

Jeff looked up at him. Kelsie could see fear in his eyes. Fear and wonder. "I don't know. Something just stopped me. Something . . ." He trailed off, shaking his head in bewilderment. "Janice told me about people who tried to leave, and couldn't. I never really believed it. But that night, standing there alone with the ax in my hand . . . I understood."

He shook his head again. "That power, Kelsie. It's strong. It's very strong."

Kelsie could see that Jeff was shaken by the memory. "But you think we can get in with the key?"

Jeff nodded.

"And those three guys, you figure they have the key?"

"I know they do," Jeff said, straightening his shoulders. "They've been charmed. They've seen the Hiding Fear and survived. They're just as much a part of that theater as Andy and Nancy are."

Kelsie clicked his teeth. "It's dangerous, then. Too dangerous."

"Any more dangerous than having your throat torn out?" Jeff asked, and Kelsie couldn't answer. "I'll be okay. I'm tougher than I look."

Kelsie regarded him, thought about this slender, gentle man who always wore a business suit. This house of his was enormous, elegant, and very expensive. Jeff seemed out of place in it.

"I'm glad you're here, Jeff," he said. "I'm glad you're around."

Jeff averted his eyes, then grabbed another log. "Yeah, well . . ." He threw the log into the fire.

"Okay," Kelsie said, shifting his weight. "You want to tell me?"

Jeff stiffened. "Tell you what?"

"What you've wanted to tell me since the first day we met, but were afraid to. Like if you said it out loud, something bad would happen."

Jeff stared at the fire.

"Come on, Jeff," Kelsie said. "No secrets."

Kelsie could see him measuring words in his mind. The conflict radiated from him. Finally he stood and moved to the chair next to Kelsie. He fidgeted a moment, then sat down. When he spoke, his voice was quiet and shaky. "I want you to stay here, I guess you know that. We're in this together, and I'll do whatever I have to, but there's something you have to know about me before we go on."

"What's that?"

Jeff took a deep breath and let it out slowly. "I killed someone."

Kelsie tried not to let his shock show.

Jeff glanced at him, then away. "But it wasn't murder."

"Why not?" Kelsie's voice cracked.

Jeff paused, and the silence was filled by the sound of the fire cracking. It was a pleasant sound.

"Because he wasn't human," Jeff said.

4

 The fire slowly died.

Jeff had brought out dressings and disinfectant to cleanse Kelsie's wounds. As he worked, he unfolded a story that made Kelsie's sense of dread deepen. But he listened, and took in everything he could to help him understand his new partner. He and Jeff were alone in this, except maybe for Karen.

And maybe, hopefully, Rozina.

Joe had changed. Something inside, growing, had changed him. This power, this thing without a name, had gotten inside and made him different.

He forced himself to concentrate on Jeff. He was swabbing Kelsie's throat gently, talking in a low, sullen tone. The firelight danced in his eyes.

"His name was Matthew," Jeff said. "I knew him in college. He was not memorable physically: fat and clumsy, he usually kept to himself and probably liked it. We had friends, but usually he hung around me only. My friends considered him arrogant, obtrusive, and intolerable. The more I hung out with Matthew, the less I saw of my other friends. And I should have been wary then, watching my group slowly diminish. But I liked Matthew. There was a sort of glint in his eye that attracted me. He'd never accept anything other than total success, sometimes to the point of obsession.

"After college, Matthew went to San Diego and plunged headlong into some kind of business—I was never really sure what it was exactly, except that it was extremely successful. By the time he was twenty-four, he was a millionaire.

"I came up here, and set up my business in San Francisco. I chose to live in Fareland because I hate the city. There's a

word San Franciscans use to describe what happens to some
people. *Citified.* For some, it's a fine thing. But for others, it's
treacherous. They get swept up into it without ever knowing
what hit them. And some people die. The city sucks them
dry, and they just shrivel up and fade away."

Jeff paused, his face drooping with sadness. Then he went
on.

"I work in pharmaceuticals, but my business was founded
on shaky ground. I didn't have enough capital. My savings
were gone by the second season. Had it not been for Matthew Malone, I would have died a slow, messy death.

"I think the bill collectors gave me my worst headache.
They were sucking me dry. Then Matthew came along, and
the collectors disappeared."

"Just like that?" Kelsie asked.

Jeff nodded. "Just like that. He shows up at my office one
day and says, 'I'll take care of it, Jeff. You just go home and
rest.' The next thing I know, I'm in the black. When I asked
him why he'd shelled out so much money, he simply grinned,
waving his hand as if to dismiss me. 'Call it a loan,' he says.
'But I like to think of it as an investment.'"

"In what?" Kelsie asked.

"That's what scared me," Jeff said. "He told me my problem was that I had no business sense. He said I needed someone who had my interests in mind. He told me to give him
full rein, and he'd make me the richest man on the West
Coast.

"For the most part I left him alone. I'd check on him occasionally, and always I'd find him leaning back in his over-
stuffed desk chair, offering me a bloated, fleshy grin and
telling me not to worry. Everything was going as planned.

"I wasn't scared, exactly, but I was uneasy. The books were
balancing too quickly. And I didn't like the look on Matthew's face. It had changed, or more exactly, it had been
weathered." He thought about his choice of words, uncomfortable with the sound of them, then shook off the feeling
with a hitch of his shoulders. "I think it came from having
been beaten down so many times. I had seen the look at
school, only it hadn't been so evident then. It was just begin-

ning to grow. There was a sparkle in his eyes that said, *I'll get you, by God. I'll get you.* I always figured it came from being bone stubborn, but I realized later that it was more than that.

"He started to eliminate my staff, his reason being that they just weren't needed. But my first real lesson in sound business came about three months after he'd become my consultant.

"We were sitting in my living room—not this one. This house came later. I lived on the other side of town. We sat many times, sipping wine and eating cheese. This one night I told him how grateful I was for what he'd done for my company.

"He challenged me. I was confused at first, then I said, 'Okay, Matt. I'm not all that comfortable with what's going on.'

"'Can you give me an instance?' he asked, so I asked him why he'd fired half my staff. He said he'd already explained that, but I said he hadn't explained it satisfactorily.

"That's when I got my first look at what Matthew had become, and I tell you, it scared the living hell out of me. His eyes grew dark, like a cat's eyes dilating. He said he'd explained it as much as he cared to, then told me if I wanted him to leave, he would. But he'd be expecting the money he'd fronted me."

"How much was that?" Kelsie asked.

"Two million."

Kelsie whistled.

Jeff nodded. "I was really getting scared, but I was more embarrassed at that point. I just sort of shut up, and we didn't talk about it again until I saw plainly that my competitors were beginning to disappear. I asked him about it, and he said, 'Simple. I sabotaged their operations.'"

Kelsie felt a sudden surge in his chest. Jeff had said it so calmly and so quickly that he wasn't prepared. Jeff saw the look in Kelsie's eyes and nodded.

"Yeah. That's how I felt." He finished dressing Kelsie's throat. "How does that feel?"

Kelsie touched the dressings gingerly. "Okay."

Jeff went back to his chair and sat down. After a moment

he spoke again with a heavy voice, weighted and somber. "He did something to their drugs. Put something in them."

"Shit," Kelsie whispered.

"He never told me how, exactly, but alluded to never doing anything you can pay someone else to do. But that was only the beginning. Five months after Matthew had joined my staff, my top competitor killed himself."

Kelsie groped for his glass of wine, found it empty, then glanced around for the bottle.

Jeff got the bottle from the coffee table and poured Kelsie a full glass. "He'd closed up his offices early one night, gone to dinner, then driven home and put both barrels of a shotgun into his mouth. The sound was heard three blocks away." Jeff rubbed his face with a shaky hand.

Kelsie lifted his glass and drained it without taking a breath.

They sat in silence for a moment as Kelsie let the wine work. Then he cleared his throat. "Why didn't you just get rid of him?"

Jeff looked at him with painful eyes. "I couldn't! God, it's hard to explain. It was like—like being in a spiderweb. I mean, it all started out so innocently, but by the time I realized just what was going on, I was trapped.

"I confronted him about Albert, the man who had killed himself. I came right out and accused him of having pulled the trigger. He didn't answer me. He just sat there, staring at me with those cat's eyes. I told him I wanted him out.

"He said—and I'll never forget this, I can remember it word for word—he said, 'Jeff, there is something you must understand. Every operation, every procedure, every sly twitch of my thumb, has been under your name. As far as the world knows, I don't even exist. You are ultimately responsible, and it is you who will burn.' "

Kelsie shook his head, bewildered. "Why was he doing this?"

"I'll tell you what he told me. He liked power. And he had power over me. Matthew had designed the web, labored over it, developed it to his precise specifications, and then lured me in. And all for the single purpose of ultimate power."

Jeff's story was beginning to ring with familiarity.

"That's when I knew I had to kill him," Jeff said quietly.

"How did you do it?" The question sounded hollow.

Jeff held up a hand. "The story isn't finished yet. I tried to kill him once, and it backfired in my face. I ended up sprawled on my living-room floor with my own gun forced in my mouth. But first he played with me, walking around me and firing the gun so close, I could feel the heat of the bullets. Then he forced the barrel in my mouth and told me I was expendable. He told me I'd better learn that lesson fast, or I'd be dead.

"He sent me on a world cruise—I don't know why—and when I returned I found he'd bought me this." He spread his hands, gesturing at the living room. "While I was away, I had learned about herbs."

"Herbs?"

Jeff nodded. "In Turkey I learned about a plant with a chemical much like curare, only cleaner, faster acting. And it doesn't leave a trace in the system. At least, none that can be detected.

"Matthew was a heavy smoker, so I bought some Turkish cigarettes and soaked them with the chemical. It looked like a heart attack."

Jeff fell silent. His face had drawn down into a tired frown.

The story had been a little too much for Kelsie to digest all in one sitting. Breathing deeply, he stood up, and felt Jeff's urgent uncertainty follow him. It came down on his shoulders like the weight of heavy hands.

Kelsie smiled, trying to ignore the weight. "Thanks for telling me."

"Kelsie, I didn't tell you all this just to get it off my chest. Or so you'd know the kind of man you've hooked up with. I'm trying to teach you something. Something you've got to learn. If you'd already known it, you wouldn't be sitting here with your throat in shreds."

Kelsie's hand crept to his throat. Part of him wanted desperately to sleep. His throat was beginning to burn terribly, and his body ached almost as much as his mind did. But the keen glimmer in Jeff's swollen eyes was holding him prisoner

of his own curiosity. After a moment of inward struggle he at
last gave in and sat back down.

"Do you remember I said Matthew wasn't human?" Jeff
said. "I really believe that. I really think he was just a kind of
. . . embodiment, you know?"

Kelsie nodded wordlessly, but he really didn't know.

"It's important for you to understand, Kelsie. I know what
we're up against. It touched me. It brushed against me and
penetrated my skin." His body slumped forward as though a
sack of stones had suddenly been thrust upon his shoulders.
He uttered a deep, hot sigh. "It lives inside me like a cancer.
Always growing. Spreading.

"Evil attaches itself to people like a parasite, sucking them
dry. And when the body dies, it simply moves on to another
host. Matthew wasn't human. That part of him had been
drained away years before. Only the evil remained. And
when Matthew's body died, the evil moved on. Part of it
moved into me."

Confused, Kelsie could only shake his head.

"It's not so difficult to understand," Jeff said, "or even
accept. People believe in God. And God is just a title they've
put on something so infinite, so constant, they just can't comprehend it. It's the same with evil. It's infinite, perpetual, and
constant. It lives, always. It breathes, and it feeds." His face
strained painfully. "It is always feeding."

"So, you think Andy was once human?" Kelsie asked.

"Once, maybe," Jeff said. "But Andy's a special kind.
What we used to call a psychopath. No conscience. Evil coex-
ists with him, effecting a balance. Which is why you are off
the track with him."

Kelsie gazed at him inquiringly.

"Killing him would be like cutting off one arm of a starfish," Jeff said. "It's inconsequential. The starfish will simply
grow a new arm, probably stronger than the severed one.
He's also being used to sway you, keep you away from the
central part, the heart of the evil. The soul of it, one might
say.

"You have to understand fully and completely what you're
up against. Evil is everywhere, always. At any given moment

it can be anything it chooses to be. It's all-knowing, all-see-ing. All-penetrating. It watches you and knows what you think, knows how you feel. You must always be looking be-hind you."

Kelsie shuddered. "It knew I was there, in the theater that night." He got up and moved closer to the fire. "I felt it. . . ." Suddenly, surprisingly, he hugged himself.

Jeff nodded ruefully. "And it knows your weakness."

Kelsie felt something hot and sudden well up from deep inside. He cast a distrustful gaze at Jeff. "Which is?"

"Your need for revenge," Jeff said.

The memories of that night, the cattle prod searing his skin, the sickly sweet smell of his own flesh burning, and the pain that filled up his world and fouled it with malignant obscenity, all of this flooded in on Kelsie, seized his senses, and turned his insides black. He wanted Andy to feel what he had felt. He wanted to see the pain twist and ruin that an-gelic face. He wanted it so much that it made him tremble.

Jeff looked at Kelsie with a firm gaze. "Put a lid on it, Kelsie. It blinds you, makes you do stupid things."

It was true. He had walked right into the trap Andy had set for him at the theater, brazen and blinded by the need for revenge, the want of it.

He nodded.

"There's more," Jeff said carefully.

"Oh, hell!" Kelsie turned on his heel and slammed his hands down on the mantel. "What else?"

"It knows your Hiding Fear."

Kelsie rounded on him, his anger now reaching the sum-mit. "You know, I'm getting pretty fucking tired of that phrase!" He began to pace, hands on his hips, his mouth drawn back from his teeth.

Jeff watched him. "You have to keep it hidden."

Kelsie took a swallow of wine. "I don't know if I can do it. I remember, that first time in the theater. It was so power-ful." He shook his head. "I'm not sure I even know *how* to do it."

"You'd better learn," Jeff said. "Fast." He poured himself a glass of wine, paused, then sighed heavily. "There's one more thing," he said, "and this is the worst. The most dangerous."

Kelsie felt the weight of his ordeal double in intensity, and he wasn't really sure he could endure any more. Already he was beginning to have trouble breathing. He downed the glass of wine. "What?"

Jeff looked at him, and the darkness on his face made Kelsie sink even farther into fear. "You've been touched. I felt it when I was dressing your throat." He paused, letting the seriousness in his eyes sharpen. "You're cold, Kelsie."

He'd expected to get angry, had even thought he might get scared, but what Kelsie hadn't anticipated was shame. He lowered his head. "I could end up just like Joe."

"Yes," Jeff said quietly, "if you're not very, very careful."

"How about you?" Kelsie said. "What keeps you from being eaten alive by it?"

"I'm ugly inside," Jeff said coldly, but in the center of his eyes was a spark of intelligent determination. "But I'm a survivor. I close my eyes to the Hiding Fear. I turn from it. Because the Hiding Fear is far worse than the ugliness inside me. Far worse. By defying the Hiding Fear I can own the ugliness. It's a part of me, and I can live with it."

Kelsie marveled at the mysterious conflict of Jeff's inner affliction. Jeff had murdered, had stood by passively while Kelsie was being tortured, had probably done a lot of things so corrupt that exposing them to full sunlight would cause the man to implode, and yet there was that spark of dignity in the center of all that ugliness. Dignity, and a willingness to own the ugliness inside. It made Kelsie feel distinctly humbled.

He wanted something to pass between them. Some kind of bond, spoken softly. And when he reached out and touched Jeff's hand, he realized the bond had already been made.

Jeff's hand was cold.

5

Across the street from the Fareland Cinema, Janice D'Lacy paced impatiently. That Andy. It was that Andy who'd brought the storm back, caused the sour rain to fall, the cold wind to blow constant. But she could stop him.

You're not strong enough, sister.

"I am," Janice said defiantly, straightening her shoulders. "I'm strong enough. I got the power too. I been touched, too, so I got the power." She took in a deep breath and headed across the street.

The theater was dark inside. She tested the door and found it unlocked.

"You're waitin' for me, aren't ya? You fucking little ghoul." She stepped inside.

The lobby was completely dark and very cold.

"Andy," Janice said, looking around.

Silence.

"Andy! I know you're here!"

A rustle, from the mezzanine. Janice looked up.

Another rustle. "Janice."

She felt a tingle go down her spine.

"Ja-a-a-a-a-anice."

"Andy, God damn you." She started up the stairs. "I can stop you. You know it."

"Come on, then." The voice floated on a gust of cold wind. It buffeted Janice's face and made her flinch. "Come here, Janice. Come here, to the balcony."

She gritted her teeth, narrowed her eyes, and went through the curtains of the balcony.

* * *

Jeff and Kelsie decided to sequester themselves from the town for seven days in order to devise and refine their plan. They knew there would be no room for further mistakes. They chose seven days for the number's mystical implications, and although this grated a little on Kelsie's sensibilities, he knew the rules of his life had changed, and if he were going to survive he would have to adapt.

Seven was a mystical number, spiritual, filled with magical connotation. Seven days. Seven eyes in the face of the sacrificial lamb. Seven horsemen with seven swords of fire. Seven keys to unlock the seven doors holding the seven mysteries of the universe.

Seven. In numerology it symbolized the name of God, and God's name had seven letters.

He called Karen to tell her of his plans, and the moment she answered the phone he knew something was wrong.

"It's Joe." Her voice was frightened, on the verge of panic. "He's different."

"I know."

"He's *changed*!"

"I know!" Kelsie took a breath. "Listen to me, Karen. I'm here with Jeff—"

"I want to come over there."

"No, you have to stay home. If you leave, Joe will get suspicious. It's important he not find out where I am."

"I'm afraid of him," she said matter-of-factly.

"Karen, if he threatens you, you go to Rozina's. Okay? Don't come here. Go to Rozina's."

"Okay."

"Promise me."

A pause, then, "I promise."

"Good." Kelsie rubbed his eyes. He was beginning to feel fatigued and had to consciously fight against the urge just to hang up the phone and lie down to sleep until this all blew over. "Jeff and I think we might have a plan, but we have to work on it. We have to stay clear of the town, and the theater's influence."

"Joe says he's going to start showing movies every night,"

Karen said. Now her voice was cold, almost void of expression.

"Stay in the house," Kelsie said. "Don't go out at all, not even if Joe tells you to. Don't go to the theater. I'll keep in touch with you as much as I can."

"All right."

"And, Karen, make sure he doesn't find out where I am."

There was a pause, then he heard Karen take a deep breath. "Kelsie, what makes you think he doesn't already know?"

Kelsie shuddered. She was right. The weight of his ignorance lay heavy on his shoulders. "I have to hang up now. Be careful."

"I will. Keep me posted, Kelsie." She hung up before he could say more.

He went into the living room, where Jeff was sitting. He had exchanged the wine for a bottle of Irish whiskey. There was a glass of it waiting for Kelsie on the end table next to the chair nearest the fire. Kelsie fell into the chair, grabbed the glass, and took three swallows.

"Is Karen all right?" Jeff asked.

Kelsie nodded. "I think so. I told her to go to Rozina's if Joe threatens her." He took another swallow. "She says Joe's going to start showing movies more often."

Jeff shook his head. "It isn't Joe. It's Andy."

"You think so?"

Jeff poured himself another glass of whiskey, then offered the bottle to Kelsie. Kelsie took it and refilled his own glass. The first few swallows had already begun to make his head feel light.

"Andy's been doing things on his own," Jeff said. "Sort of his own personal play time. He's one cocky son of a bitch."

Kelsie looked up. "Like his grandfather."

Jeff cocked his head, eyes brightening. "Yeah."

"We could use that against him."

Jeff frowned. "No. I know what you're thinking, Kelsie, but it won't happen."

Kelsie opened his mouth, then snapped it shut. He drained the glass. The whiskey hit his stomach in a blast of heat that radiated through his body. He actually thought he was on the verge of getting warm.

"We can't rely on Andy screwing himself," Jeff said. "He's a special type, like I said before. He has no soul. He has nothing to lose."

"Do you think we can destroy him?"

Jeff gazed thoughtfully at the fire. "If we destroy the beast, Andy will be destroyed. The two are connected, in more ways than one."

Kelsie looked down at his glass, rolled it in his hands nervously. "Do you know a woman named Rozina?" he asked, and Jeff nodded, swirling a gulp of whiskey in his mouth and then swallowing.

"She's safe, Kelsie. Don't worry. They can't touch her."

"Why not?"

Jeff grinned, his eyes glittering. "Who do you think taught me how to defy the Hiding Fear?"

Of course. Kelsie leaned back in his chair, and the stiffness that had shackled his shoulders for so long finally eased enough to let him breathe a little more comfortably.

"You must be very, very careful," Jeff said quietly.

"I know."

"It controls you, to a certain degree, do you understand that? It can trick you into saying things and doing things without your knowledge. Do you understand?"

Kelsie nodded.

Jeff sighed heavily. "We could die, Kelsie. We could die, if we're not very, very careful."

The balcony was even darker than the lobby had been. Janice made her way down the aisle by grabbing each seat as she passed it, one after another, until she was finally at the front rail of the balcony. From here she could see the screen.

Clean, white, glowing screen.

"Andy!"

Something inside her stirred with sudden expectation. She whirled around and saw a glow emanating from the projection-room window.

She raked in air and hit the floor just a second before a

pinpoint of light streaked out from the window. She looked up carefully, saw it laser straight and living, hitting the screen.

The entire balcony was suddenly bathed in brilliant, radiant light. Janice slapped her hands over her eyes.

"Look at the light," Andy's voice cooed to her. "Look at the pretty light, Janice."

She shook her head frantically.

"It's beautiful, Janice. So beautiful and warm."

Janice shivered. She was beginning to lose her will. She fought hard to keep it.

But not hard enough.

Slowly she lowered her hands, and when the brilliance of the screen hit her eyes she was consumed by its loveliness. She got up slowly, staring at the screen, enraptured by its cleanliness.

"So beautiful," she whispered, beginning to cry. "It's so beautiful!"

Then, suddenly, blackness.

Janice brought her hands to her eyes and found nothing there. Her fingers slipped neatly into clean, empty sockets.

She screamed in terror and fell back, landing in the aisle. She could no longer see the brilliance, but she felt it, felt its radiance, its cold, powerful radiance penetrating her like a thread of steel, sliding deep inside, deep down inside to the center of her.

Her last thought was of her son, and how grateful she was that he had been spared the Hiding Fear.

Kelsie regarded the man who sat across from him. Here was a man touched by evil, and he had prevailed. Jeff had said it exactly, in a way that needed no enhancement. Evil had brushed against him and had penetrated his skin. It lived in him like a cancer. He could have succumbed long ago, probably could have become one of the few elite spared by the beast by being a slave to it. He probably could have been spared the pain, but he fought it, hard, and the constant struggle was putting a terrible strain on him. It showed in the way he carried himself, with shoulders trapped in a perpetual slump. His face was drawn and tight, and his hands trembled so badly, he could barely hold anything in them. But his eyes sparkled with a kind of fury that gave Kelsie strength and determination.

There was much he could learn from this man.

And there was much to be done, beginning with his own weaknesses. So much invaded his thoughts, so many shards from the shattering of his mind. He was tormented by his need for revenge, his fear for the lives of the ones he loved, and the constant, tenacious feeling that Jeff was only half human and could be turned at any time.

But, so could Kelsie.

It was a dangerous game. A deadly game. A game full of rules that seemed to change only seconds after being made, and sometimes changed at the time of their making. Kelsie had to fight the need to get back at Andy. It clouded his judgment, tormenting him constantly. In his mind he could see Andy being slaughtered in a most calculating way, bloody, messy, with great suffering. The image filled Kelsie with a surging sensation that was almost sexual, and it took all his strength to flush it from his mind.

Jeff was right: It wasn't enough to destroy the arms of the starfish. He had to get to the heart, the fleshy part. He had to destroy the beast, the dominant force that had brought the wind and made it constant. He struggled to keep that in the forefront of his mind, accept it as an axiom, and cleave to it.

But in order to kill the beast he would have to see its face, hear its name. Know its secrets. And those things, he knew, were stored in the projector. The heart of the beast, from which all power stemmed.

A thing unseen, except through conjecture. A hint here, a stolen word there. Secrecy and deception surrounding it and keeping it safe. What a glorious armor it had made for itself. But armor could be penetrated with the right tools.

Seeing it, looking at it in the light, focusing in on it and dispelling its delusions. That was what had to be done. Kelsie knew this. Deep inside, in a part of him still untouched by the fear and forsaken, hungry desire, Kelsie knew it was true.

The two of them sat there by the fire, alone in their battle.

Two scarred warriors on a strange battlefield with no real plan of attack. They had to plan.

But first, they had to rest.

When they had finished the bottle, Jeff showed him to the guest room. Kelsie fell into bed without undressing and was asleep within seconds.

While they slept, a young woman with golden hair and a fair complexion stole into the room she and her husband had made into a nursery. A flicker of red gleamed in the center of her eyes as she quietly, calmly, sliced her two-month-old baby to ribbons.

During the next seven days Jeff and Kelsie intensified their bond, developed and nurtured their trust, and on the seventh day the beginnings of a plan began to take form.

During this time they had successfully detached themselves from the town, so much so that Kelsie never learned about Shari's arrival.

Shari prided herself on her patience, but patience had grown thin in the past five months. Her phone calls to Karen were fruitless, and finally she'd had enough. She piled herself into her car and took off for Fareland.

She knew Kelsie was staying at the Fareland Hotel and went there first. The man behind the counter regarded her with a sweet, almost childish gaze.

"I'm looking for Kelsie Brown," Shari said. "What room is he in?"

"Oh, he's not here right now," Alan Mayhew said to the woman. "But I can give you a key to his room. You can wait for him there."

Shari nodded. "That would be nice, thank you."

The man giggled as he handed her the key. Shari glanced at him sharply, then turned and left the lobby.

She opened the door to Kelsie's room and went inside, leaving the door open.

She began to look the place over. Some of his clothes were hanging in the closet. The covers from the bed were gone. This made her frown, but more disturbing was what she found beside the bed. The phone lay on the floor, and on the nightstand was Kelsie's room key.

As she reached for it she heard the door close behind her. When she turned, she saw the desk clerk standing there, his eyes glittering and a wide, clownish grin spanning his face.

"Are you scared?" he asked her, giggling in that wild, horrible way he'd giggled in the lobby. "Are you scared, pretty lady?"

"What do you want?" Shari said, backing up a little.

Alan advanced on her. "Are you scared yet?"

"Yeah, okay. I'm scared." Shari planted her feet, clenched her fists. "I'm scared. So what do you want?"

Alan giggled again. "I got what I want. I got it." He brought up his hand. In it he held a long, thin knife. "Do you want it?"

Shari backed up another step, bringing her hands out in front of her.

"Do you want it?" he asked again, taking another step toward her.

Shari readied herself for his attack. It came swiftly. He sliced through the air with the blade and she lurched back, hitting the end table. Her feet tangled in the phone cord and she fell face first.

He was on her instantly.

And when he was finished, there was nothing left of her.

6

 The first part of their plan was to confront Andy's goons when Andy wasn't there. It would take patience, because they had only a hoped-for coincidence on their side. They would have to watch the house where Andy lived and wait for the proper time.

It came sooner than they had expected.

Andy's house was set back on a flat, wide lawn. It was an old two-story tract house with a small garage set in back and to the side. It needed paint.

They knew Andy would leave the house around seven-thirty, but whether or not his three goons would go with him was left up to chance.

Their plan was to stake out the house, sitting in Jeff's car a little ways down the street, and watch for a pattern. Once a pattern had clearly been established, they would make their move.

It didn't quite work out that way.

On the first night of their stakeout they watched Andy leave alone. *Okay,* Kelsie thought, *that's the first step.* The next thing to do was to find out how long he would be gone.

Before he knew what was happening, Jeff had the car door open. Kelsie lurched over and grabbed him by the arm.

"Where the hell do you think you're going?"

"This is it," Jeff whispered, his voice tinged with excitement.

"The hell it is! Get back in the car!"

Jeff turned to him, and Kelsie felt a spark shoot up his spine. Jeff's eyes were moist, excited. A kind of maniacal gleam swam just under the surface.

"Jeff . . ."

"I can feel it," Jeff cried. "I know it's the right time. I've got to go now. I've *got* to!" He yanked free of Kelsie's grip.

"Jeff, no—"

"Kelsie, *please* . . . just stay here. Watch for Andy."

Before Kelsie could say another word he was out of the car and walking across the front lawn.

Ah, Jesus . . . right out in full view. Something was very wrong.

Jeff walked up to the front window and peered through it. Inside he saw Stricker and Crow sprawled in chairs, watching TV. After a few seconds he saw Harley, sauntering in from the kitchen with a six-pack cradled in one arm. He flopped himself down on the couch and threw each of the others a beer.

Jeff took a deep breath.

He stepped up to the front door and stood there for a moment, trying to calm the fire in his nerves. Then he lifted his right foot and thrust it out, against the door. It gave easily and fell through in a display of splinters. The three men jumped up from their chairs and stared at him as he stood in the threshold.

Crow moved toward an M15 propped against the chair.

"I wouldn't do that," Jeff said evenly, and Crow stopped. Jeff moved toward them. "Let's talk."

The air inside the car was beginning to turn cold. Kelsie hunched forward, wishing he'd brought a coat. Outside the night was folding in, shadows dark and thick creeping up and touching the car. He watched the street for Andy, his senses sharp and biting. His heart was pounding painfully against his breastbone and his nerves felt like piano wires stretched tight. If only he could relax. Just relax, just for a minute, just long enough to quiet his thundering heart.

Relax, just for a minute. Let the sound fade. Let the muscles smooth out. Just for a minute and then you'll be sharper. It won't hurt as much. Let your heart slow down, just a little, just enough so it won't hurt anymore.

A ground fog had begun to form, moving slowly, thick and comforting. It swirled about the car.

Thick. Comforting.

Kelsie felt his heart slowing, his muscles relaxing, a sweetness in the air that soothed his lungs. He let his eyes close, just a little.

Just enough.

It felt so good, inside the fog. So good. No need to worry. No need to think about the small silhouette creeping around the car, trotting on four legs across the lawn and into the backyard. Up the back steps. . . .

Jeff had been right. Without Andy these three snotty brats were spineless. They stood in a huddled group, herded together by their own cowardice. They watched him with fitful, stupid eyes.

"You bastards," Jeff said coldly. "You're slime, you know that? You're pig food."

"What do you want?" Crow stammered.

"I think you know."

The three stared at him dumbly.

"I want the key. Now. Where is it? Where do you keep it, you slugs?"

Crow's eyes cut to the coffee table. Jeff followed his gaze. In the center of the table was a small silver key.

Right out in the open, for crying out loud. Jeff reached for it. It was almost like it had been planned—

As his hand curled around the metal key his eye caught movement in the kitchen. His hand tightened on the key.

In the shadows, or part of them, was a slender form. It moved with elegance into the light. His heart fluttered as he saw her, registered her beauty.

"No, oh, God, no—" He tried to shut his eyes, but it was too late. She caught him, touching his eyes with her own, so feathery and soft, powdery blue, penetratingly warm. Jeff felt himself falling into them, and there was nothing he could do, nothing he wanted to do, to stop the fall. His heart was skipping and fluttering like the wings of a hummingbird. His nerves sang harmony throughout his body, lighting a small fire at his center.

He watched her, captured in the web of her enchantment, as her lips parted to display two perfect rows of white teeth. A part of him screamed in terror, but it was so far beneath the bewildered craving of his conscious mind that he heard it only as a whisper, an unimportant muttering of someone less substantial than himself.

She lifted a slender finger and crooked it in his direction. "Come here."

As if caught in a river's current, Jeff felt himself being drawn toward her. That unimportant stranger squirming inside of him fought against the current but it was too strong, too overwhelming, and before he realized what was happening he was standing next to her and she was tilting her head up, parting her full lips, and inviting him in.

He wanted her to touch him. He wanted it, and was horrified by it. It would hurt, he knew, but the pain would be exquisite.

"Don't touch me." A feeble attempt at self-preservation . . . why? Somewhere in the depths of his soul . . . something . . . "Please don't touch me. . . ."

Her hands were on him, caressing him. The small flame in the center of his body flared, radiating out, devouring every part of him. His head swam in a thick, milky haze. He felt the fire consuming him, pain so sweet, the smell of roses.

Then she pulled away, and the fire died suddenly. In its wake was the blackened ruination of his spirit. It screamed, the pain now an ache so deeply seated, it would probably never go away.

It was then, as the ache of loss cleared his senses, that Jeff realized he was on his knees. His hands were behind him, wrists crossed and bound.

His body throbbed with the ache of sexual denial.

The three boys with their stupid faces and filthy clothes stood in a semicircle around him. He peered into their faces, saw the reflection of his own sexual lust in the filth of their expressions, and a deep shame fell on him, surpassed only by his terror.

Crow had the M15 in his hand. He was advancing on Jeff, anger etched cleanly on his face. He jammed the shotgun up under Jeff's chin. "Gonna blast your fucking head off!" Spit flew from his lips.

The twine binding Jeff's wrists cut into his skin. Jeff closed his eyes. Stupid, so stupid. He would probably have let himself sink into the pool of defeat if he hadn't been so terrified. Crow wouldn't blast his head off. That would be too easy. No, things were going to get worse from now on. Death would become something he'd beg for.

I will not beg, he thought, the barrel of the shotgun digging into the soft skin under his chin. *Will not, will not beg.*

"Back off, Crow." The voice came from behind. Jeff opened his eyes to look, then shut them again, squeezing them tight. He didn't really need to look. He felt Andy there, felt it like dead fingers playing with his insides.

Crow backed away as Andy came forward and stood next to Jeff. Andy grabbed a hank of hair and slowly pulled Jeff's head back. In his left hand he held a wad of cloth.

"Well, well, well, Jeffey boy. Thought you were smart. Thought you had it all planned out." He stuffed the wad of cloth into Jeff's mouth. Jeff felt his tongue being forced back at a painful angle, making him gag. Tears squeezed out at the corner of his eyes.

"Thought you held all the cards, isn't that right, Jeffey boy?" Andy grinned. He pulled another piece of cloth out of his back pocket and wrapped it around Jeff's mouth, tying it tightly at the back of his head. "Tell me, buddy boy. Didn't you think—didn't you have the slightest, tiniest thought that maybe, just *maybe* you were being played for a fool?" He yanked Jeff's head back with a snap. "Didn't you?"

Jeff shook his head weakly.

"No," Andy said. "Of course not. Tough guy, right? Mister Big. Mister Tough Guy. I'll give you this, Mister Tough Guy. You've got balls. At least, for now you do."

He let go of Jeff's hair, pushing his head forward with a brutal thrust, and turned to Crow. "Take him out to the garage. Tie him to the workbench. I'll finish him there."

The three grabbed Jeff roughly and dragged him outside.

At the door, Crow turned. "Andy, that bench. It's too long. Ropes won't reach."

Andy tilted his head back with vague impatience. "So, nail him to it."

Crow's lips split in a lusty smile as light dawned on his stupid face. "Yeah . . . *yeah*!" He turned and lunged out the door.

Andy turned to Nancy, who was watching him quietly, her eyes narrowing. "You want to say something?"

She smiled calmly. "Be careful, Andy. Walk lightly."

Andy's anger flared. "I've waited a long time for this," he said through tight lips, pointing to the back door. "I won't be denied. Not this time."

Nancy made a sidling move toward him and he pulled back. "Then, you walk alone," she said. "Remember that, cousin."

Jeff's mind raced, trying to dodge the fear that ricocheted inside his brain. He had to keep his wits, had to, or they'd kill him. Kill him, or worse.

He fought against the panic welling up, and when he felt his hands free he kicked hard with his foot, aiming at Crow's crotch.

But Crow was ready for him, and he grabbed Jeff's foot with ease. In the same motion he grabbed the other foot and pulled Jeff up while the other two grabbed his arms. Then he was in midair, being slammed down on the long wooden bench with such force, the air was beaten out of him. Hot pain splashed against his back and he lay gasping, unable to fight as Crow tied his feet to the legs of the workbench.

Then Jeff saw him climbing, moving up along Jeff's legs, digging his knees into the large muscles of his thighs. They cramped, and the pain went into his pelvis.

On his chest now, pushing the air out of him again. It was all happening so slowly and yet without order. His mind would fly away, running wild with panic, and only glimpses of what was happening would focus in for a moment, then get beaten away by the terror. Crow sitting on him, his arms being pulled up over his head, warm hands on his wrists. Sweaty hands.

"It ain't right," he heard Harley say. Uselessly, he felt a glimmer of hope.

Crow snatched a hammer off the wall.

"Hell, it ain't right," Stricker said.

"I don't know," Harley said warily. "Who's idea is this?"

"Who do you think?"

Harley shook his head. "It ain't right."

"Shut up!" Crow growled. He held two large nails in his left hand.

"Hurry up!" Stricker said. "Fucker's strong."

Crow held up one nail, twirled it between his thumb and forefinger. "Stretch his fingers out."

Harley pried the fingers of Jeff's left hand out, splaying them flat against the surface. Jeff tried to scream, but only a muffled whimper came out through the gag.

Crow leered as he placed the nail against Jeff's palm. Jeff felt the prick of the point, and before he could scream again a blast of molten lead seared through his hand.

Then the scream came, forcing its way through the wet cloth crowding his mouth. He saw it come out of him and swirl up to the light overhead.

"Screams like a woman." Harley giggled.

Crow placed the other nail against Jeff's right palm. He felt the prick, and this time heard the hammer slam down on the nail head. Another blast of molten lead, and another scream swirled.

His hands felt like bowling balls, fire streaming out of them and mixing with the screams. His mind wanted to let go, just let go and find another place where there wasn't any pain and the world wasn't so red. But he knew if he passed out he might never wake up again, so he fought, and the pain punished him for his defiance.

Andy's voice, through the red and the pain: "Go inside."

The three groaned like disappointed schoolchildren being told it was late and time to go to bed. They moved away reluctantly and the constriction in his chest lessened. He took in a hot, moist breath.

His eyes felt swollen shut and that was okay because he knew Andy was there now, hovering over him like a bad dream.

A hand on him, lying heavy against his heart. Jeff groaned.

"Open your eyes," he heard Andy say. "Look at me. I want you to look at me."

Jeff opened his eyes. Andy wavered, swirling with the light and the screams still echoing in the stale air.

"We've met before, you and I," Andy said softly, almost seductively. "We know each other well. If you had not been so belligerent, we could have been brothers."

The hand on Jeff's heart went cold.

"When we knew each other, I tried to teach you a lesson. But you wouldn't learn, Jeff. You just didn't listen." He pulled a small knife out of his back pocket and waved it before Jeff's eyes. "I suppose you're wondering what's going to become of you. Is that right?"

Jeff stared motionless, his eyes swimming in tears. Andy pushed down hard on his chest. It felt like a ramrod.

Andy's brow knitted in genuine concern. "I'm not really sure what to do with you." He moved the knife close to Jeff's face. "If it were left up to me, I'd kill you, sure as hell." He slipped the blade into Jeff's left ear. "I'd skewer your brain. It would make a wet, sloppy, delicious sound, this knife going in and whittling your brain. Lots of blood. I like blood. I like a lot of blood."

Jeff closed his eyes.

"Open them," Andy commanded. Jeff obeyed.

Andy pulled the blade out, looked at it thoughtfully. "Death is so final. So complete. Redeeming. Death would set you free. And it is not your fate to be free, brother."

Jeff sobbed.

"I figured I could possibly satisfy the needs of everyone by choosing the path to death. I could, for instance, do this." He cupped his hand around Jeff's nose, pinching the nostrils together.

Jeff had seen it coming and had taken in a great gulp of air before Andy's hand had clapped down on his nose. He squeezed his eyes shut and fought desperately against the panic that would use up his air too quickly. Still the oxygen in his system diminished and his chest retracted.

He felt Andy's cold breath against his cheek. "Can't breathe, can you, brother? Can't breathe."

Bright spots of color exploded before his closed eyes and his lungs burst into flame. The agony heightened his senses to a defined clarity, blasting him with every inch of pain. The warm hardness of the wood against his back, the numbing in his legs brought on by ropes tied too tightly to allow normal circulation. Andy's cold dead hand against his heart, freezing it into stillness but not soon enough, oh, God . . . not soon enough. He wanted to let it come, let it end him, but his body fought against him, struggling and writhing by its own will against the killing force.

Let it come just . . .

Let it come. . . .

And then it settled in, just out of reach but he could see it, feel it. The violent blotches of color dispersed, fading to a soft white. He felt warm, safe, floating away, and it wasn't so bad. It didn't matter anymore. Nothing mattered because it was coming, and he wouldn't have to fight anymore. In this place, where Andy had thrust him, there was peace and serenity. His body was numb and warm, so warm, and it felt so very good. Yes . . . the pain was slipping away, and nothing else remained. . . .

Then the blockage on his nose loosened and his lungs fought for air. He raked it in, coughing, etching a hot path down his throat. The colors blasted away the friendly whiteness and Andy floated amid them. Reality took form and brought with it the pain.

"Torture, indeed, brother. But all too temporary. And no blood." He was loosening Jeff's tie, pulling it away, and his fingers played with the buttons of Jeff's shirt. "I think you should know, you're going to be here for a very long time." He unbuttoned the shirt and laid it open. But as he gazed down on his victim his eyes took on a sorrowful look, a hurting grimace tugging at his lips. "Dear brother, we exist on a common plane. If only you'd listened the first time." He held the small knife with the tip of it just resting on Jeff's chest. "Now we both must suffer."

As the blade pierced Jeff's skin, Andy moaned, tilting his head back and closing his eyes. He took in air, swiftly, like the gasp of a dying man, and then dragged the blade down Jeff's chest at an angle. A thready trail of blood followed the blade.

The pain snaked along the wound, striking and blinding white, a lance of silver melting like the ice beneath a skater's blade. Jeff closed his eyes and forced the scream lodged behind the wad of cloth to come forth, muffled and terribly weak.

With every inch of strength and will left to him, Jeff pulled himself away from the pain and horror, and set in his mind the image of Kelsie Brown. The silver hair, the funny quirk at the corners of his mouth. Cool gray eyes. He formed it, molded it, pulled it into himself, and wrapped it around like a woolen blanket.

The blade came down a second time, tracking in a parallel path along the first gash. Distantly he heard Andy moan again, gasping as the blade traveled down his chest, but he dared not look. He kept his eyes clamped tightly shut, fixing on his own personal screen the image of Kelsie. Pain filtered through, jarring his concentration, but still he held on to the image, clung to it like a piece of driftwood in an otherwise lonely sea.

Through the electric current of pain he could hear Andy's lusty moan as the blade came down a third time.

In the distance, on the feathers of a breeze, Kelsie heard his name.

The fog enfolded him and, like the arms of a woman, lifted him to the center of itself, wrapping protective layers around him, shutting out the sound of his name. He let it take him deep into itself. He wanted to be there, and the voice offended him, offended his serenity in the center of the warm gray fog.

It was so warm there. And the voice brought the cold. He turned away from it.

It was closer, harsh, and terribly high pitched. The whine of a bewildered, nagging soul. It brought the cold.

He didn't want to be cold, no. He turned away again, deeper now, into the warmth.

It called his name.

Annoyance swelled. The voice grew in pitch. The fog pulled on him, tugged on him, and called him into it. But the voice, bringing the cold. The voice . . .

He knew that voice.

Like a slap on the face it came to him, cold and uncaring, but terribly urgent. It swept away the fog and left him shivering.

He sat up with a jolt.

He was in a car, but the rest was unclear. His mind fought for a foothold as he looked around frantically, trying to remember.

Remember, trying to remember what the hell was he doing here?

Through the windshield he saw the circular glow of streetlamps spilling across the sidewalk. He tracked the sidewalk up to the car, then looked off to his right.

Oh, Jesus God.

He strained through the darkness, peering at the house. It was dark except for a feeble light shining in the front window. Desperately he looked at his watch.

Thirty minutes . . .

Jeff's been in there for thirty minutes.

Oh, Jesus God God *damn* it, how could he be so stupid! Jeff, alone in there for thirty minutes. God *damn it*!

He got out of the car, hunched down, and crawled along the side of it. He made a bolt for the bushes lining the side yard and crawled along their shadows on hands and knees, sweat dripping into his eyes, his heart thudding in his throat.

He pulled himself up slowly to the window ledge and peered in. In the living room were the three goons, the three rotten grapes he knew as Stricker, Crow, and Harley. They were moving about in a panicked search for something, throwing over tables and heaving cushions wildly into the air. Harley was whimpering in a blubbering, uncontrolled way

that dragged his mouth down at the corners in a horror mask
of fear. Crow moved past him, shoving him to one side and
shouting angrily as he went to the back door and shouted
Andy's name. Kelsie's attention switched to the garage. He
could see it through the back door Crow had thrown open.
When he saw Andy emerge he crouched down. Rage surged,
and he fought it down desperately.

Andy was standing in silhouette, his body bathed in clean
white light from the interior of the garage. The jagged rage
welled again and burned his eyes. He stared at the silhouette,
let it brand a scar on his heart as he held it close

Got to control it got to

and wouldn't let it go.

His fingers gripped the window ledge.

Andy came out of the garage, slamming the door behind
him. As he came into the house Kelsie crawled along the
front porch and headed for the garage. As he passed the
window he could hear them shouting in frightened anger.

"You call me in here for that?" It was Andy. The rage
flamed. "He's got it, you asshole. And I've got him!"

Kelsie made a bolt for the garage. He came up to the door
and flattened himself against it, his ear cocked against the
cracked wood. Slowly he touched the doorknob, looked back
at the house, then opened the door and rushed inside.

It was light inside, but still it took him time to comprehend
what he saw, there on the workbench, blood thick and
thready, everywhere, gleaming in the harsh light . . .

. . . hands . . .

. . . and blood, and . . .

His hand came up and clapped against his mouth. For a
second he thought about running. His legs had even begun to
move, but instead of going for the door he ran to Jeff.

Jeff's eyes were closed. His body shook in fine tremors,
and there was a soft, whispering sound coming from deep
inside his throat. Words came to Kelsie's mind. Words he'd
heard in TV shows and movies. Words like *shocky, pain-
induced coma, trauma.* Jeff's face was fish-white, and there
was too much sweat. It streamed off him in reddish rivulets.

He forced his gaze to the hands, looked at them hard, and his stomach lurched. He turned away gagging.

Through the terror his mind began to click out actions. He reached for the hammer lying nearby on the long workbench, then clambered up onto the bench and leaned over Jeff's body. He started to remove the gag in Jeff's mouth, then realized he'd better leave it where it was.

"Jeff. Oh, Jesus, Jeff . . ." He hooked the hammer under the head of one nail, then took a deep breath. "It's gonna hurt, Jeff. I'm sorry. It's gonna hurt—"

He pried the nail out. It made a clean, squeaky sound as it pulled out of the wood. Small chunks of wet flesh clung to it. Kelsie pressed his lips tightly shut to stifle another rush of nausea.

Jeff's eyes flew open. His back arched so suddenly, Kelsie was nearly thrown off. The twisting pain in his face made Kelsie's heart sob.

Kelsie went for the other nail. It made the same sound, but came out clean.

He jumped to the foot of the bench and untied Jeff's legs, then pulled him to a sitting position. Jeff's head flopped back and forth like the head of rag doll. Kelsie pulled him up and over, slinging him over his right shoulder. As he did so, he caught sight of the M15 leaning against the workbench. He grabbed it, and headed for the door.

Once outside, he ran with full force for the front yard.

As he rounded the house he saw the car and set his mind on it. It became a singular thing. *Get to the car. Get to it and take off. Get out of here. Just to the car. Maybe fifty yards, and then we're safe.*

From the corner of his eye, as he reached the middle of the yard, he caught sight of Stricker and Crow. They were rushing at an angle and it was all too clear he wasn't going to make it. They were heading him off, and before he could think of what to do they were on him, tackling him around the knees. He fell headlong and sprawling, Jeff and the M15 flying out in front of him. Jeff rolled three times before stopping with arms and legs splayed.

Crow pulled Kelsie over onto his back, his arm going high

over his head to be brought down on Kelsie with killing force. Kelsie saw the rage in his stupid eyes, burning there like streetlamps.

Kelsie pulled his knees up to his chest and then kicked hard, his feet harpooning and hitting Crow squarely in the groin.

Without waiting to see the results of his attack Kelsie grappled for freedom, crawling at first, then getting to his feet and running. He veered to one side and swooped for the M15 and as he came up he swung around and leveled it at Crow.

Filled with hate, setting his sights on the thing he hated, he pulled the trigger and emptied the barrel into Crow's midsection.

A glistening wet spray spurted out from behind Crow. His eyes bulged with surprise as his body flew backward. He landed in a trashy mound of his own flesh.

Kelsie sent another bullet into the breech and swung the M15 toward Stricker. Stricker's hands came up defensively, his head shaking from side to side, his mouth forming a perfect O. "Don't—"

"Son of a bitch." Kelsie squeezed the trigger again.

The blast hit Stricker in the head, sheering away half of it. Streaks of crimson flew into the air in graceful arcs. Stricker stood only for a moment before his body folded in on itself.

Kelsie swung around again, searching for Andy. No rage this time, nothing that primitive. His decisiveness was exact, cold, and calculating. He swung around, and searched.

Into his line of vision came Jeff, sprawled on his back, arms and legs spread-eagle. His face was even paler than it had been. But that wasn't what made Kelsie's heart lurch into his throat. It wasn't the fact that Jeff was probably already dead. That wasn't it at all.

It was Razor.

She lay over Jeff's still body, her front legs planted firmly on his chest. Kelsie could feel the constriction, the heavy weight pushing out air and not letting any more in. Razor was watching him, almost challenging him, warm blue eyes piercing the night and making it wickedly bright.

Kelsie bared his teeth. "Get off him."

Razor emitted a low, sinister growl.

Kelsie leveled the M15. "Fucking bitch, get off him!" He aimed the barrel at a spot directly between the dog's eyes.

The dog did not move. She watched him, challenged him. Unnatural eyes, sickly warm, like the ripening of infection. . . .

Kelsie felt his trigger finger twitch. The rifle went off with an explosion of light and sound. It threw him back with a numbing force, heat pounding against his chest. He fell, doing a backward somersault and landing on his knees. His ears rang.

The numbing heat was in his hands, and when he searched for the rifle, groping in the wet grass for it, he caught sight of it a few feet away. The barrel had flowered open.

He looked back at Razor. Silent, watching, he saw a smile on the dripping muzzle.

Kelsie's heart went cold. "Oh, shit . . ."

Razor turned her attention to Jeff, moving her snout down his body, nudging his crotch. The sight made Kelsie sick.

The dog's massive head moved slowly, turning toward Kelsie, regarding him with vague amusement. The snarling smile widened.

Kelsie held one hand out, pleadingly. "Please . . . don't . . ."

The dog's blue eyes glistened with quiet power. Slowly she got up, leaning over Jeff's inert body and licking blood off his chest and belly, snorting sounds gurgling out from the long, shimmering snout.

"Please . . ."

She nudged his crotch again, then ran her muzzle along the inside of his thigh. The horrible gurgling sounds resonated in Kelsie's ears. He watched helplessly.

"Make her stop," he whimpered. "Please, oh, please, God, make her stop!"

Precious

Unspoken, the word stung his brain. He froze.

Razor was up, moving toward him, her head hung low and her eyes fixed.

My precious

He was on his hands and knees, gripped in terror, unable to do anything but watch as she came up to him and touched his lips with her cold black snout.

Precious, my very precious. The stain is deep.

He went down, tumbling into the blue forever of Razor's eyes. His mind fell in on itself, laying open the fabric of his dreams.

"I want"—Kelsie felt a scream—"I want you to die."

Your hands are bloody

Kelsie looked at his hands. They dripped with sticky red syrup into a pool of bone and torn flesh.

His scream came, wrapped in terror.

7

Light stole in under Kelsie's eyelids, stinging his eyes. He shaded them with a trembling hand. The air lay cold against his skin. A primal ache had penetrated his body, making him feel old and spent. Something inside told him to go gently into the shadows of the past, and become one of them.

But something else, something inherently sedulous, prodded him to draw together the fragments of his self and bind them. He didn't want to do this, because the ache in his body was an intimate thing, a thing to be feared. It was forever.

Timidly, he opened his eyes a slit. He groaned, shied from the light.

Inside, the wildness of his spirit fought his subjugation. The conflict hurt his heart.

Then the light, blinding as it was, began to change in form and texture. No longer did it punish him with its cruel revelation. Now, it was a changing of darkness, a lessening of turmoil in his weary mind.

It was an oasis, and he fought to reach it.

Once infinite, the light now began to shrink, consuming itself and rearranging itself into something familiar, something with a reality that could be touched with the body as well as the mind. Kelsie grasped for it desperately but the light was beyond his reach. Instead, his hand thumped against something solid and cold. His fingers curled around it, and the cold seeped in. He squeezed it, felt its solidity, and focused his gaze on the cylindrical rod that seemed to tower into the sky and balance the light on its very tip.

A rod, he thought, or maybe a pole. Yes, maybe a pole.

Kelsie tried to pull himself up, but he was too weak. He lay on his back and stared at the cold, long pole with the light on its tip, and struggled to understand it.

A pole, and a light. He squeezed his eyes shut and grappled with the image. A pole, and a light. A pole. A pole and a light. Or maybe a lamp. Lamplight.

A streetlamp.

Yes . . . *yes*! Kelsie heaved a sigh. Simple and easy, thank God. Thank God. He lay there shivering, breathing in gulps of air, and stared gratefully at the simple, ordinary globe that was just a streetlamp.

The primal ache in his body began to change as well, becoming something more akin to the dull hurt of muscles having strained too much. Reality was forming around him and inside him. His fragmenting mind had begun to reassemble. Strength was slowly replacing fatigue.

His first question had to do with where he was. He was lying in wet grass; of that he was sure. But how had he gotten here?

Kelsie turned his head, trying to get a handle on what was around him, and to his right on the ground he saw Stricker. The reality he had hoped to embrace as a friend now became a treacherous thing. He could see the line of separation where the M15 had blown away part of Stricker's skull, leaving the tip of the nose and the earlobes intact. The rest was scattered in an array of bloody shadow.

Kelsie rolled over on his stomach, trying to hide. Crow lay to his left, a mass of dark wetness covering him like a blanket. Kelsie buried his face in his arms, but the memory had etched itself in his mind like acid on stone.

Your hands are bloody

He began to weep.

Then he remembered Jeff.

He looked up, frantically searching, avoiding the two ruined bodies, and finally he found Jeff, lying at a distance. Kelsie crawled toward him.

As he drew nearer, he could see the chest rising and falling in gentle motion. Kelsie struggled closer, every muscle in his body screaming. His arms and legs collapsed and he crawled on his belly until finally he reached Jeff and fell half across him, holding him, laying his head against the gently rising chest and hearing the heart beating weakly; a feathery sound. He uttered a shuddering sigh.

Razor should have killed him. She should have killed Kelsie. But she hadn't.

And that should have been a relief. But it wasn't.

Kelsie pulled the gag out of Jeff's mouth, then hoisted him into a sitting position. When Jeff uttered a feeble moan Kelsie felt a rush of relief. He pulled Jeff up and over his shoulder, staggering at first, then getting a foothold. He headed for the car.

He opened the door and laid Jeff gently on the front seat. Coming around the front of the car, he braved another look at the front yard. The sight was mercifully distorted in darkness, but still he could see the two disfigured bodies.

Your hands are bloody

Kelsie shut his ears to the resonating sound . . .

. . . your hands . . .

. . . he threw it, like a piece of trash he hurtled it out and away from himself.

It came back, embedding itself in the deepest part of his soul.

Your hands will always be bloody. You can't be rid of it.

Kelsie stood alone in the darkness, leaning heavily against the car with his head bowed.

You'll never be warm again.

He heaved a sigh that was weighted with foreboding, laced with a strange, slumbering hope.

He got into the car and started the engine. Looking once at Jeff, making sure he could see a slow, steady rising and falling of the chest, he pulled out from the curb and headed down the street.

He was sure someone would try to stop them, but as he wheeled into the center of town he saw no one, the streets dark and silent and strangely deserted, and for a moment his spirits lifted. But as he came around the corner onto Devil's Mountain Road he saw them.

They came from the shadows, moving swiftly like rats to garbage. They swarmed into the street, ramming themselves into his car with such force, he was knocked to one side. Jeff slid down at an angle and nearly went to the floor but Kelsie grabbed him, slapping his hand against Jeff's chest and holding him back against the seat.

He slammed his foot down on the accelerator and the car lurched forward. He could hear them grappling for a hold, clambering onto the roof, fingernails scraping along the sides. His heart nearly froze, and with one hand on Jeff and the other on the steering wheel, he set his gaze on a place in the distance, free of the deadly crowd, and shut out thoughts of what would happen if the mob succeeded in getting them.

But the fear was coming at him from all sides. The locals outside, bent on destruction, fueled by hate and corruption. And inside the terror and guilt weaving a suffocating fabric of tensile strength, wrapping around him, closing, shrinking . . . he could barely breathe.

Suddenly his foot slipped off the accelerator and the car began to slow.

The clamor of slamming fists and scraping nails crescendoed with victory. The car moaned beneath their deadly weight, and Kelsie saw the end of things. He saw it clearly, after everything that had happened, the car was slowing and the monsters outside were going to tear the doors away with their bare hands and drag him out.

This time they'll kill me, he thought as the car pitched and swayed. *They'll kill me, but not right away. . . .*

In the distance he saw a sign hanging over an old building in need of paint. He latched on to it, drew from it the hope he needed, and the car sped forward. He could hear the bodies falling away and the car breaking free. He drew from that, too, and his foot slammed down again.

Behind him he heard the angry cries. They faded with distance, and his hopelessness subsided.

He wheeled into the small parking lot in front of Rozina's bar and parked as close to the front door as he could. The door was standing slightly ajar.

Jeff had begun to stir, moaning weakly. Kelsie pulled him out and grabbed him around the waist, swinging one arm across his back. The angry cries were growing louder, joined by the sound of running feet.

Rozina met them at the door. She held it open and Kelsie stumbled inside.

He ran to the back of the bar. The screaming and footfalls rushed forward like a raging wave. Kelsie crouched in a corner with his arms still clinging to Jeff's limp body. His throat ached with fear.

The door exploded inward. Kelsie screamed.

But only four men came in. John Williams, Alan Mayhew, Rudy Olsen, and one Kelsie didn't recognize. Their faces were distorted and ugly, filled with rage. They searched for only a moment before seeing Kelsie, then advanced on him.

But it was only four men. Kelsie could have sworn the angry crowd that had chased was ten, maybe twenty. But there had only been four.

The realization quelled his panic, and now he could see Rozina standing between himself and the half-crazed men. She seemed so small and frail, but she stood in authoritarian repose, her hands resting on her hips.

When the men saw her, they stopped, nearly bumping into one another.

"Bar's closed," she said evenly.

Kelsie held his breath.

The men moved indecisively, squirming a little. In unison they attempted an advancing step.

"Bar's *closed.*"

They jerked back. Alan Mayhew looked past her at Kelsie, his eyes burning. But the others averted their gaze. They shuffled without direction, then slowly backed away until they were out the door, leaving it to swing closed by itself.

Exhausted, Kelsie collapsed, sliding down the wall and landing with a soft *thump.*

Rozina bent over him, hands resting on her knees.

"I fell asleep," Kelsie said, "and you woke me up. I heard you calling my name."

Rozina nodded silently.

She blurred with his tears. "I killed them. Stricker and

Crow. Wanted to kill Andy. Couldn't find him. I killed them, oh, Christ . . . I killed them!"

"You were thinking of him"—she nodded toward Jeff, now draped over Kelsie's lap—"trying to save him."

"I took a rifle . . . killed them." He gave a hoarse, pitiful moan.

"Kelsie . . ."

Kelsie hugged Jeff's limp body close to his chest. "God . . . oh God, I—"

Rozina took his head in both hands and gave him one quick shake. He looked up, surprised and frightened.

"Now, you got to be strong," she said powerfully, "for him, for Karen. You got to let it go. Empty yourself out, before they do it for you."

The strength in her eyes came at him in a wave of color and sound. D'Lacy had said it, he remembered. It fills you up, then empties you out. . . .

He nodded.

He looked down at Jeff, surprised he was still clinging to the man. Jeff's skin was pale and flaccid. "He's hurt bad. His hands . . ."

Rosina helped Kelsie up and guided him toward a small room at the back of the bar. As they moved, Jeff began to stir. His head rolled a little as he tried to look at everything, and when he tried to stand and then to walk the effort did no more than clear his senses enough to ignite the pain. He clung to Kelsie desperately, burying his face against Kelsie's chest. In the back room was a bed, a chair, and a nightstand. A naked light bulb hung from a fixture in the center of the ceiling.

Kelsie deposited Jeff on the bed and covered him with a blanket. He took one of Jeff's hands and examined it. The hole itself was surprisingly large, and the skin and flesh surrounding it was swollen and caked with blood. Andy had violated the man. He had forced his way into Jeff's spirit and denigrated it. An injury like that rarely heals. The scars run so deep they never do disappear.

Kelsie laid his own palm against Jeff's palm. Jeff cried out in pain.

"Damn you, Jeff," Kelsie whispered. "You told me you knew what you were up against."

"I knew," Jeff said. His voice was hoarse and whispery.

Tears ran freely from Kelsie's swollen eyes. "I fell asleep. God help me, I fell asleep!" He squeezed his eyes shut. "This is my fault."

Jeff took a deep breath. It was a moist sound, and it yanked Kelsie out of his misery. "There is no fault. No blame. Let it go, Kelsie."

"How!"

Jeff turned his head slowly and looked at Kelsie. Pain was still etched deeply in the lines of his face, but the eyes were bright and nearly sedate. They held the firm power of confidence. "I killed a man. I did it willfully. He was eating me alive, eating me slowly, making me watch. So I killed him."

Kelsie laid his hand on Jeff's shoulder in an effort to quiet him, but Jeff went on, his gaze fixed on a place where he must have been alone in the dark, a dead man lying at his feet, a pack of Turkish cigarettes with one missing. . . .

"The beast will use it, Kelsie, do you understand?" Jeff fixed him with a firm, penetrating gaze. "The beast will fill you up with it, and when you are so bloated with it you think you're going to rupture, it will empty you out. And everything goes. Your spirit. The knowing of self. Everything. Do you understand?"

"I—I'm not sure."

"Be sure," Jeff said gravely. "It uses everything, that beast. Uses your guilt, your fear, your rage. Uses them like a blade and cuts you to ribbons with them. You've got to own them, because if you don't, the beast will own them. And he'll own you. He'll make you betray yourself. If that happens, then the bastard won't have to do much more than scratch his ass."

"I'll try," Kelsie said shakily.

"No! Do it. Do it or suffer. Do it or suffer the Hiding Fear." Jeff gingerly slid one hand into his pocket, gritting his teeth to stifle a scream. When he pulled the hand out it was clenched in a fist. As he held the fist out to Kelsie his mouth gaped open in a long, deep wail.

Kelsie cringed, the sound of Jeff's pain searing his ears. He pulled away from the fist, not wanting to look again at the ragged hole in the palm. But Jeff held the fist out, looking at him in such a way that Kelsie was compelled to watch.

Slowly, the fist opened.

"I've thrown you a lateral, Kelsie. You've got the ball now. Run with it."

Kelsie looked with surprise and wonder at the small silver key resting in Jeff's mutilated hand.

Through the filmy mask of pain set so deep and resolute in Jeff's haggard face, Kelsie saw the hint of a smile. He took the key.

"You're going to be okay," Kelsie whispered.

Jeff nodded silently. The smile widened.

Kelsie turned to Rozina. She was standing just a short distance from them, hidden in the shadows but strikingly clear. "You'll take care of him?"

She nodded.

"Keep him safe—"

Rozina reached out and placed two fingers on Kelsie's lips. Her touch was warm and dry, and her lovely dark eyes bathed him with a feeling so empowered with strength, he started to cry. He embraced her.

She said softly, "Tomorrow, things change. Take the key. Run with it. It'll guide you. You'll know, when the time is right."

"I don't"—Kelsie stifled a sob—"I don't know what to do. I'm—I'm scared, Rozina."

Rozina stroked his hair. "So am I."

Kelsie pulled away from her, surprised. She rested her hands on her hips. "Kelsie, how can we *not* be?"

He stared blankly, befuddled, then rubbed his face hard. Rozina went to him and took his hands. "You will always be afraid, and there's nothing wrong with that. But you don't want the beast to know what it is that really scares you. That's when the danger begins. That's when the end of things becomes real."

Kelsie shook his head uncertainly. "How do you do it, then? How do you keep the beast from using your Hiding Fear?"

"I own it," Rozina said simply. "I defy it." The corner of her mouth went up. "I look the other way."

Kelsie raised his eyebrows.

"If you don't know what your Hiding Fear is, the beast won't know."

Kelsie stood very still, letting her words sink in. He didn't understand it completely, but that didn't seem to matter. Rozina said he'd know when the time was right, and he believed her.

He took a step toward her, but she held him off with a stern narrowing of her eyes. They stared at each other, exchanging a silent moment, and when Rozina finally moved away the cold returned. As she turned her attention to Jeff, Kelsie felt the empty hole of aloneness open and invite him in.

He watched for a while as Rozina bathed Jeff's wounds with water she'd brought in a bowl. Jeff was quieter now, the pain and horror gone from his face.

"Those guys," he said, "the locals, when they followed me in here . . . they were afraid of you, Rozina. They were scared shitless."

Rozina didn't answer. She continued to bathe Jeff's wounds. Kelsie shifted his weight a little, remembering how she'd just stood there, telling them the bar was closed, and how they'd simply shuffled out. "They can't come in here, can they?"

Rozina ignored him.

Slowly, Kelsie began to understand. "You didn't just happen to wind up here, in Fareland. Did you? And this place, this bar . . . it isn't just a bar." He took a step forward. "It's a safe house, isn't it? A kind of . . . what . . . a sanctuary against the evil." He looked around, as if expecting the place to acknowledge what he was saying. "You've put your own power into this place, to make it safe. That's why you're here, isn't it?"

Silently, Rozina nodded.

Kelsie went to her and knelt beside her. "Rozina, why don't you just destroy the evil? Wouldn't that be easier?"

Rozina began to wrap Jeff's hand in a clean white strip of

cloth. "Why doesn't God just wipe out world hunger?" she asked simply.

Kelsie paused, confused. Rozina sighed. "Everything anyone does has a purpose. Cause and effect. You know what that is, Kelsie? Cause and effect. The scheme of things. What you do in your life affects a lot of people. Affects events. We all got a purpose, and we all got business to tend to." She looked at him finally. "You got business too. Things you gotta do, not just for Joe, or this town, or me. You got things to do that are gonna affect you for the rest of your life. Not everything is neat and tidy, wrapped up with a pretty pink bow."

"I know, but"—he shook his head—"but you got power. More power, I think, than that theater. You could wipe it out—"

"And God could wipe out hunger. But He doesn't do it."

Kelsie frowned. "I don't understand."

She straightened her back and took a breath. "Okay, let me put it in a more personal way. When I was little, I had a kitten. One day I saw the kitten playing with a bee, and I thought, *Poor little thing, it's gonna get stung.* But when I went to grab the kitten my momma stopped me. She said, 'Let the kitten get stung.' I asked her why. I mean, why should I let the kitten get hurt when it was so easy for me to stop it? And Momma said, ' 'Cuz if you save it now, it'll never learn. It won't learn the danger of playing with bees, and maybe someday it'll try playing with a *lot* of bees, and maybe they'll kill it.' "

Kelsie rubbed his chin, thinking. "So, there's something to learn in this?"

She nodded. "Things to learn. Things to learn about evil, and about yourself." She took Jeff's other hand and began to clean it. "Life isn't easy. Never has been. We learn, or we stay ignorant. Better to learn."

Kelsie fell deep into thought, trying to understand.

"Why did you follow the soul-eaters?" Rozina asked.

"I was curious," Kelsie said. "I didn't think they could hurt me."

"You learned different, right?"

"So what are you saying?" he asked, frustrated. "Are you saying there's something Joe's supposed to learn from this?" He ground his teeth. "What good is the lesson if he isn't around to benefit from it?"

Rozina didn't answer. Kelsie got up and began to pace as his frustration and confusion mounted. "There's something you're not telling me."

From the corner of his eye Kelsie saw Rozina's shoulders bunch. He went to her and knelt beside her. "What aren't you telling me?"

When she didn't answer he took her by the shoulders. There was something in her expression; a clouding sadness— a sort of relinquishing anguish he'd never seen before in what was usually a dynamic face filled with conviction, and Kelsie began to understand.

"You're not as strong as you used to be, are you?"

Rozina looked away.

"It was the soul-eaters, wasn't it?" Kelsie said. "When you fought the soul-eaters . . . that's when it happened."

"They were killing you."

"And you saved me," Kelsie said. "But when you saved my life, you lost a little of your own." He let her go. "Why didn't you tell me?"

"No need."

"I had a right to know!" Kelsie said angrily.

"What right?" Rozina countered. "It was my choice. My decision." She sighed. "It's over now. In the past. Kelsie, don't waste energy fighting a battle of the past." She went back to swathing Jeff's hand, her lips pursed. "Things to do. Business to tend to. Get on with it."

"I can't do it alone," Kelsie whispered.

"You're not alone. I still got some power." She began wrapping Jeff's hand. "I'll do what I can. You go now. Go on. Tend to business."

He wanted to stay, just for a while. Just until he felt a little stronger. It seemed to him that with every turn, every effort he made to do what was right, someone got hurt. And now, realizing the price Rozina had paid to save his life, the mounting consequences of his actions were beginning to take on the appearance of threat and defeat. How could anything he did be of any use?

"Don't do that," Rozina said, as though she could hear his thoughts. "Don't fall prey to guilt. It's a tool of the beast. Don't play that game, boy. Not now. You don't have the time."

Kelsie pulled her words in and tried to make them a part of himself, but his mind was overloaded. He wanted to stay here, with Rozina and Jeff. He wanted to stay where he didn't have to make decisions that would affect lives.

But staying here would affect lives just as readily as leaving to fight the thing of constant wind. There was no escape for him. There was no way out of the maze, except to place his hand on the wall and grope blindly until the wall angled toward the opening.

"Tend to business."

Rozina's voice, so stern it was almost cruel, made him jump. She was bathing Jeff's chest with a white wet washcloth. It must have felt good. It looked so clean and white.

"Tend to business," she said again, and this time Kelsie obeyed. He left the shelter of the room.

The bar was dark and smoky and empty. Slivers of light played across the tables and lay like shards of ice on the dusty floor. From behind him Kelsie could hear the sound of the white washcloth being dipped in water and wrung out. It was a clean sound.

He took a deep breath.

Tend to business.

He gripped the key, the one thing given to him. The simple, unimportant thing that Jeff had risked his life for, and suddenly it wasn't enough.

8

Andy pulled Harley behind him, dragging him stumbling and struggling down the center aisle as Harley fought feebly against his cruel grip. He dragged Harley up onto the stage and stood him on his feet. Harley cowered a little, stepping back.

"You fucked up," Andy said coldly.

"Andy, please—"

"I gave you a simple job to do, and you fucked it up. Someone has to pay, and it won't be me."

Harley averted his eyes. He hopped from one foot to the other, rubbing his hands anxiously against his thighs. "Hey, listen, ain't my fault Stricker and Crow're dead."

Andy crossed his arms over his chest. "No?"

Harley began to squirm. "Oh, shit. Shit, man, it's all gone bad! It ain't s'pose to be like this, Andy. You were s'posed to take care of us. Now it's all fucked up."

"That's what I'm talking about."

"No!" Harley finally looked at Andy. "No, that ain't what you're talkin' about. No, you're talkin' about layin' their blood on me. Well, not this time, Andy. Fuck I will!" His voice rose to an angry squeak.

"Harley," Andy said patiently, "there must be balance. Do you understand that?"

"Yeah, but—"

"Things have to balance out. An eye for an eye, you know?" He took a step toward Harley, and Harley shrank away. "Someone has to pay the price."

"You can't do this!" Harley screamed. He was shaking violently, his eyes darting. "It ain't my fault!"

"Fault rides on the wind," came a voice from the shadowed house. Harley whirled around, uttering a frightened squeal.

Nancy sat in the first row, sparkles of red and silver dancing in her hair.

"It rides the wind," she said, rising. Harley groaned. "And sooner or later it's got to come to rest."

"Please . . ."

She moved with gliding ease up onto the stage. He turned desperately to Andy. "Don't let her—" A hand came down on his shoulder. His legs gave way. "No oh no no no please don't! *Don't!*"

Nancy drew him close to her.

Andy watched.

Before leaving Rozina's, Kelsie called Karen to see whether Joe was at home or at the theater. He got his answer when Joe picked up the phone.

"Go home, Kelsie." The voice was hard and alien. Kelsie felt his shoulders grow rigid with tension.

"Let me talk to Karen."

"Fuck you."

Kelsie ground his teeth. "You really like kissing ass, don't you, Joe?"

No answer.

"You were born to it, you know?"

Still nothing.

"Let me talk to Karen."

"No."

"Did you kill her too?"

"What the hell are you talking about?"

Kelsie let out a breath. "People are dying, being tortured, brutalized. And you think you're uninvolved because all you do is run the projector. Isn't that what you said? Wasn't that your excuse when you slammed your knee into my chest and tied me to your bed? You just run the projector. Am I right?"

"Yeah." Tight. "That's right."

"But it's the projector that's been doing all of this."

Silence.

"The killing, the torture. The maiming," Kelsie said, trying to control the quiver in his voice. "It's giving the orders. And you, you son of a bitch. You turn it on."

Cold silence. Kelsie gripped the phone. "Didn't think of that, did you?"

The cold breathed out of the earpiece and down his spine. Kelsie jerked away from it, his heart skipping.

"You're a fine one to talk about killing," Joe said. "Your hands are bloody, you fucker. Look what you've come to."

It's not Joe it is and it isn't . . .

Kelsie's hand trembled.

"How's your new pal, Kels? You get him killed too?"

It uses everything . . . fills you up with it . . .

"You're a real friend, yes, sir. Your pal's getting his hands speared, and you fucking fall asleep."

Don't listen don't listen to it just ignore him just don't listen don't . . .

But the voice, the strangeness of it, the truth it proclaimed so utterly . . .

. . . and the cold was getting brutal.

"You fucked with Karen, and now she's a wreck."

"That's not true—"

"What'd you promise her? What little lies did you tell her while you were splitting her up the middle?"

"Joe . . ."

"Tell me what you did to her, I want to hear it. Did you lick her blood? Did you smother your face between her legs and lick her blood? Did you slurp it out of her?"

Kelsie clutched his stomach.

Not Joe it's not Joe it's

"And when you made her suck your cock, how did it feel? How did it *really* feel?"

"You're crazy! Nothing like that happened! Why are you saying this?"

"How did it feel?" the voice went on, cold, ice burning his brain. "And while we're at it, how did it feel when Stricker's head went flying off? Huh? As good as getting head from a bloody bitch you fucked so hard, she doesn't even look human down there? And when you saw Stricker's brains, all steamy and clumpy like that on the ground, did it make you

come? Did you come all over him, Kelsie? Did you come all
over his brains? Did you?"

Sickness and rage merged together, and Kelsie felt it rise
up from the pit of his stomach to boil in his head, blurring his
vision. He gripped the phone with both hands, teeth grinding
hard against themselves. He squeezed his eyes shut.

*Don't listen don't listen to it keep it under control fills you up
and empties you out don't listen you're a dead man if you do
you're dead!*

"I'm"—he took a breath—"I'm not afraid. . . ."

A surge of cold blasted from the receiver, searing his hand.
He cried out, dropping the icy, steaming thing, and backed
away. The receiver fell swinging from the cord, and as he
stared at it, his mind and body struggling with the deadly
threads of influence now so tightly woven into his psyche, he
heard the laughter.

Long and high and inhuman, the laughter flowed on the
glacial rush of cold.

Kelsie backed away, and the laughter followed him.

Long before Nancy was through, Harley had lost his hu-
manness. Now he was only the shell of a man, hollows and
cracks meandering about the nearly indecipherable torso.
The head had caved in on one side, while the other side
puckered and blistered. The eyes were still human, but so
skewed, they could not focus as one. The left eye veered to
the outside corner of the socket, and the right stared in lu-
nacy at his tormentor.

Nancy touched him lightly on the cheek and his body trembled violently, both shrinking from the frosty touch and
straining for it, craving more. She ran her hand down the side
of his gnarled face, let her fingers dance lightly on his throat,
then touched his chest and left a mark the color of coal.

"My precious," she cooed. "My very precious."

The mark on his chest pulsated.

Harley stared at her, his one good eye imploring her.

Nancy guided him, and he moved with her touch. She
turned him, led him to the screen, and pushed him gently

against it. As his body touched the smooth white surface, it stuck there, like a bug on a screen door.

"You're a part of me now, my precious. A part of everything. Here the pain ends."

She gave him a gentle shove.

His right shoulder disappeared, into the screen.

Harley's mouth gaped in a silent scream, and he looked at her, the fear of betrayal flashing in both eyes.

His right arm sank into the screen.

Harley wept, tears streaming down his unearthly face. He turned to Andy, and Andy smiled at him.

As his right knee went into the screen, Harley found his voice. "Andy!"

A thin ribbon of white swirled out and wrapped around his left thigh.

"Don't do this please don't let her do this to me!"

Andy watched.

The ribbon of white curled around his middle, tightened. Harley wailed.

His screams rose to frightening pitch, the sound echoing in the dark and empty house. More ribbons slithered out, curling around Harley's body, hugging his chest and wrapping around his head.

In one absolute and inarguable movement Harley was pulled into the screen. Only his screams remained, fading gently into the darkness.

Andy looked at Nancy, smiling. He raised his arms in question. "Enough? Yes. More than enough."

Nancy smiled, but her eyes were hard. "Not nearly."

Andy's smile faded.

He whirled and searched the darkness of the house, his eyes moving to the projector window at the back. "I say it's enough! There is no more!"

Nancy touched him and he jerked away, his face pulling down in a fearful grimace.

"Did you really think you were going to get away with it?"

Andy bared his teeth at her. "You blocked me!" He pointed an accusing finger at her. "You blocked me! The key is lost, and you are responsible!"

"Tell me something, Andy," she said calmly. "Did you really believe eyes were not upon you?"

He looked again at the back of the house, and saw a tiny pinpoint of light from the small projector window. He smiled wickedly, then turned a loathsome eye to Nancy. "That's *my* power!" he shouted. "You think you can use my own power against me? You're crazy!"

"Your power?" Nancy sighed. "Oh, cousin. I am so disappointed in you."

She turned and walked slowly to the front row of seats, then quietly sat down.

Andy watched her and began to shake.

"It's my power . . ." he said feebly.

The cold seized him.

He stumbled against the screen and was pinned there. He tried once to struggle free but the cold had already penetrated his body, sunk into his bones, and had made itself the very framework of his body. With dawning horror he sagged against the screen. And waited.

Nancy watched him, her cool powdery blue eyes in deadly focus. She would not miss a second of this.

Andy watched in terror as the pinpoint of light became a stream, fine and silver, penetrating the dark living silence of the theater. It followed its own design, moving toward him, closer, closer.

It touched his chest, and he closed his eyes.

"You walk alone, cousin," Nancy said tenderly.

"My power . . ." he mumbled uselessly.

The stream of light thickened. Andy kept his eyes tightly shut. He felt the silver thread of light, bright and deadly, pierce his skin with its icy sharpness. It streamed through the fine slit it had made and entered him.

Now Andy opened his eyes. He looked down and saw the silver ice-thread flowing into his chest. He wanted to scream.

A rope of light now, he felt it curling and twisting inside him, fondling his organs, lacing through his intestines, curling around his spine. As it snaked down through his legs, he moaned; a grievous sound.

The rope found its end, slipping in through the slit in his chest, and Andy fell.

Only then did Nancy move, standing deliberately. She knelt beside him and turned him over on his back.

From the center of his chest the last inch of silver rope trailed out.

"It's everywhere." Andy whimpered. "It's growing."

Nancy hooked the silver thread with her finger and gave it a tug. Andy screamed as the silver thread lacing through his body was pulled taut.

Nancy bent low and whispered, "Where is your power now?"

Andy wept.

"Things never do stay the same, do they, cousin?"

"You blocked me," Andy managed to say, but his voice was weak and milky. A tiny loop of silver came up through the skin on his cheek.

"Feeling numb now?" Nancy asked, and Andy nodded. "Pain ends for you." She sighed. "Tell me what it's like, before you are no more. Do that for me, cousin. Will you?"

Andy shook his head.

Nancy watched as the fabric of his jeans deflated. She pulled them away and saw a fine web of silver where his legs used to be.

The web crept.

His thighs. His hips.

His belly first bulged, then deflated, tiny movement like thin wires curling and twisting, forming, moving toward his chest, his shoulders.

He touched his face with lacy fingers, laid them gently over his eyes that twirled as silver orbs in lattice sockets.

He opened his mouth, and a fine mesh spewed out.

In the deep aloneness of the theater Nancy watched the silver mesh writhe and squirm with life. She bent her head low, scooped it into her hands, and held it lovingly against her cheek.

"My precious," she whispered. "You will always be with me."

*   *   *

The laughter still following, still echoing in the shadowy stillness, Kelsie nearly fell against the bar. He grabbed the rail with both hands to steady himself, fighting against the power of the laughter.

Finally, taking a deep breath, Kelsie made a dash for the door. He fell through it and literally leapt for his car. He was almost there, his hand on the door, when he saw the four men. His body froze.

They were so close; closer than he would have expected, because he'd seen no one when he first came through the door. But his mind had been elsewhere. His mind had been wrapped around the growling laughter.

The men swarmed toward him. He lurched for the bar door.

Hands on him, tearing at him. Fingers digging into his back, his throat.

His hand on the doorknob; being pulled away, the cool metal slipping from his fingers. He could see them in his mind, pulling him down, smothering him, his one hand reaching uselessly for the closed door. Panic erupted.

His fingers touched the knob again, and the door inched open.

He gave a wrenching cry and lunged forward, dragging with him the swarm of angry hands and kicking feet. He fell through the door, swinging it wide, and the swarm was swallowed up in a fury of screams and painful cries, made silent by the closing of the door.

Kelsie staggered, desperately trying to take in air faster than his lungs could handle. When he looked up, he saw Rozina watching him.

He breathed raggedly, then took another fuller breath that burned his lungs. "I forgot about the locals."

Rozina shook her head disgustedly, and Kelsie sank back against the door.

Karen heard the laughter.

She was in her room, lights out, shadows deep and comforting. She'd gone there to hide, and now the laughter was invading the safe darkness. She moved to the door.

Not wanting to, she opened it and crept out into the hallway. The laughter was louder in the hallway; crisp and clear, floating up from below.

The laughter. A sinister sound. Alien. She gripped the handrail.

Her heart pounded against her breastbone, trembling moving down her arms and making them ache. She took the first step, but could go no farther.

The laughter stopped.

Karen strained her ears.

A wispy sound, like breathing. So faint, almost not there. She took another step.

"What are you doing there?"

She jumped, stifled a cry by slapping her hand across her mouth.

"What are you doing?"

She searched the landing at the bottom of the stairs. Hard darkness. She wanted to run, the need to run so violent that she had to grab the railing with both hands.

Into view, as if a single spot of light had suddenly bathed the landing, Joe emerged.

His face was hard, angry, violent in shadow and striking brightness. The two warred on that face. And his eyes . . .

"Karen."

His eyes were . . .

"My wife. My lovely wife. Come here to me." His hand came up, motioned.

Karen shook her head.

He took one step. "I want you to come here to me. I want you to come." Another step. "Love me, don't you love me? You always said you loved me."

"I don't know you." Her voice cracked.

"Oh, you know me. Yes, you do. You know me. You have known me. Always."

Another step. Karen gripped the handrail. "Joe . . ."

But it wasn't Joe. Not anymore. Maybe it could have fooled her. Maybe. Except for the eyes.

Stone eyes. Black, like coal. Hollow. She could see right through them, into his brain, and there was nothing there.

"Where is he!" she screamed. "What have you done with him?"

"Who?" Another step.

Karen backed up. "I'm not afraid of you."

"Oh?" He was there, just below her, looking up at her with hollow eyes. "Really? Not afraid of me. Okay. But you're afraid of the house, aren't you?" He reached out, suddenly, and Karen tried to pull away, but the hand enclosed her arm, squeezing it tight.

She gasped, the air catching in her chest. His hand was freezing.

A human hand, sculpted in ice.

She struggled, tugging so hard, she felt something spring in her wrist with a hot, fleeting pain. The sculpted hand dug into her flesh.

"You said it before, Karen," said the thing with nothing behind the eyes. "The house doesn't like you. Won't let you take a hot shower, remember?" He came up the last step and pulled her to him. "Want a hot shower?"

The face was very close to her. She could see into the brain, and, oh, Christ there really was nothing there.

He dragged her screaming down the hall, pulling her into the bathroom. With one hand still clamped around her arm, Joe turned the faucet, and steam billowed to the ceiling.

He forced her to her knees. "No shower this time. Maybe just a bath." He clamped his hands tightly around her head. "Nice hot bath, yes? You'll love it."

The tub filled, steam rising from the surface. Karen felt its scalding heat against her face.

"You fucked him." His voice was icy cold, etched in hate. "Did you think I wouldn't know? How could I not know?" The hands squeezed her head with a terrible jolt.

"I don't know what you're talking about!" she screamed.

"Some tub mates would be nice. A few toys, yes? Sorry I don't have any rubber duckies." He twisted her head to one side and her cheek brushed the surface of the water. The heat shocked her.

Her eyes were drawn to the junction between the tub's rim and the tile wall. There, in the crevice of the junction, was a spider. It was large and black, its shiny body beaded with tiny drops of steam. It sat there in the crevice, and her stomach tightened as she thought the thing was looking at her.

"Maybe that will do," Joe said, gripping her neck with his left hand and reaching with his right, touching the spider and coaxing it down the side of the tub.

Horror rose.

Karen struggled, but the hand held her, digging into the tendons in her neck.

With Joe's nudging the spider dropped into the water. It was at eye level, its tiny legs thrashing the surface and sending out tiny waves. Joe pushed it along with his cupped hand, until it approached her face.

The tiny legs tickled her cheek, and sickness seized her.

"There's no way out of here," Kelsie said. "I can't get past them. God, I feel like I'm in a Romero movie."

Rozina leaned against the bar. "Are you afraid of them?"

"Yes!"

"Don't be."

Kelsie huffed hopelessly.

"Kelsie," Rozina said quietly, "you can't always help being afraid. But *sometimes* . . . being afraid is just a waste of time."

He looked at her questioningly.

Rozina crossed her arms, cupping each elbow in her palms. "Remember closet monsters?"

Kelsie blinked. Slowly his mind worked over the memories of his childhood. "Not the closet," he said wistfully. "Under the bed."

Yes! Under the bed! He was six years old and the monsters lived under the bed.

"You were scared of them, weren't you?"

He nodded.

"So, how did you ever get out of your room?"

Kelsie thought.

Six, he was just six and there were monsters under his bed. They lived under his bed, waited for the darkness because they were hungry and they wanted him. They'd wait for him

to swing his feet over the edge, and then their claws would
dig into his ankles and rip the skin and they'd hook him with
their claws and drag him under the bed and horrible things
would happen because they were hungry.

They'd wait, oh, yes . . . they were so cool. So patient.
They'd wait until the middle of the night when he had to go
to the bathroom. His bladder would feel like a hot stone in
his belly until he couldn't stand it any longer and he'd swing
his legs over the edge. . . .

But one night he'd finally had enough. He'd sat upright in
bed, thrown the blankets off, and shouted, "All right! You
want me, come and get me now!"

And nothing had happened. He'd swung his legs over, and
nothing had happened. He'd walked to the door, and nothing
had happened. He'd gone to the bathroom, gotten a drink of
water, come back, rearranged his bed covers and slipped in
beneath them, and nothing had happened.

He glanced at Rozina's smiling face.

"Sometimes," she said, "being scared hurts more."

Kelsie raised himself up. "Okay," he said steadily. "Okay,
here we go." He turned and reached for the doorknob.

"Wait a minute."

Kelsie whirled around. *"Now* what!"

Rozina smiled calmly. "You know what you're going to
do?"

"Yes!"

"And what's that?"

Kelsie sighed impatiently. "Get into the projector room."

"Get into the projector room," Rozina echoed, and Kelsie
nodded. "Then what?"

He hesitated.

"You'll get into the projector room, and then what? Just
what are you going to do with the damn thing?"

Feeling a little foolish, Kelsie shrugged. He hadn't really
thought that far. "Look at it."

"Look at it," she mocked him. "What the hell good is
that?"

He shrugged again, shifting his weight uneasily. "It's a
start."

Rozina shook her head in disgust. "Got to be more to the plan than that, fool." She reached out, fingered something for a moment, and then slid it down the length of the bar. Kelsie watched as it came to rest at the edge, then snatched it up.

It was a book of matches. The name ROZINA was stamped on the cover. He flipped it over. "What's this for?"

"You'll know, when the time's right."

He glanced at her, not quite sure what she meant, and stuffed the matches into his pocket.

As he reached again for the doorknob, Rozina spoke in a low, almost lilting voice that touched him in a way he hadn't expected. "One more thing, Kelsie, and this is important. It never ends. Follow me? The wind is constant. It's constant here, and it never lets you rest. Never, not for a second, never let your guard down. Because if you do, just for a second, everything will be lost." Her face was cool and smooth. Her eyes shimmered with what Kelsie thought were tears. Who was she weeping for?

He gave her a healthy smile and went through the door.

The water scalded Karen's cheek. She gave a distant cry, and in the instant before her nose went under she drew in a deep, hurried breath and shut her eyes.

Her head went under.

The burning settled tightly on her skin. She felt it sink deep into her bones.

His head was close to her, and even through the buffer of water she could hear him breathing; a raspy, hurried sound. His weight came down on her and the edge of the tub dug into her belly.

The burning water seeped into her ears.

And then the heat, the pain, faded away, lost in the terror of no more air.

No more air, she had to breathe. Her lungs, cramping and compressing, fought against her. She struggled, her arms flailing without direction. They brushed against Joe's face and she tried to dig her fingers in, searching for his eyes, wanting to gouge them out. But she couldn't get a firm grip.

Her arms continued to flail, striking the sides of the tub, brushing against things she could only fleetingly recognize. A washcloth, the soap dish, the faucet.

The faucet . . .

. . . and in the storm of panic came a place of calm. In thought, fragile and weightless, an idea came to her.

Her lungs convulsed.

She groped with her left hand, searching for the faucet that had been there only a second ago, but now she couldn't find it . . .

. . . *find it God damn it God damn it to hell I've got to breathe got to breathe my lungs are killing me I've got to* BREATHE!

Her knuckle touched the faucet. It was warm and slick with steam.

Her throat ached, wanting to open wide to let in air that wasn't there, and she fought against it, fought against the terror and groped again, desperately searching for the faucet and the hot water running from it. It washed over her hand and she traced it up, finding the hard warm metal, and following it to the handle used to divert the water from the tub to the shower.

Her body hitched with spasm,

NO!

and her fingers lost their grip.

Bright spots appeared before her clamped eyes. She opened them, and the water burned, the fire fighting for command over her aching lungs.

breathe I've got to breathe God help me help me oh please don't let me

She searched again, groping, her hand brushing the handle.

die don't let me die please I've got to breathe can't hold my breath any longer

Her fingers closed around the handle, and she gave it a tug to the right.

As the hot water sprayed from the shower head she felt the grip on her head loosen. It wasn't much, but it was enough.

She came up out of the water, raking in the hot steamy air. In the midst of her raspy coughing she felt Joe fall away from her, stumbling, and heard a soft thud. She glanced at him quickly to see him sitting back against the wall, his hand gingerly rubbing the back of his head. He was groaning.

She scrambled away from him, crawling on her hands and knees, and as she reached the door, she used the knob to pull herself up. She heard Joe pull in air through clenched teeth and a hand came down around her ankle.

She howled, dug her fingernails into the hand until it jerked away, then stumbled out through the door. She made a lurching move back toward it, grabbing it with both hands and pulling it closed.

Joe was grappling for the door. She heard him slip and fall against it, and then he was tugging on it and she knew she couldn't keep it closed against him.

No time.

No time.

She wanted to rest, to catch her breath, but he'd have that door open in seconds, and then he'd kill her.

She climbed in a half-run to her feet and raced for the stairs.

As she reached the middle step she heard him slam open the door, wailing so horribly, it made her cry out. She took the last five steps as one and hit the front door at breakneck speed.

It was locked.

She tugged on it, expecting it to swing open, and when it didn't her body crashed against it. She fumbled for the latch, but her fingers wouldn't work.

Joe was on the stairs, taking them in easy strides.

Her fingers twitched, and the latch stayed fast. In desperation she tugged uselessly on the door.

Joe was behind her, only a few feet away. She turned, and sank against the door.

He had his hands out in front of him, his fingers curled in a hooklike way. His mouth dragged down in a snarl.

She slipped along the door to her right, searching for a way out. But there was none.

He took a step toward her, his hollow black eyes shining and glistening—insect eyes, the desire for destruction fueling the gleam. There was nothing there, except the need to kill.

But then he stopped.

He cocked his head, as though listening to a distant call. The hollow eyes rotated.

Then his shoulders slumped.

Karen braced herself against the door, watching, wondering what was going on. His hands dropped slowly, drifting like dead leaves to his sides as his face slackened and his sharp black eyes fogged over.

He shook his head, almost mournfully. "Never enough," he whispered, and Karen thought she saw a tear in the foggy, lifeless eyes. "Never enough. It challenges me." He looked at Karen, as though she would know what he was talking about. "I'm so tired, Karen. Can you help me? Can you help me to sleep?"

"Joe?"

Suddenly his face dragged down in sorrow. It was deep, primal, the sorrow of betrayal. "Why did you sleep with him? Why did you do that to me?"

She took a cautious step toward him. "Joe, I didn't sleep with him."

He shook his head. "She told me you did. She said she watched you, that night. She watched you from the stairs."

"We fell asleep, Joe. On the couch. That's all." She took another step toward him. "Joe, can't you see what's happening? Can't you see how you're being used? Being lied to?" She reached out a hand. "Come back to me now, Joe. Come back, please."

He backed away from her, shaking his head sadly. "I want to sleep." Then he turned, and walked, nearly dragging himself through the living room and out the kitchen door.

With confusion and terror finally sinking in, Karen sank to the floor. She cried, but not because of terror, and not because her senses had been stretched so taut that merely the suggestion of another strain would snap her mental stability. She cried for none of these things, because first there had been Joe, and then there had been the thing with the coal-black eyes that had tried to burn her face and drown her. And then there had been Joe again, a victim of the hiding fear and prisoner of his sorrow, imploring her to explain a betrayal that had never taken place.

In the end, as she sat on the floor of Frank Jordan's house, Karen cried from grief.

Kelsie stepped out into the night air, expecting the swarm of people to come down on him again. But the street was deserted, and the air was deadly still.

He got into the car, shutting the door and locking it in one motion. Then he sat.

The streets were deserted.

He sat, thinking, and realized he was trembling.

Where were they?

Kelsie gripped the steering wheel and set himself to the task of focusing his concentration. He had to think about what to do. And he had to think about the beast.

It uses everything, this beast. Every opportunity to get inside and scratch a scar. Every thought made to hurt, to remember, and to hurt. Remember Joe, lost love, Karen. The laughter.

The laughter, in the phone. The laughter so inhuman. So much power. So much betrayal. A primitive, ancient thing, that laughter. All-encompassing. Everything and nothing, like infinity.

The alpha and the omega.

It used Joe's voice, used his body, his mind. Made him ugly inside. Made him reek of death inside. Made him reek of power.

Something like that, it couldn't be just one thing. It couldn't possibly have a boundary, or even a limit.

Limitless power. A thing with no name.

Sadness crept in.

Everything, it uses. . . .

Where was Joe? Where had he been sent when the limitless thing stole his body? Could he really still be trapped inside? Or had Joe—the essence of Joe—simply been thrown away? Tossed into a corner like a dirty garment?

Everything.

A worn-out coat, fabric frayed and useless. No more warmth.

Karen said she saw sadness sometimes. And a limitless power with no name would not feel sad.

Joe was still there, still a prisoner within himself.

Kelsie closed his eyes and leaned heavily against the steering wheel. Trapped inside yourself. There can be no comprehension of that kind of suffering.

Everything uses everything it fills you up.

How was Kelsie going to find a way to set Joe free? How could he fight that kind of corruption, so crafty, so powerful? So evil?

His hand crept to the bandage on his throat, now damp with sweat. He let his hand trail down to his chest and belly, then rest gently on the left side of his groin.

So many scars. So many more to come.

Suddenly he felt very, very tired.

"I won't let go of him," he told the night. "I won't."

He slipped the key into the ignition.

But what good would it do? What good, looking at a fifty-year-old projector? What did he expect to see? The heart of the nameless thing. The soul of it. So what?

So what?

He turned the key.

And besides, who was he to think he could do anything about it? So far, all he'd done was screw up. Tried to help Joe, and what had it gotten him? He'd been hung up by his heels and gutted. Real great, Kelsie ol' pal. Thanks a lot. Thanks one hell of a lot.

The engine turned over.

And how about Karen? Oh, yeah, he'd been a hell of a good friend to her, hadn't he? Where had it gotten her? Was she gone too?

The engine roared, then settled into a fine low idle. He stared at the tachometer as it played gently between 10 and 20.

Was she?

He shifted the gears.

And Jeff . . .
Released the hand brake.
Your pal's getting his hands speared . . .
Kelsie fell back against the seat.
. . . and you fall asleep. . . .
A deep, sorrowful moan escaped before he could stop it.
Everything it uses everything the wind is constant here. . . .
"God, please . . ."
Fills you up . . .
He uttered a cry.
. . . and empties you out. . . .
He gripped the steering wheel with both hands, squeezing
it until his knuckles went white. He held his breath until his
lungs begged. His foot slipped off the clutch and the car
lurched forward, then sputtered and died.

He fell against the steering wheel and wept. "God, please
don't do this to me please let me go. I can't do it anymore. I
just can't do it. . . ." He let out a long, shuddering moan.

*Fills you up and empties you out don't listen don't listen to it
close your ears close your heart and don't let it in don't listen
don't listen don't LISTEN don't*

"Listen to me!"
He sat upright and pulled in air.
"Listen to me!" It was Rozina's voice.
He looked around.

Through the windshield he saw the smoky light peeking
out from the crack in the door of Rozina's bar. The light
looked warm. He let it creep into him, fragile fingers of comfort reaching through the cold darkness, touching him.

Then he saw Rozina in the window. It was just a silhouette;
just the outline of her fine soft hair, the curve of her breast,
the hand laid gently on her ample hip. He couldn't see her
shadowed face, but he knew she was looking at him and the
look went inside, lay warm against his heart, and filled his
mind with white light.

He smiled.
The soul-eaters had hovered over him, had tried to steal
inside, and Rozina had sent them packing.
He started the car again.

9

Karen sat in the darkness feeling numb and empty for a long time after Joe had left. She stared mindlessly at the shadowy shapes around her, the incongruous angles and incomplete curves and planes of the furniture and walls. Nothing really familiar; she was sitting amid the intricacies of an alien landscape, a stranger in an unwelcome land. She had no business being here.

She could hear sounds in the distance, the shuffling of feet, heavy clumping sounds, but her mind refused to register them until their distant timbre increased, growing stronger and somehow more relevant than the crippling hurt of her heart and the fatigue that weighed so heavily on her mind. Letting the sounds filter in through the cloud of dismay and utter misery was a difficult thing to do, but their persistence finally snagged her attention. She crept to the window and peered out.

Forms made black by a moonless night were moving along the road toward the house. They were hunched and hesitant, taking a few steps and then stopping, peering out, pointing, turning to one another and whispering. She couldn't decipher what they were saying, but the frightened, angry tone of their hushed voices was horribly clear. Being Joe's wife no longer held any weight with the locals, or the theater. In Joe's mind she'd betrayed him. Lies had been spread, and for a purpose.

She was a threat. She'd always been a threat. But for the life of her she didn't know why.

She crawled away from the window.

They were all there, she knew. Rudy Olsen, Al Farnwell

. . . men she'd chatted with and waved to and done business with. Now they were coming to hurt her, maybe kill her. Now she was the enemy, the means by which they'd find relief from the unrelenting, filthy hunger.

The sounds came closer.

She grimaced, feeling her burnt skin stretch and scream. She touched her cheek gently and the pain spirited to the bone. She sucked in air as she examined her tight skin for blisters. Mercifully, there were none. The burn was only third degree.

Closer still, the shuffling of feet across packed dirt and dead leaves split the dark silence outside. Hushed angry whispers gave way to shouts, and the shouts focused on her name.

Part of her wanted to curl up in a ball and let panic clean her out so there would be no feeling, no thought, no awareness of what was outside the thick shroud of insanity.

Another part of her wanted to survive.

She came to her feet and bolted for the back door.

The theater was absolutely dark.

Kelsie maneuvered his car so that the headlights shone in through the lobby doors. They pierced the darkness with lonely, lifeless light. Silence reigned.

He peered through the windshield. The shafts of light diffused into soft washes of gray, illuminating only a small portion of the lobby within. He could see the outline of the snack bar, and to the left the curving shape of the stairway to the mezzanine, diffracted and incomplete.

He got out of the car and stepped up to the lobby doors. As he laid his hand on the door handle, his heart gave a subtle lurch.

It was warm and soft, like living flesh.

He jerked back, his mind making alternate leaps from confusion to terror. He took a deep breath and waited for the violent flurry in his mind to settle, then touched the handle again.

Still warm. Still soft, almost yielding. A hand closing around his own. He was expected . . . yes. . . .

His body cut a path in the diffused light. He looked at his shadow looming up before him, lying dark against the entry-way curtains.

The curtains billowed, and his heart lurched again.

The Fareland had breathed.

Kelsie closed his eyes. *Will not panic. I will not panic.*

Fixing his mind firmly on what he had to do, he clenched his fists and moved slowly toward the stairway.

He went up the stairs slowly, looking straight ahead and not wavering.

Halfway up. His shoulders ached.

Another breath. The stair gave way and he fell to one side, his hand reaching out for the railing.

It gave, too, feeling warm and supple. Kelsie cried out and fell back, hitting the wall with a thud.

I'm inside it.

He stood shakily with his back braced against the wall as panic fingered his brain.

I'm inside it oh shit I'm inside its guts.

Panic spawned terror, and the terror spirited through him in a flash of sound. He fought desperately, grinding his teeth, fought to keep his mind from folding in until there was noth-ing left, and heard the Fareland breathe again.

Rozina.

Kelsie had said to get to Rozina's if anything bad hap-pened. Rozina would protect her.

The cold night air knifed Karen's burning face but she kept moving, protecting her painful skin with her hands. She skirted the side of the house, took time enough to peek around the corner at the angry mob now swarming over her front porch, then made a dash for the road.

Get to Rozina's.

As she ran she kept an eye on the swarm as they threw themselves against her front door, and when she reached the creek she stopped to watch them. They were like animals; large hungry bears slamming their bodies against the fragile door frame until it finally gave way in a splintering crash, and they moved inside as one.

She turned and headed across the creek. The way was difficult; trying to pick out rocks large and stable enough to bear her weight without slipping on their slick surface, she fell twice and each time the sharp edges cut jagged gashes in her ankles and shins. She had to stifle cries, squeezing her eyes tight enough to make them tear, then continue to move until she was finally across. Slender streams of watery blood traced down her legs.

Now the main road was just ahead. Behind her she could hear the rage of defeat when the ugly swarm found the house empty, then the sound of stamping feet on the wooden porch, the pause in their search, and the final wailing cry of detection when they saw her in the distance, heading for the road.

She made a lunge for the main road, hit it running, and headed for town.

The slapping of her own feet against the dusty road was a feeble sound compared to the thunder of the swarm. They had reached the road in less time than it had taken her, and were now only a hundred yards behind her. Panic rose, and she used its fury to bolster her forward momentum.

She rounded the corner and could see the town proper only two blocks away. Shadows liquefied around her, taking form and giving chase. She began to cry, her rasping sobs catching in her throat as her lungs fought for air.

The angry crowd had closed their distance to less than thirty feet. Rozina's bar was on the other side of the town proper. She would never make it.

Why are you going there?

She heard it in her mind, as though something had squirmed in through an open crack and was whispering, taunting her with its implacable logic.

Joe's okay. He's better now. No need to see Rozina. Why are you going there? Go back home, Karen. You're safe at home. Joe will be there soon.

Now she could hear the labored breath of the angry crowd, the heat of their anger a furious squall against her back.

Go back home! her fevered mind screamed at her, but she ignored it.

* * *

Kelsie struggled to slow his breathing. His lungs seemed to liquefy inside his chest, white hot and molten, steaming the air he sucked inside.

This is the plan. Frighten me. Weaken me. Get me to drop my guard. . . .

If he succumbed now to the terror, he would not survive.

But he was not without weapons. Jeff had given him the key, and maybe, just *maybe . . .* it was enough.

One chance. One slim chance. It had to be enough.

He got up.

He tested one step, and nothing happened, but somehow that wasn't very comforting. Anything could happen, at any time, and it would happen when he least expected it.

He looked up at the Fareland's ceiling. "You're a treacherous son of a bitch, aren't you?"

The disquieting mixture of rococo and Art Deco stared down at him.

Kelsie started up the stairs, careful not to touch the railing. He moved slowly, and as he reached the top he uttered a sigh of relief. He had almost expected the living staircase to heave and swirl, bucking him off and sending him to the lobby floor, where he'd break his back and lie helplessly as the Fareland slowly digested him over a hundred years—

Kelsie closed his eyes. *Stop it. Stop it.*

He looked down the long curving mezzanine, searching for the door to the projection room, but there was no door at the other end and for a moment he was confused. He moved to the first entryway and peered through the curtains.

The screen, strikingly white, burned his eyes and he staggered back, slapping his hands over his face. He stood there, breathing hard, hands hiding his face, and when he finally lowered his hands and opened his eyes all he could see was whiteness. For a long, terrified moment he thought he was blind.

But slowly images began to emerge from the whiteness. He heaved a shuddering sigh, his body still trembling, then peeked at the screen again.

It was so white, it was almost blue. And it was very, very clean.

Kelsie.

Kelsie stiffened.

Kel-l-l-lsie-e-e-e. A gentle, whispery sound.

Kelsie slapped his hands over his ears and forced himself not to listen. He tried to turn away from the screen, but found he could not take his eyes off it. That whiteness, the clean, shining brightness. It enveloped him. He was drawn to it.

As though on command Kelsie stepped through the entry-way.

The screen whispered his name, breathed, promised something. Something. . . .

His legs hit something solid—the balcony rail, yes. Kelsie leaned over it, reaching for the screen.

A promise. Something about a promise.

He stretched his fingers toward the screen, tried to reach it, touch it.

A promise of something—

"Precious, my very precious."

Kelsie whirled around.

At the head of the aisle, so slender and beautiful, so promising, the woman raised her arms to him. She was laced in shadow, moving in memory; dressed in a flowing gown of silver latticework, the gown flowing freely in response to her body as she swayed, billowing and ebbing by its own volition. Its translucence gifted him with the promise of her sleek and sculptured thighs, her flat belly, and the gentle curve of her breasts. His body responded as his eyes traveled up the silver mesh gown, drinking the vision of her supple throat and full lips, the frame of her hair around vividly blue eyes.

Powdery blue eyes.

Kelsie's throat tightened.

"You know who I am," the woman whispered.

He nodded.

"What did you expect to find, Kelsie Brown?"

"I don't—I don't know, I . . ." Kelsie closed his eyes, but the sweet fire of her beauty seared his brain. His body ached.

"What do you want, Kelsie Brown?"

"I just"—his voice croaked—"I just want to see it."

"Can you see the wind, my precious?" He felt her take a step toward him and opened his eyes suddenly.

Don't let her touch you.

He backed away, losing his balance as his legs butted against the railing. He reached behind him and grasped it.

"Only when it sways the trees," she said, smiling, and Kelsie felt the smile grip him.

"My precious," she sang to him. "So very precious, I have something for you."

"No . . ."

"A gift." She was moving closer, swaying. His body surged. "A gift for you, my precious. A gift to fill your aching heart."

He tried to step back, but his own lust, full blown and hungry, fought against him. She was very close now, reaching for him. Reaching for his heart.

Don't let her touch you, don't—

"Do you feel the cold?"

It came, sinking teeth into his skin, penetrating his center and then radiating out.

"You belong to it. You belong to me."

Kelsie writhed.

Don't let her touch me God please oh please don't—

But then her hand was on him, and his brain exploded as fire merged with ice, sending out sparks of color. His body succumbed to its own hunger.

"Come, precious," she said, pulling him close to her, her arms twining about him. He felt them trace a river of heat down his back, caressing his hips, circling in between his legs. Fire and ice licked his thighs.

She closed her hands around his and guided them to the soft fullness of her breasts. As his fingers touched the smooth warm skin, what Kelsie had thought was the ultimate of desire found a new and deadly limit.

"You're ready for me." Her breath brushed his skin. "Oh, yes . . ." Pressure against his swelling groin. "I can *feel* you ready for me."

She moved, and he helplessly followed. "You have labored, my precious. Come watch the trees sway."

She lifted him effortlessly and dropped him into one of the front seats. He collapsed into it, gripping the arms as his desire tore at his insides. She'd moved away from him, just barely out of reach, and the pain of it drove him to near madness. She could do anything to him now. Anything. She owned him.

She went behind him, still caressing, still breathing on him, her hands laid against his head on both sides. Swiftly her hands bore down, until he felt as though his head had been slipped into a vise. The fire and ice merged with fear as the vise closed down on his head. He tried to squirm free but his body fought him, craving for more of the fire, more ice, the pain pulsating and throbbing in his nerves. His legs grew hot and heavy. His pelvis was on fire. And the hands held him fast.

In front of him the screen flickered. His heart fluttered. "What will you do to me?"

"Nothing, precious. You will do it all."

"I don't"—the screen swayed, billowed, flickered—"I don't understand." He tried to look away, but his head was held tight.

"You will taste your own blood and find it sweet. Only then can you know the greatness of power. It will be a part of you, and you, a part of it. You will never be cold again."

A storm of shadow filled the screen.

"Watch, my precious. See yourself."

Compelled to watch, Kelsie lifted his face to the screen. The shadows flowered out, filling the house like smoke.

Kelsie's heart screamed.

"What do you see?"

Kelsie writhed as the terror being played out for him tried to seize him.

"What do you see?"

On the screen, shadows, images blurred and soft, focusing and then blurring again.

Kelsie watched the screen.

The center of space, whole galaxies gone cold. Blackness,

void, no sound, no light. There is nothing in the center of every-
thing that was and is. There is nothing, except an egg.

Its surface is soft, pliable, almost translucent. It glows with its
own quintessence. And there is something inside.

Kelsie ground his teeth.

It moves, inside. It squirms and struggles, trying to find a way
out. Black formless shapes scrape the inside of the egg, testing,
tapping, scraping, struggling to be free of the prison made for it.

Kelsie watched, tears streaming from his eyes. He took in
air, held it, fought.

A formless shape, sentient, in anguish, locked inside the
prison. It struggles, howls, the egg warps with its fevered strain-
ing against the pliant substance. The egg strains, nearly ripping.

The Hiding Fear.

Kelsie fought.

Hands on his head, closing, crushing. His body screamed.

"Show me what you see, Kelsie. Show me what's inside the
egg."

"No."

"Show me, Kelsie. Show me what's way deep down inside."

"NO!" Kelsie shut his eyes. "It's mine. I *own* it! And I've
buried it!" He opened his eyes. Sweat poured down his face
in salty rivulets. He smiled through his pain. "You can look
for it if you want, but you'll never find it!"

The hands clamped down on his head. "Tell me where you
buried it."

Kelsie grimaced, his teeth grinding. "No!"

"Then feel the pain."

The screen flickered, puckered. Shapes undulated, shadows exploded, focused, streaming down to clarity and burning into his eyes. He uttered a low, despairing groan.

"What do you see?"

A room.

Kelsie struggled, but the hands held him.

White room. Leather . . .

. . . straps . . .

He gave a long, pitiable groan.

Leather straps, pulled tight, pinning him to the bed with rough white sheets. People watching . . .

. . . watching . . .

Kelsie lurched in the seat, struck by the sudden pain of the image made clear. "Losing my mind! I'm losing my mind, God, they've taken it from me!"

The people . . .

"Tell me," Nancy commanded.

He gave a miserable cry. "They took it from me! Strapped me down and they're watching me. They won't listen to me. They won't believe me!" He stopped, his eyes widening. "Something in his hand. Something . . . oh, God no . . . it'll hurt. It'll hurt, they're going to hurt me!"

A needle.

The needle inching toward his arm. He struggles, fighting against the straps holding him down, tries to twist away from the needle but it comes down, penetrates his skin. He sees it, feels it slip into his skin, stab his bone. Hot wires snake up his arm, into his shoulder, his chest. Hot wires, red hot and slithering, snake into his heart.

Kelsie howled, wrapped in agony.

"There's more," Nancy cooed.

"Please . . ."

"Watch the screen."

Kelsie watched, and saw the nightmare.

"Tell me," Nancy whispered.

"It's a boy," he rasped. "Young boy. Six years old. Only six." He grimaced. "Only six!"

"What is he doing?"

Kelsie breathed hard. "Cage . . . on the lawn. Guinea pigs, eating the grass but it's hot . . . too hot . . . the sun's out and it's too hot. . . . I didn't know!"

"You knew."

"No—"

"The sun was too hot, and you forgot about the guinea pigs. You left them there, and then you found them. Smelled them. High, gassy smell."

"They're dead!" Kelsie cried.

"Tell me where you buried it," Nancy commanded.

Kelsie wept. "No!"

"Feel the pain, then. Feel them die."

It came. Furious heat, wet and smothering, soaking through his skin. His insides boiled with the heat. His skin, first dripping with his precious body fluids, now radiated the killing heat from within. Every nerve shriveled, every muscle solidified and fractured. Kelsie howled as the pain merged with the baking heat.

"It hurts!" Kelsie screamed. "Oh, God it hurts, it *hurts!*"

Nancy bent low, her breath brushing his flush cheek. "Tell me where you buried it, Kelsie. Tell me, and you won't hurt anymore."

Falling, gliding to the center of things, to the center of self. The egg, pulsing, warping, cracking open—

"NO!" He shut his mind to it, turned away, denied the Hiding Fear.

"Then feel the pain."

Again the screen flickered, and a new nightmare played itself out for him.

Karen pistoned her legs, slamming them down on the street as she ran. Her chest was on fire. She could feel them getting closer, overtaking her.

ROZINA!

Then she saw it, like a beacon in the thick foggy darkness. Rozina's bar. Light filtered out from beneath the doors. She fixed her gaze on it and ran.

Right behind her now, she could almost feel their hands on her.

She hit the door of the bar at a full run. The door gave way and she fell inside, rolled twice, and lay sprawled on the floor as the door swung shut with an audible, forceful *whap*.

Karen lay on her back, breathing hard. She brought her legs up and lay there, eyes closed, waiting to see if her heart would stop.

It didn't, and when she opened her eyes Rozina was standing over her. The look on her face was one of resolution and regret. "Been waiting for you," she said, then turned and walked away.

Karen struggled to her feet. Rozina moved silently through a door at the back of the bar, and Karen followed her.

In the back room she found Rozina sitting next to a bed where Jeff lay. His hands were wrapped in clean white cloth. Rozina was dipping another white cloth in a bowl next to the bed. She wrung it out, and began to swathe Jeff's forehead.

"Kelsie's in trouble," Karen said urgently. "Isn't he?"

Rozina nodded. "Nancy is taking him to the Hiding Fear."

Karen shook her head. "Hiding Fear . . . what's that?"

"It's what's inside," Rozina said. "Deep inside, where there is no light, no air."

"Then you have to help him."

"I have." Rozina sighed. "I've done what I can."

"I don't believe that," Karen said sternly.

Rozina ignored her. Karen took a step forward. "You've got power, I know you do. I don't understand it, but I know it's real. Your being here, this bar, the people in this town being afraid of you. All of this has a purpose." She ran a hand across her brow and huffed in exasperation. "You can't turn your back on him now. He needs you. He's not strong enough and he needs you."

"I told you," Rozina said coldly. "I already told you I done what I can. It's up to Kelsie now."

"But he's in too deep! You just said so. He needs more help. More than I can do alone. And you know that. I know you know it. Why won't you help me?"

Rozina sagged, her head falling back. "I've done my battle," she said in a tired, old voice. "Let me rest."

"I can't do it alone!" Karen shouted desperately.

Suddenly Rozina buried her face in her hands and howled. It was a terrible sound, filled with conflict and fear. It made Karen's heart flutter. She stood frozen, thinking she'd somehow pushed Rozina over a fatal edge.

Finally Rozina sighed, raised her head, and sighed again. Karen waited quietly.

"I'll help," Rozina said in a low voice. She stood and faced Karen, giving her a stern, solemn look. "But you have to be the one. You have to save him."

"Okay," Karen said. "What do I have to do?"

Rozina moved away, closing her eyes. She stood silently for what seemed a long time, and when she finally spoke it was in a very deep, commanding voice. "He's very close. Close to the Hiding Fear. If he sees it, he'll die." She looked at Karen. "You have to stop him from seeing it."

"How do I do that?"

"You'll know."

Karen exhaled. "I don't understand."

"You will, when you need to."

For a moment Karen was confused, but only for a moment.

10

When they stepped out of the bar Karen was surprised to find the street empty. They walked along, Karen keeping close to Rozina, and headed for the Fareland.

The streets were absolutely, completely empty.

"Where are all the people?" Karen asked.

"Hiding."

"From what?"

Rozina looked at her. "From me."

They continued down the street.

The front of the Fareland was open. As they reached the doors Karen could see a glowing blue light slanting out from behind the balcony curtains. They went inside, and Rozina pointed to the mezzanine. "They're up there, in the balcony." She went to the stairs and started up them. Karen followed.

By the time they reached the mezzanine Karen could hear Kelsie's voice. He was crying, begging. Her heart lurched and she headed for the curtains.

"No," Rozina said, grabbing her arm. "You wait here. Wait until I'm finished, then you come in."

"How will I know?" Karen raised her hand. "Never mind. I'll know." She sighed deeply, crossed her arms over her chest, and leaned against the railing.

Rozina pulled the curtain back and stepped into the balcony.

The brilliance of the screen was a blinding white. She reached out with her mind and knew that Kelsie was dangerously close to the Hiding Fear. It was fingering his brain, peeling back the layers of his psyche like an onion, and he was within moments of seeing it. She had gotten here just in time.

Rozina closed her eyes, reached out with her spirit, and grasped the blinding white light. When she felt its radiant cold she opened her eyes and let the light inside.

Nancy whirled around, saw her, and screamed.

Rozina felt the light stream into her, filling her heart, freezing her with its power. She cleaved to it, felt it with her soul, molded it, and merged with it until she was one with it.

There was no more light in the balcony. No light on the screen. No light peeking through the projection-room window.

The light was in Rozina.

She turned her attention to Nancy. The beautiful woman was crouched low, her eyes burning with hatred. She bared her teeth; shining white and sharp. Rozina raised her arms and held out her open hands. "Come, sister. I own you now."

Nancy shrieked with rage. "I am my own power!" she screamed.

Rozina beckoned her with a gesture of her hand. "I own you now."

"NO!" Nancy lunged at her, hands hooked into claws, and fell on her.

Rozina embraced her.

Slowly, howling with rage and despair, Nancy began to dissolve. Her body warped and swirled, losing substance, becoming light, and the light that had once been flesh flowed into Rozina's body, leaving the gown of silver mesh to fall to the floor.

Rozina knelt beside it, gathered it into her arms, and held it close to her body. "Free now, Andy. Free." She hugged the mesh and it dissolved as well, seeping into Rozina until there was nothing left of it.

Rozina knelt there, filled with the power of the light, and breathed deeply. She stayed very still, very alone in the place where her spirit soared and bellowed, bloated with the light, and wept softly.

* * *

It's time.

Karen jerked.

It's time.

She moved slowly toward the curtain. There was no light coming from the balcony. No sound, except a harsh, heavy breathing laden with sobs.

"Kelsie!" She ran through the curtains.

He was sitting in the front row of the balcony. His body was rigid, his head tilted back. He was screaming and sobbing, making horrible, heart-wrenching sounds.

Karen ran down the aisle and stood in front of him. The look in his eyes nearly made her scream. They were wild with terror, bright and wicked, rolling unnaturally. Karen grabbed his head with both hands. "Kelsie!"

He screamed. "It hurts! It *hurts!*" He tried to struggle free of her but she held on tight, bringing her face very close to his.

"Ease back, Kelsie," she said. "Ease away, come on."

He shut his eyes tight, screaming, moaning.

"Ease away from it, Kelsie." She wrapped her arms around him, hugged him. "Come on, ease back. Turn away from it."

Slowly, almost imperceptibly, Kelsie began to calm. Karen hugged him, held his head against her breast, stroked his hair. "Turn away, Kelsie, you can do it. Come on. Ease back, turn away."

She continued to hug him until his breathing slowed. Then he heaved a heavy sigh. "Oh, fuck . . ."

Karen pulled back and looked at him. His eyes were red and still a little wild, but focus and sanity had returned. He looked at her, knew who she was. Relief flooded through her like water from an overflowing stream.

Kelsie sat up, sighed again, and rubbed his face. "I don't *ever* want to go through that again." He got out of the chair, swayed a little, then steadied himself. Karen could see that he was in control again, and strong. She hugged herself, rubbing her upper arms.

Kelsie turned to her. "Thank you."

Karen shrugged, not knowing what to say. She looked around. "Where's Rozina?"

Kelsie looked at her sharply. "She was here?"

Karen nodded. "Yeah. She came in first. Told me to wait. The place was filled with light, and then it was gone."

Kelsie bent his head.

"Kelsie?"

When he looked at her, she saw great sadness in his face. "Kelsie?"

"I want you to go outside now, okay?" Kelsie said. "The rest of this, I have to do alone."

Confused, she wanted to ask further, but the look in his eyes stopped her. She nodded, hugged him, then turned and went up the aisle. When she reached the top, she turned back. "Kelsie?"

"Yeah?"

"Bring Joe back home."

Kelsie rubbed his hands together. "I'll try."

Karen watched him a moment longer, then went through the curtain.

He heard her walking down the stairs, heard her footsteps cross the lobby and the lobby door swing shut. When he was certain she was outside and safe, he sat down again and looked at the screen. There was a filmy shroud of gray covering it, the kind of shroud that only time can bring. No light came from it.

The light was in the corner, to his right, near the railing. Kelsie looked at it for a long time, feeling his heart thud. When he tried to move, his legs were stiff with fear. He walked slowly toward the light.

Huddled in the corner by the railing was Rozina. Her knees were pulled up close to her chest. Her head rested on her folded arms. Glittering light flickered on the floor and against the railing. The light was coming from her face.

Kelsie swallowed. "Rozina?"

She raised her head and as she did, as the terrible blinding light streamed out of her eyes, Kelsie felt himself sink into a pool of grief. "Oh, God, no."

He took a step forward but she raised her hand. "Get out."

Tears welled in his eyes. "I can't do that," he said in a

raspy voice laden with fear and sadness. "If I leave you—
even if I turn my back on you—you'll disappear." He sup-
pressed a sob. "You'll disappear, I know it. And I'll never see
you again!"

"Now you get hold of yourself," she said angrily. "You get
hold and you tend to business!"

"Rozina, please—"

"Get out!"

He stood there a moment longer, then turned away.

In the next instant the light was gone.

His grief flooded over him. He didn't need to look back to
know Rozina was no longer there. He hugged himself, pulled
his grief inside, and used it to make himself strong. "Tend to
business," he said aloud, looking up at the window of the
projection room. "Tend to business."

As he stood there, hugging himself, growing angry, he felt
a shift in the air. It came from behind. He looked around
slowly, and as his eyes adjusted to the darkness at the back of
the balcony, he saw something looking at him from the entryway. It was shrouded in shadow, but its presence was powerfully felt in the glare of unseen eyes.

He bared his teeth at the shadowy figure. "I can take anything you throw at me," he said quietly.

The shape moved away from the curtain. The curtain
made a whispery sound as it closed.

Kelsie followed.

He stepped out onto the mezzanine. The air was disturbingly still. He took a moment to steady his nerves.

Without looking he knew someone was standing at the
head of the stairs. He turned slowly.

Joe.

At the top of the stairs. Joe, looking so sad, so weary.
Kelsie moved toward him. "Joe?"

Joe raised his arms entreatingly. "Help me."

Kelsie stopped.

Joe's eyes went hard. *"Help* me."

"You're full of tricks, aren't you?" Kelsie said. "But that's
all they are. Tricks."

Joe laughed; a sinister sound. Kelsie took a step forward. "I'm going to destroy you," he said slowly.

The laugh came again, ice on a filthy breeze, and this time all that was left of Joe slipped away until there was nothing left but the evil. It stood like a liquid shadow, large and quietly powerful.

"What can you do?" It pulsed. "You are frail. Impotent. I still work inside you. Feel me, can you feel me?"

Cold, like ice. Kelsie braced himself against it. "I'm not afraid of you."

"That could be dangerous."

"No. I've seen you. I've seen inside of you. I know what you really are."

The eyes narrowed.

"These people," Kelsie said, "all these people, they've been keeping your secret for years, feeding you, prodded by their own shame, their own fear. Joe used to say that people were nothing more than sheep standing on two legs. It's hard for us to find our own direction, much less keep it once we do. But it's not finding direction that's the problem. Problem is, it's just easier to let someone else guide you. Make decisions for you. You exploit that. You use it to feed yourself and you're always hungry, aren't you? Never full. You never can get full so you just keep feeding and feeding, but it's never quite enough, is it? Never . . . quite . . . enough."

The thing growled. Kelsie took another step. "You fed off Joe's weaknesses. You fed off me. You *raped* me! You filled me up and then emptied me out, but I'm luckier than Joe. I'm lucky, because I never saw the Hiding Fear. I came close. Fucking close. But I didn't see it. And now it's buried." Kelsie smiled a little. "You'll never find it."

It made a hissing sound, outraged, and bent low like a cat preparing to strike. "Be careful. Be very careful. You are not as free as you would like to think."

Kelsie kept moving. "You can't hurt me anymore. You emptied me out. There's nothing left you can do to me."

A sickly smile tugged at the thing's lips. Kelsie stopped.

"How confident you are," it said. "And how stupid. How arrogantly ignorant."

Kelsie braced himself, but before he could do anything, before he could think, the thing in front of him swayed, blurring out of focus, and Joe was there again.

Kelsie tried not to look at him.

"Kelsie." It was Joe. Oh, God, please . . . it had to be. . . . "Help me. It's got me. Gotten inside me. You've got to help me."

It was true: Joe was a prisoner within himself, trapped in the center with foul substance all around. Trapped inside, screaming, clawing at his own insides, trying to get out. Kelsie felt Joe's pain in his own aching heart.

"Joe!"

But Joe couldn't hear him. His body shook, his face contorting and relaxing, responding to a power from within. It was difficult to watch, because Joe's face kept changing. At first he saw Joe as he had known him. Then he saw other things, like an overlay of cellophane. Someone else's eyes, someone else's scowling grin. His body twitched and strained, as if he was being pulled in many different directions.

Kelsie reached out to him, but Joe backed away. "Always there! Always with me! I can't take it anymore!" He threw his head back and howled, the sound resonating, vibrating the walls. His body arched in a terrible spasm, arms wide, mouth gaping.

Then he began to move. It was almost comical, like an acrobat doing a cartwheel. He stood on his hands next to the railing, and in the next instant his legs went over.

Kelsie watched transfixed as Joe's hands grasped the railing and his feet swung over. He hung there, his grasping hands sliding slowly down the rungs of the railing.

Kelsie lunged forward and grabbed frantically. He went down on his belly as Joe's hands uncurled from the railing. He held on to one hand, and looking down he saw Joe's haggard face contorted with pain. His body went limp, and the only thing keeping him from falling was Kelsie's desperate grip on his wrist.

Joe's head fell back and his mouth dropped open.

"Don't!" Kelsie screamed. "God damn you, Joe! Don't let the bastard win!"

Joe opened his eyes. His face relaxed. Slowly he pulled himself up, grabbing on to Kelsie's arm until his face was close to Kelsie's, peering at him through the rungs.

And the eyes. The eyes . . .

Kelsie moaned.

The eyes were black, rotating electrically, and behind them, nothing there. Kelsie could see the optic nerves, two tendrils of tissue streaming out and back, floating in the dark red nothing.

Kelsie hung on.

A sneer curled the lips. Slowly, watching Kelsie with the lifeless black eyes, the thing took one of Kelsie's fingers and began to bend it back. Kelsie gritted his teeth against the pain. It pulled the finger, then jerked it with one flashing move. Kelsie heard the bone snap, and the pain shot up his arm. He screamed.

Breathing hard, clinging with the rest of his fingers, he watched as the thing took another finger, bending it back slowly. "No . . ."

He fought hard against the pain he knew would come. He clamped his eyes shut and fought.

He screamed again as the second bone cracked and Joe's wrist slipped through Kelsie's broken fingers.

"NO!" he lunged for the falling body, but he could not reach it. The thing fell, but it wasn't a thing anymore. It was Joe again, eyes solid and bright with terror. Kelsie hid his face in his arms, but his scream didn't muffle the sound of Joe's body hitting the floor. He heard it: a watermelon hitting cement.

He scrambled away from the edge of the balcony, not wanting to look, not wanting to see Joe's body lying in a spreading puddle of blood, his head split open. Kelsie huddled on the floor, face buried deep in the crook of his arms.

I'm sorry, Joe. I'm sorry so sorry oh God please don't let it be . . . please. . . .

He rolled over on his back, his body racked with sobs.

Strength gone, emptied like a pail of water tilting, his heart lay open, and the cold crept inside.

Slowly the grief began to ebb. It was a subtle thing, overpowered by the cold. The cold was everything now. Everywhere. In his bones, deep inside his bones. Kelsie thought if he were to crawl up on a rock when the sun was at its zenith, if he were to lie there on his back with the heat of the baking sun washing down on him, he just might feel a little warmth for a time.

For a time, until the sun went down.

11

At last Kelsie pulled himself to his feet. He had to see one more time. He had to see Joe.

He went over to the railing and looked down.

But Joe wasn't there.

Kelsie closed his eyes and prayed.

Please, God. Please. Make it so Rozina took him with her. Please. Make it so.

There was something left to be done. His mind had grown cold and uncaring, and now he moved automatically. He found himself thinking about the sun and the rock onto which he'd crawl, when all this was over. And it was going to be over very soon.

He held his battered hand close to his chest. The fingers throbbed but there was no real pain. It was more a memory of pain, made dull with the passing of time, or possibly it was the cold.

He staggered back, without direction, and fell through the entryway curtain. The darkness of the screen seemed as brilliant as the white light it had once held. The brilliant light that was now inside Rozina. Grief tugged at his heart, but the pain of it seemed detached. He pondered this idly. How strange it was; pain a distant memory. Only the cold had substance.

Kelsie headed for the door at the side of the balcony.

He walked up the stairs slowly, moving without purpose.

He stopped at the top of the stairs and pulled the small silver key from his pocket. He held it in his open palm and stared at it numbly, then inserted it into the door.

The door swung open with ease.

The room was even darker than the rest of the theater. He moved slowly, advancing on the dark object in the center of the room, then reached out and let his hand meet cold metal.

His mind snagged on its insignificance.

A projector. A small 35-millimeter projector. Dust in the crevices, rust on its metal sides. So small. Lifeless. Kelsie ran his hand along its side.

Threaded into it was a reel of film far too large for the projector to accommodate. Where it was stuffed and squeezed into the mechanism the film was crumpled and torn.

It began to hum.

Kelsie watched, and it hummed. And then it began to breathe.

Kelsie backed away. He felt a tiny tug at his guts as the too-large film was sucked into the mechanism, devoured by it, used by it. The sound it made was wet and ravenous.

"This is it, then," he whispered. "The heart. The feeding thing."

The film writhed through and around the projector like blood pulsing through veins. It was vile.

"You're not as strong as you used to be, are you?" Kelsie said. "Rozina saw to that." Gritting his teeth, he grabbed the film in his good hand and ripped it out of the machine. It wriggled alive and wet in his grasp.

Cold air struck him from behind. But it was feeble, disorganized. It tugged at him with desperation, and Kelsie walked away from it, carrying the living tendrils of film loosely in his hand.

He heard the commotion before he stepped onto the mezzanine. As he stood at the railing, he saw the four men. The locals. They were holding Karen.

Their eyes shifted to the writhing film in his hand. Rage painted their faces.

"It's over," Kelsie said in a low voice. "Let her go."

Rudy Olsen grabbed Karen by the hair and pulled her forward, holding her tightly about the waist. He glared at Kelsie. "I'll kill her!"

Kelsie dropped the film in a heap at his feet. "You boys

best be getting home now. It's all over." He pulled the book of matches Rozina had given him from his pocket.

Rudy yanked Karen's head back farther. She yelped fearfully. "God damn it, I'll *kill* her!"

Kelsie looked at him coldly. "Ask me if I care."

Rudy froze, his mouth gaping.

Kelsie pulled a match from the book and struck it. He let the flame settle, then tossed it into the pile of tangled film.

He heard a crackling sound, and then a hiss, and then the film shot out in snakes of color and flame, moving mindlessly, writhing across the floor. He stepped away as it made a lunge for him.

Watching the tendrils of film as they searched blindly for him, he went down the stairs, feeling the heat of the flames at his back.

The crowd wailed as one. Rudy let go of Karen, pushing her to the floor.

Kelsie made a swooping motion as he passed her, scooping her up in his arms. The crowd had dispersed, all shuffling about in a daze. Kelsie stopped to watch them.

They were looking all about, some scratching their heads, some standing with their mouths hanging open. Kelsie looked around to see what they were looking at.

It was a curious thing: The lobby, slowly and deliberately, had begun to change. Dust began to settle everywhere. The wood of the railing grew dull and cracked. The entryway curtains began to fade, then fall apart in tatters. It was as though time had sped up, and the theater was growing old in a matter of seconds.

Kelsie put Karen down and whispered to her. "Look. Look what's happening."

She looked, her mouth falling open. They both went into the house. The screen was nearly black with soot. Big holes dotted it. The seats were worn and threadbare.

"Kelsie," Karen whispered, "you know what this is like?"

"Yeah." He reached out and touched one of the seats. It was covered with a thick layer of dust. "It's like the theater hasn't been used in fifty years."

They went back through the curtains and found the lobby

empty. The front doors were smeared with filth. As they pushed through them the hinges made a rusty scream.

The crowd had gathered outside. They looked as though they had just awakened from a dream.

"Where's Rozina?" Karen asked.

Kelsie bent his head. "She's gone away."

Karen's face tightened with anguish. "And Joe. He's gone too."

When Kelsie didn't answer she grabbed his arm. "He's gone, too, isn't he?"

Kelsie nodded silently. Karen's eyes filled with tears.

"I hope he's dead." She sobbed. "I hope, I pray to God, he's dead."

Kelsie took her in his arms and held her close. "Me, too, Karen."

She buried her face against his chest and cried. "You're cold, Kelsie," she said sorrowfully. "You're so very cold."

Epilogue: Into the Fray

 Jeff was sitting up in the bed. His hands were wrapped in clean white bandages. For the first time since Kelsie had met him, his face looked smooth and relaxed. The reddish hue had left his eyes.

He greeted Kelsie with a smile. "Been a long night."

"Too long," Kelsie said. He led Karen to a chair and sat her down. Then he sat down heavily next to Jeff.

They sat in silence, the sound of Karen's sobs filling the room.

"I suppose you know it isn't over," Jeff said.

"What do you mean?"

Jeff shrugged. "It was just a shell, Kelsie. Just a house. The spirit never dies."

Kelsie shook his head. "I got to the heart of it. I burned the film."

"You burned *some* film," Jeff said gently. "Old film gets thrown away. New film takes its place."

"Christ." Kelsie dropped his head in his hands. "You mean, this could all start up again?"

"It never stopped," Jeff said.

"I've failed, then," Kelsie said hollowly.

Jeff shook his head. "Not really. It depends on what you set out to do." He eyed Kelsie. "Just what did you set out to do?"

Kelsie thought. "Save a friend," he said finally, and closed his eyes. Jeff laid a hand on his shoulder.

"You set out to save a friend, and you ended up saving a town. Not a bad day's work."

"But nothing's changed," Kelsie said. "Nothing's changed. The beast is still around. Still using people. Still feeding."

"Of course it is. Always will be. You can't change the world, Kelsie. Only your small corner of it."

"What change?" Kelsie said tightly. "Joe's dead."

"Is he?" Jeff asked, and Kelsie looked up sharply. "How do you know?"

"I saw him," Kelsie glanced at Karen, then lowered his voice. "I saw him die."

"You saw what you were supposed to see. Ah, Kelsie . . . haven't you learned yet?"

Kelsie was numb.

"Joe's still around," Jeff said gently. "Still being used."

"Jesus . . ."

"It's a never-ending struggle, Kelsie. Some people are never touched by it. They go through their lives blindly. Never hurting. Never feeling cold. But some of us get touched, and once that happens, you can never turn away from it." He leaned back and closed his eyes. "Future looks pretty bleak, doesn't it?"

"Everything's changed, then," Kelsie said bitterly. "It'll never be the same. Ever."

"It's doubtful."

"So, what do I do?"

"Well, you could just forget the whole thing. Mourn the loss of your friend. Lick your wounds and crawl on back to L.A."

Kelsie narrowed his eyes. "Admit defeat."

"Precisely."

Karen was looking at him.

"And then one night," he said, turning back to Jeff, "it'll come for me, like it did Joe. There's no escape, is there? I'm damned, either way."

"But you're stronger now. You've been touched, and you survived. Gather your forces around you, Kelsie. Gather them about you and batten down."

"Is"—he cleared the tightness from his throat—"is there any hope of my ever finding Joe?"

"You'll find him," Jeff said simply. "That's not the problem. The problem is, you're fighting a war that can never be won. All you can win is a few small battles. A skirmish here, a struggle there. But never the whole ball of wax. Are you prepared for that?"

Kelsie slumped. "I have no choice."

"That's true."

Kelsie thought of Rozina. Twice now she had taken the soul-eaters and had gone away with them, leaving him safe. How could he repay that? How could he ever repay that?

"You're an unwilling warrior," Jeff said. "But most warriors are. Things never really change. You can't kill evil, ever. It'll always be there, always feeding. And as long as there are people around to feed it, it'll grow. You can't kill it." He smiled, a sheepish, cunning smile. "But you can sure give it one hell of a fight."

Kelsie nodded.

Okay, then.

Okay.

You want a fight?